sQuid

a novel by

Kenneth McKenney

Grosvenor House
Publishing Limited

All rights reserved
Copyright © Kenneth McKenney, 2010

Kenneth McKenney is hereby identified as author of this
work in accordance with Section 77 of the Copyright, Designs
and Patents Act 1988

The book cover picture is copyright to Kenneth McKenney

This book is published by
Grosvenor House Publishing Ltd
28-30 High Street, Guildford, Surrey, GU1 3HY.
www.grosvenorhousepublishing.co.uk

This book is sold subject to the conditions that it shall not, by way of
trade or otherwise, be lent, resold, hired out or otherwise circulated
without the author's or publisher's prior consent in any form of binding or
cover other than that in which it is published and
without a similar condition including this condition being imposed
on the subsequent purchaser.

A CIP record for this book
is available from the British Library

ISBN 978-1-907652-57-8

I would like to thank my old friend Kip Calderara,
without whose help and encouragement
Alice, the giant squid, would never have seen
the light of day

* * * * *

Follow me and I will make you fishers of men
Matthew 4:19

ONE – the creature rises

The giant squid first came ashore on the wettest summer the country had ever known. Day after relentless day the skies opened, rain bucketed down; the ground lay drenched and unyielding. Water gathered in huge pools, made roads impassable, turned estuaries into swamps. Villages in the Midlands were drowned in floods, houses reduced to piles of junk. Country roads, hamlets, streams and linking bridges were shattered by mudslides. The police worked around the clock rescuing those trapped in vehicles. Sewers overflowed in London, thousands of fish floated dead in the scum.

In the little Scottish town of Culloch, opposite the Isle of Mull, a sense of disaster hung in the air. The summer tourists, on whom the town depended, stayed away in droves. All along the High Street, shops, pubs and restaurants closed down. Fishing became impossible. Country walks were abandoned. Farms became quagmires. Cattle, far from decorating the countryside, remained in their stalls, lowing mournfully in the muck.

"It's about time the government stepped in," the locals complained. "This is a national disaster."

"It's bloody climate change," others declared. "Worse than terrorists."

The Media added its uncontrolled voice. The Press thundered about global warming. Pollution was out of control. Friends of the Earth issued renewed warnings about the melting ice-caps; polar bears were dying of the heat. TV pundits insisted new lifestyles be adopted. Something drastic had to be done.

But still the rain streamed down, pushing even more mud into the waters along the Argyll Coast, carrying with it the rich scent of peat and livestock into the murky sea.

In the midst of this stew the squid was lured from the depths, tugged by a hunger, driven by a subtle force it had never encountered before. Impelled from below, coaxed from above, aided by a surging tide, the enormous cephalopod - literally an animal with feet on its head, came up from the Atlantic into the Firth of Lorne. Although the Peake Deep, where it normally hunted, was flowing with nutrients, they didn't satisfy its newborn craving. The smaller creatures the giant feasted on - other squid, hake, ray, ling, prawns and octopus were plentiful, but no longer were sufficient. The giant squid was urged upward by promises of something better ahead.

It was a time of change in the waters. There were more sperm whales than had been seen for years. Twice one of the beasts chased the squid, on the second occasion catching a companion that swam by the cephalopod's side. After that the squid had hidden for a while. Shooting backwards, clouding the water with a gush of black ink, its eight arms and twin tentacles drawn close, it sought refuge in a field of kelp. There it waited, its appetite growing, until the nutrient waters in the Firth of Lorne enticed it toward the Scottish coastline and into Culloch harbour.

For centuries Culloch had been a fishing village where men in small boats braved the seas, returned with their catch to drink and feast and join their wives. But that way of life had rapidly faded. Now there were fewer fish to catch, more competition from factory ships. Common Market regulations made the fishermen's future look bleak. Even though there were some in the town who would never accept that their lives had altered, who persisted to trawl when they could, many turned their talents to the tourist trade, which for a time had flourished. They built a new hotel, opened their houses, their farms, their hillsides, made welcome all who came from afar, brought new life to an old tradition - Culloch had been a holiday resort for as long as anyone could remember. But when the fishing failed, tourism became an essential business. On it the town depended.

Men in Burberrys came to shoot grouse on the moors, paying large sums to raise their guns in the early light, to sip whisky by a fireside in the evening before supping on roasted lamb. It was the simplicity of the village that attracted many, the return to an idea of good times gone. Others arrived to walk the heathery hills, scramble across rippling streams, stride up outcrops, gaze over a rolling landscape of soft blues and lilacs to admire the sea. Some journeyed to spend a quiet week or two, to stay in a bed-and-breakfast, to wander through the picturesque streets and buy a cashmere sweater, a silver plate from Edinburgh, and to watch their children paddle along the shore. They said how nice it was to leave the rat-race behind, how good to be out of the stink of the city.

But that bright mood changed the year the giant squid came ashore. The weather put an end to it. More whisky was drunk by fewer visitors. More lambs sheltered in barns, uneaten. The stalls that sold plates and silverware, cashmere, even the furtively supplied earrings of freshwater pearls, illegal in Culloch since 1998, lost customers as the rain poured down.

It was the rain, however, that attracted the squid. Among the amalgam of vegetable matter, the outwash of farmyard soil, was the rich and wholesome tang of flesh, a taste the squid remembered vividly. Once, rising up from the Atlantic, on a day when the sun gave a warm and tingling feeling all along its eight-foot back, the squid discovered farmyard flesh. Amongst the waste from a cruise ship was an untouched leg of lamb.

Using its long tentacles, which could stretch twenty-four feet, making the whole creature more than thirty in length - not the biggest in the oceans but certainly large enough to cause a stir when it came ashore, the squid grabbed the lamb. Had there been nothing tastier among the waste, the creature might have been satisfied with the cucumber rinds, banana peel and the loaves of bread that floated past, but the meat was a treat. Drawing the flesh into its beak, a powerful tool capable of cutting through a steel cable, the squid devoured the flesh and found it good.

Now, as it came close to Culloch harbour, in the early hours of that rain-drenched dawn, there was something similar in the murky water which drew the creature on. Encouraged, the squid swam past the fishing boats tied to their moorings, went round the small stone quay at the swollen river mouth and up through the town itself. No one saw it on that mouldy morning. A dog on the riverbank barked, then ran whimpering away as an enormous eye turned in its direction.

When the squid arrived at the place where the flavour was most intense it paused a moment, then came ashore. And although not used to being out of the water, it found the going easy. The ground was wet and slippery, and there were few obstacles in its path. With eyes that were twice as powerful as those of any man, it quickly located its victim - small, easily-captured toddler that put up no fight at all. Even the mother backed away in fear. At once, the squid's great tentacles lashed out to take hold. With a powerful surge they drew their catch toward the eight waiting arms. In less time than it would have taken a cat to catch a sparrow, the giant had what it wanted, returned to the river and swam out to sea. For a moment or two the victim struggled feebly, then quickly drowned. The squid took it to the safety of a massive kelp bed where, nibbling bits off with its parrot-shaped beak, grinding them down with the rows of teeth on its tongue, it put an end to its hunger. To the squid's delight, the prey was deliciously warm, as pleasant as the sun on its normally sand-coloured back, so tasty the creature darkened with desire for more, realising that what it had achieved was luscious.

This was what it had come for. This was the place to survive. What's more, if there were other inhabitants on this fertile ground, they were a timid lot. None had interfered with the capture. No other scavenger had darted forth to pick up the scraps of the kill. There was no competition here.

Jamie McCory first heard of the squid's attack when he came down to breakfast the morning the creature came ashore. By then the skies had cleared a little, pale-grey light was filtering through, and he found his father,

William, the local vet, talking on his mobile phone in a voice that was quieter than usual. He sounded unusually perplexed.

"It was all right when I left," William McCory muttered as he closed his phone. "Right as rain last time I saw it."

"What was that?" asked Molly, Jamie's mother. "The dog with the broken leg?"

"Harry Carter's new-born foal. The one I helped him deliver yesterday. He said it had turned into a streak of slime."

"What?"

"That's what he told me. He left it in the barn last night with the mare. Gone this morning, that's why he phoned. Turned, he said, into a streak of slime. He couldn't believe it." William looked up as Jamie approached, stared a moment at his sixteen year old son. As usual, Jamie wore an old blue sweatshirt, faded jeans and a striped woollen hat pulled down over his ears. From beneath it his green eyes peered out cautiously. "You hear that?" his father asked. "You ever come across anything like it?"

"Like what?"

"A new-born foal that, well, just melted."

"Aw, come off it, Dad."

"How could you expect Jamie to know about anything it?" Molly said briskly. "It's ridiculous, anyway. Foals don't melt."

"This one did." William McCory leant back as his wife placed bacon and eggs, fried bread and tomatoes before him. "That's what Harry Carter said it looked like. There wasn't anything left but slime."

"It's a wonder we haven't all turned into slime. The weather like it is."

"What about the mare?" asked Jamie, taking his place at the table. "Is she all right?"

"She's fine. Though Harry thought something had frightened her." William picked up a fork. "What do you make of it?"

Jamie shook his head.

"Leave him alone, Will," Molly said. "Let him eat his breakfast in peace."

"He can eat and think at the same time. Anyway, you know what he's like. He knows more about animals than I do. Calls every fish between here and Oban by name."

"That's different," Molly said mildly as she poured milk over Jamie's muesli. She knew her son had funny ways, but that was all right as far as she was concerned. She loved him for what he was. If the truth were known, she wasn't too upset by the fact he was a bit different from other lads in the town. Not that he didn't get on with them, it was just he didn't lark about as much as some. He often wandered off on his own, took his wetsuit out of the garage and went diving along the coast. He was happy alone, and she admired him for that. Will wasn't always as patient with the boy, even though they got along well enough. Mind you, Jamie did have some annoying habits - he hardly ever took his hat off. A pity, really, he had nice red hair. There was that vegetarian thing, too. He ate nothing with eyes. Eggs, she sometimes managed to get into him, but he survived mostly on nuts, fruit, cheese and bread, wholemeal when he could get it.

"Potatoes have eyes," his father pointed out once. "You don't have much trouble with them."

"Yeah, right," Jamie had replied on that occasion. "They're watching me all the time to see I behave myself." Now, he stirred his muesli slowly. "Where did the slime go?" he asked.

"It didn't go anywhere. It was on the floor of the barn."

"Didn't lead anywhere?"

"I don't know, I didn't ask."

That's the trouble with people, Jamie told himself. *They don't want to know.* But he didn't say anything. There was no point. He didn't want to argue with his father.

"Would you care to come with me when I go over to Carter's?" William asked. "Have a look at the slime for yourself?"

"No, thanks. I'm going for a dive."

"In this weather? The water's like mud."

"Your dad's right," said Molly. "It's filthy with all the rain."

"I found a clear spot yesterday." Jamie's head went closer to his bowl. "Up where the current comes in."

"You be careful of those currents, my boy."

"Yes, Dad. I will."

Molly McCory turned away, began making a cup of tea. There were a dozen things she'd have liked to say to warn her son about the weather, but held them back. She didn't want to spoil his morning. Jamie loved diving, went off on his own whenever he could. But the holidays would be over soon, then he'd return to school in Oban, have only have the weekends to get into the water. On top of everything, it had been a dreadful summer, and she knew how much he missed putting on his gear and slipping into the sea. He was happy shallow diving, going under to explore then coming up for air, floating along on the surface. Sometimes he used his air-bottle, but only if he got a lift. It weighed too much, he said. He could manage it, but had enough with his weighted belt and the rest of the stuff if he had to go on foot.

She watched him diving when she could, pretending to do something else. Didn't want him to think she was mothering him. But she wasn't happy about him going out into water as dirty as this. What's more, his father was right, the currents could be bad, especially when the tides were high. Only last year two young men from Glasgow were swept out to sea and never heard of again. They didn't know these waters the way I do, Jamie had said, when told about them. But that didn't stop her worrying.

"Might help if you came to Carter's," William persisted. "Could get a clue."

"About what?"

"The slime. You wanted to know where it went?"

"Will..." said Molly, as patiently as she was able. "Let him eat his breakfast." She couldn't help it, whenever they looked like getting into an argument she had to step in between. Not that it ever came to much, they seldom raised their voices. But Will could get sarcastic and she hated that, so she did her best to stop any disagreement before it went too far. "Anyway, what *clues* could he have about *slime*? You said, yourself, you'd never heard of anything like it."

"That doesn't mean he hasn't got something ticking over in the back of his skull." William pushed his plate away. "All that time he spends on the computer? God knows, he might be on the cutting edge of foal-slime. Have a few ideas I could use."

"*Will...*"

"Maybe later, Dad." Jamie looked up at his father, then glanced away out the kitchen window. The sky was grey but the wind was down, nothing would be stirring up the water. "I can't come now. I want to catch the incoming tide."

"Suit yourself then. I'm off."

William pecked his wife on the cheek, nodded at Jamie, went out to the garage where he put Wellington boots, a mackintosh, into the back of his four-wheel drive, then set off for Carter's stables, thinking about his son. He regretted not having more children, a girl perhaps. It would have been easier if Jamie wasn't the only child, but there was nothing to be done about that. There hadn't been any option. After two miscarriages, and spending six weeks on her back, Molly had brought their son into the world. Then, on the advice of her gynaecologist, she had her tubes tied. Another pregnancy could have killed her, she'd been told.

"Pity," William murmured. "The way things happen."

He drove along the High Street, down through the little town, past white-walled cottages, stone houses with slate roofs. By the *Harbour Light*, one of the three pubs in Culloch, two men were looking upward, shrugging dubiously. Outside the Post Office, which they'd threatened to close, several women were chatting beneath dry umbrellas. *The rain seems to have lessened*, William thought, glancing up at the sky. *Don't tell me we're in for a change.*

TWO – the trail

After the giant squid had eaten the foal, dropping all that was left of the animal - the white bones, onto a patch of sand, it almost smiled with satisfaction. The flesh, the internal organs, even the hide had been consumed in slow and rewarding delight. Holding the prey with its arms, the tentacles now close to its body, the squid had picked away the flesh with its sharp black beak. After grinding it fine with the teeth on its tongue, a long ribbon that stretched back to its stomach - itself an organ so versatile it could swell to accommodate nearly everything its owner swallowed, the giant cephalopod settled to digest its meal.

It lay on a large flat rock surrounded by kelp. There, amidst the gently waving stalks, beneath an overhang of bedded limestone, it rested. For the first time in many weeks it felt safe. Even though a few green-backed crabs peered out of their holes it permitted them their curiosity. A spotted dogfish swam by, its eyes idly scanning the landscape, yet missed the huge shape tucked beneath the overhang - the squid had turned the colour of stone. The dogfish went on, untouched. The day before it might have been captured, now it was left to wander. The squid had enough to digest for a while.

As it lay unmoving it became aware of a sense of peace flowing through its veins, a feeling nearly unknown to the giant creature that had spent most of its life hunting or being hunted. Sperm whales were its worst enemy, as recent experience confirmed. Although squid usually swam alone, except for the breeding season, lately it had shared the waters with a smaller female, which had been devoured by the whale in spite of its attempts to fight back.

The giant squid drew its arms in close as it recalled the whale coming through the darkness, clicking as it sought to pinpoint its target, finally swooping on one of the pair it found. For long terrifying moments there had been a deadly battle. But the great weight of the whale, a huge beast with hair on its face, was more than the smaller combatant could cope with. It struggled as the whale, the squid's tail in its mouth, tried to swallow the rest of its body. The squid, doing its best to survive, bound the whale's mouth closed with its arms. Wrapping them tightly around the whale's jaw, surprising small for so large an animal, the squid clamped it firmly to the massive head. Arms and tentacles in a vice-like grip, a labyrinth of writhing flesh, the squid tried to ease itself free.

It almost managed to escape. The whale thrashed, felt the need for air. With a huge flick of its enormous body, the great beast shot up through the surface. There, it spouted, took in fresh breath, shook itself and, failing to dislodge the squid, plunged back into the shrouded depths.

By now the squid was tiring. First one arm lost its grip, then another. The suckers tore away, returned to the attack but with lesser determination. Although it held on as long as it was able, and its saw-toothed suckers dug into the whale's hide, leaving scars that would last a lifetime, the whale's long pointed lower jaw, with its sixty teeth, finally sprang open. With a sudden swirl, the whale broke the grip of the squid, and swallowed it whole. Even though the cephalopod weighed nearly five hundred pounds, it was less than half the weight the whale would consume that day.

The giant squid that had come ashore at Culloch remembered the fight and shuddered, grateful for having survived. It could easily have been the chosen one, shredded by those massive teeth. Now, it lay quietly, absorbing its meal, feeling surprisingly safe. There were no whales within earshot, no clicks to be heard. And it could feed again whenever it needed.

A swirl of contentment went though its huge frame. This was obviously the place to settle, somewhere to live in peace. The squid was nearly three years old, and its whole life had been spent surviving, honing its skills. It had been reasonably content in the massive Peake Deep until some curious force urged it away from the world it knew, initiated its wandering. For months it had searched the shores, once attempting to land on the Spanish coast, but the oil that seeped from a sunken vessel had proved too distasteful. The squid had lifted one of its dinner-plate eyes to see a line of black crosses set up on the beach, and had been immediately disgusted. It moved on, went further north, until it came to Culloch where the winds were bad and the rain poured down, but there was something quite welcoming in the swirling waters, something that encouraged it to stay.

Later that morning at Harry Carter's stables William McCory, Culloch's vet, examined the trail the giant squid had left when it returned to the water. Tall and angular, William bent as he stared at the slime. It had dried a little, turned a purplish hue, but remained a clear line on the concrete floor.

"Bloody funny, this," he said. "The foal was all right when I left."

"It was late-born." Harry Carter shook his head angrily. "Been a lot this year. Everything's buggered up these days. Nothing's like it used to be."

"That's true enough." William touched the slime. It felt like plastic. "But I've not seen anything like this before."

"The foal's been stolen," replied Harry, a chunky man with a weather-beaten face. "Bastards come up from the south. Take anything they can lay their hands on. Sell it for dog food, mostly."

"But they don't usually leave this sort of mess." William's eyes followed the trail as it went from the stable, disappeared on its way to the River Orchy, which ran through Culloch and into the sea. The water, although normally clear, with its share of brown trout, lily-pads and dragon flies, today was discoloured by the rain. "And they don't come by boat."

"What do you mean?"

"Look where it goes." William recalled what his son had wanted to know. He had to give it to Jamie, he mightn't say much but it often made sense. "Down there to the Orchy."

"You're not suggesting they came up the river in a boat? Dragged the foal over the grass? Then went off, leaving this mess?"

"I suppose not. That doesn't make much sense either."

"Nothing that's happened over the past few years has made much sense." Harry Carter moved closer, his red-veined face angry. "First it was the Mad Cow disease. Took all the stock I had."

"I know, I helped you put them down."

"Bloody awful, wasn't it?"

William nodded, remembering the long hours spent culling herds, killing hundreds of healthy animals, obeying official orders. What had hurt most was working on the smaller farms where every animal was known by name. Some were treated as household pets. The first cases turned up in 1986. Ten years later nearly two hundred thousand had been confirmed, and still the government remained in denial. Under pressure from the meat industry, where so much money and manpower were at stake, they refused to acknowledge the epidemic. One minister gave his daughter a hamburger on television to prove the safety of British beef.

"Mad *Cow* Disease?" muttered Harry. "It was the officials in charge that were mad."

"You're right," William replied. "They should've vaccinated the herds."

"They said that'd give our beef a bad name. Could've hit the export market."

"Couldn't have hit it any worse than it did."

"Makes me sick to think about it."

William agreed. Some of the cattle had to go, but there'd been ways to protect the rest. Those in which the disease was fully developed were no longer able to stand. They stumbled, their fore-legs doubling beneath them as they moved away from the herd. Although their milk supply remained adequate, and was sold along with the rest, there came a time when William, and men like him, had to put them down. Especially after cats began dying from infected pet food, showing how readily the disease could move from one species to another.

First it was pigs that suffered from Scrapie, their version of the disorder. When their remains went into cattle-fodder, cows became ill. Next were the domestic animals. But only when they realised how many humans might be infected did the government give in. Even then, instead of vaccinating all cattle without symptoms, they decided on mass slaughter. Officials claimed that too many animals had been moved from one part of the country to another to consider any alternative. There was uncontrolled spread of Mad Cow Disease, they said. Elimination was the only remedy. All potential victims had to die. The Army was called in. Four and a half million cows, calves and bulls were slaughtered, most of them healthy, in the prime of life.

"My Friesians." Harry spat contemptuously. "Some of the old girls I'd had for years. Bursting with life, they were."

"You're right. It was a dreadful waste."

William saw again the trenches being dug, the bodies hauled by trucks, pushed by tractors, the legs stiff, the stomachs bloated. They were burnt in fires that lasted for days. He could still smell the smoke, the stench that spread across the countryside. He remembered Jamie seated before the television, staring at the graphic scenes, tears streaming down his cheeks. They boy been no more than a child, and the deaths touched him deeply. *As they'd affected every one of us*, William thought. *However we might have reacted.* For his part, Harry Carter had refused to give in. He'd moved from cows to horses, establishing a riding school that had done well until this disastrous summer arrived.

"Then they mucked up the fishing," Harry said. "It wasn't enough to kick the farmers in the balls. They had to get the fishermen too."

"That's not quite the same."

"The hell it isn't. Try talking to their wives and children."

"I know." William cleared his throat. He'd learnt it didn't pay to argue with men like Harry, their minds were too deeply wounded. Nevertheless, he found it impossible not to add, "But, in many ways, the fishermen are to blame for what happened. They've taken what they could for years. Never put much back. Not like you. You were always breeding cattle. Putting new seed in the ground."

"What about the salmon farmers?"

"They're doing something," William agreed. "But they're not like the trawler-men. They don't have nets that are miles long. Don't drag up everything they can, then throw the little ones back. Dead, of course, never given a chance."

"It's the Spaniards who do things like that. And the Japanese." Harry kicked at the scattered hay. "Now they're stealing my bloody foals, leaving this shit behind."

"I doubt if the Spanish or the Japanese are to blame for what happened to your foal," William replied, in an effort to lighten the mood. "The culprits are closer to home."

"You're could be right there. This looks like home-grown bastardry." Harry lifted his cap, scratched his balding head. "I talked to Tony Croft, the sergeant. But there's little he can do. No one saw anything. He's got nothing to go on."

"Except this." William touched the trail of slime with the toe of his boot. "Though, I must confess, it doesn't tell us much."

"You sure it didn't come from the foal?"

"I don't know, but I'll take a sample." William fished through his mackintosh, found a small plastic bag, scraped up some of the purplish stain. "I'll get it tested."

"What's that going to tell you?"

"Who knows." William smiled wryly. "It might've been left by aliens."

"Is that all you've got to say?"

"For the moment, yes."

With that William waved goodbye, returned to his vehicle, drove across the mud-caked courtyard, back along the High Street, hoping to catch the mail van before it left for Oban. He'd send the sample to Malcolm Stewart, a vet who ran a larger practice with all the facilities he needed. William usually sent his bone, blood and tissue samples to Stewart for analysis.

Harry Carter watched him go, wondering what had happened to his foal. They'd been stolen before, but never like this. He'd hoped the vet might've had a reasonable explanation, but the man had given away nothing. As for that crack about aliens, it wasn't even a decent joke. Specially when you thought about that boy of his. Always in the same old clothes, woollen hat pulled down to his eyes, off on his own, talking to animals. A weird kid if ever there was one. God knows what planet he came from.

On the other hand, Harry didn't know much about kids. Never married, never had any. Only boy he ever got close to was his sister's youngest, and look what happened to him. Spent five years on a fishing boat, lost his job, took an overdose of something and died with the needle in his arm. Bloody awful world they lived in. And it was getting worse by the day. Harry Carter turned back to the stable, thinking he'd try for the Town Council next time round. They needed a voice like his. All the bastards there did was talk about new sets of traffic lights, getting more in taxes. In the meantime, the best thing he could do was sit up at night with a loaded shotgun, see if the thieves came back. When they did, he'd show them a thing or two. A man had the right to defend his property.

When Jamie McCory reached the sea, the need to get into the water came in a rush. It had been that way as long as he could remember. When he looked into the depths, saw the seaweed, the glint of fishes, it mesmerised him - it never stopped changing shape. He gazed at the shadows, all that lay beneath, and it beckoned him to enter. It was magic, he could never get enough. As a toddler, walking along the small quay in Culloch harbour, holding his mother's hand, he used to lean over to watch the sprats swimming in shoals. He'd point at the crabs shuffling over the rocks, almost falling in.

"Be careful," his mother would warn him, her lean body angling back. "Or you'll have us both in there up to out necks."

He'd laugh at that, lean out further, reach for the sea.

Once, with his father, who didn't always hold his hand, he'd jumped from the steps of the Port Bridge into the River Orchy to land in the shallows, where he'd seen the tail of a brown trout protruding from under a smooth black stone.

"For God's sake be more careful," his father sputtered, dragging him back by his jacket. "What do you think you're doing?"

"Fish," replied Jamie, one of the first words he learnt. "Fish, there."

"Not any longer," his father growled, as by then the trout had gone. "Now, let's get you back before you freeze to death."

William had taken his son home, lecturing him sternly. But when Jamie was four, his father had arranged swimming lessons, bought him a mask, snorkel, fins and a miniature wet-suit fitted with water-wings. Nevertheless, his father continued his warnings about the perils of the sea, perhaps because he'd never dived himself - he couldn't even swim.

"Be careful," was his constant warning. "Watch out for the currents. And the tides."

"Yes," his mother always agreed - she couldn't swim either. "Don't take any risks. And please don't stay in too long."

As soon as he could Jamie began diving alone, walking over the hills near Culloch, coming down to the water by rocky pathways, some of which he felt he'd discovered on his own. If his mother drove him, or his father had time, he took his air-bottle. Then they went along the coast road to one of the many bays and inlets along the Firth of Lorne. But, in fact, he was happier without the bottle, just floating on the surface, holding his breath to go down. That way he felt part of the world in the hollows between the rocks and outcrops, not something from another world needing bottled air to breathe.

Now, with a scent of change in the morning air, Jamie McCory pulled on his wet-suit. He put on his weighted belt and fins, spat on the inside of his goggles to prevent them steaming over before pressing them into place. With the breathing end of the snorkel between his teeth he lowered himself into the water, welcoming its first icy shock. Almost immediately he became used to the cold, and began idling out to sea.

    It was always the same, yet different. It didn't matter how well he knew each little cove, how often he'd swum around a rock, there was always something new about it, something that hadn't been there before. Such as a crab that had taken up residence in a crevice, or a piece of driftwood jammed beneath a stone, a flounder trying to make itself invisible in the sand with only its eyes peering out. Once a basking shark swam over shoulder, came gently up behind, almost touching him before going on. Jamie had barely moved as the big shape went past, his heart racing with joy. It was amazing, this wonderland he was allowed to enter, and it became more exciting each time he went in. It wasn't a silent world, as Jacques Costeau had said, there was always something clicking, some small sound to keep him company. He loved being in the water and never felt alone.

THREE – at first sight

William McCory failed to catch the mail van to Oban with the slime sample he'd taken from Harry Carter's stable. Before he was half-way down the High Street, he received a call from Ian Chattan who, with his twin brother Alec, was setting up an organic farm three miles down a side road in the hills. Their task wasn't easy, the weather had flattened a row of multi-bay tunnels, almost wiped out the soft fruits they were trying to raise. Raspberries, strawberries and the recently fashionable blueberries - said to contain the seeds of life, had been damaged by the basketful. However, the old varieties of Scottish apples they were grafting onto existing stock had survived the storm.

Ian Chattan rang because there was a problem with one of the Ayrshires in the herd. When William last saw the cow she'd been heavily pregnant with twins, another late-birth in this unusual season. Now, her time had come, and the first calf was breeched, Ian said, his voice rising over the phone. One back foot was sticking out. He thought the other was doubled inside. If William didn't get there quickly he was afraid they'd lose both calves, even the mother.

"How far along is she?" William asked. "What's she doing?"

"She's down. She's having trouble breathing."

"What condition's the road in?"

"Not bad. We put gravel down last year. Most of it's still there."

"I'm on my way."

William turned his four-wheel drive around, cut through the Common, took the road to the south, knowing he'd spend the rest of the morning reaching into the pregnant cow, trying to save the calf. There was always the danger the head could twist in the process and the infant emerge stillborn. He hoped its twin was aligned for a normal birth.

"I mustn't forget that sample," he murmured, as the vehicle splashed through a puddle sending muddy water high. Then he caught a glimpse of blue hills in the distance, glowing below layers of drifting cloud. "Look at that, don't tell me we're in for a spot of sunshine."

The sight of clearing skies turned his thoughts back to Jamie, wondering if his son was already in the sea. Curious, this obsession the boy had with diving as neither of his parents swam. In a way, William realised, he and his wife they were partly to blame. They'd encouraged their son to spend as much time as he could splashing and paddling when he was younger, vaguely expecting the phase to pass. It hadn't, and these days you couldn't keep Jamie out of the water. He went in whenever he was able, whatever the weather, and never seemed to feel the cold. That had something to do with being struck by lightning, the specialist in Edinburgh had decided.

Not that it'd been a direct hit. Jamie had been standing near a metal-framed window when the ray came down, cracked the glass, buckled the window and threw him across the room. That had happened five years ago, and ever since he'd been able to stay in the water as long as he liked. At times until he was blue with cold. Everyone made brass monkey jokes, but Jamie just shrugged them away, often through chattering teeth. He always said everything was fine, he knew how much cold he could take.

"Let's hope he doesn't stay in too long today," William said, as he turned up the hill to the Chattan farm. "This good patch isn't going to last."

When Jamie McCory got into the water the sea was murky. He couldn't see more than five or ten feet, but could feel a current coming in, sweeping away the dirt. He swam slowly out toward it, grateful for the visibility it brought.

"*Been a week since I was in,*" he told himself, as he coasted along, grinning around his snorkel. "*Starting to get withdrawal pangs.*"

He never talked much about his love for the water. Said a bit to his mother, but that was all. There were others he'd gone diving with but none of them felt the same as he did. And after that prick from Glasgow speared the pollock, he hadn't taken anyone with him. The prick been staying with Betty, who lived next door. She was the boy's aunt or something.

Jamie didn't really object to spearfishing. If somebody caught a fish, took it home and ate it, that was all right. He didn't do it himself, killing wasn't what he got into the water for, but he could understand why others liked fish. But, Jesus, that kid from Glasgow was something else. Jamie wouldn't have taken him in the first place if his mother hadn't talked him into it. *Betty's a good friend*, she'd said. *Her nephew's only here for a day or two. I'll drive you if you like.*

Jamie hadn't wanted to be driven, didn't want to make a big thing out of it. He'd walked the nephew, Alf, over the hills and down to the rocks. Not far, even though the prick said it was like walking miles. When they'd put on their gear and were about to get in, Alf pulled a small speargun out of his pack.

"Don't use it," Jamie told him. "We're just going to look."

"Got to get something," Alf replied, pulling the rubber back, hooking it into the metal spear. "Got to take something home for the pot."

"Not with that, you won't."

"Why not?"

"There's no cord. Nothing tied to the spear."

"Shit." Alf examined the speargun. Jamie pushed it away as it turned toward him. "I was going to get some, but forgot."

"Leave it here. Let's just get in."

"Christ, no. I'll have to make sure, that's all."

"Make sure of what."

"I get it in the head."

Jamie stared at the kid, his green eyes darkening with anger. He had a good mind to call the whole thing off, start walking home. But the pull of the sea got to him. It was a sunny day, not a cloud in the sky. They weren't even wearing wet-suits, just tight pullovers to hold back the cold, and the water was so clear he could see the bottom. He couldn't turn away from it now, no matter who was with him.

"Leave the gun," he said. "There's nothing to spear."

"Bullshit." Alf pointed at a number of delicately patterned wrasse picking at the weed. "Place is alive with them."

"They're too small."

"There'll be something bigger." Alf, unused to wearing fins, splashed clumsily through a rock-pool and fell into deeper water. "Jesus, it's fucking cold."

Jamie said nothing as he slid into the sea, keeping behind Alf, who was waving the speargun around, looking for something to shoot. It didn't take long. The tide was coming in, bringing hungry fish with it. Soon a big olive-green pollock cruised up beside them, showing no signs of fear. It looked familiar. Perhaps it was one of the many Jamie had swum with before.

As soon as he saw it Alf turned with the gun. Jamie tried to stop him, but wasn't fast enough. The spear shot out, hit the pollock, went halfway through and stopped. The pollock flicked in the water, tried to escape, but the weight of the metal turned the fish on its side. The last Jamie saw of the beautiful creature was it limping away in the water, dragging the spear with it, going out to sea to die.

"Shit," shouted Alf, head above the water, snorkel out of his mouth. "You see that? Fucking enormous."

Jamie didn't reply. He turned back to the rocks, climbed up, took off his mask and fins, reached for his towel. "You getting out?" Alf called, and when Jamie said nothing, added, "We only just got started."

Jamie took off his wet pullover, dried himself without saying a word, then pulled his woollen hat down to his eyes. He stared at Alf, who was trying to put the snorkel back between his teeth. A wave caught him, filling his mouth with water. The prick coughed, went down, shot up again.

"Hey," he shouted. "You going to leave me here?"

"Suit yourself," Jamie said. "I'm going home."

"You can't. You told my auntie…"

"I said I'd take you snorkelling. That's all."

"No, wait." Alf paddled to the rock, holding the speargun in one hand, attempting to climb out, but spluttered and slipped back. "Give me a hand."

Jamie walked to where Alf clung to a ledge and took the speargun away. "Try it now," he said, and watched Alf scramble ashore.

"Yeah, right. Fucking exciting…." Alf began, then stopped in mid-sentence as Jamie went back to where they'd left their clothes, jammed the end of the speargun in a cleft in the stone and bent it double. "Shit…," he yelled. "What you done?"

"You won't need that again."

"You fucking smashed it."

"Nothing to what you did to the pollock."

"It was only a fish."

"It was more than that."

They didn't speak again all the way home. Alf went back to Glasgow a day later. That had been a year ago and he hadn't seen the little prick since. Now, as Jamie drifted along through slowly clearing water, an untouched pollock swam slowly past, giving him a curious glance. But, hey, what was that in the distance? The ghostly shape of a dolphin moving in and out of the gloom? He hoped so, it could mean the weather was going to improve.

"*That'd be nice*," he murmured to himself. "*Get the bottle out. Go down deeper. Been a while since that happened.*

Jamie moved on, splashing as little as possible, trying not to disturb his fellow-creatures in their magical world. They'd be nervous after all the storms, and would scatter if he frightened them. He'd just take a quiet look around, see what there was to see.

William McCory spent most of the morning on the Chattan farm working with the pregnant cow, trying to ease the breech-born onto the stable floor. It wasn't easy. As Ian Chattan had told him, only one hind foot was visible, the other was back, awkwardly placed - there was a chance of it puncturing the womb. Normally the forefeet emerged first, soles down, the nose resting between them, the little head alert. But it wasn't like that this time. There was every chance the calf was doomed.

William began by reaching in, trying to get the misplaced foot into a normal position. He grasped the leg, it felt like plastic, and slowly eased it out to join the other. Then, he tried to turn the calf, but found the task impossible. The pelvic area wasn't large enough, the head had twisted sharply to the left and, as the cow hadn't given birth before, she resented his intrusion. He had no forceps with him, so had to do everything by touch, knowing he had little time.

"She going to make it?" Ian Chattan asked, his face concerned. "She doesn't look good."

"She'll make it," William grunted. "Hold her head. Don't let her get up."

"Do you want a rope to drag it out?"

"I'd rather not. I've seen them come apart like that."

For another hour they worked, Ian kneeling beside the mother, stroking her head. William, his forearms covered with blood, gradually manoeuvring the breeched calf out. In the end, the hind quarters emerged, and he was able to reach the head. Pulling with one hand, pushing with the other, wondering if the life would last, he brought a baby bull into the world. It slid free and lay gasping. William urged it to its feet, saw that it remained steady, then handed it over to Ian who took it to the mother. She sniffed her newborn thoroughly, began licking it clean.

"That's the first," said William. "The other'll be easy."

"Is it normal?"

"I think it is," William replied, and soon another male came out to be set up on spindly legs. "Let's get them together. See that she accepts this one too. Sometimes the second's rejected."

Both men watched, crooked smiles on their faces, as the second calf was welcomed by the mother. Ian turned to William. "Thank you," he said simply.

"We were lucky. The mother was good. By God, it never fails to impress me how animals are able to support so much pain."

"If it'd been one of us....?"

"Don't even think about it. Now, I suggest you leave them together for a few hours. Let them bond. See she gets plenty to eat. She'd going to need extra nourishment for a while." William looked at his arms, the blue overalls he wore – they were thick with blood. "I'll clean up and leave you to it."

He drove away, beneath clearing skies, with the sense of satisfaction he always felt when something like a breech birth was successful. He never boasted, told anyone how clever he had been. It was enough to know his skill and patience had given another life a chance.

When William got home, he put his overalls and shirt in the washing machine he used for work clothes. As he turned it on, his wife came into the laundry. "Jamie back yet?" he asked, although he knew the clearing skies could keep the boy away for hours.

"Not yet," Molly answered. "But, I'm sure he'll be here soon."

"He'd better be careful about the weather. This change isn't going to last."

"Don't say anything to him, Will."

"He's not always as careful as he should be."

"He knows what he's doing. Now, there are two women in the surgery with dogs waiting for injections. And a little girl with a hedgehog that's got a broken leg," Molly said firmly, turning the conversation away from her son. "You really do need an assistant."

"I've got Lucy. Isn't she there now?"

"She is, but she's getting on. And she's only a nurse. You really should look for someone younger. Someone qualified who wants a place."

"Perhaps you're right," replied William. "I'll talk to Malcolm Stewart about it. I've got a sample to send him in the fridge."

"That's a good idea. You could certainly do with some help."

"Let's see what turns up. And, even though you'd rather I didn't, I will have a word with Jamie when he returns."

"Please don't be too hard on him."

"I'll try not to." William turned away, his mind elsewhere. "Now, I must get that slime off to Malcolm. The sooner we find out what it is the better."

When the giant squid saw Jamie McCory it became completely still. Its mantle, the great shroud covering its body - usually cylindrical but flattened now, turned as dark as the rock surrounding it. Even its huge eyes became practically invisible. Unmoving, it watched the approaching creature, trying to determine what sort of fish it was. Although the thing had twin tail fins similar to its own, it was unlike anything the squid seen before. It had arms, two at the front, two at the back, and seemed to hunt on the surface. The squid wondered if it was good to eat. It would certainly be easy to capture.

One flash of the twenty-four foot tentacles, their end pads covered with powerful suckers, capable of clamping onto any surface like a pair of tongs, and the clumsy beast would be done for. What's more, the creature seemed unlikely to put up any fight. It had nothing as big as the sperm whale's lower jaw, large enough to swallow a squid whole. Nor was there any sign of the rows of razor-sharp teeth some sharks possessed. In fact, the squid could see little in the way of a mouth. There was a thin tube protruding upward, but that was probably some sort of sexual organ, no danger at all. The creature, which looked a bit like a starfish, was there for the taking.

On the other hand, the giant squid was not particularly hungry. It had eaten well recently, and knew there was more to be had along this well-stocked coast. So, it watched and waited, and only felt the slightest sense of apprehension when the thing above it paused, its curiously glazed eyes peering down at the white bones, the remains of last night's supper, which lay half-buried in the sand.

Jamie McCory wasn't surprised to see the bones. Although he knew every detail of this little cove, there was always something new to discover, and the bones looked especially interesting. The thing to do was come back later and take a closer look with the air-bottle. He'd have no trouble finding the place again. Most of the features he swam amongst he'd given names to. There was the Castle, the Tombstone, and the Place where the Pollock was Murdered. This overhang of limestone, which completely hid the giant squid, was the Grotto. He'd often gone down with the bottle to see long-clawed lobsters, their feelers testing the currents, and those spider crabs covered with bits of seaweed they'd stuck on to camouflage themselves. He liked to remain as still as he could watching the crabs, the lobsters, the multitude of little fishes spinning in and out of the patches of light. That way he was almost part of their world.

There wasn't much light down there now, and the water was still too dirty to be sure what the white things were. But they were something he'd like to examine. He wondered if they'd been washed out to sea by the rain, or fallen off a yacht, though that was unlikely so close to the rocks. Still, anything was possible in the water. He remembered the small stainless steel box he'd found jammed beneath the Tombstone that had taken several dives to release. When he finally got it to the surface it was empty, apart from sand, shells and a few wriggling worms, but it was a treasure all the same. He emptied the contents into the sea, cleaned it, dried it and put it in his room. He used it for his DVDs.

"*But these white things aren't like that*," he told himself, then glanced at his watch and made a face. "*If it's fine tomorrow I'll come back. But if I don't get home right away, Dad'll have my guts for garters.*" He laughed, blew a string of bubbles. "*And that'd be pretty messy.*"

He turned back and climbed out of the water, took off his gear and dried himself with a freshly-washed towel. He grinned as he rubbed his skin briskly. This was another of the good things about diving, the feeling of rough cloth when he got out. It brought a new tang to his body, told him he'd be ready to go back again soon. Come to think of it, the sea was where he'd be for the rest of his life if nothing changed his plans. He was going to study marine biology, work with the water, find out how to protect the creatures that dwelt there. It sounded daft, and he knew it, but the sea was in his blood.

FOUR – stirring the pot

As Jamie McCory climbed out of the water, leaving the bones and the huge watchful eyes behind him, Harry Carter, owner of the squid's last meal, walked into Culloch's police station looking for Sergeant Anthony Croft.

"Tony around?" he asked the constable behind the front counter. "I talked to him earlier. Said he'd be here."

"Out the back." The constable, Murdoch Roberts, a fresh-faced young man, licked his thumb, turned over another page in his notebook. "Won't be long."

"He say anything to you?"

"About what?"

"My foal the buggers stole last night."

"What buggers?" The constable looked up, saw Harry's angry face and softened his tone. "I mean, you got any names? Descriptions, things like that?"

"If I had, I'd have given them to the sergeant over the phone." Harry turned away as Croft, a middle-aged man with mournful eyes, came into the office. "Tony?" he asked. "You got anything?"

"I got a dodgy tummy, if that's what you mean. Think it was the steak and kidney pie," Croft replied sourly. "But that's not what you're after, is it? As for your foal, I haven't a clue. When these bastards come up they usually get away with a truckful. This time, no one else has lost anything. Are you certain yours was stolen?"

"I'm bloody sure it's not there now." Harry lifted his cap, scratched his head irritably. "At first I thought it was some disease. That's why I called the vet."

"What'd Will say?"

"Thought it was aliens."

Sergeant Croft sighed heavily. The constable smirked.

"Might sound funny, but I've got nothing to laugh about." Harry Carter's weather-beaten cheeks reddened. "This is my livelihood we're talking about. Christ, I just got going after they shot my Friesians, then the weather turned to shit. Now they've taken a new-born foal, and all you lot can do is laugh."

"Hang on," Croft replied patiently. "Tell me why Will said anything about aliens. He doesn't go around cracking jokes."

"It was the slime that did it."

"What slime?"

"The purple stuff that went from the stable to the river. He thought the thieves had come up in a boat. He took a sample. It's going off to Oban for a test."

"All right, Harry, let's start again. Give it to me nice and slow, all the details." Croft tapped the notebook Constable Roberts held. The constable picked up a ball-point pen. "Then we'll see what we can do." He winced as his stomach gave a rumble. "Tell Roberts all about it, everything you know. I'll have a word with Will McCory. Now, excuse me a minute. I've got to take some bicarb."

"You don't think Angus Douglas should know what's going on?"

"Mister Douglas? The Chairman of the Town Council?" Sergeant Croft slowly shook his head. "It's not his cup of tea."

"What if there's more stuff stolen?"

"Then, we'll see."

"Now, Harry," Murdoch Roberts began patiently. "It was a foal, you say?"

When Jamie arrived home, hungry and quietly excited, his mother toasted him a cheese and tomato sandwich, which he wolfed down with a glass of milk, then ate an apple out of the bag Ian Chattan had given his father. It was a Stirling Castle, one of the many old Scottish varieties the brothers were grafting onto existing stock. It was delicious.

"What'd Dad say?" Jamie asked, between bites. "Anything else?"

"He was worried you'd be away too long," Molly McCory replied. "We both were. It looks as if it's going to rain again."

"About the foal, I mean."

"Oh, I'd almost forgotten about that. It was before he delivered the calf, wasn't it?" Molly ran her fingers through her short gray hair. "There's so much going on. It's been a busy morning."

"He said it'd melted. The foal. It had turned to slime."

"So he did. I think he's got a sample of something he's going to send to Oban." Molly took her son's plate away. "I'm not sure what it is."

People don't ask enough questions, Jamie thought, but didn't say anything. He seldom criticised his mother. She was the only real friend he had. Funny, that? He wasn't a mummy's boy. He had one or two mates at school. He liked girls, but the only person he trusted was his mum. He could talk to her about anything for however long he wanted.

"He's in the surgery, if you'd like a word with him," Molly added. "Lucy's there, so he won't mind being interrupted."

"I'll leave it till later."

"What is it, Jamie?" Molly glanced at him. He was balancing a fresh apple on top of another, his green eyes serious. "Anything wrong?"

"Not really," Jamie said, but there was. He'd had this feeling ever since his father mentioned the slime. He didn't know why. It was stupid, but he'd like to know if it led anywhere. If it told anyone where it came from. "It's just a bit unusual, that stuff he was talking about. It could have come from the sea."

"The sea?"

"You never know."

"You'll have to talk to him about that." Molly began drying the plate. It was quite normal, she supposed, living where they did, but Jamie had a real obsession with the water. Wanted to save whales, clean oil-slick off clotted birds, preserve as much of the dwindling fish stocks as he could. He'd spend his life underwater if it were possible. Probably would, if it came to that. When he left school he wanted to study at Dunstaffnage, the marine science college near Oban. There was nothing to stop him. After that he'd go wherever it took him. Down into the depths most likely. "Oh, there was something else I had to tell you," she added, giving her mind a rest. "Your father's going to get an assistant. Someone to help him in the surgery."

"What about Lucy?"

"She's getting on. And she's only a nurse. He wants someone to work with smaller animals. All those little ones that come in."

"Sounds good."

"You don't think that, one day, you'd....?"

"Come on, Mum. You know that's not for me."

"You like animals."

"Yeah, but I prefer them with fins."

The giant squid came ashore for the second time in the early hours of the following morning. The weather had turned sour during the night, more rain poured down converting the rivulet, which ran over the cliffs from the Chattan farm, into a tumbling stream bearing the flavour of fresh-born calf.

The squid didn't move until Jamie McCory had swum away, had lain dark and almost motionless, inhaling only enough seawater to keep its twin hearts beating. It knew, instinctively, how to survive. Years of genetic memory, half a billion since its ancestors came to life in the primeval waters of the earth, kept it safely hidden until the thing above turned and went away. Not that the four-armed creature, a misshapen starfish without any doubt, had issued any threat. On the contrary, a sense of harmony filtered down as it swam over the squid - a pleasant change in a world where attacks could be started by the twitch of a fin. Still, it was time to find a new shelter, so the squid moved on to just below the Chattan farm where, to its delight, a new and tempting taste began flowing over its gills, making it realise that its appetite wasn't quite so satisfied after all.

First, however, the squid had to discover if the source of the flavour was accessible, and then whether it was worth the hunt. Making its mind up wasn't new to the giant creature. In its short and vigorous life it'd had to make many choices - whether to attack or flee, what food was needed at a given time, what appeared most readily caught – these decisions were made on a daily basis. The only choice it had ever suppressed had to do with bonding. The picking out of an attractive partner, who would insert sperm beneath her mantle, had so far been avoided. In fact, the squid was still a virgin. There were a number of reasons why.

To begin with, she knew that mating was a dangerous game. After a mother's eggs were fertilised they had to be attached to the seabed by little stalks. This was an exhausting process - there were times when the female died from sheer fatigue. Apart from that, she'd never seen another of her tribe who attracted her sufficiently. But, above all, there was that recent substance filtering through her veins - the curious and compelling impulse of something, which, after driving her out of the Peake Deep, was urging her to find a new and exciting partner. Although she had no idea what that might be, the force had brought her here, taken her to where she hung in the water below the Chattan farm, where the problem of the moment was how to scale the wet cliffs above the swelling sea.

As it turned out, climbing the rock was easier than first appeared. The water running down was fresh, yet rich with oxygen. The squid tested it with a tentacle and knew she could survive in it for as long as needed. Lifting herself with her eight powerful arms, the tentacles withdrawn, the body raised like that of a spider, she began to make her way up the bed of the rivulet. Moving her arms in unison, clinging to the cliff, she soon reached a bed of flat rock at the top. Once or twice she loosened a boulder, as a sucker plucked too vigorously, to send it crashing down into the sea. However, no one heard the falls. Nor did anyone witness her progress, see the spider-like creature, its eyes enormous in the night, rising out of the water. There was no one to tell Ian and Alec Chattan what was about to happen to their calf.

When the squid arrived at the cow-shed, standing high on the banks of the stream, she paused. Here the water was heavy with flavour, enriched by the closeness of the new-born calves bedded with their mother. The squid paused to calculate the quickest way to catch the prey, how much time she would have to remain out of the water.

She knew she could manage for a few moments without oxygen. That lesson had been learnt when she'd taken Harry Carter's foal. By moving fast, keeping moist in the grass between the river and the stable, she had caught the foal with her tentacles from a distance of twenty feet. But, here, the victim was surrounded by other members of the herd, protected like young whales in a school. The capture would not be as easy.

Briefly, the squid considered returning to the sea, but the flavour was too tempting and the food so close. So again, with spider-like movements, she lifted herself out of the stream. Gripping at rocks, ripping out tufts of grass, she approached the building, slid up the half-open stable-door to examine what lay within. Almost at once, with her powerful vision, she saw what she wanted and attacked.

Immediately, a wave of uneasiness went through the herd. Cows skittered, thumped in their stalls, mooed, lowed and rolled their eyes. The mother came to her feet as one giant tentacle, and then another, reached out to take her offspring. She thrashed on her chain, kicked back against the cowshed wall, then came to the defence of her children, impelled by the pain it had taken to bring them into the world.

She lowered her head, her short sharp horns directed at the squid. Her mooing turned into a threatening growl as the tentacles gripped her new-born calves, binding them together in an enormous bale. Snorting in anger as her infants struggled, the mother attacked the intruder, now hanging on the stable door, its huge eyes peering in.

The mother lurched toward the beast, but her chain stopped her with a jolt. She pressed on, snapping the shackle, and attacked the tentacles that were dragging her babies away. Her horns went into the soft rubbery flesh, jerked up and ripped free. She butted and the monster's arm yielded. She lunged a third time with greater success. The tentacle which held her first-born, the calf William McCory had delivered with such loving care, withdrew, releasing its catch. The calf staggered and fell against its mother, as its twin was carried away.

By now the cow-shed was alive with the sound and movement of terrified Ayrshires. The giant squid, nursing her wounded tentacle, grasping the prey with the other, managed to draw the calf within her arms and enfold it tightly. Once held, the calf stopped struggling. Without hesitating a second longer, the squid slid off the stable-door, fell back into the bubbling stream, allowed the water to take her away, and was washed down the cliff to the sea.

Inside the cow-shed, the mother held her remaining baby close. Trembling in a mixture of rage and fear, she began licking the creature, restoring its faith. While all around the noise rose to a level that finally awoke the Chattan brothers, who sprang from their beds, told their wives not to worry, pulled on Wellingtons and stumbled into the night to find out what was causing the uproar.

Later that morning, Sergeant Anthony Croft, his stomach on the mend, replaced the telephone on the front counter of the Culloch Police Station and turned to Constable Murdoch Roberts.

"That was Alec Chattan," he said. "They've had a terrible night. Something got in amongst the herd. Attacked a cow and her calves. There were two of them, fresh-born. One's got little circles all over its hide. But there's no sign of the other."

"They know what took it?" Murdoch asked, reaching for his notebook. "Cattle thieves don't usually go up there in the hills."

"They've no idea," Croft replied. "Thought it might've been wolves."

"Been no wolves on these islands for three hundred years."

"Might have escaped. There's some that's kept as pets."

"That's illegal."

"Doesn't mean it doesn't go on."

"What we going to do?"

"You write a report. I'll have a chat with Will McCory."

At that moment Harry Carter walked into the station, red-eyed and tired. He'd sat up all night in his stable, a loaded double-barrelled shotgun by his side, a bottle of whisky close at hand. Cursing the bastards who'd taken his foal, muttering insults against the police, the Town Council, even the vet with his ideas about aliens, he'd finally came to the conclusion he'd get nowhere on his own. By the time pale light began to filter through rain-sodden cloud, the chill of the dark deep in his bones, he'd had enough. A man had the right to defend what he owned, but there were times when he needed help.

"What's happened?" he asked, as both the sergeant and the constable looked up with watchful eyes. Carter's face was more flushed than ever, there was a threatening note in his voice. "Got any idea who took my livestock?"

"It was a foal, wasn't it, Harry?" Croft asked quietly.

"Aye. Know anything about it?"

"Now, well..." The sergeant hesitated, aware he was under no obligation to tell this angry farmer what Alec Chattan had said. On the other hand, in a town as small as Culloch it would take little time for word to get around. And there were curious similarities linking the two events. "We haven't discovered anything more about your foal, but there's been another incident."

"You telling me the thieving bastards came back?"

"We're not quite sure what happened, Harry," Croft replied, feeling his stomach starting to churn again. "But the Chattans lost a calf."

"Who took it?"

"We don't know yet."

"The thing is, Harry," Constable Murdoch Roberts said softly, hoping to calm Carter down. The whisky fumes on the man's breath were fierce. "There's something a bit odd about all this. We've not had anything quite like it before." He paused, glanced at the notes he'd been taking. "Ah, who was with your foal when it was taken?"

"No one. If I'd been there I'd have shot the sods."

"Was the foal left on its own?"

"She was with the mare, if that's what you mean."

"How was the mare when you found her?"

"Frightened half to death." Harry put both hands on the counter and raised his voice. "What the hell's this got to do with my livestock? Mind telling me that? Either you know who took the foal or you're wasting my bloody time."

"Now, Harry," said Croft. "Let the constable ask his questions."

"Oh, for Christ's sake," Harry Carter spluttered. They were all the same, these buggers with authority. There was a computer behind the sergeant, a filing cabinet beside it. Give them a bit of equipment and they think they're running the country. But what could he do? He was only paying their salaries. "Get on with it."

"Were there....?" Constable Roberts cleared his throat, checked his notes for confirmation. "Were there any strange circles on the mare?"

"What?"

"Round marks? Anything like that?"

"Like what?"

"Like mini crop circles, for example."

"For Christ's sake, don't tell me we're back to fucking aliens." Harry Carter looked from face to face. They weren't a bad pair of coppers, but what did they think they were up to? The whole bloody place was going to the dogs. It was about time someone did something about it. "You better get hold of Angus Douglas. He should be told what's going on."

FIVE – fishy business

Angus Douglas, chairman of Culloch Town Council, a rotund man with what he liked to think of as a Churchillian figure, was sitting in his study, wearing a burgundy dressing gown, a port and brandy in one hand, watching the morning news on the BBC, when Sergeant Croft phoned him.

"Sorry to disturb you, sir," Croft began carefully. He felt uneasy in Douglas's company, even over the phone. He'd known the man for most of his life, yet always found him cold and distant. "But I think this is important."

"What is, Sergeant?"

"There's been some cattle stolen."

"Nothing unusual about that, as we're both too well aware."

"Very true, but the stock's normally taken from the fields. And then by the truckload. This went from someone's stables."

"Not really surprising, there's little enough left out in the fields these days. Be up to their knees in mud." Angus sipped his drink, watched a car bomb explode on the screen, and wondered why he'd been called. There was nothing new about stolen cattle. "Who were the unfortunate owners?"

"The Chattan brothers and Harry Carter."

"What was taken?"

"A foal, sir. And a calf. Both new-born."

"For God's sake, man, don't tell me you've interrupted my morning just because a foal and a calf have disappeared. Got nothing better to do?"

"It's not as simple as it sounds." Sergeant Croft's voice hardened. The encounter with Harry Carter had been enough for one day. It had taken half an hour to get the angry farmer out of the station. Only by promising to tell the chairman of the Town Council what was going on had the man been persuaded to leave. So the sergeant wasn't in any mood to be brushed aside by Angus Douglas - an overweight relic who thought he owned the town. His ancestors might have, but that was a long time ago, the world was very different then. "There's a sort of slimy residue that's been left behind in both cases," Croft continued. "At the Chattan farm there are funny circles on another calf."

"What sort of circles?"

"Like mini crop circles." Sergeant Croft swallowed, his stomach was playing up again. "Harry Carter didn't see anything like that, but he wasn't exactly forthcoming. It seems the vet made some crack about aliens that got up his nose. I suggest we call a council meeting. I've talked to Will McCory. He feels the same as I do."

"Aliens, eh? Now, that sounds a little more intriguing."

Angus Douglas sat back in his chair. Born into a once-wealthy family, he now lived alone in the Big House on the hill. He had no children and his wife had left years ago. These days, if he looked out the window of his study, he could see a collection of new houses built on what used to be his land. Without the money they'd brought in he'd have been on the bones of his well-padded arse. But he seldom looked at the toy-houses. The sight of them sickened him. What he really wanted to see was a return to the glories of the past. The fishing boats coming back to harbour. The cattle returning to the sheds at night. The smell of fresh-scythed grass. But, unfortunately, that was behind him now. All he had left was a flock of Blackface sheep - direct descendants of those established by James the Fourth in 1503, yet a mere token of what once had been a grand holding. What's more, this house of his was badly in need of repair. Perhaps, just perhaps, the sergeant had come across something that might put Culloch back on the map, bring a little money into the town, some of which would end up in his pocket.

"What do you think, sir?" Croft asked, puzzled by the silence. "Shall I send out some notices? Sort out a meeting?"

"Ah, let's not make it too formal," Angus replied in a milder tone. "I suggest you get a few of us together for a drink in the *Harbour Light*. You, me, the vet, of course. You might invite the Chattans. But, I don't think Harry Carter'd be much help. He's not exactly one of us."

"Perhaps not."

"While you're at it, put a call through to the *Oban Times*. They might like to send a reporter down. Crop circles on a Culloch calf?" Angus Douglas gave a chuckle, watched bodies being carried out of a bombed building without wondering who they were. "There's probably a news story in that. Could do us all the world of good."

"I'll get going right away, sir." Sergeant Croft replaced the receiver carefully, not quite sure what he'd begun. The call had been made innocently enough – in part to placate Harry Carter, in part to make sure that everything was done by the book. But the respone of the Chairman of the Town Council had surprised him. Everyone knew the town needed something to lift it out of its sombre mood, but the chairman's reaction seemed too extreme.

The giant squid lay motionless in a cavern quite close to the cliffs below the Chattan farm. She'd eaten the calf. The few hard bones that remained, the scraps, the extraneous bits and pieces, had fallen into a crevice, where they were immediately attacked by eager crabs, a swarm of flittering prawns.

Even though her hunger had been satisfied, the squid made no effort to move. The damage the cow's horns had done to her tentacle meant she would have to lie quietly for a while, give her body time to recover, allow the blood from her twin hearts to carry out its process of repair.

In her voyages through the oceans, before that unknown substance had urged her away, the squid had seen many of her companions lose suckers, parts of a tentacle, even an arm or two. Their flesh had healed, in time the survivors had gone on to live with the stumps the appendages had become. She was confident she'd also recover and be able to return to the place where the four-armed creature had hovered on the surface. Strangely enough, for a person so used to living alone, she was tempted to see the starfish again. It had issued no threats, given no sign of aggression. In fact, the little eyes behind the great orbs it used to peer through had been gentle; she had to see them again. Perhaps the time had come to mate, although how anything could be accomplished with the tiny sex-organ the starfish possessed was something she'd need to investigate. However, it might be less painful than with one of her kind – some of them had penises three feet long.

It was a curious tug, more powerful than any the squid had known before, that urged her back to the place where she'd lain, almost invisible, watching the creature stare down at the foal-bones lying in the sand. Nothing she'd encountered was quite like the starfish. And, nothing she'd ever met in the water had seemed so unthreatening, had issued such a sense of good fellowship, of wanting to belong.

No matter how bruised the squid now felt, how long it took to recover from the battle with the cow, she was certain she'd return to the shadow below the overhanging rock, and wait for the strange creature to reappear. She felt certain it would. Perhaps contact might even be made. Certainly there was no danger in the hovering. The starfish-like thing had neither teeth nor jaws, tentacles or arms that were big enough to harm her. There was even the faintest chance she'd discover what had sent her away from the world below; she might learn what had brought her to Culloch harbour, to the food that lined the shore.

William McCory stared at the circles on the bull-calf's hide, ran his fingers over their indentations. In all his years of study, working with animals both great and small, he'd never come across anything that resembled the rings on the calf. The circles were all much the same size, about three inches in diameter and looked as if they'd been made in a series of attacks. Many were laid one over the other, like lash marks on the flanks of beaten cattle.

But these were not as deep, and their edges were serrated. The only thing that came to mind were the biscuit cutters Molly used in the kitchen. He doubted, however, if the Chattan brothers had anything in the cow-shed like that. He turned to them, a pair of almost identical men with short greying hair, open country faces, and eyes that were creased with worry and confusion.

"What do you think caused this?" he asked Ian, the closer of the two.

"No idea," Ian replied. "We heard a row, and came out running."

"It was about four," said Alec, glancing at his brother. "The whole place was in a state. Look at them." His eyes went to the Ayrshires, uneasy in their stalls. "They've not settled, even now."

"The only thing we found was this." Ian put his hands on the cow, now guarding the remaining calf. He turned her head toward the vet. "As I told the sergeant, it's some sort of plastic. It's all over the horns. And it stinks of fish."

"It's purple." William stared. "Like the slime I scraped up at Harry Carter's."

"What happened there?" asked Alec.

"He lost a foal. Whatever took it left a trail that went down toward the Orchy. He thought the foal had melted."

"Aye, Harry would." Alec made drinking motions with a hand. "Bit of this and Harry'd think the world had melted."

"Maybe, but the same stuff was all over the floor. Probably too much hay here for it to stick. There's some on this, though." William went over to the stable door.

"It's just like the sample of Harry's I sent to Oban for analysis."

"What'd they say?"

"Haven't had a reply yet."

"What do you think it was?"

"To be perfectly honest," William replied. "I've no idea."

The vet then examined the calf's wounds, discovered they were superficial and gave the animal an antibiotic injection. He remained silent as he worked, as did the twins. Before he left, William told the Chattans that as soon as he got back to his surgery he'd call Malcolm Stewart and find out if the sample had been tested.

"Will you let us know what it is?" Ian asked.

"Of course."

"You see, we've got a few ideas of our own."

"Like what?"

Ian shrugged, turned to his brother. "Salmon farmers," Alec admitted.

"You think they might have taken the calf?" William sounded unconvinced. "And Harry's foal? Just one off, miles apart?"

"Hard to tell with that lot. Some of them let their livestock swim in shit," Ian grunted. "God knows what they feed them."

"Can you take me, Mum? This afternoon?" Jamie, pulling his woollen hat down to his eyes, gave his mother an appealing look. "I want to have a go with the bottle."

"This afternoon?" Molly McCory frowned as she put finishing touches to the macaroni cheese she was preparing for Jamie's supper. Later she'd grill chops for her husband and herself. She'd become used to preparing split-meals, as she called them. Will certainly liked his meat, but as far as she was concerned, it mattered little what she ate. "This afternoon's a bit tricky, Jamie. I promised Gran I'd take her over some fresh eggs."

"Fresh eggs?"

"Yes, you know what people are like. They come into the surgery with their cats and dogs, quite often bringing something from the garden. At the moment, we've lots of eggs."

"Couldn't it wait till tomorrow?"

"I'd rather it didn't." Molly rubbed her forehead with the back of her hand. She always found it difficult to say no to her son, but she really should go and see her mother, who lived on the banks of Loch Awe, ten miles inland. What's more, she didn't want to take Jamie to the coast and leave him there. She loved watching him diving, was proud of his ability in the water. And it didn't hurt to keep an eye on him, although she usually pretended to be reading a book. But her mother had called twice this week. The weather was getting into her bones, she'd said. And she'd been told that poached eggs on spinach would do her the world of good. "I've promised Gran. I don't want to let her down."

You can't look after everyone, Jamie thought, but didn't say anything. His mother would take him if she could.

"Why today?" Molly asked, grating parmesan over the casserole. "You went yesterday. I'd have thought that'd keep you happy for a while."

"I saw something. I wanted to take another look at."

"What was it?"

"Not sure, it's just...I don't know." Jamie shrugged. "But I can leave it till tomorrow."

"Listen..." Molly straightened her long angular body. "If you really want to, I suppose I could give Gran a ring."

"It's okay. The tides aren't heavy. It'll still be there tomorrow."

"What was it?"

"I don't know." Jamie began to fiddle with a spoon by the sink. It was funny, but he had to see those white things again. They weren't like the tin box he'd found, not as good as that. But they were different and he wanted to check them out. "Don't worry, it's okay."

"Tomorrow, I promise," Molly said, feeling guilty. She knew he didn't really mind, but that wasn't the point. She also knew she could phone her mother and make an excuse. It was just that, well, it was always like this. She ended up being the meat in the sandwich. She shook her head, began chopping parsley to sprinkle on the macaroni cheese. "We'll go in the morning."

"Right."

"I won't let anything get in the way."

"Anyway, I've got other things to do," Jamie replied, deciding to melt down the lead he'd been collecting for weeks - bits of old piping, sinkers he'd found caught on the rocks, some with hooks and lines still attached. He'd make another slug for the weighted belt he wore in the water. It was time he did it, the bigger he got the more lead he needed. "Don't worry, Mum. Tomorrow will be fine."

"You sure?"

"Yeah, don't give it another thought." He banged the sink with the spoon, making his mother jump. "Don't worry about it."

But she did, it nagged at her for the rest of the morning. She was still thinking about it when William came home.

When William arrived there were two messages waiting for him on the kitchen table. The first was a note Molly had scribbled after a phone call from Sergeant Croft, asking if her husband could join Angus Douglas and several others for a drink that evening at the *Harbour Light*. The second was a fax from Malcolm Stewart saying he'd run an initial test on the material taken from Harry Carter's stable. It seemed to be some sort of shellfish. Perhaps the old chap had been putting cockles in his haggis. To be sure he'd send it to the marine laboratory at Dunstaffnage for confirmation. He also said he'd found an assistant who might suit Will. She was a Spanish girl, who'd studied at Derby and worked in a clinic there. A country lass, she'd come to Scotland hoping to find a place in a practice. Malcolm hadn't been able to fit her in, but if Will was interested he'd have a word with her.

"Things are moving fast," William said, looking up from the messages to his wife. "You've read the fax, I suppose?"

"Yes, when Lucy brought it in from the surgery." Molly ground black pepper over the chops she was to grill later. "Sounds quite promising."

"It does." William tapped his wife's note. "Tony Croft give you any idea what this meeting's about? Who the other people are?"

"Not really, he just said Angus Douglas wanted to get together. But he did mention that a reporter from the *Oban Times* might be there."

"What for?"

"I don't know, Will. You'll have to ask him yourself."

"You all right, Molly?" William queried as something seemed to be troubling her. She was grinding pepper forcefully. "Anything wrong?"

"Not really."

"What is it?"

"Well..." Molly sighed. "It's just that Jamie wanted me to drive him up the coast this afternoon. I said I couldn't because I'd promised Gran I'd go over."

"How did he take it?"

"All right, but it set me thinking. He's always alone. I know he's got a few friends at school, but whenever he can he's on his own in the water. It's a wonder he doesn't come home frozen stiff."

"He can't," William said lightly. "He got struck by lightning, remember. That chap in Edinburgh told us that."

"He mightn't *feel* cold, but still." Molly put down the pepper grinder, picked up the macaroni cheese dish, put it in the oven. "It's the way he's so *often* on his own that gets to me. That's why I feel bad about this afternoon. Do you think I should...?"

"Don't worry about Jamie, he's all right. And the last time he took anyone with him was a big mistake. Remember Alf? Betty's nephew?"

"He was a nasty piece of work. His language was disgusting."

"Most kids talk like that when their parents aren't around. I've heard our little boy use a ripe expression or two. Anyway, Jamie's better off without someone who wants to kill his friends."

"That's true enough." Molly's eyes softened. "You *do* understand him, don't you, Will? I mean, sometimes...."

"I know, I should learn to hold my tongue." William turned to Malcolm Stewart's fax. "Now, this Spanish lass? Should we invite her for supper sometime?"

"That sounds like a good idea. What's her name, again?"

"Blanca González."

"That's White something, if I remember anything from that Spanish course I took. I wonder what she looks like."

"I'm sure we'll find out soon enough. I'll ask Malcolm to set up a meeting." William turned on the electric kettle. "How about a cup of tea?"

"Yes, please." Molly smiled. "And have a good supper before you leave. It does you no good drinking on an empty stomach."

SIX – gathering of clans

When William McCory arrived at the *Harbour Light* he found Angus Douglas seated in a corner of the bar. With him were Sergeant Tony Croft and Alec, one of the Chattan twins, who said his brother was still busy at the farm. All had drinks before them on a scrubbed pine table.

"So, you've turned up at last," called Angus breezily, picking up his whisky. "We'd just about given you up for lost."

"Sorry about that," William replied, after telling Jack, the barman, he'd have a pint, the same as Alec. Sergeant Croft appeared to be drinking soda-water. "I was just leaving when someone came in with a dog that'd been hit by a car."

"Put the little bugger down, did you?"

"I managed to save it, actually."

"Very noble." Angus glanced at his watch "Well, now that you're here, I suggest we begin. It looks as if the *Oban Times* isn't going to make it."

"What's this about?" asked William. Like Sergeant Croft he had little patience with Angus Douglas, yet was aware of the weight the man carried in the town, both literally and officially. "Tony's call didn't say much."

"I suggested that." Angus sipped his drink. "I didn't want the story to get out too soon. Not until we're good and ready."

"What story?"

"Crop circles on calves. *Your* theory about aliens, Will." Angus beamed, pleased with the frown his words provoked. "Isn't that what you told Harry Carter?"

"That was a joke."

"Harry didn't think so." Angus turned to Tony Croft. "Isn't that right, Sergeant? Carter took it seriously enough?"

"He wasn't greatly amused."

"See what I mean?" Angus's eyes gleamed cleverly. "We need lots more like him, because that's what we want people to think. You don't have any other explanation, do you, Alec?" Angus faced the Chattan twin. "You've no idea what happened to your calf?"

"Not really. All we found was that slimy stuff."

"I took a sample of the same stuff at Harry Carter's," William said. "It went to Oban for analysis."

"What did they find?"

"It seems to be some sort of shellfish."

"Shellfish? I've heard there are giant cockles off the Orkneys. Perhaps they're on the march." Angus chortled. "That'd make an even better story."

"If you want my opinion, it's the salmon farmers," Alec Chattan grunted. "They treat their stock like battery hens. The bastards give the same stuff to their fish as goes into cattle and poultry feed. Wouldn't surprise me if they're taking new-borns to add to the fodder."

"Leave the salmon farmers out of it." Angus Douglas put his hands on his knees and leant firmly forward. "Let's stick to crop circles on calves."

"But that's absurd," said William. "I made that remark as a joke. Not to be taken seriously."

"You're right, it makes no sense," Sergeant Croft agreed. "It sounds fantastic."

"Precisely why we'll go with it," Angus replied briskly. "It's the sort of thing that interests people. The more absurd the better. Gets them talking. Brings them running to take a look for themselves. We've had a bloody awful season. The fishing's shot to hell. There's talk of closing down the post office. Even the police station's on a condemned list. All the more reason to put the story out. We need every bit of publicity we can get. And there's nothing like crop circles, UFOs or aliens to whet the appetite. That's why I wanted the *Oban Times* along. Pity the silly buggers didn't show up. They've missed their chance. But you're all here, so, how do we go about it?"

No one replied. All were stunned by what the chairman had said

"Nothing wrong with the idea, is there?" Angus moved his eyes from face to face. "It's not going to harm anybody. In fact, it could do the town a world of good."

"The only thing about it," William said. "Is that it isn't true."

"Are you absolutely certain?" Angus sat back in his chair, knowing he'd played a blinder. Their expressions told him that. They'd be crapping in their own nests if they turned against him now. He stared squarely at Tony Croft. "What do you say, Sergeant? We're not breaking any laws."

"I, ah, well..." Croft looked at his soda water, wishing he'd ordered scotch but his stomach wasn't up to it. The thing was, the chairman had a point. He might be a pain in the arse but his thinking was sound. Culloch badly needed a push. "There's no evidence either way, is there?"

"Thank you, Sergeant, that's good thinking." Angus turned to Alec Chattan, fully aware that his brother was on the town council. There'd be no trouble there. "You prepared to go along with this? That organic farm of yours could do with a bit of publicity."

"Very well." Alec nodded. "I'll talk to Ian."

"That's settled then." Angus waved at the barman, ordered another round of drinks. "Put them on the council's bill," he said. "This has turned into municipal business." He smiled widely, showing uneven teeth. By God, they'd know who ran the town before this show was over. They'd be lifting their caps to the man who put Culloch back in the limelight, got the money rolling in. He glanced at the vet. "You've no objection, Will, I take it?"

"I don't suppose I have." William drank, let the ale cool his throat. The theory was ridiculous, but if anyone was silly enough to believe it, it could do very little harm. And the chairman was right about the season, it had brought nothing but disaster and discontent. "Unless I get something much more definite from Oban, you'll hear no complaints from me."

"Let's toast that," Angus said, as the barman arrived with fresh drinks. "To crop circles on calves in Culloch. Just wait till the story gets out. Pity that reporter didn't turn up, but I'll give old Charlie Coots a ring. He's editor of the *Oban Times*. Now that we've got some real drama, he'll be all over us like a rash. Next thing you know there'll be TV cameras from half-way round the world. Let's not delude ourselves, we need the attention. We need something to put life back in the town." He peered at the window, saw dribbles running down the pane.

"Look at that, for God's sake, it's started to rain again. But, my friends, don't let it get you down. The sun's about to shine."

In spite of the showers during the night, the following morning dawned clear and clean. The sun shone brightly for the first time in days, and Jamie McCory was ready to go diving even before he'd had breakfast. He arrived in the kitchen, his woollen hat set at a cocky angle, to find his mother grilling sausages for his father. A bowl of muesli, a pot of yoghurt, were waiting at his place at the table.

"Great," he said, sitting down. "I've been looking forward to this."

"You were up early," Molly replied. "I heard you in your room."

"Putting that new weight I made yesterday on my belt." He ate a spoonful of muesli, chewing the hazelnuts slowly. "This is good."

"Glad you like it. It's a batch I put together myself. And you've no need to worry. I'll take you up the coast this morning." Molly smiled. "It's lovely outside. Haven't seen sun like this for ages."

"The sea's perfect. I could see from my bedroom window." Jamie tore the lid off the yogurt. "Where's Dad?"

"Still in the bathroom. He was late last night. I was asleep when he arrived home." She turned as William came into the kitchen. "That meeting must have been interesting. It was after midnight when you got back. What was it all about?"

"Don't ask." William shook his head in disbelief. "The whole thing's bloody ridiculous." He turned to

Jamie. "I don't want to keep you out of anything, son. But you'd better be careful what you say about what I'm going to tell you."

"What on earth's going on? If you can't tell Jamie...?"

"I'll tell you both everything. Just listen to this."

While he ate William McCory told his wife and son what had occurred the evening before. He mentioned Harry Carter's missing foal, the remaining calf at the Chattan's farm with the strange circles on its hide, the slimy material that was left behind in both places. He talked about the report he'd had from Malcolm Stewart, who thought the sample might have come from a mollusc. He spoke about Angus Douglas, and the story that was to be released about crop circles on new-born calves. The aliens, yes *aliens*, that had visited Culloch. The story mightn't do much damage. It could even boost the tourist trade, but could easily be discredited. As far as he was concerned, he added as he reached for a cup of coffee, he wouldn't contradict anything Angus Douglas said until he discovered what the real cause was. And the sooner he did that the better.

"You see, I'm partly to blame," he admitted, pushing his empty breakfast plate away. "I made a joke that misfired. I told Harry Carter I thought his foal might have been taken by aliens."

"You didn't?" Molly said.

"I'm afraid I did."

"What made the circles, Dad?" Jamie asked, more interested than usual by what his father had said. "The same thing that left the slime?"

"I've no idea."

"Like me to look into it?"

"On an alien website?" William began, then held up an apologetic hand. "Sorry, I didn't mean to take it out on you, but I'm really concerned about all this. Find out as much as you can. I need all the help I can get. And, let me tell you something. You were right the other day. That slime did lead somewhere. It went down to the River Orchy."

"All the way?"

"Yes, it left a clear trail."

"Okay." Jamie's head was beginning to buzz. "I'll do what I can."

With that William McCory left the table. When Jamie finished his breakfast he looked questioningly at his mother. She gave him a nod, saying they were ready to go. He immediately went off to get his gear, telling himself he'd think about what his father had said when he was diving. Being in the water often helped clear his head. *That's half the trouble with people*, he told himself. *They don't go off someplace quiet and sort things out.*

With the sun shining through crystal clear water, the giant squid began to move again. She extended her arms, let them feel their way over the pebbly bottom, testing their strength. She put out the good tentacle, watched it rove through stalks of kelp that were almost still in the now-calm sea. It was as flexible as ever. The battle with the cow had done no harm. She tried the tentacle that had been attacked and, to her relief, it was also working. With her huge, saucer-shaped eyes she examined the wounds that had been so raw and saw that scar tissue was already forming, beginning to cast a seal over the damage. It would need looking after, had to be kept retracted for a while but, restored by the recent meal, the squid knew she could swim almost as fast as ever, and wondered if it was time to return to the place where the starfish dwelt, to see if she could learn more about the creature.

She eased out of the overnight refuge, and with the funnel that emerged from beneath her mantle directed a stream of water into the crevice, jetting herself away. Normally, when shooting through the seas at speeds that could reach twenty-five knots an hour, twice as fast as a marauding whale, the squid travelled backward, her arms and tentacles trailing behind like the tail of a wind-driven kite. This morning, however, there was no need for haste, so she swam slowly forward, steering herself with her fin-like tail, heading toward the place that Jamie McCory called the Grotto.

Molly McCory drove her son along the coast road, the sun coming into her Volkswagen with refreshing warmth. She drove over bright green hilltops, through firs forming picket-fences along the skyline, beech leaves turning golden as the season came to a close.

"It's beautiful, Jamie," she murmured - her heart always lifted on days like this. "It's absolutely perfect, isn't it?"

"Yeah, I can't wait to get in the water." On his own, Jamie seldom took the coast road. He preferred walking up over the hills, where he could stop and look down at the sea, watch the shapes that moved as the ripples flowed. He liked to follow the beds of limestone sloping down into the water, wondering what they hid in their hollows, what secrets they held. If he lifted his eyes over the Firth of Lorne there was the Isle of Mull, rising like a soft cloud on the horizon. "It's magic."

"What do *you* think's worrying your father?" Molly asked, a little later, her mind going back to the breakfast table, the concerned look in her husband's eyes. "The idea of aliens is ridiculous, but those circles on the calf, they're really strange."

"Weird."

"You said you'd look into them."

"I didn't find much though, nothing that made any sense."

The evening before Jamie had spent a long time on his computer searching for something to explain the markings on the calf. He'd found a report on ring-worm in cattle, but the condition was rare and occurred mostly in the tropics. Even though it had been passed on to humans in Australia, it seemed to have no connection with what had happened at the Chattan farm. *Anyway*, he'd told himself. *If it was that, Dad would have known about it.* Still, there had to be a logical answer somewhere. He didn't believe in aliens any more than his parents did. And there *was* something in the back of his head he couldn't quite get clear - a picture he'd seen somewhere of circles on the skin of an animal, but he couldn't think where. Finally, he had given up and gone to bed.

"I looked for a good while," he added to his mother. "But I didn't get anywhere."

"You will keep trying, though?" Molly changed gear, turned into a side road leading down to the sea. "Your father'd really like it if you could work together."

"I'll have another go later on."

"Did I tell you he's getting an assistant?"

"Yeah, who would that be?"

"A Spanish girl, Malcolm Stewart's met. Fully qualified, and really good with small animals. She and Lucy could do most of the work in the surgery."

"Speaks English, I suppose."

"I'm sure she does. Where was it she studied?" Molly drew the car to a halt beside a block of bedded stone. "Derby, I think."

"Sounds good. Dad could do with some help."

Jamie slid out of the car, filled his lungs with the sea, the kelp, the tang of fish. It always got him right away. He couldn't wait to start. From where he stood it was only a few steps to the water, then round the point to the Grotto. Today, he wasn't directly in front of the Grotto, where the lobsters and the spider crabs dwelt, not like when he was on his own. But he had his air-bottle, and that made a difference. Even though he liked to be alone, it helped to be driven. And his mother would give him a hand with the bottle, although he could manage on his own. Once on his back, it was easy. When he got in, he didn't do any of those tricky things you saw on TV. Like sitting on the side of a boat and falling backwards. He just found a place to enter and then slid quietly in without disturbing anything, without making a splash. He didn't want to startle the fishes, send them scooting away thinking he was something to fear.

"Right," he said, his voice quickening. "Let's get started."

The giant squid swam slowly up the coast, away from the cliffs below the Chattan farm. She knew where she was heading, remembered the overhang of rock she'd hidden beneath after eating the foal, and recalled the place where the bones had fallen onto the sand, the little creatures that scuttled out to pick them clean.

Recalling events, making choices, had enabled the squid to survive in the depths and semi-darkness where most of her life had been spent. There, she had been forced to choose between hunting and hiding, attacking or retreating to escape. As her huge body had grown, so had her brain. It wasn't quite as big as a sperm whale's, which was the largest of any creature that has ever lived, but certainly large enough to know when and how to react, what to look for, where to go.

Now, close to the surface, she realised that the emptiness of the depths had made life quite difficult in the past. The waters below lacked the signposts that were so useful now. Here, with her brilliant eyesight, the sensitivity that lay at the ends of her arms and on the suction pads of her tentacles, she could see and touch and map her way along the rugged coastline. And here, in spite of the constant clicks and scrapings and washing of weeds, there were none of the signals that came from whales, the sounds that filled both her hearts with fear.

Moving slowly, knowing where to go, the giant squid made her way to the Grotto. The sea was still, there was barely any movement in the water, and all around was the promise of a bright new day.

Jamie McCory slid into the sea, felt it take the weight of the air-bottle, and was lifted once more by the excitement of being in the water. He half-turned to wave at his mother, standing uneasily on the shore. She'd watch him go under, look at the bubbles that followed his trail, then return to the car and pick up a book, not reading a word on the page. When he came out she'd be waiting with a dry towel, a thermos of hot milk. She'd ask him how the water was, what interesting things he'd seen.

They'd sit together, after he'd changed his clothes, and talk about the dive. She was especially easy to be with then, although she seldom went into the water. She sometimes paddled at low tide near the shore, but that was all. Like his father, she wasn't a swimmer, which was funny when you thought about it for people who lived by the sea. He wondered how they could keep out of it.

He'd tried to interest them in diving, but got no further than getting them to try on a mask in the dining room. Both had spluttered, said it made them feel they were suffocating. As for the snorkel, they just shook their heads. They had their own lives, he knew that, and he sometimes joined them on walks over the hills to take part in what they did. But the water was his own special kingdom, and he didn't mind being alone. He knew what they said about diving without a companion, but it didn't worry him all that much. It was a whole lot better than having to share the water with a prick like Alf.

SEVEN – deep waters

When Angus Douglas rang Charlie Coots, editor of the *Oban Times*, he expected a more positive response. After all, he'd known the thin, white-haired journalist for more years than he cared to remember. They'd played golf together, visited each other's houses, shot grouse on blustery mornings, drunk malt by the bottle. So, when Charlie burst out laughing at the suggestion that aliens were responsible for the circles on the Chattan's surviving calf, Angus's blood pressure simmered.

"Listen here," he replied sharply. "There's no other explanation. The vet's seen nothing like this before. The Chattans have no idea what took one calf and mutilated another. Or what reduced the rest of the herd to a state of absolute terror. What's more, they left some sort of material behind that hasn't been fully identified."

"What sort of material?" Charlie Coots enquired. "Ectoplasm?"

"Something considerably more substantial than that," Angus replied, telling himself he'd better keep calm. "More like plastic."

"Cocaine residue?" Charlie blew his nose on a Kleenex. "Some of the lads that steal cattle go in for that sort of thing."

"For Christ's sake, Charlie, listen to me." Angus Douglas was determined not to give in, there was far too much at stake. What had begun as a suggestion in the *Harbour Light*, a search for publicity to put new life into the town, had now hardened to a conviction. Above all, he had to stick to his guns, or risk sounding like a buffoon. "We've got real evidence here. Something everyone can see for themselves. Why don't you send one of your people down? Let them take a look?"

"I would if I could," Charlie replied a little more seriously. "But I can't."

He quite liked old Douglas, though felt a bit sorry for him. There'd been a time, before his wife left, before he took to drinking heavily, when Angus had been excellent company. A little stuck-up, perhaps, a relic who longed for a return to the past, to the authority that came with the blood, but bright and entertaining enough. Now, living alone in a semi-ruin, scraping along with what was left of the money from the land he'd sold, he'd become tiresome. It was surprising he'd managed to hold on to his position as Chairman of the Town Council. That was just as well, without it he'd have had nothing. Which explained, of course, why he was trying to drum up interest in Culloch now. No one could blame him for that. But *aliens*, for God's sake? Quite pathetic really.

"The thing is, I've got my hands full," Charlie added. "Every man-jack, and jill-woman in these PC-days, is out on something or other. Haven't got anyone to send."

"Come down and take a look for yourself."

"Impossible. We're only a weekly, I'm up to my eyes in it."

"Then, by God, I'll take some photographs. Bring them up to Oban."

"Just a moment, Angus. Think what you're doing before you take it any further. Crop circles on a calf, or my backside, for that matter, are old hat. They were all over the country a few years ago. Since then, dozens of theories as to what caused them have been made public. Books pronouncing them as frauds have sold by the ton. People aren't interested any more. They want something new, nowadays. They want something that's completely different."

"I suppose so, but..."

Angus took another swig of the port and brandy he'd poured to reinforce himself before making the call, recognising that Charlie Coots might have a point. But it didn't mean that the calf-circle story had to be thrown out the window. He knew his old friend would do something if he could. A few years ago he'd helped save the Douglas herd of Blackface sheep. When an over-zealous official suggested putting them down at the height of the Mad Cow epidemic Charlie had come to the rescue. After several front-page stories in the *Oban Times*, the BBC had taken up the cause. In the end, the herd had been left untouched. It had to be sequestered for a time, but the blood-line that went back to the sixteenth century remained intact.

"Are you suggesting we wait a while?" Angus asked in a milder tone. "See if anything more interesting turns up?"

"That's a good idea. Ask around, see what you can find."

"More circles? Something like that?"

"More anything, Angus. Even..." Charlie was about to say flying saucers, but resisted the impulse. "Even more of that plastic stuff you mentioned."

"Right, then, I'll make some enquiries. Let you know what I find."

Angus Douglas put the phone down thoughtfully, took his drink to the window and stared out at the rows of new houses on what once had been his land. They looked relatively decent with the sun on their white facades. The line of their chimney-pots made a nice pattern against the calm blue sea.

"Hate the thought, but there'll be many more of them if I have anything to do with it," he muttered. "I'll get evidence of something that'll bring them in, even if I have to conjure it up myself."

It didn't take long for Jamie McCory to find the foal bones. Once under the water, he glided gently toward the Grotto, loving the sense of being balanced in the sea. That was the great thing about the bottle, he didn't have to think about going up for air, and he knew what to do to keep safe. Before his father bought him the gear, he'd taken him to Oban for a course in scuba diving, where he'd learnt he could only stay under for a certain time, had to calculate how long his air would last, and to get out if he felt cold. He knew that if he went deep, he had to return to the surface slowly to avoid the bends. He'd read somewhere they were called the bends because the pain was worst in the knees and elbows. It was so intense people doubled up in agony. That was because of the nitrogen that went into the body under pressure in the water, and if you came up too quickly it turned into bubbles - like opening a can of Coke. The bends could kill you if you weren't careful, if you didn't let the gas get slowly back into the air in your lungs. Jamie had learnt about things like that, but he seldom went very deep, not much further than a hundred feet, there was enough to see in shallower waters.

Go really deep one day, though, he told himself as he got closer to the Grotto. *Love to see what lives down there.*

He'd been down deep on the internet, seen photos of fish with enormous heads, huge mouths with teeth like iron gates. There were things with stalks that had lights on them so they could see in the dark, and huge creatures no one knew much about. He'd watched films, taken with remote cameras, of crabs and fish and worms that lived in super-heated water coming out of hot springs on the ocean floor. There were octopus with fins and amazing shapes, some of them looked like Dumbo. It was incredible way down in the depths, he couldn't wait to take a look for himself. But that would have to be later, after he'd studied at Dunstaffnage.

Jamie swam on, his mind jumping, other thoughts creeping back. What was it his father said at breakfast about a trail of slime and funny circles? He'd looked for a while on the internet without much success. Yet, somewhere he'd seen a picture of something that left those sorts of marks, but couldn't remember where. It didn't sound like anything on the surface. *Wait a minute, you're getting carried away,* he told himself. *You came here to look for those white things. Do it before the tide begins to turn. It'll be going out soon enough, and the currents can get strong. You don't want to end up fighting them.*

He turned the corner of a weed-covered rock and immediately saw what he was looking for. They were still there by the Grotto, a collection of white things half covered with silt and sand. He moved closer and picked one up.

The giant squid became aware of Jamie's presence before she saw him. Built into her nerve endings was a sensory system so finely tuned it could detect movements in the water long before whatever created them came into sight. It was a sort-of radar, developed over the thousands of years her fellow creatures had lived in the oceans of the world. Without it they might never have survived. Most of the time, however, the messages she received were ignored, accepted as unthreatening. Only when they came from something as dangerous as a sperm whale did she responded - then, as quickly as she could.

Now, as the squid searched for the starfish, she knew what signals to expect. She'd registered them earlier, stored them in her memory along with the knowledge that the thing issued no threat, seemed to be quite friendly. So, before Jamie entered her field of vision, she sensed his presence. At once, she stopped, remained almost still, quivering a little to hold her position in the water. She retracted her arms and tentacles, made herself as small as she could, though that presented a problem. Even with all her appendages withdrawn she measured more then eleven feet. Nevertheless, doing her best, she waited to see what would happen, quite eager to make contact with the starfish again.

Soon it came into sight. It wasn't up on the surface this time, but swimming deep, almost down to her level. And its body had altered, grown bigger, turned orange along the back. The giant squid's quivering increased as she wondered if she should change colour too, go from a neutral grey to something vivid in order to make herself more attractive. But, she hesitated, suddenly shy. This wasn't the appropriate moment, she should wait a little longer, find out more. Perhaps the best method would be to catch the thing, gently draw it closer, see what it was like.

Jamie McCory turned the bone over in his black-gloved hand, a little disappointed. He'd expected something more exciting, like the tin box he'd found once. All the same, it was unusual to discover so many bones together on the bottom like this, as if someone had put them there. Even though they were surrounded by prawns and crabs, crawling with sea lice, there was something ordered about their placement. He scratched around in the sand, making a slender eel race away, other small creatures scatter, the crabs back off defensively, claws held high. It took a moment or two for the water to clear before he was able to examine the bones more closely. He saw the skull when a worm slid out of an eye socket.

Looks like a grave or something, he told himself, picking it up, wondering what it came from. *I'd better take this back for Dad. He'll know what it is.*

Jamie blew a stream of bubbles, glanced at his watch. He'd been in the water longer than expected - crazy how time drifted by down here. He had to get out or his mother would start to worry. She'd be sitting in the car, a book on her lap, trying not to look at the shoreline, waiting for him to climb out and join her so she could give him a mug of hot milk.

Yeah, he thought. *Got to go now.*

As he turned to leave he saw a shape in the distance that looked like a bank of weed. It was almost on the bottom, not quite clear in the silt he'd stirred up. He stared, and with a jolt that went right through him, that set his heart going like a train, he recognised it as a living creature. It was less than thirty feet away, and by far the biggest thing he'd ever seen in the water. It was just hanging there, watching him with eyes like dinner plates, waiting to see what he would do.

Get out of here, he told himself, his mind a whirl. He was scared, fear prickled all through him. He was sweating under his wet-suit. He couldn't believe anything that size would be right here in the Grotto. *Leave it alone.* He began paddling backwards. The thing kept staring, it didn't move, and somehow its calmness made him feel a bit better. Whatever it was, it didn't look like it was going to attack him. It just sat there, sort of trembling, staring with those enormous eyes.

Hang on. He had to clear his head. He couldn't race off just because he'd got a fright. *Maybe it's an illusion. Things look bigger underwater. It's not doing anything. It might be sleeping. But, what the hell is it? Some kind of ray?*

There were many rays along the coastline, usually lying flat on the bottom, trying to hide. Once, he'd gone down behind one, grabbed its tail like someone in a film he'd seen. He'd expected to be pulled along like the other diver but got a powerful shock instead. It went up his arm, like the lightning that stopped him feeling cold in the water, and made him let go with a gurgle, feeling as if he'd touched a live wire. Later, he identified the ray as one of the electric ones.

But this thing wasn't like that. It wasn't like anything he'd seen before. In spite of his heart still racing, he had to take a closer look. And he was feeling a bit easier about it now. The first shock was dying away. *Can't just go and leave it,* he thought. *Might never see it again. Got to know if it's real. Got to find out what it is. This is a chance in a lifetime.*

Very slowly, Jamie moved toward the squid, going carefully, so as not to give it a fright. It was like that in the water, if you just drifted along sometimes the fish didn't take much notice, swam with you some of the way. Then, unthinkingly, he blew out a stream of bubbles, and the creature disappeared. One moment it was hanging there. The next, in a flash, it had gone. Jamie felt the water move, like a blast from a garden hose, and found himself alone in the Grotto. There was no one else with him apart from the usual number of curious fishes, and the skull that was still in his trembling hand.

"Amazing," he spluttered, blowing a stream of bubbles. "Never seen anything like this before. But, I can't tell anyone about it yet. Not till I know what it is."

As soon as the giant squid saw Jamie pick up the bone, she felt sorry for the creature. From somewhere deep within, among the records she kept in her complex brain, came a motherly reaction, a desire to protect. Even though she'd never had children of her own, she realised that this ungainly starfish needed to be cared for, perhaps given something to eat. It was obviously hungry. Why else would it be looking for food on the bottom of the sea amongst something she'd left behind? Behaving that way was most unusual for so large a creature. Underwater dwellers as big and as well-equipped as this weren't scavengers, they hunted their food and ate it fresh.

However, the starfish *did* look a bit like a remora, those pathetic hangers-on, with suckers on their backs, that clung onto sharks and rays and sea turtles eating the scraps their hosts left behind. And she'd watched the starfish pick up the remains of her meal and look them over carefully. Finally it selected a piece, after chasing away the rest of the scavengers, and seemed about to eat it, even though the squid couldn't see how it would fit into the starfish's tiny mouth. It didn't seem to have any teeth, only that tube which went up to its back. Perhaps it was a sexual organ after all.

Then, when the giant squid was about to take a closer look, the thing moved toward her and blew out a chain of shining bubbles which gave her such a fright she had to retreat. The only other creature that did anything like that was the dreaded sperm whale - this was no time to take any chances. With a powerful surge from the jet beneath her mantle, she shot away knowing she could return any time she wanted. There was no doubt the starfish would be back. One thing she'd learnt, in her short time in these waters, was that the creatures that dwelt there liked the places they lived. She'd watched them swim away then circle back to where they knew as home. So, off she went, into a bed of kelp, changed colour to blend in with the darkness of the weed, and realised she was quite peckish again.

Jamie McCory climbed out of the water, eased the bottle off his back and made his way to the car, wondering what he'd seen. It might have been a swirl in the currents, a type of mirage. The water had been a dirty, and the hanging creature had vanished in a flash. *But no*, he told himself, with a shake of the head. *It had been there as clear as day.* And, strange as it might seem, in the brief moments they'd spent together, he'd felt a connection, almost like he'd known the thing. Like he'd known that pollock Alf shot. While he'd watched the pollock limp away to die, its pain had been inside him. It was the same with the thing that looked like a ray. He'd seen something in its eyes. And those eyes, they were familiar. Like the marks on the calf his father had talked about. It was all coming together slowly, he had to really think about it now, had to find out what it was before he told anyone about it. After all, he was only a kid, no one was going to take him seriously until he had some proof.

"If must have been cold in there today," his mother said, helping him off with his wet suit. "Your face is as white as a ghost's."

"A bit." Jamie rubbed himself dry, pulled on a heavy sweater, his woollen hat. He felt better with that in place. Then he picked up the skull he'd found on the bottom and showed it to his mother. "Look at this. It's fresh. I bought it for Dad to see."

"Why should he be interested in that?"

"Just thought he might."

"Well, you never know." Molly smiled fondly as she reached for the thermos. He was a funny boy, she had to admit. Always bringing strange things home. Still, it was better than sitting in front of the television like some of the others. And he was kind, that was one of the best things about him. She'd seen him pick snails off the road so they didn't get squashed. Most other kids would have stamped on them. "Here, get this into you. It'll warm you up." She handed him a mug of milk from the thermos. "When you've finished, we'd better get going. It looks as if the weather's about to change again."

"Right." Jamie stared at the dark clouds coming over the Isle of Mull, wondering when he'd get back into the water to see if that hanging thing was still around. It had frightened him, but he'd got over the worst of it now. And it had made him think how small he was, but that was okay too. In its own way, it had told him he didn't really belong in their world. But it hadn't been aggressive, you had to give it that. It could have wiped him out, if it had wanted to, but it let him stay and look it over. Only, when he got too close, it vanished. And that was another lesson to keep in mind. He'd have to be a lot more careful next time. Show it he was a friend. "It's going to rain again," he said to his mother, getting his thoughts back to his world. "The fine spell's not going to last."

"Yes," replied his mother. "We've had a dreadful season."

Jamie didn't say anything. He couldn't think of a more interesting time. While it was wet he'd get onto the internet, maybe find out something about that thing with the enormous eyes. He'd get back into the water soon as he could. In the meantime, there was plenty to do.

EIGHT – storm brewing

"Harry Carter's giving us a bit of bother," Sergeant Croft said to Constable Roberts, in the back office of the Culloch Police Station, as they began their report of the week's events. "He was drunk again last night."

"Nothing new about that." Roberts frowned, pen in hand. "Don't tell me you want to record it?"

"No, but we should keep an eye on him." Sergeant Croft popped an antacid tablet into his mouth - his stomach was feeling better. His wife said it was the meadowsweet tea she'd been brewing. He thought that keeping off whisky might have had more effect, though he wasn't prepared to admit it. "The poor sod was tossed out of the *Harbour Light* last night."

"Not the first time that's happened either."

"No, but last night he was having a go at the Chattan brothers, accusing them of getting special treatment He said no one took any notice when his foal disappeared. But Angus Douglas was happy enough to give the Chattans a hearing when a calf was taken from their farm. Just because one of them's on the Council."

"Well, something funny is going on. You were at that meeting, weren't you, sir?" Constable Roberts coughed discreetly. "The one with Alec Chattan and the vet in the *Harbour* Light. Is there anything you'd like me to put in the report about it?"

"Not really, no action's to be taken yet."

"I see." The constable scratched the back of his neck with the ball-point pen. It didn't all add up. Yesterday the sergeant got a call from Angus Douglas, then made a few himself. After that, there was this meeting in the pub. This morning the sergeant comes in looking perplexed, as if he had no idea what to do. Then, half an hour ago there's a second call from Douglas, and the sergeant starts whistling, saying how his stomach's on the mend. The old feller was hiding something, there was no doubt about it. "You sure you don't want me to report *anything* about the *Harbour Light*? Wasn't the business between Harry and the Chattans a faction of the law?"

"No really." Croft looked blandly at Roberts. He understood the constable's curiosity, but there was no point in telling him anything now. "The meeting didn't come to much, and we can handle Harry Carter on our own."

"What about the foal he lost? And the Chattan's calf? That's theft, isn't it?"

"Not unless we've got somebody to accuse. They could've been lost, for all we know. Let's see if anything else gets taken. In the meantime, say nothing about it."

"You, ah, wouldn't like to share something with me, sir?" Constable Roberts smiled knowingly. "Something I'd keep it strictly between ourselves."

"Not at the moment."

"Even though Chairman Douglas seems to have been extra busy?"

"He's only trying to stir up interest in the town."

"Nothing more than that, sir?"

"No, there's not," Croft replied firmly. "Anyway, this place could certainly do with a push. That's one of the things he underlined when he called half an hour ago."

In his second conversation Angus Douglas had told the sergeant he'd spoken to the editor of the *Oban Times* who wanted more evidence before he ran any story about crop circles on calves. The chairman said he now felt the same. He didn't want to start anything that turned into a joke. As for aliens? That was out of the question. Apparently the entire population of a town in Romania had run away because they thought some disco's lights was an invasion from outer space. They became the laughing stock of the country. No one wanted anything like that in Culloch. So, in the meantime, Douglas told the sergeant to bide his time, see if anything else occurred.

"We've got more than enough to report as it is," Croft added to the constable. "There's the stuff that was taken from that holiday home. The one that was abandoned after the rains."

"We think we know who did that, sir. The couple from Aberdeen."

"Then put in all the detail you've got and ask Aberdeen to check the couple out."

"Very good, sir." Constable Murdoch Roberts made a further note. *Time for a bit of detective work*, he thought. *Find out what's going on. Talk to a few of my friends.* "I'll get this ready for you to sign. It'll go off this afternoon."

"Thank you. That'll be all for now, Constable."

—⋙—

"Leave it in the garage," Molly McCory said, as Jamie took the foal's skull out of the car. He'd already rinsed his wet suit, hung it up to dry alongside the weighted belt he wore. His goggles and fins were arranged neatly on a shelf, and the bottle was in its rack. He was a tidy lad, even if his father thought he was a bit too fussy at times, but she couldn't complain about that. "It pongs a bit."

"I want Dad to look at it soon as he can."

"Then come and get it when you see him. I don't think it'll walk away."

"You said it *ponged*." Jamie grinned. "You told me once my trainers ponged so much they could walk away on their own."

"That's true enough, I caught them half-way out the door." Molly laughed. "Now, get inside. Your father's probably in the surgery. If he is, leave him alone. You'll have plenty of time later to show him that old bone."

Jamie went into the house, images of the hanging thing sweeping through his mind. He couldn't get over the enormous eyes, and the way it had suddenly disappeared. While he waited for his father he'd go to his room, get onto the computer again. There had to be a link between the marks on the calf, the bones he'd found and that creature he'd seen in the water. He knew he might be crazy, thinking this way, but there were too many coincidences for it all to be accidental. There *had* to be a connection. He only hoped he'd discover what it was before anyone else. It would be amazing if he was the only person in Culloch who knew what was going on - especially before he showed the skull to his dad.

While Jamie was busy on the internet, William McCory remained in the surgery - part of the house on the corner of the High Street and Harbour Road. Having just castrated a tomcat, he was watching his nurse, Lucy, put a couple of stitches in the lesion, thinking how good it would be if the Spanish girl, Malcolm Stewart had recommended, joined the practice. They could use an extra pair of capable hands.

"I can manage on my own now," Lucy said, peering up through pebble glasses. "If you wanted to get away, that is."

"There's no hurry," William murmured. "When you're done, I'll be able to tell Missus Webster her moggy's fine with an absolutely clear conscience."

Lucy nodded and turned back to the cat - an elderly ginger fellow with tattered ears and a limp, which an old lady had brought in saying she didn't want it to wander any more. The other night it'd almost been hit by a car.

"You'd think he'd know better at his age," the owner had added. "You'd have thought he'd have given up that sort of thing by now."

"Some never do," William replied. "And perhaps it's all to the good. Survival of the fittest, that sort of thing, you know."

"I wouldn't have called him one of the fittest," Mrs Webster replied, handing the cat to the vet. "Though he was very handsome in his day."

Leaving her in the waiting room, William had taken the cat into the surgery, knowing the operation would be relatively simple, even though the animal had eaten that morning, which made a general anaesthetic risky. Unconscious, the tom could choke on its vomit. When told of this, the old lady had been reluctant to take the cat home, starve it and return the following day, so he'd injected a tranquilliser, then a local painkiller, and after a snip or two the operation was over. Now, as Lucy tied the last of the stitches, and William was about the leave the surgery, the telephone rang. He picked it up to hear Malcolm Stewart, who, after a hurried greeting went on to say he'd had a report from Dunstaffnage Marine Laboratory about the sample taken from Harry Carter's stables.

"I told you I thought it was a mollusc," the vet from Oban went on rapidly. "And I wasn't too far off the mark. Just wait till you hear this"

"What exactly?"

"A cephalopod. They're part of the mollusc family, even though the shell's inside the body."

"You saying it's from an octopus?"

"They seldom come this far north. So that's unlikely." Malcolm gave a snuffling laugh. "And, from what you've told me, this Carter chap doesn't sound as if he goes on holiday to Portugal."

"What then? A cuttlefish? Their backbones get washed up round here. The locals put them in the cages for their birds."

"Close, but no cigar." Malcolm laughed again, stringing out the exchange. Will McCory took everything far too seriously, here was a chance to take him down a peg or two. "Try again."

"Then it has to be a squid. They pull them up by the thousand over in Moray."

"Almost, but not exactly. It *is* from a squid, but the chaps at Dunstaffnage aren't sure which. The DNA doesn't exactly match the local variety. They're sending it on for more tests. Like to guess where?"

"Not really, just get on with it." William tried to hold back his impatience, tiring of Malcolm's little game. "Where did it go?"

"New Zealand."

"Why all that way?"

"They didn't tell me much more than that. Got all mysterious. Shut up like clams, if you'll forgive the pun. However, if you want my humble opinion, I'd say they're looking for a squid. A deep water monster nobody knows much about. Care to chance your arm on that?"

William frowned, the only cephalopod that came to mind was one he'd read about but hadn't studied – a creature that belonged more to the world of myth and science-fiction than a stable in Culloch. He began to wonder if the vet in Oban was playing some elaborate trick.

"No idea?" Malcolm persisted. "Then, let me tell you what I think. I'd guess they're in touch with the Natural Science people at Wellington University."

"Why?"

"Because that's where the most recent DNA match is likely to be stored. That's where most of what I'm thinking about have been found. Local fishermen caught the first live one the other day, though it died almost immediately."

"Malcolm?" William measured his words. "Unless I'm very much mistaken, you're suggesting that the material I collected from Harry Carter's stable, and from the Chattan's farm, came from a giant squid."

"Well done." Malcolm Stewart's laugher hit a new high. "Right on the mark. I've no idea how it could have got there. And we won't know for certain if it is *Architeuthis* until there's a New Zealand match. But, don't worry, as soon as I hear anything, you'll be the first to know."

"Good God...."

"What?" Lucy looked up from the cat, which was beginning to squirm, her eyes wide behind her glasses. "Did I do anything wrong?"

"No." William gave her a reassuring smile. "It was just something Mister Stewart said."

"I'm sorry, I thought you were talking to me." Lucky returned to her work. William went back to Malcolm. "When are they likely to know for sure? Dunstaffnage? They give you any idea?"

"None, we'll just have to wait." Malcolm changed his tone, his voice became suggestive. "However, there's something else I've got to tell you. This Spanish lass, Blanca González, could come for supper Saturday night. I wouldn't turn her down if I were you. She's a knock-out."

"Thanks, I'll tell Molly to expect her."

"As for the big-eyed monster, just watch this space. If it *is* the creature from the deep, I'd like to know what it's doing ashore? It's not their thing, is it?"

"Not that I know of," William replied. "But from what little I have read about them, they're pretty much of a mystery. They've never been studied alive."

The giant squid remained in the kelp until the world began to grow dark, until the light that came from above had faded. She was hungry again and knew it was time to search for food in this wonderland of plenty, even if not always easy to hunt. And she should find a particularly accessible catch this time as her injured tentacle still throbbed painfully.

Normally, she ate more regularly than of late. Smaller squid, prawns, octopus, medium-sized fishes made up her diet. Occasionally a dogfish or a ray was added. On a good day she could get through a hundred pounds of food or more, although the energy spent on obtaining it burned up a lot of her catch. Lying quietly off the Culloch coast meant less nourishment had been needed and, when caught, came in large helpings. As was her custom, she'd eaten her catches slowly. In fact, she didn't have any option as her oesophagus passed through her brain on its way to her stomach. She had to be careful how big a bite she took - too large and it gave her a headache.

But now, with interest in the starfish pumping through her veins, hunger was making its presence felt in ever increasing waves. It was time to climb onto the land above and seek fresh fodder there. S0, slowly, not using anything like her normal speed, she eased her way out of the kelp and swam toward Culloch harbour. There was no question of going back to the cliff where she'd last hunted - the battle with the cow had made her wary of that. Her first impulse was to return to the site of her earlier success, so she entered the river running through the town but, on a whim, before reaching Harry Carter's stable she turned right, up a tributary of the Orchy, near a big house that stood on a hill.

From the paddocks surrounding the mansion came a familiar scent, one that set her juices flowing. It reminded her of the leg of lamb she'd once found floating in the wake of a passing ship, a treat she had never forgotten. Impelled by memory, the giant squid swam eagerly up a tributary toward Angus Douglas's herd of Blackface sheep.

It was evening before Jamie McCory and his father had a chance to discuss the skull. By then, the rain had lessened and the weather forecast was good, so as he went into the garage to collect the bone, he was sure he'd be able to go back to the Grotto in the morning and see if the hanging thing was there. He wouldn't need his bottle. In fact, if he had to move quickly, the less gear he had the better.

"You know what this is?" he asked his father, when he returned to the house and unwrapped the skull from the newspaper he'd used to carry it in. He didn't want anyone complaining about a smell in the sitting room. "I found it today."

"What is it?" William McCory had finished in the surgery and was going through a magazine which, as far as Jamie could see, was full of pictures of sharks and whales. As he turned to his son he closed it quickly. "Where'd it come from?"

"Along the coast. It's been there a couple of days."

"How do you know?"

"I've seen it before, but I didn't have the bottle then. I got hold of it up this morning, when Mum took me in the car."

"It's a cranium," William said as he examined the skull, turned it over in his hands. "But, you'd know that, wouldn't you?"

"Yeah, but what's it from?"

"Something small." William paused, the conversation with Malcolm Stewart had set his mind racing. The possibility of a giant squid leaving traces of its DNA in Culloch was bizarre, seemed absolutely incredible. In order to find out as much as he could about *Architeuthis* he'd picked up the first reference he found when he came out of the surgery - a National Geographic article on creatures of the deep, and was glancing through it when Jamie interrupted him. He'd closed the magazine almost furtively, he didn't want any more rumours in the town, especially if they came back to him. His comment about aliens had been quite enough. However, as soon as he touched the skull, he knew immediately where it had come from, and a prickle ran down his spine. "Fresh born. The bone's soft."

"It's been in the water a while."

"That shouldn't make much difference."

"There were other bones with it," Jamie said. "Quite a lot."

Jamie had spent as much time as he could searching the internet while he waited for his father.. It hadn't been easy. He started with hanging things in water and shower curtains came up. That had been stupid. Then he found sites about those jelly-fish with poisonous tentacles, up to one hundred feet long. Portuguese Man of War, they were, and could kill you if you had a dodgy heart. But it wasn't until he said the thing looked like a bank of seaweed that something worthwhile appeared. There was a report from a nineteenth century sailor about a patch floating on the surface near Rangoon. The man first thought it was a mass of weed, but it turned out to be more ferocious than that. When disturbed, it attacked a boat and almost dragged it under. *My God*, Jamie said to himself. *Was that what I saw in the Grotto?* The thought made him go hot and cold. He turned to other possibilities, things that might supply a different explanation, wondering if he'd just imagined the enormous creature. After all, it hadn't touched him, and had disappeared in a flash. Maybe he'd had a brief attack of nitrogen narcosis, that feeling of intoxication some divers get if they go down too deep. But that didn't seem likely, and it had never happened before. His brain was starting to bubble over when his mother called him, saying his father had come out of the surgery. So he switched off the computer, relieved to get away, but even more certain he couldn't say anything to anyone until he had undeniable proof.

"The bones were in a bunch," he added, watching his father's response – the old man suspected something. "They were half-covered with sand."

"Nothing else with them?"

"No, but they looked like they'd been piled up."

"It's..." William McCory licked his lips. He knew exactly where the skull came from, and was torn between telling his son not to return to the water and the alarm his words would raise. "It's from a foal," he said finally. "Probably the one Harry Carter lost. My guess is that it got washed away in the huge downpour the other night."

"Is that what you really think, Dad?"

"Well, it's quite possible with all the rain we've had."

"What about the slime trail?"

"That? Slugs, I'd say."

"I suppose that's possible," Jamie replied, knowing his father was avoiding the truth, and understanding why. They both had to be certain before they confided in each other. His father wouldn't jump to conclusions, and he couldn't say anything until he'd taken another look. If he came across the thing again, it'd be amazing, but at least he'd know it was real. *And Dad feels the same,* he told himself. *It's a stalemate.* But he couldn't push the old man too hard. If he did that his father might get sarcastic, tell him to stop sniffing glue or something. "It *could* be slugs," he added quietly. "Those big yellow ones."

"They leave a lot of mess." William handed the skull back to his son. "Put it in the garage. We don't need it in the house."

"Mum said it pongs."

"She's right, it does." William looked into his son's eyes, saw the uncertainty, but had no chance to do anything more - Molly began calling them to supper. "We'll talk about it again later if you like."

"Do you want to?"

"Yes, I do." William left for the dining room. "Come on, it's time to eat."

Jamie waited a moment before following. He really didn't know what to think. All the stuff he'd turned up on the net had got him going. Made him wonder if what he'd seen was true. On the other hand, the look on his father's face, when he said he knew where the skull came from, had told him all he needed to know. And there was that magazine his father had been looking at before he picked up the skull. The one with sharks and whales. Probably one of the hanging things too. A giant squid they called it. A creature hardly anyone had seen alive.

But, why didn't he say something? Why didn't he say what he thought? He trusts me, doesn't he? Why didn't he let on?

Jamie went into the dining-room, hat pulled down tight. He wasn't sure what he was going to do now. He wasn't looking forward to talking to his father again. And his appetite had gone away.

NINE – when in doubt

It was nearly closing time when Harry Carter was thrown out of the *Harbour Light* for the second night in a row. He'd sat at the bar for hours, drinking pint after pint, with a whisky added every now and then. He'd sold the mare that had recently foaled so had money to spend, but the more he consumed the louder he complained until four men, playing cards at a corner table, told him to shut up.

"That's the trouble with you lot," Harry shouted back. "You never open your bloody mouths. Just take what you get."

"Put a boot in it, Harry," one of them replied, glancing at a group of tourists at the far end of the bar. "Or you'll frighten this lot away. There's precious few around these days."

"Probably them's the bastards that took my foal. The Chattan's calf as well." Harry turned in the tourists' direction. "Hey, you..." he began when Jack, the barman, a stocky chap with arms like fence posts, cut him short. "Out of here," he said firmly. "Or I'll get in touch with Sergeant Croft."

"Tony Useless Bloody Croft, a lot of good he'll do. Christ, when I told him..."

At that, Fred leapt round the bar, plucked Harry from his stool and frog-marched him to a side door. "Go home.

Get some sleep. Don't come back until you're sober," he said, pushing the red-faced stable owner into the night.

Harry Carter stood unsteadily outside the *Harbour Light* for a moment or two breathing heavily. Then he raised his voice to bellow, "Fuck the lot of you," before spitting and turning away.

Fumbling in his overcoat pocket for the keys of his van, he came across a half bottle of whisky he'd bought earlier with the intention of spending the night inside the stable, a loaded shotgun by his side - to be ready in case the thieves who took his foal came back.

"Well, bugger me, look at that," he muttered. "There's a bit of luck."

Cheered by the find, Harry stumbled across the High Street to the Common, cursing several cars that braked to avoid him. He made his way to a shelter by the river where townsfolk waited for busses, where amorous couples got up to whatever they could, to find it empty. Pushing aside a plastic bag, an old newspaper or two, he sat down on the bench, look a long swig from the bottle and, quite soon, slumped back and fell asleep.

The giant squid paused before she reached Angus Douglas's holding, the only section he could call his own after selling up for the new estate. She hesitated because, although the night was now dark enough to move ashore, there were too many creatures on the land, running about, raising their voices, warning her to keep hidden until they'd gone. At least the things that lived here were active for a change, and their raucous cries were loud and clear.

Even though she swam beneath the surface of the river, the squid was able to register sound through the water. She had no ears, but her receptor cells - lodged in lines along her head and arms, were sensitive enough to record noise wherever it came from. And the sounds coming from above were loud and threatening, telling her she needed to be more cautious than before.

The first night she'd come ashore had been dark, wet and windy. A dog had barked, but that was all. On the second occasion, no living creature had made any sound as she climbed the cliff to the cow-shed. But tonight was different - she knew she had to wait. That, however, wasn't of any great concern, all she required was a place to hide, somewhere safe in this tributary of the Orchy.

The river water wasn't as salty as the sea, but it flowed quickly, bubbling over boulders, picking up all the oxygen she needed. The bed of the stream was honeycombed with caverns, washed out of the limestone by centuries of wear. Soon, she found herself waiting in what had once been a fisherman's paradise, full of salmon, brown and rainbow trout, though their numbers had dwindled in recent times.

Nestling deep into a pool beneath an overhanging bank, making herself as small as possible, the giant squid settled on a bicycle frame that had been thrown in some years before. Quite comfortable, she knew she could wait as long as it took for the sounds from above to die away. Then, when all was quiet, she'd climb up to where the delicious water-borne scent was coming from, and eat her fill of the flesh that held such vivid memories.

"Malcolm Stewart suggests we invite this Spanish lass for a meal tomorrow evening," William McCory said, when they all were seated around the dining table. "Does that sound all right?"

"Fine," Molly replied, passing him a plate of roast lamb, boiled potatoes and carrots. She knew he preferred his vegetables roasted, but cooked that way Jamie wouldn't touch them. Split-meals weren't always easy - she sometimes wished they were more like her, less fussy about food. Never mind, to give them what they wanted was part of her job, she supposed. "I wonder what she'd like to eat?"

"The same as us, I imagine. She's lived here a while." William glanced at his son, who was sprinkling grated cheese on his vegetables. "I only hope it's something with eyes."

"You never know," Jamie murmured. "She might really care about what goes into her stomach."

"Don't worry, I'll keep it simple," Molly said quickly, glancing from Jamie's face to William's, neither was smiling. She wondered if they'd had words again, and hoped it wouldn't spoil the meal. "I'll make a nice big salad. With side dishes of cold meat and cheese. She can help herself to whatever she likes. So can the rest of us."

"What's her name?" Jamie asked his father.

"Blanca González. White something, your mother says."

"What part of Spain's she from?"

"I'm not sure," replied William. "All I know is, she's been here for a few years. Did her degree at Derby University."

"You don't know much about her. But you're giving her a job?"

"I'm not sure what I'm doing. I haven't met her yet."

"When will you make up your mind?"

"There's no hurry," Molly said, wondering where the touchiness came from. When she talked to Jamie about the girl that morning, he'd barely seemed interested - wondered if she spoke English, that's all. Now he was asking all sorts of questions. "We'll have supper with her. See how we get along."

"That's right," William agreed. "Get to know her, then decide."

"You want me here too?" asked Jamie.

"I certainly do."

"I mean..." He lowered his head. "It's got nothing to do with me."

"I want her to meet everyone," William said, his voice hardening. "And while I'm at it, what have I said about wearing that hat at the table? Just see you don't do it tomorrow night."

"It doesn't hurt anyone."

"Stop it, both of you." Molly put down her knife and fork with a clatter. "And tell me what's going on? You're ruining my supper."

"It's nothing," William replied. "We often talk like this."

"That doesn't make it any better."

"It's the skull I found." Jamie had to get something out. His father hadn't told him anything. *What, if that thing I saw really was a giant squid? And he knows it? What the hell am I going to do?* "Dad said it came from the foal Harry Carter lost."

"It's possible," said William. "Though, I can't be sure."

"You said you knew." Jamie stared at him. "You thought it got washed down in the rain."

"I know, but..."

"Are you trying to tell me you're arguing over that stupid old bone?" Molly shook her head in disbelief.

"You're sitting there, being nasty to each other, because of *that*." She turned to Jamie, her voice unusually sharp. "If this is all I get for taking you diving, you can forget about any more in the future."

"Mum?" Jamie blinked, his mother rarely spoke as bluntly as this. "It wasn't, well, I just wanted to know what Dad thought."

"Then ask politely." She turned to her husband. "And why don't you tell him what you know?"

"I have a doubt or two, that's all," said William said, feeling guilty. He should have said more to them both. "Anyway, Jamie and I often have different opinions."

"And you know how it upsets me."

"Mum, take it easy." Jamie put both hands on his woollen hat. He needed it badly right now. "Like Dad says, we often have a go at each other."

"Then, stop it immediately." Molly swallowed, her heart was beating too fast. She'd need to take a sedative, otherwise she'd get no sleep. "Let's see if we can finish the meal in peace. And, for goodness' sake, both of you, try to act more like gentlemen when our Spanish guest arrives. If you want Miss González working with you, Will, you'd better convince her she's going to be happy here. I'm sure she'll be most *unhappy* if she finds herself in the middle of a family row."

At that very moment, Blanca González was looking forward to a quiet life in the country, where she could become part of a small practice and work with the animals she loved. She came from Cantabria, had grown up amongst its gently rolling hills, and had always wanted to be a veterinary surgeon. As a child she'd seldom played with dolls, spent more time with plastic animals, arranging them in a toy farm her father built in the corner of her bedroom. She had a soft, woolly dog called Raffa, which she dressed in a range of tiny garments, and whenever anyone asked what she wanted to be when she grew up, she always replied, "*Una veterinaria.*"

At school she'd scored high marks in biology and, to her surprise, English - somehow the language came readily to her tongue. Later, at the University of Leon, she studied veterinary medicine. While others in her year wavered, changed from philosophy to psychology, from law to commerce, she became even more convinced that working with animals was exactly what she wanted to do. At Leon, another event changed the course of her career - before she'd completed her degree she went to England on a student exchange program and decided she quite liked the place.

After that life leapt along at a speed she found difficult to keep up with. When she graduated from Leon, she obtained a place at Derby University where she did a master's degree in small animal therapy. She chose the smaller creatures, not only because of her childhood games, but because she felt she lacked the strength to work with larger beasts. This was almost a traditional decision, in her own country bigger animals were nearly always treated by male vets it was accepted as a *macho* task. Blanca, on the other hand, was slight, with long black hair and dark eyes that often sparkled. When she left university for a second time, she worked in Derby's Veterinary Hospital for nine months.

"It was like a pregnancy," she often said.

Then, on a walking holiday in the Scottish Highlands, she thought of moving further north. The countryside was similar to her part of Spain. At home, she'd accompanied both parents on hikes along the Picos, the mountain range separating Cantabria from the south. Making a few enquiries, she'd discovered a mutual friend who introduced her to Malcolm Stewart. He, in turn, suggested William McCory, a vet in Culloch, who had invited her for supper the following day.

Now, going through her wardrobe, trying to decide what to wear to meet a family she knew very little about, she finally selected a pair of well-washed jeans, a purple pullover, a beige suede jacket. *There's little point*, she told herself. *In dressing up for the occasion. They should see me as I am.*

"I've been invited to talk about work," she murmured aloud. "I'm not going on a date."

Nevertheless, she hoped she'd be readily accepted, and was looking forward to living in a smaller town, somewhere she could get to know those who brought their pets into the surgery, make friends with the neighbours in her street. And she was doubly excited by the thought of being by the sea. That, too, would somehow keep her close to home. She came from Comillas, a coastal town that once had been a fishing village, loved the water, and spent as much time diving in it as she could. And she was very proud of her latest possession, an underwater video camera which she intended to use to photograph whatever the Culloch waters held.

The giant squid came out of the water when the world above was still, although it took a long while for the sounds she was unfamiliar with to settle down. The car horns, the music from a hillside disco, the shouts of distant strangers took their time to die away. When she finally emerged the rain had gone, although the rocks beside the stream were wet enough to travel on. The grass she'd have to cover to reach the barn, where Angus Douglas's Blackface sheep sheltered for the night, glistened under a lifting moon.

Crouching, her back up, using her eight arms like legs, the giant squid climbed out of the pool. Spider-like she crawled over the rocks onto the damp field, but moved less confidently than on her two previous occasions. The first had been uncomplicated, yet left her with the knowledge that carrying prey over land was much more difficult than in the water. The catch struggled, had to be contained, gave her fewer arms to move with. The second experience had been brutal. Her wounds were still painful, and she had to nurse the damaged tentacle.

So, with extra caution, the giant squid approached barn. Before arriving, she paused to survey the darkened scene. She could afford to wait as the grass contained all the moisture she needed for the moment. Raising her head, her eyes enormous in the night, she saw that the creatures in the barn were small - that, at least, was a promising start. None was the size of the mother who had lashed out with sharp horns to protect her young on the last occasion.

However, on closer examination, she saw that they were curious stock, these things with the delicious scent, quite unlike the piece she'd found in the wake of the passing ship. They were covered with what appeared to be a growth of dense white seaweed. Perhaps they used it, the way some crabs did, to camouflage themselves. A nuisance, really - it would have to be stripped away. What's more, they had spikes above their black faces, like some of the rays the squid was familiar with - but these were more elaborate. They were long and curled, with hook-like endings, and would need to be avoided. They reminded her of the cow. Nevertheless, it seemed these creatures could be overcome, especially if she put to use the lessons she'd already learnt. So, lifting herself on her powerful arms, the giant squid moved cautiously toward the barn.

Inside the wooden structure, the sheep began to stir restlessly, disturbed by the new and threatening odour coming closer in the damp night air. None had any idea what it meant. None had smelt anything like it. But, its presence was unwelcome, suggested nothing that was friendly, and as it steadily approached, the herd shifted uneasily in their stalls.

"What's on your mind, Will?" Molly asked, slipping into bed beside him. An hour earlier she'd taken half a valium, and now felt a little calmer. "I know you and Jamie have your ups and downs, but tonight was really awful."

"It wasn't that bad," her husband replied, hands behind his head, staring at the ceiling. "Anyway, you shouldn't let it get to you like that."

"I can't help it. I love you both. I hate it when you pick on each other." She leant on an elbow, facing him. "There *is* something, isn't there?"

"It's..." William began and then hesitated. He wasn't certain, and too well aware of how quickly rumours could spread. His joke about aliens had been enough to involve the *Oban Times*. He dreaded to think what Malcolm Stewart's suggestion – that the slime came from a giant squid - was likely to provoke. The National Geographic article he'd been reading, when Jamie brought in the skull, was about an attempt off the New

Zealand coast to film what they called the *near-mythic creature*. Now, it seemed, they'd caught the first one alive. And the thought that an *Architeuthis* had come ashore to attack the local cattle was bizarre but undoubtedly exciting – he and Malcolm could be the first to get a close look at a living specimen, go down in the record books as scientists of renown. However, at the moment he didn't have enough evidence to talk to anyone. The specimen he'd sent to Oban still had to be confirmed. There might be a dozen other explanations for the missing cattle and the trail of lime. With all these uncertainties stirring his mind, the last thing William wanted was to involve Molly. "What did Jamie say this morning?" he asked. "When he came out of the water with that skull?"

"Nothing really. Though, I must say, he did look awfully pale. White as a ghost."

"What had happened, do you know?"

"I'm not sure. I think he got very cold, that's all. But you know what he's like, he never says much. Just showed me that skull and said he wanted to talk to you about it. Isn't that what he did?"

"Yes, I told him, I thought it came from Harry Carter's foal."

"What was it doing in the water?"

"It probably got washed in."

"But you're not sure, are you? I know you, Will, you're hiding something."

"Well, there are a couple of things I want to check, that's all."

"Will...?"

William turned and kissed her, put a hand on the small of her back "Let's leave it for the moment. When I've got it sorted out, I'll tell you more. In the meantime,

I'm sure we can find something better to do." He pulled her close.

Molly sighed but said nothing more. She trusted him and was prepared to wait. Soon, their bodies were entwined.

In the bus shelter Harry Carter woke, staggered to the bank of the River Orchy and urinated copiously. He looked up at the sky and grunted sourly. It was clearing; the air coming up from the south carried a reassuring warmth. He returned to the bench he'd slept on, picked up the whisky bottle and took a long and greedy swallow. For a moment he considered looking for his van and driving home, then put the thought aside and drank some more.

"Fuck it," he muttered. "Let's wait till it gets light."

He collected another newspaper, rolled it up as a pillow, lay back on the bench and within a few minutes was snoring loudly, his only company a red squirrel which had hopped across the Common. It sat on the bench beside him, watching him with bright button eyes as it nibbled a potato crisp it had found in a half-empty bag.

TEN – nessie

As the giant squid approached the barn, the Blackface sheep stirred restlessly, their hoofed feet pawing the scattered hay. Above, the sky had grown pale, a pink glow lay along the horizon, tinting thin layers of cloud. Apart from bird-song and bleating, there was no human sound so, without any further hesitation, the squid moved quickly over the grass, almost running on her powerful arms, tentacles curled tightly beneath a mantle the colour of the morning mist.

Circling the barn was a barbed wire fence, but this presented no problem to the cephalopod. She had the ability to condense, extend or squeeze her body though what appeared to be the most unlikely spaces. Once, she'd managed to creep through a cleft in the rocks to escape a sperm whale, an act so seemingly impossible that the pursuing beast had thumped the stone with its monstrous head in pure, uncontrolled fury. So, the fence was easily handled. The squid stretched out, became a long elastic band and continued toward the barn.

On arrival she paused, lifted an arm over a wooden gate, found a drop-latch and opened the entrance. It was a simple manoeuvre, one that came easily to a creature accustomed to moving stones in order to capture lurking crayfish or retreating crabs. Without any problem, she pushed the gate ajar.

As soon as it opened, the herd of Blackface sheep retreated into a tight defensive circle. Then, a long-horned ram, bigger than any of the others, moved forward to face the invading creature, the unsavoury stench it bore. All the animals were wary now, yet as a brave and hardy breed they were determined to protect their young. Amongst their number were two late-born lambs, whose scent had attracted the squid.

The ram stamped its front feet vigorously, challenging the trespasser. Apart from its presence, the opening of the door had come at an unusual hour – this was no time to be disturbed. Later, the man who tended the herd, Tommy Tranter, the only employee Angus Douglas still retained, was due to fork out fresh hay, usher them into the paddock if the weather was right. Sometimes Angus himself came to look them over. Smelling of whisky and cigars, his odour was accepted. But this new presence seemed distinctly hostile. They prepared for the worst.

Asleep in a chair before a television screen, where a pornographic movie had agile people doing impossible things, none of which he witnessed, Angus Douglas dreamed of seeing his photograph on the front page of the *Oban Times*, heralded as the man who'd saved Culloch, brought the town back from the brink of financial despair. He imagined talk-shows, television interviews, long elaborate lunches in the handsome Scottish parliamentary building, where he would take his fill of wonderful treats surrounded by expensive architecture, being welcomed by beaming politicians.

"Well deserved," he heard someone say. "We need more like him."

SQUID

Angus murmured as he slept, blissfully unaware of what was happening on the screen, where someone was doing something so acrobatic it threatened to handicap him for life. Angus's smile grew wide as he heard what he took to be a round of gentlemanly applause in his favour. It was, in fact, the frantic bleating of his Blackface herd as the giant squid moved closer.

The squid slid past the open door, not moving quite as comfortably once inside the barn. The surface was dry, straw stuck to her arms making them less sensitive, the wounded one twitched painfully. She paused some ten feet from the ram, searching for the aroma of the new-born lambs, creatures similar to those she'd already taken. But they were not so easily encountered. And, before her, more ferocious than the cow that had fought to defend its calf, was the largest of these seaweed-covered animals, snorting ferociously, stamping the ground.

The giant squid hesitated. In both her hearts she was a peaceful being with no taste for unnecessary violence. It had offended her when the sperm whale bashed its head against the rocks. There was no call for anything so brutish. Even though force was essential to catch what was needed to survive, she'd tried to live her life as harmoniously as possible. So, facing the hostile ram, she concluded it might be better to slide quietly away, return to the peace of the inshore waters. She had a sudden desire to renew her acquaintance with the starfish, the creature that had sent out wave after wave of simple goodwill. Another other good reason for wanting to leave was that the ram was about to attack.

The Blackface lowered its head, its horns ready for battle. All around were sounds of disturbance. Fear was spreading throughout the herd. As alpha-male in the enclosure, the ram had little choice in the matter. It had to defend its flock. Without a second thought, it hurled itself toward the sliding creature that had barged in at such an unexpected hour. But, as soon as the ram began its charge, the invader turned and fled. It lifted its body on its many legs and ran through the open door. Encouraged by this cowardice, the ram sped after it.

The giant squid retreated to the barbed wire fence and slid hastily beneath it. It would be a pity not to feast on tender flesh, but this had become a matter of survival. On the far side of the fence, she took to her legs and kept running as the ram plunged on. Spurred, the horned beast made no effort to slow its speed, leap or to avoid the barbed wire. With a loud snort from its jet-black nostrils the Blackface smashed straight through.

The impact halted the animal for a moment. It paused, shook its well-armoured head, as the squid ran untidily over the slippery grass. But her withdrawal only inspired the ram to further feats of glory. With its head down, the sharp curled horns protruding forward, it resumed its charge at even greater velocity.

The giant squid had barely reached the riverbank above the pool she'd sheltered in, when the ram crashed into her. Instinctively her arms came and gripped the hairy beast with their powerful suckers. She and the ram became a single thrashing creature. They teetered an instant on the river bank before falling into the water. On their way down they bounced over rocks like some gigantic football before splashing into the pool. Their descent only came to a halt when they landed on the bicycle frame.

As soon as she was in the water, the squid lost part of her fear. Although still wary of the beast, she was in her element now. The ram, on the contrary, was doomed in the depths. It snorted, water filling its nostrils, and struggled as best it could. It made its way to the surface once, took in a lungful of desperate air, before being hauled below again. Together, the ram desperately attempting to escape, the squid increasingly certain of her meal, they were washed away by the current and carried toward the sea.

Harry Carter was zipping up his trousers after using the River Orchy as a urinal again, when the squid and the ram swept down toward him. He blinked at the sight, wondering if a dog had tumbled into the stream. Or some idiot tourist had gone for an early swim. In both cases they deserved to drown. But his eyes opened wide in disbelief as the struggling creatures came closer. He almost soiled his underpants when a tentacle rose from the water like an enormous snake.

"Jesus Christ," he whispered. "What's that?"

Harry rubbed a hand over his ruddy face, as the tentacle turned toward him - its paddle-shaped end resembling a head. In his hung-over state it appeared to be staring directly at him. It was as frightening a sight as he'd ever seen. And all the photographs ever taken at Loch Ness sprang to mind.

"It's Nessie," he cried, his voice cracking. "Here in Culloch."

Harry Carter stumbled back, slipped and almost fell. Recovering, he stared again at the muddy river, hoping to catch another sight of the beast. But, by now, the currents had taken the squid and her prize away, carrying them under Port Bridge and out to sea.

"Got to tell someone about this," Harry muttered, turning toward the Common. In the distance he could just make out the blue and white Police Station sign. "Tony Croft. He's got to know."

In a staggering run he started off, frightening away the red squirrel, which had remained beside him for most of the night. "He's not going to be there now. I'll have to haul him out of bed. But just wait till he hears this," he gasped, his lungs burning. "Nessie in Culloch."

Later that morning William McCory called Malcolm Stewart, wanting to know if the Oban vet had heard anything more about the sample he'd sent to New Zealand.

"Not yet," Malcolm replied. "Nothing till Monday, at the earliest. They're on the other side of the world, remember. While they work we sleep."

"I'm surprised the people at Dunstaffnage weren't more specific when they tested it. They've got a pretty good reputation."

"Perhaps they'd better things to do." Malcolm's snuffling laugh drifted down the line. "You heard about their *Ig Nobel* prize?"

"What for?"

"Herring farts."

"What?"

"You heard me. Herrings breaking wind."

"You're joking." It was a pity Malcolm couldn't resist his little games, but this was no time to discourage him. "What's next? Crabs belching?"

"I'm serious. The Scottish Association of Marine Science has found out that when herrings fart it's their way of talking," Malcolm added. "I told my wife if it happens to me, not to be offended. I'm only paying her a compliment."

"I see, so we have to wait until Monday for any news from Down Under?"

"At the earliest." Malcolm paused a moment, when he continued there was less flippancy in his voice. "But just wait till New Zealand confirms what you and I are pretty certain of. That'll be world-wide news. God, Will, we'll be famous."

"If our suspicions turn out to be true," William replied cautiously. "In the meantime, I suggest we keep it to ourselves."

"There's no need to jump the gun, I know. But when we get the evidence, we'd better move pretty damned fast. We don't want anyone else getting the credit for a discovery as important as this."

"Still, we don't want to make fools of ourselves."

"Christ, Will, you know as well as I do, that if it is *Architeuthis*, we'll have a first. No one's managed to get a decent look at the thing alive. The only photographs that have ever been taken were of that half-dead creature the other day, wriggling around in a net. All the others that have been brought ashore have been dead before anyone got a chance to examine them. Think of what would happen if we managed to capture a living specimen? Put it in a tank and studied it? We'd be celebrities overnight. The scientific world knows more about dinosaurs than giant squids. They're the last great beasts that remain on this planet no one knows anything about."

"You've obviously looked into this."

"As far as I've been able to, but there's bugger all to learn. I've been trying to get hold of a book by a man called Ellis. Unfortunately, it's out of print. I've been on to Amazon. They're sending me a second-hand copy, but that could take days. We're on the front line with this, Will. We can't afford to let anyone from Dunstaffnage or New Zealand get credit for our discovery."

"I still think we'd better go easy," William replied quietly, a little surprised by how quickly Malcolm Stewart had jumped in to stake his claim. Still, he could understand the man's desire to become involved. If a giant squid had come ashore along the Culloch coast, it would be of international importance. And if they were able to capture it, examine a creature that was still a mystery to most, they'd certainly become famous. There could be more than an *Ig Nobel* prize involved. However, they'd need to be very careful until they were absolutely certain. There had been too many false claims by scientists and medical men in the past few years to expect any sympathy if they turned out to be wrong "Let's wait until we hear from New Zealand before we take it any further," he added firmly. "After all, a day or two won't make any difference, will it?"

"All right then, but only if you agree not to say anything without consulting me." Malcolm replied. Will McCory might be a little overcautious, but that didn't mean he wouldn't try to claim everything for himself. "We're in this together, right?"

"You have my word on that."

"Okay, then there's one thing more we ought to be looking out for."

"What's that?"

"This giant squid's already come ashore a couple of times, there's every chance it'll be back."

"That's quite likely."

"Then we'd better put our thinking caps on. Work out a way to catch it."

"Have you any ideas?"

"No, but let's see what we come up with." Malcolm's laughter returned. "God alone knows what number-sized hook we'd have to use."

William McCory said good-bye, Malcolm's words ringing in his ears. New possibilities were opening up at an amazing pace. It wasn't that he was bored with what he did. He loved his work, the ability of his hands to cure the wounded and the sick, but it would be wonderful to enter a world nobody else had ever explored before, to be one of the first to examine *Architeuthis*.

"I must talk to Jamie," he murmured. "Find out more about that skull. This time I'll tell him what I know. I don't want him going back into the water unless I'm sure. Until this is over he'd better keep well away from the creature."

"The ram's gone, squire. Went in the night," Tommy Tranter, cap in hand, told Angus Douglas. "Right through the fence into the stream."

"I beg your bloody pardon?"

"The rest are there." Tommy moved his feet uneasily. It was his job to get the Blackface out in the morning, put them away at night. The laird did his block if they weren't looked after properly. "But not the ram. Something must've got him."

"What the hell are you talking about?" Angus poured whisky over the porridge Tommy's wife, Sarah, prepared each morning. She also left him cold cuts and boiled potatoes for the evening. At midday he went down to the *Harbour Light*, where he had shepherds pie for lunch, accompanied by two pints of ale. The ritual gave him a sense of security long gone in other sections of his life.

"What do you mean, the ram went right through the fence?"

"Snapped it wide open. Smashed through it like a truck."

"You been drinking, Tommy?"

"No, squire. Haven't touched a drop since Saturday night. Then, I must confess...."

"Spare me the gory details," Angus interrupted, sprinkling sugar then reaching for a spoon. Tommy was pretty reliable, never turned up late. Sarah, his wife, a younger woman, prepared good food, occasionally allowed him to stroke her bottom and, quite often, a little more. It would be a bloody nuisance if he had to get rid of them. But if Tommy were no longer capable he'd have to start looking for someone elsewhere. "When did this happen?"

"Had to be quite early, squire. They were all there last night. I came back this morning to find the fence in a mess, the ram gone." The stocky man glanced across the dining room at his wife, standing by the door, drying her hands on an apron. "Sarah'll tell you that."

"That's true," she replied. "There was n sign of the ram this morning. And the rest of them were in a terrible state. All huddled together. Scared, I'd say."

Angus Douglas frowned, tapped the sugar bowl with the spoon. What Sarah had said rang a distant bell. He'd heard some sort of racket in the early morning. Enough to get him out of his armchair, turn off the television and go to bed.

"There were no tyre-marks, squire," Tommy went on. "Or footprints, anything like that. Only the mud the ram dug up. And some sort of slimy stuff."

"*Slimy stuff?*"

"Like snail marks on the grass." Tommy shuffled his feet, feeling an idiot. Snail marks didn't make sense. He wouldn't have said anything about them if the boss hadn't accused him of being pissed. "But darker, they were. Purple, I'd say. There was more of the mucky stuff on the barbed wire. First I thought it was ram's blood, but it was stickier than that."

Angus Douglas put a spoonful of porridge in his mouth, his mind picking up speed. What was it Tony Croft had said before they got onto those bloody croft circles? About some sort of slimy stuff left behind when Harry Carter's foal was taken? And the Chattan's calf disappeared? The vet had taken a sample and sent it to Oban to be tested. By God, something very curious was going on. Croft circles on calves was only the beginning. This had many more possibilities than he'd first imagined. He'd better get on the prowl, make the most of it. He took another spoonful of porridge. It had never tasted so good.

"I wonder if you'd make a couple of phone calls for me, my dear?" he asked Sarah Tranter, his voice unusually calm. "I'd do it myself, but this breakfast of yours is so awfully good, I don't want to let it get cold."

"Who do you want me to call?"

"Tony Croft, the sergeant. And Will, the vet. I'd like to have a chat with them in the *Harbour Light* at lunchtime. That is, if they've nothing better to do."

"I'll phone them now."

"Don't say anything about the ram until I give the word." Angus gave each of his hirelings a doughy smile. "I don't want to get any tongues wagging."

"Of course," Sarah replied, turning away to wink at her husband – it looked like he was off the hook. "I could fry you an egg, if you fancied it," she said to Angus. "With a little bacon on the side."

"What a splendid idea."

Smiling, Angus returned to his porridge with the feeling that life had taken a turn for the better. He might be the last of his ilk in Culloch, but things were on the mend. Given the chance, he'd turn this whole curious business into a public relations masterpiece. He'd have his little town front page news all over the world. As for being the last in the line, didn't someone say that the vet was getting a female partner? Perhaps a little new blood could be added. Or was that going too far?

Blanca González was up early that morning. By the time Sarah Tranter had made Angus's phone calls, the Spanish vet had tucked an overnight bag into her Ford van and was looking up at the clearing skies. The day was full of promise.

"A good idea to start early," she murmured. "I don't know the way, and I want to have a look at the town. Who knows, it might be my home for years."

With that thought, she drove out of Oban, following a narrow coastal road. On her right, the waters in the Firth of Lorne were calmer than she'd expected. The night had been wet, with winds coming up off the sea, but the day had dawned bright and cheerful, the air was tangy as it drew her on.

"Like home," she said. "We get sudden changes there, too."

The recollection gave new edge to anticipation. It would be wonderful to live somewhere more like Comillas, the little town she'd grown up in, where you could watch the boats go out through the waves, then return with their boxes of fish. Perhaps Culloch would be like that. On her left, rose layers of heather-clad hills, purple and blue in the morning light. They weren't as high as the Picos, but they carried familiar patches of snow. All around were pines reaching up to the sky. It was really lovely country.

Even though she had little idea of what Culloch was like, she felt comfortable with what she'd heard. And Malcolm Stewart had assured her that William McCory was a decent man. He worked hard, which was why she was needed, and would treat her well. He was happily married, had one son, although Malcolm confessed he knew very little about the boy. He appeared to be a solitary character, fascinated by the sea, and who spent a lot of time in the water.

"Perhaps we can dive together," Blanca said, with glance over the Firth of Lorne. "If he doesn't know how to do it, I could teach him."

Happily, Blanca González drove on, little knowing what lay ahead.

ELEVEN – wonder-land

"Haven't a clue," Tony Croft told William McCory, when the vet arrived at the police station in the hope of discovering why he'd been told by Sarah Tranter that Angus Douglas wanted to talk to him again. "Got a similar call myself."

"She asked me to be in the *Harbour Light* at noon. Didn't give a reason, but her voice suggested Douglas wouldn't be too pleased if I refused."

"She can sound authoritative when she wants to. Does a bit more than cook for the old feller, if you know what I mean?"

William smiled wryly, recalling a woman's description of an affair she'd had with a London politician. *Like being under a wardrobe with the key still in the lock.*

"Funny thing is, last time I heard from Angus, he was putting everything on hold," Croft continued, stifling a belch - his stomach was playing up again. "The *Oban Times* wasn't too interested in crop circles on calves, and that set him back a bit."

"He said the same to me." William glanced around the sergeant's office. A government poster about putting a stop to yob culture caught his eye, reminding him that last night had been extra noisy in the town. "Has anything else happened?" he asked carefully. "Is there anything new?"

"Well..." Tony Croft scratched his cheek. He liked the vet. Will was a good citizen who did what he could when needed. If there was no ready cash after a job was done, he'd wait more patiently than most. There couldn't be a better person to talk to about what had occurred earlier that morning. "As a matter of fact, Harry Carter knocked me up at sparrow-fart with a story that didn't make sense."

"What was it?"

"He said he'd seen Nessie in the River Orchy."

"The Loch Ness Monster?" William frowned, uncertainly. "Was he sober?"

"Not entirely. But he swore he saw Nessie clear as day. Went past him down the river, splashing all over the place. Lifted its head, looked at him, then shot off out to sea."

"My God," William whispered. "What did you do?"

"Told him to go home and sleep it off. Said I'd have him for being drunk in a public place. Making a nuisance of himself. Stuff like that to quieten him down. In the end, he went away. But he'll be back, sooner or later, shouting his head off."

"What do *you* think he saw?"

"Could have been anything, being him. He'd been tossed out of the pub again. Spent the night in the bus shelter by the Common. A bottle of whisky to keep him company." Sergeant Croft shrugged dismissively. "Why? Are you taking him seriously?"

"Probably not, he's had a bad time lately. But, ah, was anything else taken?" William asked carefully. "Any more reports of theft?"

"I haven't heard of anything," Croft replied. "The vicar's garden gnome was nicked, but it's not the first time that's happened. Constable Roberts is looking into it now. What have you got in mind?"

"No livestock?"

"Not that I know of." The sergeant reached for a packet of gum. His wife suggested that chewing might sort his stomach out, get the juices flowing. "Why do you want to know?"

"It could be important."

"In what way?"

"Listen, I can't tell you much, I'm not sure of the all details yet, but I've got the feeling something very strange is going on," William replied. The need to talk was urgent, if only to clear his head, and he knew Tony Croft could be trusted. "We've known each other a long time," he went on. "So, please bear with me on this."

"What would *this* happen to be?"

"These animals that have been taken. I don't think they've been stolen. I know Harry Carter reckons it was someone after dog food. Alec Chattan blames the salmon farmers, but it's not as simple as that."

"What then?"

"This thing Harry saw in the river...I mean, it could have come down from the Big House, from Angus Douglas's place."

"You trying to tell me Nessie's responsible for the missing cattle?" Croft popped a stick of gum in his mouth. "For God's sake, Will? Are you out of your mind?"

"No, I don't think I am."

"But, Nessie, come on? No one really believes in her. From what I've heard those photographs at the lake were fakes. Even the ones taken by a clergyman."

"That doesn't mean there wasn't an animal up there at the Big House." When the packet was pushed toward him, William took a piece of gum, as he would have taken a cigarette in the days when they smoked - it gave them something to share. "I'm not certain yet, but I believe there's a creature that comes out of the water looking for food."

"What sort of *creature*?"

"I can't tell you until I have more proof."

"Are you saying what Harry saw this morning wasn't due to drink?"

"I don't know, but there might be a way of finding out."

"How?"

"When we talk to Angus Douglas, let's see if he's lost any sheep. This creature's come ashore in two different places, the Big House could be a third."

"Jesus...." Sergeant Croft sat back, his mournful face even more bleak. "Sounds crazy to me, Will. And I won't say anything to anyone about this. But now, you've got to tell me more."

When Jamie McCory reached the coast, the sun was breaking through clumps of cloud, he smiled widely as he looked up at the sky, his whole body humming with anticipation. He was scared, there wasn't any point in trying to hide it, but he was more excited than he'd ever been in his entire life. It was always great getting into the water, but this was special, today was way over the top.

"What am I going to do?" he whispered, as he pulled his wet suit out of the bag. "If this really is one of them, what's going to happen to me?"

After last night's edgy supper, when he and his father had circled each other like growling dogs, neither prepared to confide in the other, he'd disappeared into his room and gone back to the computer. He'd visited the sites he'd discovered earlier - the things that were found in the depths. He went past worms and crabs that lived in hot water, beyond the strange shaped octopus with fins, through the seaweed stuff, until he arrived in the world of the giant squid, the site he'd had to close down earlier when his mother called him to the table.

But after supper, as soon as he got onto the cephalopod page and saw the long body, the huge eyes, the trailing arms and tentacles, he was certain that was what he had seen in the Grotto. There was no doubt about it any more. There were even pictures of circles the creature had left on the bodies of whales, they were the same as the ones on the calf he'd tried to identify earlier.

"To think I've been that close to a creature some people spent a ton of money trying to get a look at. And they haven't even got a decent photograph yet," he'd whispered to himself, his heart racing. "Even the one they caught the other day, it's just a mess spread out in a boat. My God, they've got no idea what it looks like in the water."

Exploring further he'd discovered something else, something that was really scary. All over the world writers and film-makers had turned *Architeuthis* into a monster. But no one had ever said why. Was it because they didn't know enough? Did they make movies where it pulled boats down to the bottom, murdered sailors, attacked like some wild beast, just because nobody knew what they were talking about? One writer had it climbing the Statue of Liberty; another the Eiffel

Tower. Were they just trying to scare people with fantastic images?

"It wasn't like that, not the one I saw," he'd said, shutting down the computer, saving a little power. Then he'd put both hands on his head, pulled his hat down tight. "I should've asked Dad more questions. And he should've told me what he knew."

Now, in the bright and clear morning he slipped on his fins, checked the clasp on his weighted belt, his mind running all over the place. He wanted to get in immediately, but was a bit frightened of what he would find. Last night he knew he'd have to take another look, see if the giant squid was still in the Grotto, even if he crapped his pants while he was down there. He'd lain awake a long time planning what he'd do in the morning. He had to get up early, not say a word to anyone, just grab his gear and go. Well, now here he was by the edge of the sea, looking into the water, feeling scared, but knowing he had to get in.

That's what being brave is, they say. Having the shits but doing it.

"Come on," he said, loud enough for a black-backed gull to take to the air. "It's only a bloody great shellfish. It's not going to eat you up."

After the giant squid had been washed out to sea, the dead ram in her arms, she'd returned to the cavern where she'd sheltered after taking the Chattan's calf. She knew the terrain, all the twists and turns of the landscape, and felt safe enough there to eat her catch. But, in spite of her hunger, she'd had to prepare the meal slowly - getting the flesh off the thing was no easy task. Its body was protected by the seaweed it wore - a coating as tough as kelp. The fact that her wounded tentacle had not yet fully recovered made peeling the ram a painful process. First the outer layer had to be cut into with her beak, then pulled back by her arms. However, she soon discovered that once the skin had been opened it slipped off quite readily. After that, she could dig into prey, eat it like any other. Snipping pieces off the carcass, her file-like tongue rasping away the flesh, she ate her fill, while around her the water grew red with blood, became infested with tiny scavengers.

The meal, nevertheless, was less satisfying than the earlier two. The first had been exciting, had led to the discovery that there was plenty of food to be found on the land. The second had been a warning, told her those creatures that lived above were defensive beings, especially when it came to their young. But this third had been quite frightening, had forced her into a hasty retreat.

The time had come to make a further decision, one that was critical to survival. Throughout her life she'd made many choices, deciding which fish to catch, what lobster to gather, whether or not to venture forth when the sperm whale's clicking filled the darkness of the depths. But this time it was different, she now had to deal with the unknown, and she didn't know whether to stay or leave.

The force which had urged her away from the Peake Deep was starting to fade. At first it had been extreme, impossible to resist. But as the days went by, as the currents swept the waters clean, its effect had been lessened. In the beginning, there'd been other members of her gigantic family accompanying her, but gradually they had disappeared. Some had fallen prey to whales - she'd seen one taken from her side. Others just seemed to have vanished, returned perhaps to the world they knew. Yet, she'd remained, managed to survive, and was now tempted to stay a little longer, strangely drawn to the starfish that had looked at her with kindly eyes, although she knew in both hearts it was time to depart.

But the starfish had a curious attraction, unlike any she'd known. She wondered if it had anything to do with the search for a mate, one who would bond to produce a host of young. The thought confused the cephalopod, made her turn a little pink. She was a virgin, after all, with no experience of such matters. And, she asked herself, if it *was* her duty to attract the swimming creature, what colour should she assume? Dark or pale, streaked or spotted? A bright and robust red? How should she behave? Would being coy seem appropriate, or would a direct approach be more effective?

It seemed all too much for the moment, especially now that her stomach was full. On the other hand, there was no time like the present. Anyway, if how she acted and what colour she wore failed to attract the starfish, she could always eat the thing. It would be far easier to skin than the last of her catches.

William McCory and Sergeant Croft tramped down the Culloch High Street past Boots, the chemist, Grants, the hardware store, the post office that was threatened with closure, toward the *Harbour Light*, concerned about their imminent meeting with Angus Douglas. He was old blood, Chairman of the Town Council with friends in high places, and they weren't quite certain what he should be told. They'd discussed the matter of the giant squid for a long time before leaving the station where, in spite of insistent prodding, the vet remained evasive, said little more than that there might be something which came out of the water and took livestock. Well, the sergeant had assured him, he'd have to be more precise than that if he wanted to get anything from Douglas – after all, the man was a politician.

"If this *creature*, as you call it, has come ashore a third time?" Croft persisted, stepping aside to let a woman with a pram go past. "What's it going to tell you?"

"That it might be settling here."

"What's *settling*?" Croft's voice sharpened. "Come on, you've got to tell me more."

"I'm afraid I don't know much more."

"If you don't confide in me, Will, I don't know how I can help you. We're either together in this or you're going to be left out on your own."

"Very well, but for God's sake, don't tell me I'm going crazy." William watched Croft nod, and decided to confide in him completely. There was little point in holding back any longer. If confirmation came from New Zealand, and that could be any day now, the whole world would know. "I don't want to sound dramatic, but we might be about to solve one of the great mysteries of the deep."

"Like what?" Tony Croft stopped again; he needed to know a great deal more before they went into the *Harbour Light*. The pub was just across the street, its freshly-painted sign catching the sun. "You're not talking about Nessie again?"

"Nessie might have been one of them."

"What do you mean? A conger eel? Something like that? Come to think of it, maybe that's what Harry saw, a bloody great eel lifting its head out of the water."

"Not an eel, Tony. A giant squid."

"What?"

"You've never heard of them?"

"Not a lot They're like an overgrown octopus, aren't they?"

"Only very much bigger." William then told Croft what he'd gleaned from the *National Geographic* and a couple of sites he'd searched on the surgery computer. "For centuries sailors have come back with stories of monsters half as big as their boats. A few specimens have been caught or washed up on beaches. They captured the first one alive the other day, but it died almost immediately. The thing is, no one knows much about them."

"You really think that's what we've got here in Culloch?"

"I do, but the really strange thing about it is, it comes ashore to hunt. Nothing like that's ever been heard of before. These creatures usually spend their time way down the bottom. Miles deep."

"Do you believe this, Will?" Croft stared at the vet, wondering if he was telling the truth. After all, he'd made that crack to Harry Carter about aliens. "Are you telling me that one of these monsters has come ashore, here of all places, and taken new-born cattle for food?"

"I'm almost certain it has. I'm just waiting for final confirmation."

"My God, if what you say is true, we'd better be very careful what we tell Angus Douglas. If he thought crop circles on calves would put Culloch in the news, he's going to wet himself over this."

"That's why I didn't tell you much before."

"You could have, I'm not as obsessed as he is."

"I'm sorry about that." William shrugged apologetically. "I was just afraid of starting another rumour. The first one was bad enough."

"I'll second that, but if you're right we'd have something here like nowhere else. A *Free Willy* type of thing? I, ah, saw the movie again the other night," Croft cleared his throat - there was no point in admitting it was his favourite film. "We'd have a first."

"I know, I can't stop thinking about."

"Once the word got out there'd be people from all over. It'd change the town completely."

"That's why I want to be sure before we say anything to Angus Douglas. Within the next day or so I should have the evidence I need. The sample I took from Harry Carter's farm has been sent to New Zealand for further tests. If they come back positive, we'll know for sure."

"I can see why you want to keep a lid on it." Croft paused, thinking of something else *Free Willy* brought to mind. "That, ah, boy of yours? He's always in the water. Has he seen anything funny?"

"Not that he's told me. Though he found some bones that could have come from Carter's foal. That's what got me thinking."

"Did he say where he found them?"

"Off the coast somewhere."

"Do you know if he's been back there again?"

"My God, I hope not." William McCory swallowed uneasily. He should have told Jamie more, should warned him to keep out of the water. He reached for his mobile phone. "I'll give him a call. Find out where he is."

"Then we'd better go across to the pub. Douglas will be getting impatient."

TWELVE – signals

Jamie McCory didn't hear his phone, he was swimming toward the Grotto when it rang, his heart beating uncertainly. He'd had some bad moments in the water, but nothing like this. Once he'd been caught by the tail end of the Corrievreckan current, swept out to sea. Though he'd been anxious when the tide took him, he kept his head, waited until a swirl brought him closer to the shore where he managed to hang on to some kelp. It took a long time to get out, and then he had to walk miles back to where he'd left his clothes. Still, it taught him not to venture out too far, and gave him a new respect for the sea. But this was a different sort of creeping fear, there were no currents near the Grotto - but maybe, just, maybe, a giant squid was waiting around the corner.

It's scary enough to think about sitting in front of the computer. Let alone being in the water, he told himself. *I'm an idiot, but I can't help it. I've got to be sure it actually exists.*

Then, out of nowhere, like a pop-up on the screen, it was below him. Spread out in the Grotto, its body spotted red. Not trying to hide as it did the first time. Just hanging there, looking up with eyes as big as dinner plates, watching every move he made.

"Jesus," he whispered, making bubbles in the water. "What the..."

Suddenly he felt the water swirl around him, like the back-draught from a passing car. The thing was moving – coming up, stopping, then going back again. He could see how it made the currents – with a tube between its eyes. With it, just by squeezing, the squid could move any way it wanted. Now it was using the jet to circle him. Staring up with those enormous eyes like it was looking him over, seeing if he was real. It was amazing, it really was – but the squid was checking him out.

"What?" he said. "What are you trying to do?"

The squid turned sideways, one eye peering as if making up its mind. That way on, Jamie could see it was longer than he first thought. Its body was bigger than his, and he was no runt. With the arms, all held together, it was like a rocket streaming through the water, going around him like it wanted to be sure there was no more to him than it could see.

"You real?" he bubbled, keeping his place in the water, his fins marking time. Once again he wondered if he was suffering from the rapture of the deep - being drunk on nitrogen that had got into his blood. He'd read about it making people see things that didn't exist. There was one poor diver who took his mouthpiece out, tried to give it to a fish. But, hang on, that was only if you'd been down and came up too quickly. He'd only just got in. This was actually happening - but he mustn't let the thing get into his head. Then he had an idea that was absolutely ridiculous. It was insane and he knew it, but it was all he could think of to do. He pushed one hand down toward the giant squid, the tip of the forefinger and the end of the thumb making a circle, the international underwater OK sign. "Look at that," he said. "I'm your friend."

SQUID

The giant squid watched the starfish stop a little clumsily, but that was only to be expected, they weren't the most mobile of creatures. She'd seen bottom-dwelling members of his tribe, some large enough to eat, drift from rock to rock with a trembling, but quite graceful, motion. Although, this one was clumsier than most, it seemed almost crippled. Perhaps it had been hurt, the way she'd been hurt by the cow. Yet all its parts were moving. And now it had an arm out and was making a curious gesture with the tiny tentacles at the end. However, it appeared content just to watch. There was no aggression, nothing like that. Most importantly, the squid couldn't see any teeth. It was time to take a closer look.

When they reached the *Harbour Light* Sergeant Croft and William McCory found Angus Douglas in a buoyant mood.

"Hello there," the portly chairman called as soon as they walked in, beckoning them toward his table. He couldn't wait to hear what they had to say for themselves. As far as he was concerned, he was way ahead of the game. He'd already found slime on the barbed-wire fence in the Blackface enclosure, the same sort of stuff the vet had spoken of earlier. His ram was obviously the third in a series to be taken. It was time to see what these two johnnies had to say for themselves. "Come along, let's get started."

"Sorry if we're a bit late, sir," Sergeant Croft muttered apologetically. "I got held up at the station. Will was waiting for me there."

"No problem," Angus replied, then asked if they'd like coffee. When they nodded, he ordered the same for himself with a splash of brandy. "Now, let's put our cards on the table," he continued. "What's known about the foal and the calf that have gone? And that slimy stuff you were checking out?"

"As far as I know, we're still waiting for further evidence," Croft replied, popping another piece of gum into his mouth. "There's nothing new yet. Isn't that right, Will?"

"I spoke to Oban yesterday. They're doing another test."

"Is that really necessary?" Douglas peered from face to face, both men were stonewalling. Well, let's see how long they lasted. "Wasn't it something that could be identified easily? It looked to me just like..." He stopped immediately, realising he'd blundered. "Ah, here's the coffee," he went on quickly. "Sugar? Or is it saccharine these days?"

"Looked like what?" William asked bluntly.

"I, ah, can imagine what it looked like."

"I might have mentioned some sort of slimy material. But I didn't go into any detail." William stirred his coffee pointedly. "Where was it exactly? The stuff you saw?"

"There was no need to actually see it," Angus stumbled on. "Your description was enough."

"Come to think of it, sir," Croft said quietly. "I believe it was me who was more specific about the material. Some sort of residue, I think I said."

"Precisely." Douglas reached for his cup. "Know what it is?"

"What have you lost, Angus?" William persisted. "Has one of your Blackface gone?"

"I, ah..." Douglas sipped, thinking frantically. The coffee was hot and the brandy helped. There had to be some way of regaining the advantage. "You obviously expect me to say, yes. If I did, would that add another piece to your puzzle?"

"It might."

"Let's put our cards on the table, shall we?" Angus Douglas replied, slowly gaining ground. "How about telling me exactly what is going on? You thought I was daft when I wanted to make something out of croft circles on calves. But that's only half the story, isn't it? There's a lot more to it than that."

"We think it might be conger eels," Sergeant Croft said quietly. "They could be attacking our livestock. Matter of fact, Harry Carter saw one this morning in the Orchy. He thought it was Nessie, but you know what he's like."

"Nessie?" Angus Douglas spluttered, anger replacing unease. "Harry Carter? Conger eels in the Orchy? Who the hell do you think you're talking to?"

"Something to do with climate warming, sir." Tony Croft found it difficult not to smile. It felt good to have the upper hand over the Chairman of the Town Council. "I was reading a report the other day. Seems cod stocks are slumping, albatross are dying of hunger. They say it's all to do with the plankton. Wouldn't surprise me if conger eels are coming ashore."

"Balderdash. No conger eel could've taken my Blackface ram."

"So that's what you lost," murmured William. "Pity you didn't say so sooner."

"Don't tell me *you* believe this eel claptrap, Will? For God's sake, man, you're a vet." Ignoring the others, Angus waved at the barman, ordered a double brandy. "Now, let me warn you, both of you, if you don't tell me what's going on I'll call a special meeting of the council. I'll have you denounced for withholding information. Information that could be of public interest."

"I wouldn't do anything for a while," William replied. "As I told you, I'm waiting for certain results to be confirmed. Until I get them, it would be most unwise to make any sort of statement."

"What about you, Sergeant?" Angus turned impatiently to Croft. "Don't tell me you're part of this bloody conspiracy?"

"I..." began Croft, when his mobile rang. He answered and, as he listened, the lines in his mournful face twitched into a smile. "That was Constable Roberts," he told the others, closing his phone with a snap. "It seems everything's all right."

"Good." Angus leant forward. "What exactly has been solved?"

"The vicar's garden gnome's been found, sir," Croft replied politely. "It was on the Common with a condom over its head. That's not the first time that's happened."

"For God's sake, just leave me alone," Angus Douglas growled, reaching for his brandy. They'd pay for this. He'd show them. There's no way they could treat him like a fool and get away with it. "I expect a full report when you finally find out what's taking the local livestock. In the meantime, get out of sight."

With courteous nods, William McCory and Sergeant Croft rose and left the *Harbour Light*, trying to hide their grins.

Jamie thought he was going to die when the giant squid touched him. For long moments they'd hung in the water, keeping their places, examining each other from afar. Then Jamie decided to move down closer. It seemed the only thing to do. How was he going to find out anything if he just stayed back and waited? He wasn't as frightened as he'd been at first. Nothing menacing had happened. The creature had changed colour once or twice, each time becoming a little brighter, but that was all. As the moments passed, he felt more comfortable in the company of the squid.

It's not going to hurt me, he told himself. *Last time it ran away.*

In none of the items he'd found on the web were there any stories about squids attacking people. There were some old reports about sailors being torn limb from limb, but nobody was certain if they were true or not. All the bad stuff had been in novels and films.

Anyway, I've got my knife, he thought. He carried it strapped to his leg, although he knew he'd never use it. *I could always poke its eyes out.*

He took two or three deep breaths to clear his lungs - he could stay under longer that way, then let his weights take him down to the level of the squid. And, as soon as he got near enough, the squid put out a tentacle and touched him. It reached out and patted him on the back. He thought he was going to die.

The squid watched the starfish's ungainly movements, saw it make a sign with its tiny tentacles, blow bubbles like a whale, then come down and move in closer. To her surprise, she turned bright red. A rush of tenderness swept through her as she stared into its curious eyes. She knew she had to protect it, yet had little idea how. It was such an incompetent creature, things could go wrong if she moved too fast, although it was critical that she did something to reassure it she meant no harm, make it known she was a friend. She certainly didn't want to give it a fright, behave like those sharks she'd seen in these waters. There was nothing gentle about their movements, nothing friendly about their great mouths with rows of razor teeth. She'd seen smaller squids panic in their company, swim frantically away at the sight of them. So, as she didn't want anything like that to happen, she'd better be very careful.

Moving as gently as she could, the giant squid reached out with a tentacle, the suckers almost closed, and touched the starfish on its back. She brushed it softly, letting it know she'd do nothing that would endanger it, cause it any pain. To tell the truth, the starfish had found its way into both her hearts. And, as soon as she made contact, her emotions overcame her. Changing colour with remarkable speed, much faster than any chameleon, she went from red to silver, to pale green with iridescent stripes, then back to bright blood red again. It was a wonderful experience.

Jamie's whole body shook when the squid's tentacle touched him. At first he couldn't believe what was happening. Things like this didn't occur in the water. When he'd gone down, the squid it was sideways-on, one great eye looking upward, staring. Then it turned full-face and the tentacle came out, waving as it went through the water. It must have been twenty feet long, and it curled around him before it actually made contact. Then it patted him on the back, like it was an old friend, sending a shock wave right through him - he thought it was the end of his days.

It was like that when the lightning struck him. He felt as if he was burning up. But this didn't leave him half-conscious, lying on the floor, wondering if he'd ever get up again. And it wasn't like the jolt he got from the electric ray - that nearly blew him out of the water. This was different, it didn't hurt, it didn't last long either, but it was way beyond anything he could ever have imagined. Then the squid patted him a second time, and a strange warmth swelled up inside him, making him feel good. His fear seemed to melt away, and he stopped thinking about dying.

This is awesome, he told himself. *This is unbelievable.*

He turned and touched the tentacle, had to do it quickly as he was running out of breath, but had enough time to make contact. The squid felt soft through his wet-suit glove, and for a second or two they held hands. Then he shot back to the surface, broke through gasping for air. He stayed there a moment, refilling his lungs, hoping to go back again immediately. But when he looked down the giant squid had gone, flashed away as quickly as it had before, vanished in the water. This time it didn't worry him, he was certain it would be back. He knew he hadn't seen the last of this magical creature.

Alice, he told himself, his eyes searching for traces of where it might have gone, knowing that he had to name it, make it quite unique. And he had no doubt it was a girl. The way it touched him was like his mother when she made him take his hat off and stroked his hair. *Alice, that's what I'm going to call you. You live in a wonderland.*

The giant squid fled quickly once contact had been made, confused by the way the starfish had returned to the surface. At first she thought she'd been too violent, although she'd done her best not to harm. But you never knew with those suckers of hers, they could scar the skin of a whale. Then she realised the creature was like a whale in some of its habits - it needed air to survive. That made it all the more primitive, of course, it hadn't much idea of how to live in the sea. She had to be patient, she told herself, give it time to get used to her before she got in touch again. It wouldn't take long, she was sure of that, those air-breathing animals had their routes. Given time to recover, the starfish would be back swimming the same old waterways, following the paths it knew. Then, she'd be able to discover more, find out if it really was a mate she could bond with. She went a little pink at the thought, but in the kelp where she hid none of the life around her seemed to notice.

When Jamie got out of the water he was shivering. It wasn't the cold but the excitement of touching Alice that made him shake all over. *Jesus*, he thought, as he towelled himself dry. *It really was there*. It wasn't his imagination any longer. He picked up his anorak, looked at his mobile phone and saw the message from his father. It told him to keep out of the water. That could only mean one thing. *His father knew about Alice too*. He had to talk to him as soon as he could. Not over the phone, but face to face. They had to work out some way of saving his new-found friend before word got out about her, before someone else discovered her. If they did, they'd catch her if they could.

Blanca González drove slowly down the narrow road to Culloch, admiring the heather-covered slopes, the golden gorse, tasting the salty air. It was too long since she'd seen a coastline that looked so much like Cantabria, with its long fingers of rock reaching out to sea, the small sandy beaches nestled between. They were similar to the ones she'd come to know well when her father took her octopus fishing.

"Ay, Papá," she said, stopping at a lookout point, her eyes on the scattering of islands below. "You would love it here."

Her gaze drifted up to a small hotel on the hill above, a white-walled building with bay windows and a tower block – it tempted her to rest awhile. There was no hurry, so Blanca drove up a winding path, through a host of daffodils, and went inside. On a glassed-in balcony with a view of the hills and the water, she ordered coffee and a plate of oatcakes. In the distance she could see a herd of deer, darkly sculptured against the skyline.

"Is it usual to see them in the daytime?" she asked the middle-aged man who served her. "I have heard they are in this part, but I did not expect to see them before dark."

"The red ones, aye, they're all over the place any time of day." The man gave Blanca a second look. "You must be new to this corner of the world."

"I have been to the Highlands," she explained, finding it easy to talk to the man, "But, now I am going to Culloch. I hope to be working there."

"You won't find much in Culloch, lass. It's been hit bad of late."

"Oh, in what way?"

"They've had the worst weather on record." The man leant over the back of a chair, watched the foreign woman nibble an oatcake. She'd like that all right, but when it came to the coffee it'd be a different matter, none of them found it strong enough. "There's nothing doing there. Tourist business's gone down the drain. The weather's affected us all over. To tell the truth, I might have offered you something here, if things weren't so slack."

"Really?" Blanca frowned, local expressions often left her stranded. "Thank you, but I think I already have a job."

"Only hope it's a good one. Culloch's a quiet place at the best of times. Right now, it's as dead as a doornail." The man straightened, began to leave. "Anyway, enjoy yourself while you're down there. There are some good folk in the town."

After he'd gone Blanca ate the oatcakes but let most of the coffee grow cold, wondering what lay ahead. She wasn't worried by what the man had said, was sure that her work would keep her busy. Nevertheless, as she'd be living on her own it would be nice to make a few friends in the town, especially if they were interested in diving.

THIRTEEN – breaking news

Angus Douglas, last in the line of those who once ruled Culloch and all that it contained, spent a long time in the *Harbour Light* after William McCory and Tony Croft left, thoughtfully sipping brandy. He knew they'd handed him a plate of codswallop, and he was determined to find out why. What's more, they'd better not try taking him for a fool or he'd be down on them like a ton of bricks. It didn't matter too much what the local vet was up to, but Sergeant Croft should watch himself. If he, Angus Archibald Douglas, Chairman of the Town Council, set his mind to it he could break the man.

"Conger eels and Nessie," he grunted, loud enough for a group of tourists at a nearby table, drinking lager and eating bags of crisps, to give him curious looks. "What do they take me for?"

Something was attacking the local livestock, there was no doubt about that. Whatever it was, and wherever it came from, it had now laid hands on his Blackface ram - and that made it personal. So what was his next move going to be? There was no point in getting in touch with Charlie Coots again. But what about that vet in Oban and the slime sample he was testing? The man shouldn't be too difficult to find. In fact, a short conversation with Lucy, Will McCory's assistant, would do the trick. Her father, poor old sod, had been found wandering around

Culloch not knowing where his clothes were. With help from Angus he'd settled in an old people's home in Inveraray. Lucy would tell him all he needed to know, locating the Oban vet would be easy.

"We'll see who runs this bloody town," he muttered. And when the tourists turned to him again, smiles on their smug faces, he lifted his brandy in a toast, emptied it in a swallow. "Enjoy your stay," he told them. "Welcome to Culloch. A little town whose days aren't yet over."

After he left the *Harbour Light*, William McCory tried to phone Jamie again, but only received a recorded message saying the number wasn't available. He checked the text he'd sent earlier. It hadn't been picked up, and he became increasingly concerned about what he should do. There seemed little point in searching for his son, he had no idea where he'd be - there were dozens of little coves and inlets Jamie explored. He was also reluctant to call his wife for fear of upsetting her. If she thought the boy was in any danger she'd be off looking for him immediately, worrying herself sick. He was anxious enough himself, and had no wish to frighten anyone else.

"I'd better go home for lunch," he told himself, glancing at his watch. "And try to behave as normally as possible."

He was walking down the High Street toward his house his phone rang. Eagerly he looked at the screen, but the call wasn't from Jamie. It was from a farmer, ten miles inland, near the shores of Loch Awe, whose old bull had become trapped in a bog made deadly by recent rains.

"I'll come now," William said, after learning what had happened. "Don't shoot him. Let's see what we can do."

With that he hurried home, found both Molly and Jamie were absent, told Lucy where he was going and jumped into his car. Although he assured himself that his son would be safe wherever he was, concern nagged him steadily along every twisting mile of country road.

Late that afternoon in the *Black Watch*, Culloch's other public house, Harry Carter started talking about Nessie - until then he'd held his tongue. Tony Croft's crisp words, when hauled out of bed at dawn, had kept Harry silent all morning. The sergeant hadn't been too strident, but his tone of voice would have made anyone think. What's more, Croft had suggested Harry lay off the tonic. Alcohol, the sergeant warned him, was beginning to rot his brain. The best thing he could do was go home, get some breakfast and sleep it off. If he wasn't careful, he'd end up facing a magistrate on public nuisance charges.

Subdued, Harry had gone back to the stables. He didn't sleep, but sweated out the booze cleaning stalls, rubbing down horses, working himself into a lather. Four tourists came in after lunch, drawn by the change in the weather. They took mounts for the afternoon and paid in cash. Harry left the lad who worked for him to wait for their return, to see that the horses were properly treated, and to shut up for the night. Feeling almost human again, Harry then drove down to the *Black Watch* and ordered a double whisky. When the second glass was set in front of him, he had no doubt about what had happened that morning, and couldn't keep his mouth shut about his close encounter with Nessie.

"Bugger them," he said, as he ordered a pint to go with the scotch. "If no one believes me, that's their business. I can only tell them what I saw."

The *Black Watch* wasn't as good a pub as the *Harbour Light*, but they weren't as likely to throw him out. He began by talking to Billy, a young waiter with a pock-marked face, and soon a small crowd gathered around him. Fishermen who hadn't been out in their boats for a week, waiters whose summer had been ruined by the weather, closed in when he offered a round of drinks. As long as Harry bought them a pint, they'd listen to whatever he said. Even when he began talking about Nessie, the Loch Ness Monster, they nodded their heads in agreement, albeit with a wink or two.

"I really did see it," he persisted, after he'd told his story twice. "With my own eyes. Nessie in the Orchy. Lifted its head and looked at me. Scared me shitless, it did."

"Yeah?" said Billy, becoming bored. "What was you on?"

"On?" Harry shook his head. "A drop of Scotch, that's all."

"You want to see monsters, I can let you have this." Billy took a few tablets wrapped in silver foil out of his pocket. "You'll have them eating out of your hand with this stuff. Man, you'll be talking on first-name terms."

"Oh, fuck off," Harry replied, but without any real animosity. He was tired, wanted someone decent to believe him - Tony Croft, Will McCory, even Tommy Tranter if it came to that. He'd had enough of the boozers here. He paid for a final round, and decided to get a good night's sleep, see what the morning would bring. "Believe what you like," were his farewell words. "But, I tell you, I'm sure I saw Nessie."

After he left, the group chatted a little longer then went their separate ways. However, the rumour mill had begun to grind. Before the night was through half of Culloch was talking about Nessie, the monster that had come down the Great Glen to the Firth of Lorne, stuck its head up in the River Orchy and waved at Harry Carter. A cleaner claimed to have seen it too. Someone else said they saw it twice.

"Where's Dad," asked Jamie, when his mother served him lunch, a small marrow cut open, stuffed with nuts and sweet corn, covered with grated cheese. "He sent me a message earlier. But he didn't say where he was."

"He's over by Loch Awe, someone's got a problem with a bull," Molly explained with a puzzled frown - it wasn't like William to call his son. "What did he have to say?"

"Nothing, he just wanted to get in touch." Jamie bent his head to his plate, hat down low. "This is good. I really like sweet corn."

"That's why I got it for you." Molly picked up her cup of tea. There were a couple of fresh trout she'd have with her husband when he finally returned. "Where were you when Will called? The same place we went yesterday?"

"Yeah, I was just poking around." Jamie knew he couldn't say anything yet. But it wasn't easy sitting there, knowing what he did. Like Harry Carter, he was bursting to talk about what he'd seen. "Taking advantage of the weather. Who knows how long it's going to last."

"That's true enough," Molly replied, knowing she'd get nowhere asking direct questions. When he was in the right mood he'd talk to her about anything. When he wasn't, he was impossible. "I just wondered what your father wanted. He's got something on his mind, you know. He mentioned it last night in bed."

"What's he concerned about?"

"I'm not sure, really. He did say something that old bone you found, but I don't know if that's what's worrying him."

"Like he said, it probably came from Harry Carter's foal." Jamie felt his face grow hot. This was awful, holding it in. He wanted to tell everyone about Alice, but couldn't say a word until he was certain she'd be all right. They might do anything to her. Catch her. Kill her. Stuff like that. He had to talk to his father first. Get him to help. Get him on side. "But he wasn't sure, was he?"

"What do you think, Jamie?"

"About what? The skull I found?" He hated keeping things from his mother, but didn't have any choice. He glanced up, found it difficult to look her in the eye. "I don't know much about bones."

"I don't suppose you do." Molly gave an inward sigh. "Unless they belong to fishes."

"Yeah, right." Jamie scraped his fork around his empty plate. His mind had been so busy he hadn't realised he'd finished his lunch. "Ah, that was good," he said, grateful for a change of subject. "I don't suppose you've got any more?"

"I have, as a matter of fact." Molly took another marrow from the oven. "Diving always gives you an appetite. I've got another one right here."

"Thanks a lot, Mum. You're great."

Little was said while Jamie ate the second marrow, both were too busy with their thoughts. Once he asked about the Spanish girl who was coming to dinner, and Molly reminded him her name was Blanca, adding that she was expected about eight.

"Just one more thing," Molly said, as she cleared the table. "It wouldn't hurt to give your father a call. Tell him you got his message."

"I've already done that," Jamie replied. "I called him when I was walking home."

All afternoon the giant squid hovered in the kelp, hidden amongst bronze stalks that waved softly in the swelling tide. She had never been so excited in all her life. She had touched the starfish. It had returned the touch. Now she wondered if the time had come for bonding. She was aware what took place when that happened, had witnessed, too young to take part of course, the frenzied process that ensued when the male, often smaller than his mate, placed his sperm inside his partner's mantle.

It wasn't very dignified, she knew, as a brightly-coloured wrasse swam past which she made no attempt to capture - there too many thoughts racing through her brain to think of food. All the writhing and squirming that went on during the sexual procedure, all those arms locking and unlocking lacked a certain charm. Given her choice, she'd much prefer a gentler approach, something that matched the look she'd seen in the starfish's eyes.

As she trembled in the kelp, ignoring a large lobster that crawled out from under a rock, Alice wondered what part of the starfish might be used to join her. At first she'd thought it could have been the tube that came from its tiny mouth. Then she'd discovered that was used to breathe with. Anyway, the starfish was a primitive creature, unable to live entirely in the sea and would know very little of its reproductive customs. Where babies came from, for example, or how they were made. She might even have to show it what to do. The thought was so overwhelming that Alice turned a bright and glimmering red, a sight attractive enough to draw several small fishes to her side. These, also, she left alone. She had more important matters to consider.

William McCory glanced at his phone when he arrived at Matt Andrews' farm, relief flooding through him when he realised that Jamie had come to no harm. He'd talk to the boy as soon as he could - in the meantime there was a bull to attend to.

"Got stuck in the muck last night," Matt said, a big man with a grizzled beard. "Tried to pull it out by the head, only went deeper." He lifted the shotgun he carried. "I thought of putting this behind his ear, but Gordon suggested we call you first."

"He's been a good old boy," said Gordon, an elderly man with a missing front tooth. "I wanted to give him a chance. He's a beautiful beast."

"Not too beautiful right now," Matt grunted. The coat of the West Highlander, normally loose and flowing, was clotted, caked with mud. The pale mane above its eyes stuck to its forehead in dreadlocks. "It's a bloody shit pile."

"I'll clean him up when we haul him out," said Gordon.

"How are we going to manage that?" Matt put the shotgun over his shoulder. "Getting the rope over his head was bad enough. He knows how to use his horns."

"Let's see what we can do," William said, studying the bull's position. It had slipped down a rocky bank into the bog. Its hindquarters were almost covered, but its front feet had found some support. Although it had stopped struggling, its head, moving uneasily from side to side, was still fighting the rope around its long curved horns. A tractor stood nearby, the other end of the rope attached. "Exactly how long's he been there?"

"Must've been early this morning he went in," Gordon said. "Don't know what the old sod was doing. He should know enough to keep away from stuff like that."

"He's getting on," Matt said. "I reckon he's past his best."

"So am I," replied Gordon. "But that doesn't mean you're going to blow my head off.?"

Two men standing by the tractor laughed. "You never know what Matt'll get up to," one of them said. "I wouldn't put it past him."

"How much more rope have you got?" William asked, moving toward his four-wheel drive. "Enough to make a sling?"

"Got all the rope you'll ever need," Matt replied. "It's getting it onto the bull that'll be the trouble. He won't let us close a second time. He'll panic, go down deeper."

"I'll give him a shot." William took his surgical bag from the car, as well as a pair of chest-high waders. "Not to put him out. Just enough to make him easier to handle. His head'll go under and he'll drown if I give him too much."

"It could be worth a try." Matt Andrews turned and called to his men, who took a coil of rope from a truck by the tractor. "But be careful getting it into him. He's mean."

"He'll be all right with this." William held up a tranquilising pistol. "I bought it a while back, but haven't had any need for it till now."

"Let's hope it does the job," said Gordon, his tongue working the gap in his teeth. "I'd hate to lose him now. He's like an old mate to me."

William McCory said nothing more as he loaded the pistol, hoping that this wouldn't take too long. He wanted to return to Culloch as soon as he could and talk to Jamie. However, he soon discovered that working with the bull was neither quick nor easy. The first tranquilising dart had little effect, sat like a poppy on a well-padded shoulder as the bull tried to wriggle it free. It took a second before the animal began to calm down. Then, in spite of Matt's warning and Gordon's constant advice, William put on his chest-high waders and eased himself into the bog.

"Come on, old chap," he said, taking hold of a horn, knowing that if he spoke gently to any animal, no matter what size it was, its fear often faded. "We're going to get you out of here. Don't make things any worse than they are."

The bull made a half-hearted thrust at him, but there was no real force behind it. "Get the rope, make two slings. One for the front, the other the back," William called to Matt Andrews, his voice barely rising above a whisper.

"Lads," shouted Matt, then reduced his tone – the vet seemed to know what he was doing. "Double rope, you'd better make it. Though how we're going to get it under him, I'm buggered if I know."

"With you lot beside me," William said. "All of you, all four."

After a few doubtful comments, the others moved into the bog. One of the men from the truck, accompanied by Matt, took the rope to the bull's hindquarters. Gordon and the other joined William by the head. All the while they worked, the vet spoke softly, telling the animal that everything would be all right. But, even though putting the rope under the forequarters was relatively simple, reaching beneath the after-end seemed impossible in the deep and cloying muck.

"We're not going to get it round his backside," Matt said, after a third attempt. He was close to the bank the bull had slipped down, standing chest-deep in mud. The end of his beard was black from the bog. "Can't we pull him out from the front?"

"That might break his back," said William softly. "Let's try again."

"Sod it. I'm going for the shotgun. He won't feel a thing."

"Give me a go," said Colin, the man by his side. "I've got an idea."

"Then be quick about it." Matt handed the man the dripping rope. "I want to get over with, no matter what we have to do."

Colin took the rope, felt beneath the bull then, with a deep breath, disappeared into the bog, sludge closing over his head. "Christ...," muttered Matt, new concern in his eyes. But a moment later Colin's head broke the surface, black with bog but grinning widely.

"Got it," he spluttered. "Even cleared his balls."

After that, the process went relatively smoothly. Slings were attached to the tractor, and slowly the bull was sucked from the bog. Only once did the rescue look like failing - when the front sling slipped and the animal's head went under, but William immediately tugged it out by the horns. Soon after that the bull scrambled onto firmer ground and staggered forward clumsily. Free from the slings it fell to its knees, snorted loudly, then came up again, its head lowered aggressively.

"Look at the old bugger," said Gordon proudly. "Still ready to have a go."

When they had washed up, hosed the bull clean, William was eager to leave. But Matt Andrews insisted they share a malt whisky, happy that the Highlander had survived. The further delay meant that soon after William arrived home, while he was still under the shower, Blanca González knocked on the door, giving him no chance to speak to Jamie.

FOURTEEN – breaking bread

Blanca waited uncertainly for the white-painted door to open, not quite sure what to expect. She'd arrived promptly, fully aware that people in this part of the world were more punctual than in her own, yet realising she knew very little about the family who'd invited her for supper.

"He's well-thought of, though you might find him a bit dull," Malcolm Stewart had confided, putting a hand on her knee. He'd taken her to a cosy pub to wish her well, moving moved a little closer each time he bought her a drink. "I don't know much about his wife. They've got a boy, but I don't know much about him either."

"You have not worked together?" Blanca removed his prying fingers. He had a wife, twin daughters, and she didn't find him particularly attractive - his high-pitched laugh became more unappealing each time she heard it. And she had no intention of going to bed with a man merely because he'd given her a reference, there were many more delightful reasons. "I thought you knew him well."

"Well enough," Malcolm replied quietly, beginning to have doubts about William McCory – the man was far too cautious. If this test on the giant squid came back positive, they'd have to move like lightning to gain the glory, there were many others waiting in the wings.

"We've met at conferences mostly, sat on panels, that sort of thing. Would you like another gin and tonic?"

"No, thank you. I have to keep sober. I'm driving in the morning."

"Of course, I understand." Malcolm moved away knowing he'd get nowhere with this one. Pity, she looked like a screamer. "Still, don't get me wrong," he added. "Will's a bloody good vet." He gave another of his short snuffling laughs. "I'd go to him myself for treatment before many of the quacks I know."

"I'm not sure I am working for him yet. He's not said yes, so far."

"He will, and I'm sure you'll be happy in Culloch," Malcolm said, wondering if confirmation from New Zealand was about to alter all their lives. "You're good. And he needs help badly."

"I hope you are right."

"I usually am," Malcolm Stewart had assured her.

Now, standing before the white painted door Blanca González wondered what William McCory was really like. However, when the door opened it was not a man who greeted her but a tall woman with short greying hair. "Come in," she said. "I'm Molly, William's wife. He's having a shower. He only got home a moment ago. He'll be with us as soon as he can." She held out a welcoming hand.

"Hello." Blanca smiled, shook hands and went inside. The house, although small was spacious, and she found herself in a comfortable room with a fire cheerfully burning in the grate. A table, at the far end, had been set for the evening meal. "Oh, this is very nice."

"Thank you, come over here. It's not cold, but the fire helps keep out the damp. But, you don't look cold, my dear. You're not even wearing a coat."

"I walked down the road. From, what is it called, *Rose Cottage*?"

"Yes, that's Sarah Carrick's bed-and-breakfast."

"I have taken a room for the night there. I thought, you know, if I am staying here, I would look for an apartment in the morning."

"That's a good idea," Molly replied, warming to this sensibly-dressed girl with long dark hair and sparkling eyes. "Oh, what are these?" she asked, as Blanca handed her two brightly-wrapped gifts, one obviously a bottle of wine. "You shouldn't have."

"I thought you would like some Spanish wine. And the other, I hope you like it too. In my country, when you go to a house for the first time, it is good to take a present."

"Thank you very much." Molly put the wine on a table. "I'll leave that for Will, but I must take a look at this." She removed the paper from a deep-blue glass bowl. "That's lovely, I'll use it for salads." She smiled broadly. "You know, I think you'll like it here."

"Yes, I think I will."

Blanca González had spent much of the afternoon walking the narrow streets of Culloch, admiring the white-fronted houses, the nests of grey-slate and red-tile roofs. She'd gone out along the harbour wall, looked down on the few fishing boats moored in the quay, the piles of lobster pots, tied down against wind and wave. The port reminded her of Comillas, where she'd often swum in the summer, first went beneath the surface of the sea to explore what lay below. Later, she strolled up Culloch's High Street, peered into the few shops that were open, doing what business they could. Some still had sandbags piled by the door in case the rains returned.

She'd paused by William McCory's surgery – in was in an extension attached to his house. It was closed, being Saturday afternoon, although there was a number for emergencies on a card inside the window. All in all, she liked what she saw, and felt she would be happy in Culloch in spite of what Malcolm Stewart, or the man who served weak coffee in the hotel, had said.

"There's Will now," Molly said, hearing a door open. "I'll give him a call."

Blanca smiled, hoping that the vet would be as welcoming as his wife.

When William McCory came out of the bathroom, rubbing a towel through his hair, Jamie was waiting for him. "I must talk to you, Dad," he said, hat in hand in the hope of making a good impression.

"I got your message. Read it just before I arrived at the Andrew's farm." William replied, the excitement in his son's eyes making him pause. It had been a great relief to discover that Jamie was safe, and he wanted to share what he knew with the boy, but this was neither the time nor the place. What's more, there was no doubt that Jamie had seen something in the sea, and both needed somewhere quiet to discuss it. "I'm glad everything turned out all right."

"What were you worried about?"

"The currents, for one." William dried his ears, put the towel in a basket by the door, each gesture done deliberately, playing for time. "You know what the tides are like."

"The tides were okay, but..." Jamie couldn't understand why his father wasn't being straight. He wanted to tell him about Alice, to trust him with the news, but the old man was backing off. *Okay then, there was nothing to do but jump in.* "Listen, there's something I've got to tell you, something that's…"

"Is that you, Will?" Molly's voice echoed down the hall. "Our guest has arrived."

"Be there in a minute."

"Come now, she's dying to meet you."

Jamie and William stared at each other, both affected by the call - William grateful for the interruption, Jamie exasperated.

"I don't know how I can help you," Malcolm Stewart told Angus Douglas, the mobile phone clamped to his ear. "They're still running tests on the sample. The results haven't come through yet."

"I understand it was some sort of shellfish?" Angus said. After a little prompting, Lucy, Will's assistant, had given him Stewart's number, but as soon as he started asking questions the Oban vet avoided them. Obviously, he and McCory were concealing something. And it had to be pretty damned important, otherwise there'd have been no a cock and bull story about conger eels or Nessie in the River Orchy. If they weren't a damned site more careful, they'd have a conger eel up their arse. "So it shouldn't be too difficult to identify. Dunstaffnage is just up the road."

"They're still working on it," Malcolm replied. He wasn't giving anything away. At least, not until he found what Will was up to. As for this blundering fool, a man he'd never heard of, who claimed to be Chairman of Culloch Council, he'd get short bloody shrift. "Anyway, when the results come through, I'll send them on to Mister McCory. It'll be up to him what he does with them."

"Will it now?" Angus Douglas's voice dropped to a growl. "Then listen to me very carefully, *Mister* Stewart. There's something fishy going on, and I'm not talking about things that live in shells. Three items of livestock have been taken. One of them from a stable owner who claims to have seen the Loch Ness Monster in the River Orchy. On top of that the local vet, your *Mister* McCory, and Sergeant Croft have something up their sleeves. Something they're not telling me about. Now you, who I believe knows as much as anyone about all this, is acting like a silly bugger. And if you've got any sense, you'll put a stop to it immediately. Now, tell me exactly what's being tested. And what you think you'll find, or I'll have you indicted along with the rest."

"Indicted?" Malcolm swallowed, reassessing the caller. "For what? There's no law that's been broken that I know of."

"How about a few you don't. Like withholding information. Failing to make known a conspiracy that could affect the welfare of the State. Keeping secret a practice which might be of interest to the police." Angus sat back in his armchair, reached for his whisky. He was playing another blinder. "In these days of international terrorism, *Mister* Stewart, there are probably at least a dozen laws that have been broken. Some of which could see you behind bars for a very long time. Are we clear about that?"

"Well, yes, but...."

"No buts, *please*. Just tell me what you think Will McCory's up to."

"I, ah..." Malcolm cleared his throat, wondering what had gone wrong. Will had said nothing about Nessie. In fact, he'd only mentioned two pieces of missing livestock. Now this chairman, or whatever he happened to be, was putting on the pressure. Well, by Christ, no one was going to push him aside. He'd done the groundwork. If anyone scored it was going to be him. "I'd like to tell you more," he continued, his tone conspiratorial. "But not over the phone. Why don't I come down to Culloch?"

"On the other hand, why don't I come up to Oban?"

"Well, I suppose...." Malcolm paused, thinking furiously. If he put a call through to New Zealand tomorrow evening, where it'd be Monday morning, he'd get the latest test results. With them, it'd be time to think about capturing the squid. He'd already planned a number of ways. Might even discuss them with this Angus Douglas. A little local help could be useful. Whatever happened, *he* intended to be the international expert. It'd be *his* face on the front page of the newspapers. *He'd* be all over the TV. It'd be *him* who got the gongs. "How about coming by for a drink?" he continued. "Sixish?"

"Why not now?"

"Can't, I'm tied up till tomorrow evening."

"Very well." With a pudgy paw, Angus scribbled Malcolm Stewart's address. The delay wasn't important. In fact, it'd give him a chance to look into the rumours circulating the town. And take a look through his library. With books on just about everything, there was no doubt he'd find what he was looking for. "Just don't keep me waiting."

"I won't." Malcolm replied. Closing his mobile phone he noticed it was damp with sweat. No wonder, this was exciting stuff. "But you'll have to move pretty damned fast to keep up with me," he whispered fervently. "You can bet your balls on that."

"Very thoughtful of you," William said, holding up the bottle of wine Blanca had brought. "From the Rioja."

"You are familiar with our wines?" Blanca asked, wondering what was troubling the man she hoped to work for. He had come into the room with a frown, formally shaken hands, then poured three glasses of sherry. His son, who followed him, had spoken once, but now sat silently, sipping Coca Cola. It was obvious that they had disagreed about something and she hoped it had nothing to do with her. "Spanish wines are very good. Especially from the Rioja."

"We know they are, my dear," said Molly, annoyed by William's behaviour. He was usually at ease in any company, but at the moment his face was closed. He and Jamie had been arguing again; they should know better with a guest in the house. "She also bought that nice blue bowl. The one with the salad in it."

"Very pretty." William glanced at the table. "A lovely colour."

"It's just right for the dishes I've prepared." Molly turned to Blanca. "Cold meats, cheese and salads. I hope you like that sort of thing?"

"Very much. It is what I eat at home. Not so much at my real home. But when I am cooking for myself in this country."

"Where are you staying at the moment?" William asked, already accepting the girl. She was relaxed, talked easily, and had square competent hands. He'd gone through the CV she'd faxed and found her qualifications excellent. He was tempted to tell her right away the job was hers - the sooner he got it over with the sooner he could talk to Jamie. The boy, who'd been bursting earlier, now sat saying nothing, almost in a sulk. He should have given him a moment longer when they met outside the bathroom, and he shouldn't have kept what he knew to himself. "Have you a flat in Oban?"

"I have accommodation there," Blanca replied, trying to access the man. He seemed cold on the outside, but must be nice as his wife was charming. "But I am staying in Culloch for the night."

"She's with Sarah, at *Rose Cottage*." Molly wanted to give her husband a good shake. He was being far too indifferent, almost rude. She'd be disappointed if he turned Blanca down, the girl seemed perfect. On top of everything, Jamie was quieter than usual. There *was* something going on between them, and the sooner they cleared it up the better. "Blanca thought, if you wanted her to stay, she'd look for somewhere in the morning," she added pointedly. It was time somebody broke the ice, and it was up to her to do it.. "Have you made your mind up yet?"

"I thought we'd have a private chat first."

"You must know whether you want her or not."

"Well, yes, I do," William replied, smiling with relief – at least that was out of the way. "I'd like her to start immediately."

Blanca laughed out loud. They were talking as if she wasn't present, yet somehow it didn't offend her. They didn't hide their feelings, and she welcomed their directness.

"Well?" Molly turned to her. "What do you say to that?"

"Oh, very good. I will begin on Monday, if that is all right with you?"

"Suits me fine." William picked up his sherry. "Let's drink to it."

After all had raised their glasses, Blanca looked across at Jamie. "What about you? Do you think you would like me here?" she asked.

"Me?" Jamie shrugged. It didn't have much to do with him. She seemed all right, but he had other things to think about. They were welling up inside, yet he couldn't get them out, no one wanted to know. "Yeah, Dad could really use some help."

"What about you? Do you think you will work with your father, one day?"

"I'm not sure yet."

"Jamie's much more interested in things that live in the sea." Molly looked at her son. "He spends as much time in the water as he does on dry land."

"You go diving?" Blanca's eyes lit up. "Underwater?"

"Yeah, a bit."

"Perhaps, I could come with you some time?" Blanca glanced at William. "That is, when I am not working, of course."

William nodded, watching his son.

"I like diving very much," she went on. "It is my *afición*, my hobby. I have bought a new video camera for underwater."

"What?" Jamie's back straightened. "What sort?"

"I am not very good with names. It is a Bluefin, I think."

"A Bluefin with camcorder?" *Jesus, that was exactly what he needed. Something to show the others what Alice looked like.* "That it?"

"I think so. If we went together, you could show me some good pictures to take, no?"

"I suppose I could." He'd just *have* to tell them everything now. All of them. Say what he'd seen that morning. Tell them what had happened when Alice touched him. All he needed was a chance, and maybe this was it. It didn't matter if Blanca was here. She seemed okay. She must like living creatures, she worked with them. "Yeah, I could take you along."

"Is the water clear here? And not too cold?"

"Depends what you wear. But there's something you should know before..."

"Let's talk about it at the table," William interrupted quickly – he needed more time to think, to decide what he should reveal. "Come on, I'm starving."

The others made no reply as he picked up his drink, reached for the bottle of wine and headed toward the table. All followed, each in their own way angered, perplexed or deeply concerned.

"I'll stay a little longer, if you like," said Sergeant Croft. "The town's a bit wild tonight."

"Well, it is Saturday, isn't it?" Constable Murdoch Roberts replied, putting aside the bag of cheese and onion crisps he'd been eating when the sergeant came out of his office. "Won't be any worse than usual. I can manage on my own."

"There seems to be more activity tonight. It's all those bloody rumours."

"About Nessie?" Roberts grunted. "You can thank Harry Carter for that. Anyway, no one really believes what he said. There's nothing to worry about."

"All the same, he's stirred things up." Croft unwrapped a fresh stick of gum. His stomach hadn't felt so good in years. "And there's others getting on the bandwagon. Some of them reckon they've seen Nessie for themselves."

"Don't worry about it, sir. Go on home and get a good night's rest. Any sign of trouble I'll give Jack, the barman at the *Harbour Light*, a bell. He and couple of mates are on call any time."

"Your vigilante committee?" Croft raised a staying hand as Robert's young face hardened. "Don't worry, it's all right with me. No names, no pack drill. Like you, I want Culloch kept nice and tidy."

"You can count on it."

"But no rough stuff, is that clear?"

"As day, sir." Constable Roberts looked squarely at his sergeant. He admired the old man, straight as a die. But there were times when it didn't do any harm to pour a pail of cold water over a couple of scrapping kinds, or toss a binge drinker into a cell for an hour or two. It all depended how you did it, who was with you at the time. Up to now, there'd been no complaints. And as far as he was concerned, there never would be. "We'll keep it decent and clean."

Sergeant Croft nodded, said good-night and went out in the evening air. It was nice for a change. Above him hung a few clouds, a scattering of stars, in one corner of the sky swung a sickle moon. He hoped it would stay that way for the remainder of the season. But after his conversation with William McCory he had his doubts. He turned his eyes toward the sea. It was calm, flat, reflecting the lights along the waterfront. Culloch was lovely at moments like this. When he got home he'd put on the *Free Willy* CD again, it never failed to lift his spirits.

FIFTEEN – gathering storm

"I saw her, she's real," burst out Jamie McCory, unable to keep silent about Alice any longer. He'd sat, holding it all inside him, while his mother served the salad, passed around the plates of cheese, the cold cuts for everyone to take what they wanted. He hadn't said anything while his father poured the wine, held his glass up to the light. *He's putting it off*, he thought. *That's the trouble with Dad, he keeps too much to himself*. But when his mother started talking about the town, telling Blanca what dreadful weather they'd had this summer, he had to let it all come out. "She touched me. And I touched her. We've got to do something. We've got to look after her."

"Jamie," William said quickly. "I don't want to talk about it now."

"Why not? You've all got to know she's there."

"What *is* this?" asked Molly. Jamie had sat, silently squirming, ever since the meal began, clearly eager to talk. His father hadn't been much better, the looks he'd given his son. At least she'd now find out what was going on. "What are you trying to say?"

"Alice. I saw her this morning."

"*Alice?*"

"That's her name."

"A girl you've met?"

"Just a minute," demanded William, it was all too clear what Jamie had seen. "Not now."

"I've got to talk about her, don't you understand?" his son went on - nothing was going to stop him now. "She's important. Mum's got to know about her. Blanca should be told, too."

Molly McCory stared at her son; she'd never seen him so excited. At mealtimes he usually sat bent over his plate, hat pulled down, barely speaking. Now, his back was straight, green eyes gleaming, red hair catching the light. In spite of her surprise, she couldn't help thinking what a handsome lad he was.

"You know what I mean, Dad," Jamie continued. "You've been looking into it. I checked your computer. I know I shouldn't have, but you weren't here. When you came out of the bathroom you wanted to say something, but you didn't. I'm sorry, but I can't wait any longer." He glanced at Blanca. "She has to know about Alice too. She's got a camera."

"I am sorry." Blanca held up her hands in appeal. "But when you talk so quickly, I do not understand everything."

"In this case neither do I," said Molly. "What *is* this all about?"

"Let me try to explain," replied William, knowing it was time to disclose what he knew. Jamie's honesty had shamed him, made him aware that he'd kept too many people in the dark. He hadn't told Sergeant Croft as much as he should. He'd been careful to say little to Angus Douglas, even though he knew the man's curiosity would become even more inflamed. As for Malcolm Stewart, although they'd spoken openly about *Architeuthis*, he'd not called to say a Blackface ram had been taken. Or that someone claimed to have seen the Loch Ness Monster in the local stream. It was time to speak openly, to tell his family the truth. As for Blanca González, she was part of the mystery now. "You see, there's something that's been taking local livestock. A creature that comes out of the sea."

"What sort of creature?" demanded Molly.

"I think it is some sort of cephalopod."

"It is," said Jamie. "I know exactly what it looks like."

"Are you suggesting that something from the sea took Harry Carter's foal? And the Chattan's calf?" Molly stared at her husband. "You said you had no idea what had happened to them."

"I didn't at first."

"But you took some sort of sample?"

"It's still being tested in New Zealand." William replied, there was no point in denying anything now. "It's not only a foal and a calf that have gone. Angus Douglas has lost one of his Blackface sheep."

"The same way as the others?" asked Jamie.

"Yes," replied William, with a sigh of relief. Whatever else lay ahead, a barrier was coming down between himself and his son. "In all three cases there were trails of slime."

Blanca González looked from face to face, desperately trying to understand every word, waiting for her chance to speak. Who would have thought that this simple meal could reveal so much.

"Are you telling me that Jamie's been swimming in the water with something dangerous?" continued Molly. "And you've done thing to stop him?"

"I didn't want to frighten him. Or you."

"Mum, I'm all right," Jamie said. *She had to calm down. They all did. If word got out that Alice was dangerous, anything could happen. He knew what people were like.* "She's my friend."

"This, ah, friend of yours? It steals food?" asked Blanca, now quite captivated by this family that seemed so quiet on the surface, yet fumed inside. She'd been involved in some animated conversations at home, but nothing quite like this. "You mean like an octopus? I have seen them take crabs that were out of the sea. They can reach from the water, you know. They can walk on rocks."

"It's not exactly an octopus," said William.

"Some *pulpo* are very big. My uncle, he caught one that was more than two metres long. It took an hour to pull it out."

"Alice's much bigger than that. She's huge," said Jamie. He felt good about Blanca. She didn't seem worried at all. And, boy, that was a welcome change. "She's the biggest thing I've ever seen."

"How big?"

"As big as this room."

"*Dios mio*, it is not a *pulpo* then."

"How often have you seen it?" asked William.

"Twice. The first time it just hung there. Like a bunch of seaweed. That's how I found out what it was. There's a story about some sailors who saw one and thought it was seaweed. They said it pulled their ship down. But I don't believe it. I think they made it up. Alice wouldn't do a thing like that. She's gentle. She touched me."

"She touched you?" demanded Molly. "Where?"

"On the back. It didn't hurt at all."

"So, what is it?" asked Blanca. "This creature you have met?"

"A giant squid," Jamie said, his face flushed. They were talking about Alice. There was nothing to hide any more. He was going to get something done. "The biggest cephalopod there is."

"He's right," said William. "In fact, *Architeuthis*...."

"Stop it, both of you." Molly raised her voice. "If this thing's been eating livestock? Taking things from the shore? My God, don't you realise Jamie could be next if he's in the water?"

"I won't be, Mum. You've got to understand. She touched me. Like I keep telling you, she won't do me any harm."

"I'll make damn sure she won't. You're not going near that water again. Not until this thing, squid or whatever you like to call it, is dead and gone."

"You can't..."

"Wait a minute." William picked up his fork. "Let's eat our supper. I'll tell you everything I know as calmly as I can. Then we can decide what we're going to do."

For a moment the others stared back in silence, then Molly took up a lettuce leaf, a token the rest responded to. While they ate, William told them what he'd learnt about *Architeuthis* and what he had yet to have confirmed by the sample sent to New Zealand.

"This Nessie you was talking about, I got news for you." Billy, the waiter with the pock-marked face who'd offered Harry Carter something wrapped in silver paper the night before, muttered out of the side of his mouth. "One of me contacts, a lass who likes a wee smoke, told me a thing or two."

"I bet you get lots of stories like that," Harry Carter grunted indifferently. He'd slept, worked hard, rented out every horse in the stable, paid his lad and was beginning to feel almost human again. After frying a pan full of sausages, which he ate with a bottle of beer, he decided to go back to the *Black Watch* for a whisky. Ignoring the comments that came from a group at one end of the bar about aliens, Nessie, the conger eels Sergeant Croft was suppose to have seen, he'd just seated himself in a corner table with a double scotch when the pock-marked waiter appeared, whispering rubbish in his ear. "The stuff you sell, people'd tell you anything."

"This is straight, believe me. I got it from a reliable source."

"Who would that be?"

"Someone who winkled it out of old Douglas." Billy gave a furtive laugh. "And a winkle's about as big as it gets."

"You're taking the piss." Harry turned away. "Bugger off."

"No, listen, this's important."

"What's it got to do with me?"

"Might help you find out what happened up at your stable." *Might also do me a bit of good*, Billy told himself. *Get away from being a waiter. Show the world I'm into something bigger than pushing weed.* "It's my hour off. Mind if I sit with you for a bit? Get a pint for myself?"

"So long as you pay for it."

"No problem. I could fetch you another scotch if you like?"

Harry nodded, certain he was wasting his time. He should clean himself up, try for the Town Council, get something done instead of sitting in a second-rate pub talking to the likes of Billy. He'd been doing all right, until the foal was taken. That'd set him back, got him into fights in the *Harbour Light*, given him a name for seeing things. No one took him seriously any more. About time he straightened himself out, especially as business was picking up again.

"It's something old Douglas said," Billy said on his return, crouching over his beer, pushing a whisky in Harry's direction. "The old sod's off to Oban, tomorrow. He's got a meeting with the vet."

"Will McCory?"

"No, the one who works up there. Who knows what got off with your foal." Billy took a long pull at his drink. "What got the others too."

"What others? I only heard about the Chattan calf."

"Didn't I tell you? Douglas lost a ram, as well."

"Where'd you get all this?"

"Like I said, one of my customers. One who does for old Douglas. Know what I mean?" Billy winked suggestively. "Seems, the old fart and this vet in Oban are putting their heads together. Like I say, the vet reckons he knows what's responsible for all this."

"Nessie?"

"Not Nessie. Locusts."

"*Locusts*, Jesus Christ," Harry snorted contemptuously. "You're out of your head."

"I'm serious. In Africa, they eat everything. Get through every blade of grass."

"They don't touch livestock."

"That's because they're *land* locusts. Not the ones that live in the sea. It's *sea* locusts that's taking the stuff round here. They come ashore at night."

"Bullshit." Harry lit a cigarette without offering one to Billy. "Nothing like that got hold of my foal. It was something bigger than a bloody locust. Left nothing but a line of slime."

"That's it. That's how this vet knows what they were. *Sea* locusts. They're like snails without shells. Think about it." Billy leant forward knowingly. "You've seen what snails can do to a patch of lettuce. Imagine what a giant sea slug could do to a new-born foal."

"You talking about them soft things that get caught in the nets sometimes?" Harry watched Billy nod. "They're sea *slugs*, about as big as my cock, if you want to know."

"Then you've got a whopper." Billy sniggered, realising that in spite of the crack, Harry was beginning to take him seriously. "There's a plague of them in Culloch harbour, hiding under rocks and things. They've eaten all the stuff out there. Now they're coming ashore at night."

"You telling me one of those little shits ate a whole fucking foal?" Harry finished his first scotch, reached for the second. "You want to be careful, son. That stuff you deal is turning your head."

"Never touch it, myself. But I tell you, they were here all right. Giant sea slugs. Left evidence, like you say. A trail of slime. Even up at old Douglas's."

"For Christ's sake, there was only one line of the stuff."

"Right, they come in their fucking thousands. All in single file. Same as those caterpillars in the springtime. Walking head to tail. Doesn't look like it, but they know what they're about."

"Why are they coming out of the water now? It's never happened before."

"I don't know, but think about it. The stuff that gets washed out there. I saw in the paper just the other day - there's Prozac in the drinking water. Goes out in the piss." Billy sniggered again. "Going to put me out of business if I'm not careful. People will get their trips from the tap."

Harry Carter took a sip of scotch, rinsed it around his gums. What Billy was saying was ridiculous, yet somehow made sense. If there *was* any sense to be made out of anything that happened in what Culloch was going through. First, it'd been Mad Cow Disease, he was still suffering from that. They'd shot all his Friesians, burnt the carcasses down the road. Then the fishing got well and truly screwed up by those Common Market buggers, who spent most of their time sitting on their arses drinking French wine, living off their expense accounts. After that, the weather had turned against him, bloody near ruined the riding business he was just getting off the ground. Now, this doper was trying to tell him that giant sea slugs, *sea-fucking-slugs*, had taken his new-born foal. It was impossible to know what to believe these days, but this wasn't as daft as Will McCory's aliens or Tony Croft's conger eels.

"Now, I'll tell you what we've got to do," Billy continued. When Sarah Tranter told him what Angus Douglas had said, his reaction had been like Harry's. But the more he thought about it, put it together with what he'd read here and there, the more possible it became. If locusts could eat up half a country, why shouldn't something like sea slugs be doing that here? And what was wrong with the things coming out of the sea? Christ knows what was really down there. "We got to put a stop to it."

"How?"

"Poison them, like they do in Africa."

"What?"

"Put something in the water. Get rid of the lot."

"That'll kill everything."

"Only for a bit. But it'd sort out of the problem, wouldn't it?" Billy leant closer. "You and me, we clean this up, we'll be local heroes. Write our own ticket. Name our price when the reporters come. They pay a fortune for stories like that."

"Where we going to get the poison from?"

"Thought I'd leave that up to you, Harry. Pesticide, something like that. Haven't you got any? Something you used on slugs before?"

Angus Douglas regretted telling Sarah Tranter anything about his trip to Oban, but she had him by the short and curlies at the time, quite literally. "You wanted one for the road? Got to pay for it, you know," she'd said, giving his pubes a tug.

"What do you want?" he asked. She'd been smoking that stuff again, he could tell from her eyes. He'd tried it with her once, but didn't like it. It made him want to hide. "I'm just off to look around."

"Don't give me none of that." She'd heard him on the phone talking to the vet, and knew she'd get it out of him or he'd get nothing into her. The thought made her want to laugh, but she held it back. "You after a second opinion?"

"About what?"

"You know bloody well what I mean." Sarah lifted her skirt, teasingly. He'd talked to Will McCory, she'd made the first phone call herself. Now, he was off to see a vet in Oban. There were rumours flying all over the place. She wanted something to add to them when she met her friends later, something that put her in the know. "Your ram's gone. So has Harry Carter's foal. There's calf from up the hill that's missing. What's the story? What's going on?"

"Nothing."

"Nothing it'll be then." Sarah turned away, shook her head. "Two can play at that game."

"Come here," Angus said, a note of resignation in his voice. She always did this to him. And it always worked. What the hell, he'd tell her something, anything would do. She didn't have a brain in her head, but it wasn't brains he was after. "Its, ah, sea slugs," he said. "There's a plague of them. Like locusts."

"What's that?"

"Giant sea slugs, we've got a problem all along the coast. That's why I'm going up to Oban. To talk to the vet about them there."

"Sea slugs, is it?" Sarah came back, sat on him. She wasn't wearing any knickers. "You know, I think you might be right. I can feel one of them down there now. Tell me more about them and I'll see if I can get some life into the one down there."

SIXTEEN – picking sides

"Right, so you know what I've seen is real," said Jamie, when his father finished talking about giant squid. "The thing is, are you going to help me save Alice or not?"

"What do you want me to do?"

"Help me keep her safe, that's what." While his father spoke about what he'd discovered, what Malcolm Stewart had said, his voice had lifted with excitement. On the other hand, Jamie's mother's face had clouded with concern. Blanca had listened intently, saying nothing even though once or twice it seemed she was about to interrupt. But it soon became clear that neither parent was going to do anything either unless he pushed them, made them realise how important protecting Alice was. "We haven't got much time," he went on urgently. "We've got to think of something fast."

"What exactly?"

"How to get her away from here."

"I'd really like a chance to study her first," William replied, spreading Scottish brie on a piece of crunchy bread, trying to appear impartial. He understood how Jamie felt about living creatures, had seen him pick worms off the road to save them from the wheels of passing cars. But this was different, this was dealing with an organism nobody knew anything about. He felt the need to respond to the world of science, to the institutions that had made him what he was. In many ways he was duty-bound to find out all he could about *Architeuthis*. "You see, so few people have seen a giant squid alive."

"That doesn't mean we shouldn't help her."

"But it does mean we should learn all we can about her."

"So what are you going to do?" Jamie asked, his voice rising. He didn't have to study Alice. He had to save her, but couldn't do it on his own. He needed help, and he needed it fast. "Do you want to put her in a cage? Like those monkeys they use for experiments?"

"I didn't say that."

"What *do* you want from this…Alice, Will?" asked Molly. She'd remained quiet long enough. Her husband was a good man, but didn't see the world the way Jamie did. Living creatures weren't as personal to him. Life and death passed through his hands all day long. If he saved an animal, it gave him pleasure. If he didn't, he went on to the next. "It's about time you told us what you really want to do."

"It's not entirely a matter of what I want to do."

"It sounds like it."

"Listen…" William paused uncomfortably, there was so much more to this than Jamie understood. "I mean, we've all got to consider.…"

"There are only two things *you've* got to consider." Molly's voice sharpened. "The first is if Jamie is in any danger. And the second is whether you want to save this monster squid or not."

"I, ah…"

"Please, pardon me," Blanca interrupted, already feeling part of this family – it was quite clear she'd been accepted. "This is not my field, but I did one year at university on marine biology. And I learned that squid, *calamar*, as we call them, do not live very long in captivity. Not like *pulpo*. Octopus can survive for years, but squid soon die."

"I wasn't thinking of catching it," William replied, guilt darkening his cheeks. "It's just that, well, the giant squid is like a creature from another planet." He wiped his face with a napkin. "My joke about aliens wasn't that far from the truth."

"So, what *are* you going to do?" Jamie demanded. He'd touched Alice. She was his responsibility now. If his father talked like this, what the hell would Malcolm Stewart sound like? Or any other scientist? *That's the trouble with the world. Everyone's out for what they can get.* "We can't wait, you know. We can't hang about any longer."

"What's the hurry? The squid's been in the water around Culloch for several days," his father replied evasively. "We know that from the livestock it's taken. There's no reason why it shouldn't stay longer, is there?"

"There is, Dad, and you know it. Someone will go after her. There's all this talk of Nessie. There are probably people getting their gear together now. I'm not the only one who dives along the coast. They come down from Oban, other towns too. Once the word gets out they'll be all over the place looking for Alice. They'll do their best to catch her and won't care if she gets hurt."

"I thought most divers went across to Mull," replied William, torn between his son's demands and what he might personally achieve. "Or further out, where the wrecks are."

"What about the tourists here? Some of them get in with spear guns. Remember Alf? The little shit that killed the pollock."

"Jamie, there's no need for that sort of talk," admonished Molly, even though she shared his feelings - Alf *had* been a nasty little turd. She glanced at Blanca, whose eyes were bright. "You must forgive us," she added quietly. "Mealtimes aren't usually as stormy as this."

"No, this is wonderful. I like it." Blanca smiled at Jamie, wanting to give him a hug. She loved his passion, the way he didn't give in. "But I have a suggestion that might suit everybody."

"What's that?" asked William. Whatever Blanca suggested could give him time to get confirmation from New Zealand. "What did you have in mind?"

"I am going to Oban in the morning. I will come back with my camera. Then I could take some pictures of Jamie and the Alice squid. So *everyone* can see what it looks like." Turning to Molly, she added, "And you can *see* that your son is safe."

"Wouldn't you be afraid?" asked Molly. This girl was quite amazing. She'd only just arrived, yet was beginning to take over. Still, she seemed to know what she was talking about. "This squid sounds quite dangerous to me."

"If Jamie is with me, I am sure I will be all right." Blanca's eyes went around the table. "Well?" she queried. "Do you all agree?"

For a moment no one replied. Then Jamie nodded, his heart leaping, even as he wondered how Alice would react. Molly's mind grappled with concern. She didn't want Jamie to dive again until this thing was dealt with. She worried about him each time he went into the water – but with a creature like Alice around? However, in the end she gave in, and merely made him promise not to do anything rash. William murmured his assent, knowing that nothing would happen until the following afternoon, knowing that, if at the last moment he thought the dive unsafe, he could always put a stop to it.

Later, walking up the hill to *Rose Cottage*, where she planned to extend her stay for at least a week, Blanca González could barely keep the smile off her face. She'd come to Culloch hoping to be offered the chance to join a practice, now she was part of something she found incredibly exciting. She stopped on the crest of a little hill, looked over the town. It seemed peaceful, even though it was Saturday night. She could see the blue and white Police Station sign. There was no activity there. The *Harbour Light*, near the Common, had its doors open, a few drinkers were at tables, enjoying the mild evening, more were inside watching a game between Celtic and Rangers, making their presence felt with roars of approval or contempt. Culloch seemed quite different now. It was no longer an unknown dot on an unfamiliar map, but a place where she belonged. She'd get up early in the morning, collect what she needed from Oban, and be back by afternoon to dive with Jamie. She hoped the sun would shine as she'd need good light for her camera. She'd used it once or twice before, but never for anything as important as this. Before Jamie got up from the table to go to bed, he'd looked at her, his eyes appealing. She'd smiled and kissed him goodnight, and promised herself not to disappoint him.

Next morning, the sky shot with pink and vermilion, a warning some said of storms to come, Jamie quietly picked up the diving gear he'd assembled in the garage the night before. After his parents had nodded their approval to Blanca's suggestion, even though his father said he'd rather wait until he heard from Malcolm Stewart, and his mother cautioned him about doing anything rash, he'd excused himself, saying he was tired and was going to bed. Before he left, he said good-night to Blanca. She'd replied warmly, got up from the table and kissed him on both cheeks. The act surprised him, but he liked it. She was okay. She wanted to help.

He'd gone to his room, waited a while, then crept down to the garage to put mask, snorkel and fins, wet suit and weight belt in a rucksack beside the door ready for the morning. It would be Sunday, the surgery closed and, unless there was an emergency, his parents would remain in bed watching the news on television. *That's what people did when they grew up. Got in a rut. It wasn't going to happen to him.*

"I'll bet they're not even awake yet," he whispered now, as he picked up the rucksack, moved away from the house. Getting going had been easier than he'd thought. He'd slept in most of his clothes, needed only to pull on a pair of trainers, an anorak to work up a sweat before he got into the water - he kept warmer that way. "They won't miss me for hours."

He felt great as he walked up the hill toward the coast. The morning was brilliant, the sea like glass. He wondered if Alice knew he was coming. Whether she'd be waiting for him near the Grotto? What she'd do when she saw him? If she'd be as friendly as she'd been before? He had to work out a way of communicating with her, make her understand what he had to say. The first time he'd given her the OK sign, but didn't think it was enough. He'd have to come up with something better, something that was special between them.

The giant squid was waiting for the starfish to return. She knew it would. They had their habits, these slow-moving creatures, they never wandered far. And neither had she until something drove her out of Peake Deep toward the Culloch coastline. Now she waited, not in the cave of the Grotto, but beside the Tombstone, a monolith that remained visible in almost any tide. There, she hung in its shadow, turning dark to hide from the rising sun, and was beginning to feel quite secure - until she saw the shark.

As soon as the torpedo-shape appeared, its dorsal fin carving through the water, mouth as mean as any she'd seen, with rows of teeth sharp enough to slice her to pieces, she knew she had to be wary. She'd seen its kind before. They followed schools of salmon, mackerel and herring, eating the trailing members, occasionally attacking the body of the shoal, snapping up all they could. Although, she had to admit, they did have moments of charm. Just before she reached the coast of Culloch, she'd seen a pair chasing each other, playing a mating game.

This shark, however, wasn't at all debonair. It was swimming steadily, clearly in search of food which had been in short supply of late. Alice had noticed a scarcity of fodder, even though schooling fish weren't what she hunted - there were far too many of the tiny creatures darting all over the place to be bothered with. The energy required to catch a decent meal wasn't worth the effort. But this shark was desperately looking for a shoal, its eyes were rolling, it was obviously hungry. It swam with the air of a predator searching for a meal.

When first she first sighted the shark Alice remained perfectly still, fearful she might be attacked. Then, recalling why she was waiting, her twin hearts froze in fear. She knew the starfish would be in great danger. It was much more likely to be targeted by the marauder, and far less able to protect itself. The primitive creature had no means of defence at all.

When Jamie got into the water, once more charged with the thrill of entering the sea, a thrill that never faltered, he swam slowly toward the Grotto, fully expecting to find Alice there. The water was clear - he could see all the way to the rocky bottom where cup corals with their fluorescent colours, spider crabs and dozens of small fishes carpeted the way.

"Magic," he whispered, through his snorkel. "A wonderland."

Yet, the sea was strangely empty. He passed a jellyfish or two, saw a pollock which darted off rapidly, and was beginning to wonder if Alice had scared away the locals, when he saw the shark. It was swimming in a circle around the Tombstone and would soon be very close.

"Shit," he said, treading water. "A porbeagle."

He recognised it immediately. The short thick body was about five feet long. The blue-grey back, the spots on the white belly, made it clear what it was - a close relative to the mako and the somewhat maligned great white. He even knew how it got its name. Someone once said it looked like a mixture between a porpoise and a beagle - the description stuck. While few attacks against divers had been recorded - even though one fisherman claimed a porbeagle sprang out of the water and tore the shirt off his back - the world record porbeagle, a specimen of more than five hundred pounds, had been caught off Scotland not long ago.

"This one's not so big," he reassured himself. "Not as big as that basking shark that swam over my shoulder once."

Even so, he felt uneasy. The basking shark had given him a sense of belonging. The porbeagle made him want to back away. He didn't know why, but the sensation was powerful. Usually he felt at home with everything in the water. Even the ray that sent electricity up his arm hadn't scared him, just given him a shock - he accepted that as self-defence. But this was different. The way the porbeagle rolled its eyes made him anxious.

Let's hope it doesn't notice me, he told himself, recalling what he'd read. If he'd been on the bottom with his bottle, he'd have nothing to worry about. But up on the surface, especially if he kicked, the shark might think he was a wounded fish, an easy target. *Keep as still as possible.*

Keeping still wasn't easy. The lead on his belt wanted to take him down, sink him gently toward the bottom. He'd be all right down there for as long as he had enough air, but when that ran out he'd have to kick back up again. Now, to stay afloat he had to tread water, without making any splashes.

He watched the porbeagle swim past in a long slow arc, its movement sinuous, its tail swaying from side to side. He wasn't exactly frightened, but knew he had to be careful. What had he promised his mother? *Not to do anything rash?* Well, he wasn't doing anything rash at the moment, just hanging in the water, hoping the porbeagle would get tired of swimming in circles like one of those roundabouts that came to the Common each year for the summer fair. He just wanted it to bugger off, leave him alone. Then, like the squid, he remembered why he was in the water. The thought flashed through him, turning him cold all over.

Alice? I wonder where she is?

"Jamie's gone," said Molly, hurrying back to her husband. "He's not in his room. I've looked in the garage. He's taken his diving gear with him."

"You sure?" William snapped his eyes away from the TV screen, where the American president was justifying the continuation of the war in Iraq. "He's not using the computer?"

"I've looked everywhere. There's no sign of him." A little earlier, Molly had slipped out of bed to make a pot of tea, and hoped to surprise Jamie with cheese on toast and hot cocoa as he'd been so good the evening before - promised to be careful in the water and hadn't argued too stubbornly with his father. "I'll bet he's gone off after that squid."

"Do you really think he'd do that?"

"I'm sure he would," replied Molly, fighting a wave of panic that threatened to overwhelm her. "Now, get dressed. We'd better see if we can find him."

"Yes, of course." William reached for his clothes, his mind churning. He was both angry with Jamie for going off on his own and increasingly alarmed for his safety, at the same time understanding why he had disappeared as soon as it got light. His son had become obsessed. Alice had become personal. Jamie believed she belonged to him, that she was in danger, and he would do whatever he could to protect her. "Where did he see the squid?" he asked. "You were with him, weren't you?"

"It was..." Molly began, then hesitated, torn between wanting to grab Jamie by the scruff of the neck, spank him soundly, and losing his trust. If she ran after him now he might close up on her the way he did with his father - she couldn't bear the thought of that. On the other hand, she had to make certain he was safe. "One of those bays along the coast," she added vaguely. "Where there are mostly rocks."

"Which one?"

"I don't know. Jamie has names for them, but I don't remember what it's called."

"Come on, Molly, the name doesn't matter, just as long as you recall where it is." William stepped into a pair of jeans, watched his wife reach for a coat which she dragged on over her pyjamas. "Take it easy, we'll find him. But it'd be easier if we knew where to start."

"Oh, my God, let me think. Those bays are so much alike." Molly paused, realised she was letting fear overcome her. She removed her coat and began changing into a skirt and a heavy pullover. "Yes, I know which one it was. But I can't think what its name is. I should remember, shouldn't I?"

"Molly?"

"Sorry, I'm not much help, am I? It's just...I don't want him to come to any harm. But I *do* want to believe in him. He said...well, he must know what he's doing. He said he feels safe with this thing. My God, I only hope he's all right."

"He'll be all right," replied William. "But let's go and make sure."

SEVENTEEN – fighting back

The giant squid watched the shark move its head from side to side as though sniffing the water, take a long inquisitive turn past the Tombstone and begin to come in close, obviously aware of food. The squid knew she had little time to act, but wasn't quite sure what to do.

Each time in the past when she'd had to make up her mind the choices had been simple. Picking out one lobster from another, knowing when she took the first the second would disappear, had been decided without a second thought. Wondering whether to go deeper into the ocean's darkness, where her sight gave her an advantage, or to seek food at a higher level where there was more in greater danger, had been easy compared to this. Now she had to choose between saving her own, almost transparent hide, or try to help the starfish which had no visible form of defence. The problem set her divided brain on fire, made her stomach squirm.

She could see the starfish now, paddling helplessly near the cavern of their first meeting. It clearly had no idea what to do. With her other eye, which could move independently, she watched the shark make a decisive turn. There was no doubt in its mind what it intended to do - the decision had been immediate, made at first sight of the starfish.

Jamie saw the porbeagle half-roll in his direction, and felt a rush of real fear. He remained as still as he could, barely keeping afloat, as the sleek shape swam past. He stared at the short nose, the mouth with its file-like teeth, the eye that was fixed on him, and tried to work out what to do. Two choices came to mind. Either he could ease away, as smoothly as possible, making little movement in the water, and then slide out onto a rock. Or he could let the current take him, keeping his eye on the shark, toward the Tombstone. It wasn't far. It wouldn't take long. There, he could hide in one of the crevices until the porbeagle found something more interesting to attack.

Neither option appealed. He'd be more vulnerable if he swam away, especially getting out of the water. If he got stuck by the Tombstone, God knows how long he'd be in the water. Even if he didn't feel the cold as much as most divers, he had no desire to be pinned against a rock all day.

They're not that dangerous, he told himself, as the shark made another turn. *They've taken fish from spear fishermen's buoys, but that's all right. The fish shouldn't have been there in the first place. Anyway, if I have to do something, they say the best place to hit a shark is on the end of the nose. It hurts a lot more there.*

But he didn't fancy that either, and was still undecided when he caught sight of a new movement in the water. He turned to see the first tentacle lash out, curve like a snake through the sun-split sea and wrap itself around the porbeagle's gills. Immediately a second joined it. Together they bound the thrashing shark, whipped it around a corner of the Tombstone.

"Let's go in my car," Molly said, as William picked up the keys to his four-wheel drive. "The roads are narrow. We'd be better off in the Volkswagen."

"All right," he replied. "You drive, if you remember where we're going?"

"It's along the coast. I think I know where it is."

"I'm sure you do, just take it easy."

"What if he's not there?" Molly asked a little later, as she turned along the waterfront, went past the sleeping Culloch cottages, their white facades lovely in the rising sun. "He might not be where we went the last time. He might have gone somewhere else."

"Do you think he's off to visit a girlfriend?" William asked deliberately, hoping to reduce the tension. His wife's knuckles were white on the steering wheel. "Taken his diving gear to show off?"

"I don't think that's where he went for a moment." Molly changed gear on a hill, grateful to be at the wheel – she'd be worried sick in the passenger's seat. "I meant somewhere new along the coast. Not where we went last time."

"You never know," William persisted, determined to settle Molly down. His normally calm wife was in danger of breaking down. "But while we're talking about girls, does it ever worry you he hasn't got a steady girlfriend?"

"Not much. There'll be plenty of time for that."

"At his age I..."

"You weren't like him at all."

"That's true enough, I just wanted to get into your knickers." William tenderly touched her knee. "Jamie's not like me, we both know that. Now, stop worrying about him. I'm sure we'll find him safe and sound. And we'd better not let him know how concerned we are. He'd only laugh at us."

"You're right, he would." Molly turned off the main road, began down a rut-filled track. The small conversation had helped, settled part of her anxiety. "What do we do when we get there?"

"Leave the car out of sight." William could now see the sea. "Find somewhere to park and walk the rest of the way."

"If he...if he really needs help, we'd better both get in. Neither of us is very good in the water. But together we'll get him out."

"I doubt if there'll be any need for that," replied William, keeping his voice light. "There, behind that rock. Pull over, and we'll get out and take a look."

In fear and fascination Jamie McCory followed the churning water, the shreds of bright white foam, around the Tombstone to find the porbeagle imprisoned by the giant squid's tentacles, gripped by four of the python-like arms. The other four were clamped to the rock, locking Alice and the struggling shark in place, bound together thrashing combat.

My God, he shouted within the confines of his heart. *What's happening?*

The porbeagle struggled, beating the water with its powerful tail. Its ferocity sent Jamie even closer to the Tombstone, into the protection of the rock. He remained as still as he was able, only his snorkel out of the water, his eyes fixed on the strangest sight he had ever seen.

Amazing, he told himself. *I can't believe I'm seeing this.*

Alice had turned a vivid red, her colour enhanced by sunlight. The porbeagle, its belly facing Jamie, gleamed white against her brightness. As she fought to protect the starfish, the squid tightened into a ball of muscle, grew smaller as she increased her grip. The porbeagle slashed at the water again and again, creating curtains of froth which obscured the combatants.

The shark's going to die, Jamie whispered. *And there's nothing I can do about it.*

Even as the thought filled him with fear – he wanted nothing to die in the sea around him, the porbeagle appeared to escape. It slipped forward. Jamie heard the roughness of its skin against the rock. It twisted its short thick body, was about to sink its teeth into one of the tentacles, when the squid brought forward her other four arms, let go of the Tombstone and wrapped herself completely around the shark; all her suckers digging in. The porbeagle was now enmeshed in Alice's coils, suffocating slowly. It could barely move, let alone open its gills to fill them with the fresh seawater it needed.

She's incredible, Jamie said. *I wish she wasn't. But she is.*

As he stared, the shark began to lose its strength. Jamie could never have said how long it took, whether it was only a moment stretched to infinity, or a period of endless waiting. He didn't see the end of the struggle, which was unsettling at the time, but later he was glad he hadn't. That way he could always convince himself that the shark might have got away.

No longer tied to the rock, the giant squid and the failing shark were taken by the tide. In the brilliantly clear water, Jamie watched them go. Only once, in the whole fierce struggle, did Alice look towards him. As the current eased her outward, she gazed back with one of her outrageous eyes. She was trying to tell him something, although he was never certain what it was. She may have been signalling a long good-bye, she might have been asking him to wait a little longer. Whatever, he felt suddenly cold and knew it was time to get out of the water.

Blanca González returned to Oban, it was to find Malcolm Stewart waiting for her. His expensive sports car was parked outside her bed-and-breakfast. He was chatting to the landlady, and waved cheerfully as she drew up in her Ford.

"Hello," he called, coming toward her. "How'd it go?"

"Quite well, I think," replied Blanca, reluctant to say much, recalling his hand on her knee, his less than flattering comments about William McCory. "I'm going back this afternoon to finalise the details."

"Don't tell me it's not all signed, sealed and delivered?" Malcolm gave a snuffling laugh. She certainly was a looker, pity he'd moved so fast; he could have got her if he hadn't been so eager. "I thought it might be, the way he sounded."

"I think it will be all right." Blanca hoped he didn't intend to stay very long. As it was, she had enough to do and no desire to waste time talking to a man she had little respect for. She turned away and smiled at the landlady. "Now, if you will excuse me, I have to go inside."

"Don't have time for a chat? How about a glass of something on the waterfront?" Malcolm moved closer, determined to find out as much as he could before his meeting with Angus Douglas. "Elevenses? A very British custom."

"Thank you, but as I say, I have many things to take care of."

"Be rude to turn me down on a day as nice as this." Malcolm's tone became more pointed. "After all, it was me who got you the job."

"I don't know that I have it yet."

"I'm sure of it. I can tell by your smile." He indicated a pub at the end of the street. "If the waterfront's too far, let's just hop down to the corner."

"Well..." Blanca looked at her watch, gave an inward sigh. Her morning had been blissful until this irritating man appeared. She'd made arrangements to stay on at *Rose Cottage*, had driven back over wonderful hills covered with the gold and green of bursting gorse, the soft purple of heather. Hares had leapt across the road, rabbits nestled in the grass. In many ways it reminded her of Cantabria. *There'd been rabbits all over this place*, her father often said. *Until we ate them. There was a time when a squirrel could swing from tree to tree all the way to the south of Spain. Then we cut the trees down.* "Just a quick drink, then," she agreed - it was a lovely morning. "We can sit outside."

"Fine, by me." Malcolm locked his BMW and, as they began walking toward the pub, took her arm. "So, how was Culloch?" he asked conspiratorially. "What's all this I hear about Nessie?"

"Nessie?" Blanca frowned, the name had been mentioned at supper the night before, but no one had paused to explain why. "Who is she?"

"Nessie, the Loch Ness Monster, you must have heard of her." Malcolm's annoying laugh broke out again. "She's famous. I've even seen road signs with her picture on them. Painted-over cattle notices, turned into warnings about our Ness."

"Oh, yes, of course, I have heard of it."

"They tell me she's been coming ashore and taking livestock all along the Culloch coast. Did Will tell you anything about that?"

"No." Blanca widened her eyes innocently, now even more determined to say nothing to this man, quite sure he was not to be trusted. "I don't think anyone mentioned that."

"More's the pity," Malcolm replied, aware she was going to be tough to crack. "Give it a thought while we sit in the sun. You might remember something."

When Jamie got out of the water his parents were standing on the shore. He could see they'd dressed hurriedly, and knew he was in deep shit. "Hi," he said, unzipping the front of his wet suit, his mother coming forward to give him a hand.

"Hello," she replied quietly, as they'd decided to say as little as possible, to give him all the time he needed to explain why he'd gone off alone. "What was the water like?"

"Brilliant." Jamie reached for his towel, still stunned by what he'd seen, and a little wary of saying anything to his parents. They were the last people he'd expected when he got out of the water. His mother sometimes accompanied him. His father had only done it once or twice. But they'd never appeared together. That meant they were worried, so he'd better say nothing about the porbeagle while they were in this mood or they'd never let him back in the water again. "It's the best it's been for weeks."

"You were off early."

"After the talk last night, I wanted to see if Alice was still around."

"Was she?" William leant against a rock, arms folded across his chest. It wasn't easy acting like this, there were a dozen questions to be answered. "Was she still in the same place?"

"Yeah, she's still around." Jamie nodded and pulled his woollen hat down hard. "What are you two doing here?" he asked, as casually as he could. "Bit early, isn't it?"

"When we'd found you'd gone, we thought we'd take a look around ourselves," William replied. "I also wondered if there'd been any more livestock reports."

"Were there?"

"I haven't heard anything."

"That's good." *And you won't, not today*, thought Jamie. *The porbeagle will keep her going for a while.* "The town's quiet, then?"

"Any reason why it shouldn't be?"

"Well, you know, with all these rumours about Nessie. Who knows what's going on?" Jamie began repacking his rucksack. "Next thing, there'll be people everywhere having a look for themselves. The government will probably send down a team of Navy divers."

"Was the squid all right when you saw her?" Molly asked, packing his mask and fins. "Alice, I mean? Did she try to touch you again?"

"No." *He wanted to tell them the truth. That she might have saved his life. But if he put a shark in the picture, they'd flip. They really would.* "She was a bit shy this morning. She went off fast."

"Do you think she'll be back?" William asked.

"Hope so, Dad," Jamie replied and wished he had more time to think. He wanted to tell them how he'd worked out a way to communicate with Alice and would have tried if it hadn't been for the porbeagle. But turning up like this they'd really thrown him. In a desperate attempt to reduce the unease, that hung in the bright morning air, he managed a lop-sided grin. "She'll have to come back, won't she? Blanca's going to take her picture this afternoon."

"You're right about that," replied William, evasively. They weren't getting anywhere like this. He'd have to talk to the Spanish girl, make sure she knew what to do in the sea. "Blanca will be disappointed if she doesn't turn up."

"Well, we'll just have to see what happens." Molly wanted to pull Jamie close, hug him, tell him how worried she'd been, but knew she couldn't. That would only make him cringe, could even send him off on his own again. She smiled, picked up the towel he'd dropped on the rocks, and tried to assure herself that he'd be safer in the water with someone to dive with. "I suppose Blanca will still be keen, having slept on the matter."

"She'll be keen," said Jamie, grabbing his rucksack. "I'd bet on it."

His parents looked at each other, but made no reply. All walked quietly toward the Volkswagen, the sun warming their uncomfortable backs.

The giant squid was desolate, downcast in both her hearts, desperately afraid she'd never see the starfish again. The poor helpless creature had been terrified when the shark arrived - its eyes had bulged with fear - so, without a second thought, she'd flung herself forward in defence. Then, what began as an attempt to save her friend turned into a frantic struggle. She'd felt the shark's anger rise as soon as she touched it.

SQUID

Fury came through her tentacles in a powerful surge; she realised at first contact that she was fighting for her life.

Immediately something primitive took over. She became, once again, the huntress, resorting to the skills she'd learnt in fending for herself - at times slashing out with her tentacles when the water was rich with food, on other occasions extending just one of her arms, its tapered end trickling over the sea bed, seeking what was hidden in the rocks. All her life she'd struggled to survive. As she'd developed she'd refined her talents, fine-tuned them to a point of perfection. Without them she would have died much earlier, like so many of her tribe.

So, what began as an attempt to rescue the starfish turned into a fight to the death. When the porbeagle opened its jaws, showed its razor-sharp teeth, all she could do was strike back. Gone was the intention of simply shielding her friend, lost was the idea of protecting it as she'd seen families of dolphins do - by slapping the water with their tails, practically making it boil to frighten sharks away from their young. All that went in the struggle to save her own incredible life.

Only when it was almost over, when she was drifting away with the tide, the moribund porbeagle in her arms, did her thoughts return to the starfish. She looked back with one eye to see it clamped against the rock, too terrified to move. That was when sadness overtook her. She didn't know if she would ever see the helpless creature again. *She* would come back, she had to, in the hope it might be waiting, but felt desperately uncertain if it would ever recover from its fear and return to the Grotto again.

The only compensation was - now she had the shark, she might as well eat it. She'd tried smaller ones before, and found them exceptionally good. They had much softer skeletons than most other fishes, none of those sharp little bones. As for their flesh, it was excellent, would taste particularly good after the last of her prey, which had been covered in so much seaweed it quite spoilt the meal.

EIGHTEEN – say cheese

"This should do it," said Billy, the waiter with the pock-marked face, touching a rusty drum of DDT with the toe of his trainer. "Kills slugs, don't it?"

"You too if you're not bloody careful." Harry Carter replied, replacing the canvas the drum had been hidden under until Billy uncovered it. "Should've got rid of that years ago. It's banned, can't use it these days."

"What you got it for, then?"

"I never got round to shifting it." Harry had been going through his books when Billy turned up, looking cocky, reminding him of their conversation the night before when, after several whiskies, he'd agreed to think about getting rid of the sea slugs Angus Douglas said were responsible for the missing livestock. It had slipped his mind until Billy arrived. That was the trouble with going on the piss these days, you forgot what you'd been up to, sometimes never remembered a thing. "I used it when I had the farm. I'd forgotten it up till now."

"Used it to kill pests, right?"

"Aye, it worked," Harry admitted, not sure he wanted to have anything more to do with Billy. On the other hand, the waiter was the only one who took him seriously. Will McCory didn't, hadn't been back since he took that sample. Tony Croft was a joke, only listened to what old Douglas said. Billy mightn't be all that welcome, but at least the little shit was keen. "It cleared them out."

"Let's give it a go."

"You want to put it in the sea?"

"Yeah, but we do it with precision. We pick our spot. Get the tides and the currents right. Then, bingo, goodbye sea slugs. Get our names in the paper. Show everybody who we are." Even though he'd told this old fart he never touched the merchandise, Billy sometimes gave his nose a jolt - but only when needed, like this afternoon. Now he was really sparking. "What do you say to that?"

"I don't know." Harry lifted his cap and scratched his scalp. He'd like to show the rest of them he wasn't past it. Christ, he was one of the ones who fought back after Mad Cow Disease. He got the stables working when others gave in, but no one seemed to notice it these days. Still, he didn't want to poison the harbour, that was going way too far. "I'd have to think about it."

"You know what they say about you, Harry?" Billy looked down his nose at the stable-owner. "They say you've given up. All you want is a bottle of scotch."

"Who says that?"

"Everyone. Look at yourself. Sleeping in the bus shelter. Banging on about Nessie." Billy wrinkled his nose. "When's the last time you changed your shirt?"

"Now, wait a minute..." Harry glanced at his cuffs - they were rimmed with dirt. Perhaps it was time to smarten up, show the town he hadn't given in. "All right, let's talk about this," he said, indicating the DDT. "Where do you think you'd use it?"

"Pick a spot, like I said." Billy winked. "Don't you worry, I've got that sorted. There's a place on the coast that looks good. I've seen the vet's kid up there, but no one else. You know him don't you? Funny little feller. A wonder he's not one of my customers, but he ain't."

"When were you thinking of doing this?"

"Like I told you. First I've got to check the tides. But tomorrow night might be all right. Sunday, the town will be empty." Billy kicked the drum again. "It's liquid, isn't it?" Simple, then. It's a doddle? Just open it up. Chuck it in. It wouldn't take a minute."

Harry Carter didn't reply, but he was beginning to think the little shit might be on to something. At least DDT would have some effect. Sitting up all night with a shotgun hadn't been worth the wait.

"So, you're off this afternoon." Malcolm Stewart leant back in his chair, his face toward the sun. Things were going nicely, she was starting to relax, even though all she'd drunk was Diet Coke. But she'd already admitted that she was driving back to Culloch later on, giving the game away. "I'd say you were home and hosed."

"Pardon me?" Blanca frowned, he'd lost her again. "I don't understand."

"Colonial racing term. Means you've won the race, been washed down." He smiled knowingly. "Doe that apply to you?"

"You are talking about my work?" Blanca couldn't avoid returning the smile. He'd been on his best behaviour since they'd arrived at the pub, admired her purple pullover, said he liked the way the sun caught the highlights in her hair, obviously hoping to find out all he could about the giant *calamar*. Last evening William McCory said that he had obtained a great deal of information about *Architeuthis* from this man, yet she felt she should say little – there was something she didn't trust about him. "I think I have the job, but I haven't signed anything so far."

"You will." Malcolm sipped his lager. She was looking great. Pity, but you couldn't win them all. "By the way, what did you make of the family?"

"They were nice, very friendly."

"Even the son?"

"Jamie? Yes, he is very, what do you say, intense? But I liked him." And before she knew it the fateful words were out. "He said he would take me diving this afternoon."

"Did he, now?" Malcolm's interest grew a hundredfold. "He say exactly where?"

"No, not really." Blanca could have bitten off her tongue. *You should think before you speak*, was what her mother was always telling her, but she'd never been very good at it, words just bubbled out. "I like diving. I have told you that before."

"Of course, and you've got a new camera, haven't you?" It was almost time to put a call through to New Zealand. Might mean hauling someone out of bed, but he didn't give a toss about that. He was meeting Angus Douglas about six and, if things kept moving the way they were, he'd be well prepared by then. "Will you be taking it out this afternoon?"

"I might, just to practice. I haven't used it much before."

"Tell you what, why don't I come down? Give you a hand. I take a few snaps myself," Malcolm offered with a smile, fully knowing she'd refuse. "I've worked on dry land mostly, but there can't be that much difference."

"That is very kind, but I think I can manage on my own."

"Well, it's entirely up to you."

"Thank you, but I will be all right." Blanca finished her Diet Coke, her smile breaking out again. She couldn't hold it back on such a lovely day. "Well, I should be going now. As you know, I am going to have a busy afternoon."

"I bet you are." Malcolm leant forward. It was time to pull the longbow. "I'm not sure if I told you this, but Will McCory and I've been working together recently. The fact is, he sent me up a sample to get tested. Has he mentioned it?"

"What...what was the sample?"

"Some sea-based organic stuff I sent on to Dunstaffnage. He say anything about it?"

"I don't think so," Blanca replied, her mother's voice ringing in her ears. Clearly, this man was thinking about what he might gain for himself. Everything about him, from his too-ready smile to his annoying laugh was insincere. He didn't deserve to be told what she knew. "We talked mostly about the animals he handles. And the work that I will do."

"Didn't say anything about a giant squid?"

"What?" Blanca frowned convincingly. "Oh, I think I have heard of them. I studied some marine biology. Didn't I tell you that?"

"Did you tell Will?"

"No, although it would have been on my CV. Have you met his wife?" Blanca went on smoothly. "She cooks very well, you know."

"Never had the pleasure." Malcolm Stewart finished his drink. She was good, he'd give her that. Perhaps he'd have better luck with Douglas. Whatever, from now on he'd have to go it alone. "Enjoy your dive," said, as they were walking back. "I'd like to see your pictures when you get the time."

"I will show them to you."

"And if, by any chance, you happen to come across a giant squid," he added, laughing through his nose. "Don't forget to tell it to say cheese."

Blanca nodded briefly, understanding him well enough. When she got the chance she'd talk to William McCory, warn him not to trust this man.

"So there was nothing special to report last night?" Sergeant Croft asked Corporal Roberts as they filled in the day-sheets. "Seemed quiet, from what I heard."

"Quiet enough. The football ended in a draw, which meant there wasn't much brawling." The constable looked up, pursing his lips. "However, there is one thing we should talk about. Though I don't think it's important enough to go in a report. Harry Carter and Billy the Dealer had their heads together in the *Black Watch* last evening. They were at it for a while."

"You telling me Harry's changed his poison?"

"I don't think so, no one saw anything pass between them."

"Billy's quick. Still, if your lads were watching they were probably just having a drink. Harry's short of mates these days." Tony Croft paused thoughtfully. "We know what Billy's up to, and it's an advantage letting him do business in a pub. We know where to look if anything goes wrong."

"And it tells us who his customers are." Roberts tapped his chin with a ballpoint pen. "The thing that worries me though, is they were together again this afternoon. Up at Harry's stables."

"Doing what?"

"Don't know, but I'll find out. If Harry's moving into the dope business we better put a stop to it right away. He'd be in a good position to push stuff, dealing with tourists the way he does. He could be setting things up for himself."

"You do that. But talk to me before you make any moves. He's not too bad yet, old Harry. But I wouldn't want him to slip any further down the pole."

"Course not." Roberts sometimes wondered if the sergeant didn't see himself as more of a father figure than a copper to the town. Never mind, he was straight and that was something these days. "I'll keep an eye on him."

Sitting in front of his PC screen, Jamie McCory was ready to explode. He couldn't wait to tell someone, *anyone*, what had happened, it was murder keeping all inside. It was like those times when he'd eaten too much. That wasn't often, but at Christmas or his birthday, when his mother made him something special and he ate it all, he felt he was going to burst. Right now it was just as bad - especially after what he'd turned up on the computer. He'd found a clip that made him realise how exceptional Alice was, especially when she saved him from the shark.

"She's unbelievable," he whispered. "She leaves this for dead."

He'd discovered a fight between an arrow squid and a dogfish, captured on a camera lowered by rope to over two thousand feet. The squid had embraced the dogfish, wrapped itself around it, the same way as Alice had done. For a few moments they'd struggled together, but then the dogfish escaped. The people with the camera were chuffed with what they'd got, said it was a first.

"That was only a three-footer," Jamie muttered, going through the clip again. "About half the size of the porbeagle that was after me. And the squid? Tiny compared to Alice." *That's the trouble with people like that. They've idea what else there is out there.* "All they got was a few pictures. No one even saw it happen. Wait till Blanca brings her camera down. We'll have something that'll blow their minds."

But he had to wait. That was the worst part. His parents hadn't said anything about this morning when they'd turned up to see what he was doing in the water. Christ, if they found out about the shark, he'd be locked in his room and they'd throw away the key.

"What about Blanca?" he asked himself. "If I tell her, will it put her off? She should be all right. She's a diver. Might have even seen a shark before."

He leant back, eyes on the screen, heart racing. What would it be like when he came close to Alice again? He was ready, had dried his wet-suit, had everything packed. He only hoped, he really did, that he wouldn't have any trouble with his parents. He didn't want them to try and put Blanca off, and he had to get moving quickly. Once word got out, and it wouldn't take long, just another mention of Nessie would be enough, the place would be crawling with people. On a day like this, there'd be divers everywhere. He looked at his watch. It was getting late, it was time Blanca González got here.

"Are you really letting him go ahead with this?" Molly McCory poured two cups of tea. "You're not going to try and stop him?"

"I don't think that would be wise." William picked up a scone, put it back on the plate. They'd been sitting in the kitchen for half an hour, and still hadn't made their minds up. Both were reluctant to prohibit Jamie from going back into the water, neither was happy to take the blame. "The thing is, it's important we respect what he's doing. He's not a baby, after all."

"He is as far as I'm concerned."

"Come on, Molly, you know what I mean. He's been diving for years. Others, who've gone out with him, say he's a natural."

"There haven't been that many. He usually goes alone." Molly placed a cup of tea before her husband, then vigorously stirred sugar in her own. "And he's *never* been in the water with anything like this...this Alice creature."

"He assures us he feels quite safe with the squid." William put both hands around the warmth of the cup. "And he'll have Blanca with him."

"I know, I keep telling myself that, but what can she do if this...this thing...?" Molly sighed heavily, closed her eyes. "I don't want to argue over this, but you don't know how I feel. You look at it objectively, as if it wasn't part of our lives. It was the same when he was struck by lightning. You just stood there, saying he'd be all right."

"He was, wasn't he?"

"We didn't know it at the time."

"Listen, Molly, I'm as concerned as you are. I don't really want him to go out again, but I don't want to stop him either."

"What if I said, no?"

"If you do, I'll support you."

"Then it'll be my fault, won't it?"

"No, it won't." William reached across the table, took one of Molly's hands in his. "You know, perhaps we're not seeing this as clearly as we should."

"What do you mean?"

"If everything Jamie's said is true, and I've no reason to doubt him, he's made an incredible contact with the creature. No one has ever been in touch with a giant squid before. More scientists have gone into outer space than have been to the depths of the oceans. And if Blanca manages to get them together on film, I tell you, it would be amazing, absolutely amazing."

"Would you be prepared to go into the water with them?"

"If I could dive as well as he does, yes."

"You'd benefit too if they got some pictures. It could make you famous."

"I'm trying not to think about that," William replied honestly, then sighed. "But, whatever it could do for me, Jamie's safety must come first. To tell you the truth, I'm reluctant to stop him. And I'm just as reluctant to let him go ahead."

"Then it's up to me," Molly replied. "I really don't want him back in the water."

"You'll have some explaining to do."

"I don't care. I must do what I think is best."

"That's what I'm so doubtful about. I'm not quite sure what *is* best."

"Well, I am. I think I know what's right for my son."

"In that case, as I say, I won't go against you."

"Just see that you don't." Molly McCory was about to say more when the doorbell rang. After a quick glance at her husband, she went through the house to be greeted by the bright eyes of Blanca González peering in. "Hello," the Spanish girl said. "I hope I have not arrived too soon? Is Jamie ready?"

Angus Douglas set off for Oban early in the afternoon, driving his ancient Bentley through orange-tinted light. He'd spent most of the morning making phone calls, finding out all he could about Malcolm Stewart. What he discovered pleased him. It seems the man had been in practice in Glasgow until an unfortunate incident with a client put an end to that. An attractive woman with twin poodles, which she brought in to be shampooed, had found herself threatened by a more personal hose. After a series of threatening letters the vet had sold his practice and moved to Oban.

"I might live in a house that's falling down," Angus said as he replaced the phone after the final call and picking up his whisky. "But, by no means am I out of touch."

He also spent a long time in his extensive library, in what he called the Marine Section, where he turned up an old book, *The Natural History of Norway*, which described in detail a sea monster the author called a Kraken. The name rang an immediate bell. It reminded Angus of a novel he'd read years ago about kraken, or was it triffids, he wasn't sure which, anyway, it was about some mysterious creature that rose up from the deep.

"Bullseye, right on target," he said, after reading a passage describing the horns of the beast which, when they came out of the water, were as large as the masts of a good sized ship. Angus went over the section twice convinced that, however mysterious this Norwegian creature might have been, something very like it was taking livestock along the Culloch coast. "No wonder these bloody vets have their heads together. Not surprising that sergeant Croft's blathering about conger eels. They all know what's happening, and the bastards are keeping it to themselves. I'll bet they've already got the test results. I'll wager they know exactly what this Kraken thing is. Come to think of it, Norway's not all that far from here. And it's linked directly to Scotland by the Gulf Stream. I'd put a fiver on that's precisely what this local cattle-thief is. By God, if anything's going to bring the tourists flocking back to Culloch, it's this monster from the deep. The Kraken is exactly what I need."

He poured himself another whisky, read on to discover that *kraken* was the Norwegian word for an uprooted tree, that the body and the many arms of the monster bore great resemblance to a trunk and its earth-free roots. In fact, could have been taken for Nessie by someone who was stone cold sober, not nearly as drunk as Harry Carter had been..

"Conger eels? Got to give it to you, Sergeant Croft. You weren't that far off the mark. Lot closer than I was with my sea-slugs." He chortled. "Mind you, they worked well enough at the time."

He closed the book, finished his drink and slept for an hour. He wanted to be clear-headed when he met this vet at Oban - when he put the little bastard through the mill. What's more, when that was done, he'd give his old mate Charlie Coots a call. There'd be no kicking the story into the long grass this time. Culloch's Kraken would be front page news.

Angus Douglas whistled as he drove along the winding road, set a brace of pheasant cluttering from a ditch, breathed deeply the country air. It was good to be back in action again. Good to feel he wasn't quite over the hill. With any luck, when this was done and dusted, he'd be Monarch of the Glen once more, wear sporran and kilt not only on formal occasions.

NINETEEN – ready when you are

"If you are worried, you could come with us?" Blanca suggested when she realised how concerned Jamie's parents were, especially the mother, who'd been almost unable to smile when she came to the door. "Then you could see everything was all right."

"Be better if they didn't," Jamie said quickly. He'd hurried out of his room as soon as he heard the Spanish girl's voice, bursting to go. "I mean, they wouldn't be able to see us all the time. It might only make things worse."

"I'm afraid he could be right," said Molly, not giving her consent, yet unable to carry out her threat of preventing Jamie from going back into the water. His excitement was too great to suppress. She turned to her husband in the hope he would decide one way or the other. "What do you think, Will? Would it help if we were there, just in case?"

"I doubt it," William replied, also reluctant to deny Jamie what could be the opportunity of a lifetime. He glanced at Blanca González. "That is, not unless you need help with your car? Fitting in all his gear and things?"

She shook her head. "There is room in the back, where I put the animals that are sick," she said, even more aware of the parent's dilemma, yet also carried by Jamie's excitement.

"How, ah, how do you feel about all this?" persisted Molly. The Spanish girl's eyes were bright, yet she seemed quite calm, her hands were steady. "Aren't you just a little worried?"

"I am really very, what do you say, wound up. But not frightened. Not after what Jamie has told me." She smiled at the boy – his eyes were grateful. "It sounds very nice, this squid."

"She's great, she really is." Once again Jamie's heart went out to Blanca. She was terrific, she really was. "Come on, let's go. I can't wait for you to meet Alice."

"Are you sure she will be there?" Blanca asked, glad the conversation had moved on. "It is not usual for big calamar to stay so close to the coast."

"She'll be there," Jamie assured her, even though he wasn't sure. After the porbeagle Alice might have gone for good, but there was no point in thinking about that. "She's probably waiting for us. Getting impatient, if you know what I mean."

"Oh, Jamie, don't you think….?" Molly began when William gently interrupted. "Just be careful," he said quietly. "Both of you."

"Right, Dad, we will."

Without another word all went outside, put Jamie's rucksack in the back of Blanca's Ford, where her own diving equipment was neatly stacked. Before she got into the driver's seat, she turned to William. "Oh, I almost forgot, I saw Malcolm Stewart this morning. I did not mean to, but I told him I was going to dive with Jamie when I got here," she said, a little guiltily.

"I don't suppose that'll do any harm."

"No, but I also told him I had a camera. And, before he left me, he made a joke about taking pictures of a giant squid." Blanca sighed. "I don't want to say anything bad about him. He has been good, he sent me here. But, I do not trust that man. He is, how do you say it, a bit sneaky."

"Oh, I think he's all right," William replied, guardedly. "What else did he say?"

"He told me you were working with him on a sample. And he wanted to know if you had said anything about it to me."

"Nothing unusual about that."

"I suppose not, but he did *not* say the sample had been sent to New Zealand, like you did. You said you were waiting for a result that would confirm it was from *Architeuthis*."

"Perhaps he didn't want to say too much until he'd heard from there," William said, even as he suspected that Malcolm was playing another of his tricky games. "Don't worry about it, I'll give him a call later on. I won't tell him that you mentioned it, I'll just ask if he's got any results."

"Maybe, I should not have said anything to you."

"I'm glad you did." William smiled briefly, knowing that Blanca was now part of his team. "Well, off you go. And, for God's sake, both of you, be very careful."

"Yes," whispered Molly. "Come back soon."

"We will, Mum, don't worry."

Molly McCory didn't reply. Silently, she watched Jamie leap into the Ford, then sighed as Blanca drove away. It took all her resolve not to run after them, shouting for the car to stop. She wondered what she was doing, allowing her son to go off to face a creature he said he trusted, but no one else in the world knew much about. At the same time, she didn't have the heart to stop him. He was so full of excitement. She swallowed and turned to her husband, who put his hand on her shoulder as the car, packed with diving gear, disappeared around a bend in the road.

The giant squid hovered in the kelp, not quite certain what to do. At times she edged toward the place where the starfish dwelt, then abruptly darted back into the cover of the tall branched weed. It was impossible to know whether the thing she'd accepted as a companion would ever come back again. Her last image of the helpless creature had been of it clinging to a rock, terror in its prominent eyes. For all she knew it had gone forever, would never return to the quiet place where they'd swum together, made their first gentle contact.

She moved forward again, drawn by the recollection of the touching, the way she'd allowed it to respond. It had been an unusual coupling. Its skin had been durable, like that of a shark's but without the roughness. As for permitting it to run its tiny tentacles over her own, that was something that had never occurred before. She had no personal experience of the squirming and tangling that took place when two of her kind got close. She had seen it only from a distance, and it hadn't attracted her.

A further consideration nagged at her as she hung in the weed. Should she risk going back to the towering rock where she'd fought the porbeagle to the death? The image of the long sleek shape, the way it circled before the attack, filled her with doubt. Perhaps there were others out there, members of the same ravenous horde. They might have already swarmed in, overwhelmed the starfish and torn its helpless body to shreds. At that hideous thought, the giant squid retreated even further into the kelp. She blew out a jet that drove her back, her arms trailing behind her like a long-tailed kite, her twin hearts beating rapidly. For the first time in her life she was uncertain what to do.

What's more, the tentacle damaged by the cow was weak again. It had almost healed before the shark arrived, but the fight had renewed the injury. It wasn't open, the way it had been before, but it ached when she moved it, throbbed tenderly all the time. So, if there was more danger out there, she wondered if she'd have the strength to save the starfish again.

For a long while the giant squid hung indecisively, trembling, not knowing what to do. The only satisfaction she'd had, on this dreadfully demanding day, was the meal she'd made of the porbeagle. It had been delicious, right down to the very last piece, and its energy it began to renew her spirit. She *would* try, one very last time, to see if the starfish had returned to its haunt. If it wasn't there she'd move on, go back to the depths she's come from and try to forget it had ever entered her life.

"Tony," William McCory said, mobile phone pressed to his ear. "You and I'd better get together. Things are starting to move."

"Move?" Sergeant Croft reached for his chewing gum, knowing that last night's peace had been too good to last. He looked through the door of his office at Constable Roberts, who was talking to Jack, the barman from the *Harbour Light*. Their voices were low but nothing in their body language that anything was wrong. "What things are *moving*? What's happened?"

"I'm not sure anything's happened yet. But I've no doubt we should be prepared."

"Prepared for what? Come on, Will, don't beat around the bush. It was hard enough getting you to tell me what you knew in the first place. Now play it straight or you'll get no more help from me."

"Right, but I'd rather do it face to face."

"To hell with that, tell me now what's on your mind now," Croft demanded. "I want to know exactly what you're talking about to before I get in any deeper. I'm in enough trouble as it is. Old Douglas didn't take too kindly to my story about the conger eels."

"What did he say?"

"He didn't have to say anything. One look was enough. He scowl was fierce when he stuck his head in the door saying he was off to Oban for the night. As chairman, he thinks the police should know where he is twenty-four hours a day."

"Douglas has gone to Oban?" fresh concern prickled down William's spine. "Did he tell you why he was going?"

"He's meeting that vet you know. They're getting together this evening."

"Malcolm Stewart?"

"Isn't he the one you sent that sample to?" Croft's mournful face grew longer. "If he and Angus put their heads together, that can only mean bad news."

"My God, Angus was bad enough with crop circles. God knows what he'll be like when he finds out a giant squid took his Blackface ram. As for Malcolm Stewart, he's determined make a name for himself. Become a celebrity." William ran a worried hand over his forehead. - whatever thoughts he'd had of his own fame and fortune were pushed aside by new fears for the safety of his son. "After what Blanca González told me, I don't trust him an inch."

"Blanca González?"

"The new vet I've hired. She starts tomorrow. Right now she's off with Jamie. They're going to film the squid. I tell you, Tony, things are really moving fast. We've got to get some sort of control over this, otherwise God knows what Stewart and Douglas will get up to."

"All right, just settle down, Will," Sergeant Croft said, disturbed by the alarm in the vet's usually calm voice. "I'll go along with you, but answer me just one question." He leant forward - apart from anything else, he needed to know the facts, separate them from the fiction. "Are you sure there *is* a giant squid out there? I mean, anyone can make a mistake."

"I'm sure, I really am. Jamie's touched it. He calls it Alice. I know he's got a vivid imagination, but I believe him. That's why I didn't stop him going back into the water with Blanca. They're probably out there now. She's got an underwater camera."

"Fucking hell," Tony Croft whispered, his words unusually blunt. "You'd better get round here as fast as you can."

"I'm on my way."

Jamie was dressed to dive, had mask and fins ready, before Blanca was half-way prepared. As soon as he got out of the car he tore off his outer garments, tugged on his wet-suit. It was dry again, he'd sprinkled fresh talcum powder in the arms and legs, helping it to slip on easily. He pulled on his boots, tugged the hood into place and stood waiting, fins in hand, as patiently as he was able for her to appear.

She'd gone behind the Ford to change into her woolly-bear, a thick padded outfit which reminded her of the romper suits babies wore. It was close-fitting, just what she needed to keep warm. Then she pulled on her dry-suit, which took some getting into as it fitted tightly around the neck and wrists and zipped up at the back.

"Would you help me with this," she called over her shoulder, when the suit was half-way on. "I can't do it on my own."

"Yeah, right." Jamie put a hand on her arm, pulled the zip up her back and was surprised by the effect she had on him. She was old, must have been twenty-five or something, yet felt like a girl. *You're getting a hard-on*, he told himself. *Stop it. You're not here for that sort of thing.* "Is that okay?" he asked, with a cough. "Not too tight?"

"Fine, thank you." She ran her eye over his diving gear. "Are you warm enough in that? It is just a wet-suit. You don't wear anything more?"

"I've got my underclothes on," Jamie replied. "I don't feel the cold all that much."

"You are very lucky. Even at home, in Spain, I cannot stay in the water long. Not without this." Blanca tapped her suit. "And, usually I wear gloves too. But today, I will have cold hands." She reached into the car, took out her video, encased in its silver housing. "I have to work the controls. It is easier without the gloves."

"It looks great." Jamie touched the camera. "Have you used it often?"

"The video, quite often. But, underwater not so much." Blanca smiled, a little crookedly, excitement pumping through her veins. *This is incredible*, she thought. *We are talking about a camera, not about what is going to happen next. We are being very calm, but *what if I am about to take the first pictures of a person and this giant calamar? My God, I had no idea Culloch would be as exciting as this.* She picked up her fins, which she'd slip on when she reached the water. Her suit had boots attached. "Come on, we will get in. I do not want to keep your friend waiting any longer."

"Right," replied Jamie, wondering if he should tell her about the shark, but quickly put the thought aside. She knew what she was doing. And he wanted to get into the water so bad it made him sweat. "It's best to go in slowly, so we don't give the fish a fright."

"I always get in like that."

"If you see her, don't move," Jamie added. He had to warn her about that, it was only fair. Alice had been quite friendly with him, but he had no idea what she'd be like with Blanca or anyone she didn't know. "I'll go ahead and see if I can touch her."

"Do not worry. I will follow you, wherever you go." Blanca raised the camera. "And I will keep this running all the time."

"Yeah, get everything."

That was the last thing they said before they got into the sea, eased into the cold and clear water that made everything seem bigger, that made the wonderland look so much larger than life.

Malcolm Stewart rang New Zealand before the antipodean dawn had broken and was surprised when the voice at the other end sounded so wide awake. "Hello, there, expected you to call me well before now. Name's Susie, by the way," a young woman said as soon as he'd introduced himself.

"I, ah, didn't want to disturb your sleep."

"Hasn't been much of that. I've been up with this all night." Susie let out a long low whistle. "Crikey, this is the most interesting thing I've been given to work on since they thought they'd found a coelacanth off Leigh."

"Really, what...?"

"Had to send the sample down to Kaikoura for a final check. Where they go whale-watching. You know, the thing the Maori run that's been such a great success. There's a big trough, comes right in close to the shore down there. They looked for *Architeuthis* in it once but didn't get a sniff. I suppose you've heard of the place?"

"I believe I have."

"I tell you straight, when they put this sample of yours through their lab, they thought they were going to have kittens. Wanted to get on the telly right away. Wanted to know who sent it to us. Do you mind if I give them your name?"

"Hang on a minute." Malcolm tried to guess what the girl had been taking to keep awake all night. He wondered what she looked like. "Before we go any further, tell me exactly what you've found."

"What you thought it was. *Architeuthis*, of course," Susie replied, pronouncing it *Arky-toothies*. "Just like the joker that was caught the other day. I suppose you know we go back a long way here with these beauties. They reckon the largest specimen ever recorded was washed up on Island Bay in eighteen-eighty. Dead as a dodo, though. But this one, the one you sent us. Fresh isn't it? Came from something that's still alive, didn't it? Like I say, just the same as the one those fishermen caught off the coast of Antarctica. Theirs was about forty foot long, how big was yours?"

"I, ah,..." Malcolm avoided a direct reply. He had all the confirmation he needed and no desire to tell this over-excited girl any more. "I'm not quite sure of that. The specimen was sent to me by a friend. I'd have to check with him."

"Like to give me *his* name."

"I'd better have a word with him first. But, don't worry, I will be back," Malcolm said, trying to sound like Arnold Schwarzenegger. "Thanks for all your help."

"No problem. I'll be here for the rest of the day. And I'll tell them down in Kaikoura to hold their horses until we hear from you."

"You've been very helpful, Susie, we should keep in touch." Malcolm managed to control his laugh. "I wonder if you could send me a picture of yourself. I'd really like to know what the person I'm talking to looks like on the other end of the line."

"Sure, will do."

Malcolm Stewart put down the phone, ready for Angus Douglas. *We'll see who does the manipulating now*, he told himself. *Who's prepared to work for or against the public good*. There was a fortune to be made if this giant squid could be captured alive, put in a tank, exhibited all around the world. There were prizes to be won that few would be able to resist. If anyone was going to score from this, he had no doubt who that would be. Probably end up with his own reality series, be a king of the box.

TWENTY – camera…action…

The giant squid left the safety of the kelp and eased her flexible body toward the Grotto where she'd first seen the starfish. To her dismay it wasn't there. She swam on to the Tombstone where she'd last glimpsed its terrified face. But there was no sign of the thing there either - it had obviously been frightened off forever. Heaviness drew her twin hearts down as she realised that the fight with the porbeagle had been more than the delicate creature could bear. She should have let the half-dead shark get away, gone back and comforted the starfish as she'd done before, raising two arms in that gesture of friendship so well-known amongst her kith and kin. There were a great many things she could have done to assure the helpless creature that all was well. Instead, about to win a magnificent battle, with a meal clutched close, she'd thought only of herself and had left the starfish alone.

Desolate, she turned toward the open sea, to the currents that had brought her here. She would have to go back to the darkness she knew, to the deeps she'd been nurtured in and recapture the life she knew. It would be depressing to return on her own – but she had her memories to sustain her. She would never forget the odd creature that swam so clumsily, who had no idea of the ways of the sea. Who wasn't even capable of drawing oxygen from the water but had to breathe in air like a whale. Perhaps she could have taught it something of what life was like in this world of hers, but instead she had spoilt her chances. It had gone, she felt sure of that. She would never see the starfish again.

The giant squid swam slowly past the Tombstone, aware of another change in the seas. The curious tang in the water, which had driven her toward the shore, had almost disappeared. That was something else she'd never forget, the way it had altered her emotions, given her a lift that changed her life, sent her on her way. When it first filtered through her giant body she had flushed a deep, impelling red. She'd been filled with a desire seek something new, to go somewhere that was fresh and exciting. That emotion seemed to have lost intensity, and its absence would make the leaving a little easier, help her move back home.

"What are you up to now, Harry?" Constable Roberts asked, after leaving the police car, walking up the gravel pathway to the stables to stand with his hands on his hips. "What are doing with that drum?"

"What drum?" Harry Carter grunted, lowering himself quickly onto the DDT. "What drum are you talking about?"

"The one under your bum."

"This?" Harry raised his cap, casually scratched his head. "It's nothing. I'm just doing a bit of sorting out, that's all."

"That stuff should've been got rid of years ago." Roberts bent to take a closer look. "Banned in the eighties, if I remember right."

"It got forgotten in the back of the shed."

"I'd be careful with it, if I was you. Rusty drum like that could break open any time. Then it'd leak all over the place."

"That's why I'm clearing it out." Harry leant forward defiantly. It wasn't so bad when Tony Croft had a go at him, but he wasn't going to take any lip from this young copper, who had a face like a baby's backside. "What's it got to do with you?"

"Maybe nothing, Harry, and maybe a lot," Roberts replied, his voice easier. He didn't want to get the old chap's back up, but there was a great deal more he wanted to know. "I'm just following up a lead, to tell you the truth. That new mate of yours has been shouting his mouth off."

"What new mate?"

"Billy the Dealer. He's telling everyone he's got something going with you."

"I've got nothing to do with him. I don't touch his stuff."

"Glad to hear it. But what Billy's on about is a bit more interesting than that. This lad says you two know what's been taking the livestock. He reckons you're going to get rid of conger eels, even Nessie if it comes to that." Roberts indicated the drum. "I hope you're not thinking of using this."

"Don't be daft, DDT's illegal."

"So is selling drugs. That's why we keep tabs on Billy. Better the devil you know, as my mother says. We keep a close eye on him," Roberts added significantly. "Don't tell me we've got to keep a close eye on you too?"

"No need for that. Like I said, I'm getting rid of this."

"Good. There's a place in Oban that'll take it off your hands." Roberts asked himself if he wasn't turning into another Tony Croft, becoming a bit of a nanny. Well, there were worse ways to go. "If you like, just drop it off down the station. We'll see it gets to the right place."

"Might do that," Harry grunted, as Roberts turned away. "I could bring it down later."

Harry Carter sat brooding long after Roberts had gone. He was in deep shit now and he knew it. Billy the Dealer had put him there. After the little creep talked about using DDT to get rid of the sea slugs, Harry had opened a fresh bottle of scotch and turned things over in his mind. If those slugs from the sea *had* taken his foal and the other stuff, the whole of Culloch could be in danger. Christ knows what they'd be after next - one of the kids along the waterfront? And if he helped to clean them out, he'd be the local hero, no longer a layabout in a dirty shirt. It had all made good sense then. But Constable Roberts, with his hands on his hips, had put a dampener on it. Made him realise that Billy was like the stuff he sold – just something that turned your head. Harry sighed and stood, looked down at the drum. He'd need to be bloody sure what he was doing before he went any further with this. The more he thought about it the more stupid the idea of using it became. He'd be better off if he left it alone. But it was bloody hard to decide what to do. And there could still be a way of making his name.

Jamie swam slowly, leading Blanca to the Grotto, looking for the giant squid. When they arrived he stopped, breathed in and out a couple of times, took a shallow dive and peered into the cave where the lobsters hid, the spiders crabs camouflaged themselves with bits of weed, and the multi-coloured sponges grew. But the hovering shape was not to be seen. There was no sign of Alice. He surfaced, jerked his thumb in the direction of the Tombstone, asking Blanca to follow.

She nodded, and they moved on. She was comfortable in her dry-suit, the woolly bear beneath it; she found the sea less cold than she'd expected. The camera weighed nothing in the water. Her hands were fine at the moment.

This is wonderful, she thought. The water's so clean. I will be able to get everything *if* the calamar is here. She didn't doubt that Jamie had seen an *Architeuthis*; his description had been too vivid for him to be telling anything but the truth. Nor was she disappointed to see no sign of Alice in the Grotto. Blanca knew, from fishing with her father, that octopus had areas they frequented, so if Alice wasn't in the first place Jamie explored, the creature may not have gone far. On the other hand, with something so enormous, its life-style might not be the same as the cephalopods that inhabited the rocks at home. Will we see it? she asked herself. Will we?

Jamie paddled on to the Tombstone where he paused to take a long look around, his heart beating rapidly as he thought of the last time he'd been here. But there were no sleek shapes sliding through the water, no sign of any shark. Though, Alice wasn't there either. He felt a sudden anxious pang run right through him. The fight had been too much for her. She had gone. She was dead. Or perhaps, just perhaps, she was hiding somewhere waiting for him to call.

"There's got to be a way of letting her know I'm here," he muttered, then remembered the method he'd worked out to make contact. The idea seemed okay in theory, but hadn't been put into practise. "A sound that tells her it's me?" he questioned. "But is it going to work?"

He turned to find Blanca beside him, her eyes wide, the silver camera catching the light. She was as excited as he was. That was something else, he couldn't let her down; she was part of the operation to save Alice now. He held up a hand, asking her to wait, then dived again and found two small stones.

Blanca watched, wondering if this was part of a ritual Jamie and the giant squid performed together. She saw him return to the surface, clear his lungs and begin knocking the stones together, uncertainly at first, but quickly developing a steady rhythm that was a bit like an audience responding to a concert in Andalusia.

As she watched she recalled a man she'd read about who lived in Fiji, who fed groupers that came to his call. Each morning a number of the huge fish, each weighing fifty or sixty kilos, would be waiting on the beach, their noses almost out of the water. When the man gave them mullet he'd caught the day before, they'd open their huge mouths to wolf it down. More came when the man banged the metal bucket he carried the mullet in. Now Blanca realised that Jamie was doing something similar, and immediately turned the video on.

Jamie saw that the camera was running, and banged harder. *Come on, Alice*, he urged. *She's going to make you famous.* He clapped the stones together more rapidly, hoping he wasn't too late.

"I've got to talk to Tony Croft," William McCory told his wife. "Sorry, I don't like leaving you on your own, but it's urgent."

"What do you need to talk about?" Molly asked, vigorously beating eggs for an omelette. Doing nothing while she waited for her son and Blanca to return from the sea was driving her mad. Cooking didn't solve the problem, but it helped. "Has it anything to do with Jamie?"

"Yes."

"What?"

"Angus Douglas and Malcolm Stewart are meeting in Oban." There was no point in hiding the truth from Molly. "My guess is they're planning something. Douglas will probably try to catch the squid as a tourist attraction. Malcolm will do anything that puts him in the spotlight. And Sergeant Croft's the only person I can trust. We've got to find a way of saving Alice."

"Saving....*Alice*?"

"If she means that much to Jamie, We must do what we can."

"You...?" Molly looked down at the mixture in the bowl. It was too thick, she'd gone too far. That didn't matter. With this she could always start again. With Jamie in the water, her husband talking of saving a giant squid, there was nothing she could do. "You're as bad as he is. *Alice*? How on earth can you save something only Jamie's ever seen?"

"I don't know, but I intend to make an effort. If Douglas, or anyone else, gets word to the Media, there'll be people all over the place. As Jamie says, they'll probably send in a team of Navy divers."

"Wait a minute, Will. For God's sake, it's only a squid."

"No, for Jamie it's much more than that."

"Whatever it is, it's with him now, doing God knows what." Molly closed her eyes, things were moving far too fast. She'd resisted calling Jamie back when he set off with Blanca in the car. That had been her first mistake, left her feeling helpless. Now Will was becoming as obsessed as her son, suddenly wanting to save, not study, the squid. "For all we know, it might be attacking him at this very minute..."

"I don't think so, Molly."

"How do you know?"

"I don't, to be perfectly honest." William put out a hand to touch his wife; abruptly she pulled away. "I don't know anything, but I don't think it will."

Molly McCory stared at her husband wanting to believe him, glad he had so much faith in their son, but wondering if he had lost his mind. What had happened to the scientist she'd married, the man who demanded answers to every question he asked? She wanted him to assure her that Jamie was safe in the water, but had no time to say anything more before he turned and walked out the door. With a heavy sigh, she returned to her omelette, threw out the mix she'd been working on, began breaking fresh eggs and beating them as vigorously as before.

The giant squid was almost out of hearing when she became aware of the faint clicking in the water, the short distinctive bursts. She was swimming forlornly into deeper seas when the signals came to the hair-cells in her head, those running through her mantle, part of the delicate system that gave her a sense of sound. For a moment she ignored them, taking the clicks might be shrimps snapping their claws, wrasse searching for prey amongst the rock-weed, smaller squid eating. But as they persisted, became louder, more regular in their rhythm, hope within her huge body lifted to the call. She turned and listened more intently to make sure the bursts weren't being sent by a whale. Then, spinning, trailing her arms and tentacles behind her, she shot backwards in the direction of the Tombstone, homing in on the sound. She felt certain it was a message from the starfish. She knew he wanted to see her again.

Blanca González was first to see the giant squid. She had her video trained on Jamie, who was looking the other direction, steadily banging the stones, when out of the corner of her eye she saw a long streamlined body shoot up behind him, halt as if it had braked in the water, open its arms, making the lines of suckers clear, and move in close. Automatically, she widened the zoom, her mind in a turmoil.

Dios mío, she thought, as she stared at the unbelievably large creature, many times bigger than the boy, eyes as large and as round as a *paella* dish, tentacles long enough to wrap around Jamie a dozen times or more. It is attacking him. No it isn't. It is...I don't know what...

Jamie turned, recognising the swirl in the water, to see Alice so near he could touch her. He dropped the stones and waited She came even closer, near enough for him to peer into the cavern of her mouth, to see the blackness of her beak. It seemed that she was smiling in the clumsy way that dogs do, not quite mastering the lip movements, but nevertheless showing their joy.

"Alice," he shouted through his snorkel, almost exploding with delight. "You're here. That's great. I thought you'd gone. I even thought you'd died."

The giant squid was so pleased to see the starfish her huge eyes failed to record anything else. She stared as the awkward creature turned, blew a stream of bubbles out of the strange thing it used for air. She reached out a tentacle, touched its curious skin. It was warm, she felt it tremble. The starfish was full of happiness to be with her once again. She looked around, to make sure it was safe, and became aware of its companion. Sudden rage swept through her divided brain.

It has a mate with it. Worse still, its companion is carrying a bright and shining offspring. They have brought their child here.

Angrily, the giant squid withdrew her tentacles, closed her arms and hovered, changing from the bright red of welcome to a more unattractive grey. She waited, her whole body quivering, to see what the smaller starfish, obviously a female, would do. Then, to her surprise, it offered the child to her, pointed its round black nose in her direction, in an act of pure affection, and held it steady. Oddly enough, the youngster had no breathing tube. Perhaps it got air from the mother.

They are such fools, Alice thought. They know nothing of the sea. And why they're stupid enough to bring a child into the water is beyond my understanding.

They should have realised, as any creature worthy of its fins would have, that the young of all tribes are the most vulnerable, often the tastiest of prey. Any other of her companions would have taken the offspring immediately, devoured it without a second thought.

But they trust me, Alice concluded. In turn, I must respond.

At once, she changed back to a warm and glowing red, began to dance for the family. She shot away a distance, spun on her tail and returned. She touched the male starfish, felt its tiny tentacles on her own. She swam around the mother, a little distantly at first, then did an elegant pirouette for the child, first spinning in one direction, then the other. All the while she kept one of her enormous eyes on the male starfish and saw that he was pleased. She went on, curling and twisting and changing her hues, showing them what she could do. If it was impossible to bond with the starfish, and she'd always had her doubts about that, she'd become a friend to the entire family and perform for them whenever she could.

Blanca González could not believe her eyes. When the giant squid turned on her, trembling with rage, cold fear ran through her, making the woolly bear feel clammy against her skin. She'd been frightened before, but nothing like this. Once, an Alsatian that needed an anti-rabies injection had cornered her. She'd been led to believe the dog was docile, so she'd approached without any thought of danger. But as soon as she touched the back of its neck, the hypodermic ready, the dog became a snarling beast. It snapped savagely, left a long red mark where its teeth scraped her skin. In panic, she moved backwards, stumbled over the dog-bowl and fell, trapped between the kennel and a split-wood fence. The dog leapt at her, growling, the hair on its back a ridge, to be pulled up at the last minute by the chain around its neck.

"You bastard," the owner shouted, running forward with a stick. "I'll flatten you for that."

"Don't hit it," Blanca cried in spite of her shock. "It was this." She held up the syringe with a shaking hand. "It must have had a bad injection before."

"It's the dog that's bad." The owner held the stick aloft, the animal cowering beneath him. "Although it's never bitten anyone before." He glanced at Blanca. "Are you all right?"

"I'm fine." Blanca scrambled to her feet. "Hold him, will you. I'll inject his backside."

The image of the snarling dog flashed through her mind as the giant squid hung trembling, anger in its fantastic eyes. Then, to her amazement, its mood changed completely. It became tranquil, swam slowly past, its gaze on the camera. It came close, opened its arms, suddenly spun away, looking lovely as it glided toward Jamie and beyond. Then it began to dance. That was the only way she could describe it. It was like a child learning *flamenco*, not quite sure what to do, but full of gypsy spirit.

Amazing, she told herself, as she followed its movements with the camera, at times recording the squid alone, at others as it circled Jamie, touching him with its long elegant tentacles, once even pulling him through the water as if he were a partner in the dance. This is, absolutely incredible. *Dios mío,* you have to see it to believe it.

As for Jamie, he was thrilled. This was more exciting than he could ever have imagined. He was playing with Alice, there was no doubt about that. They were inventing games, making up the rules as they went along. Sometimes Blanca was part of it, but mostly it was just himself and Alice in a sort-of hide-and-seek, playing touch, even dancing. Once or twice she disappeared completely, only to reappear behind him, tapping him on the shoulder, gripping him with her tentacles, surfing him along. And the most incredible thing about it, she was enjoying herself. You could see it in the way she moved. She was beautiful, a giant mass of splendour, filling the sea with joy.

TWENTY-ONE – bad weather ahead

"I've had a call from Jamie. Got it just after I left the house," William McCory told Sergeant Croft when he arrived breathlessly at the police station. "He's fine. He's out of the water, and tells me that Blanca's filmed the squid."

"She actually got live pictures?" Croft asked, wondering if the vet needed something to restore his customary calm. His face was flushed, his hands were trembling. The man obviously could do with a scotch. Perhaps they both needed one. "You're, ah, sure about that?"

"I'm sure. I'll show you the video when he brings it home."

"I certainly can't wait to see it." Croft jerked his thumb in the direction of his office. "But come through here and tell me all about it in private."

Ten minutes later, after they'd calmed their nerves with a little malt from the bottle the sergeant kept in his desk for medicinal purposes, and William had regained his breath sufficiently to recount what Jamie had said about Alice in sentences that made sense, Croft sat back and let out a long low whistle.

"My God, man, what you're actually saying is that we've got a tame monster off the Culloch coast. A giant squid that's been taking livestock- but only because it's hungry? You're quite sure it's not going to come ashore, with Christ knows how many of its friends, and have us all for breakfast?"

"That's right, it's harmless."

"So what do you suggest we do? Put a chain round its neck and introduce it to the tourists?"

"We've got to let it go."

"Now, just a minute, that's not what you had in mind the other day." Croft poured a little more whisky into each glass - it was soothing his stomach nicely. "Then you were on about *one of the great mysteries of the deep*. And gave me the impression you'd like to get your hands on it. Pull it to pieces, see how it worked."

"I've changed my mind about that. Jamie made me. He convinced me that the squid is good." William reached for his malt whisky, downed it in a single swallow. "He says it saved him from a shark."

"Bugger me," whispered Tony Croft. "This goes from bad to worse."

"I know it sounds absurd. Jamie blurted out the story over the phone. I've got to question him more closely when he gets home, but that's what he told me. He's sure this squid's his friend." William shook his head in wonder. "He was so excited he didn't make a lot of sense."

"Neither do you."

"I was afraid of that."

"Has he seen this video that Blanca took?"

"Not yet. They had to get out because her hands were cold. She didn't want to touch the camera until she'd stopping shaking. We'll be looking at it later. Do you think you could come over?"

"Wild horses wouldn't keep me away. Even if they came out of the sea." Croft smiled, the whisky was having a pleasant effect. "However, here's something *you* should know," he added, his face becoming serious again. "Our old friend Harry Carter's up to something. Constable Roberts caught him with a rusty drum of DDT."

"What's he going to do with that?"

"Constable Roberts isn't certain. Word has it that Harry and Billy the Dealer are working hand in glove. Billy's told Harry that sea-slugs, *sea-slugs* for Christ's sake, are responsible for what happened to his foal. We're not sure what they're up to. We can only watch and wait. Harry said he'd drop the DDT round here, but Roberts wasn't all that convinced he will."

"My God, if they actually put it in the river...."

"Don't even think about it, it scares the hell out of me too. We've had enough shit dumped in the sea to last us several lifetimes. The Government's even had to pay compensation for military explosives our locals have hauled up in their nets. And there were those surfers that got burnt by flares washed up along the coast. Christ, imagine the damage DDT could do if it was poured into the harbour."

"It could ruin what's left of the fishing for months, even years. Especially if they dumped the poison in at low tide."

"That's why we've got to keep our eyes open. All of us, you too, Will. Roberts has a few friends around town. They'll be on the lookout."

"Let's hope they don't miss anything." William held out his glass for more whisky. "My God, this place is turning into a nightmare."

"Did you get it all on tape?" asked Jamie, pulling his striped hat down to his eyes. He really needed it after all the excitement in the water. It made things real again. "Are you sure?"

"I am sure," Blanca replied, her hands wrapped around the cup of hot milk Jamie had poured from the thermos flask his mother had put in his rucksack. "I have everything with you and Alice together. And some of her when she was alone. She was incredible, no?"

"Awesome. And isn't she clever? When I got those stones and banged them together, she knew it was time to come. Just like she knew it was time to go when we swam back from the Tombstone."

"I am glad we did, my hands were freezing. I couldn't have stayed in any longer."

"You were great too." Blanca had surprised him as much as Alice. She'd been scared at first, but got in there with the camera, worked it until she couldn't take the cold any longer. She was still in her dry-suit, with that woolly thing underneath. She'd stopped trembling, but her face was grey. If she'd been a feller he'd have rubbed her down with a rough dry towel, but that was out of the question, although it would have been kind of exciting. He'd changed as soon as he got out of the water, now wore jeans, pullover, anorak and his hat. He felt fantastic. "I can't wait to see the video."

"You will, when we get to your house. But, don't worry, you will be pleased." Blanca sipped the milk, felt it restore her a little. She'd been silly not to wear gloves, but with them she wouldn't have been able to handle the camera. She was sure she'd got almost everything right. Some of the zooms might be a bit uneven, but the rest would be clear and sharp. It was wonderful how everything had come together like this. She wondered what had brought her here, to Culloch, at such an amazing time. "Do you believe in God?" she asked, quietly. "You know, something that controls our lives?"

"What?"

"Up there." Blanca glanced at the open sky. "In the heavens."

"I, ah, I don't know." Jamie wondered if she'd been in the water too long. "I mean, I don't think about it all that much."

"Not even when you see something like Alice dancing for us? That is what she was doing, you know? And those chimpanzees which are so human, they make you think." Blanca drank a little more milk. This was not the moment to be talking about such things, but she couldn't help it. She'd just done something that was incredible, almost beyond belief. And it made her realise that there was so much mystery in the world around her, so much she could never explain. "My family is religious. But my father also says we have our places on the planet. All of us are different, but, there are times when we cross over, become part of another group. I feel it sometimes, you know, especially in the surgery."

"You mean, we're all the same, but different?"

"Yes, something like that."

"I do too, in a way." Jamie pulled his hat down tighter. "I don't eat anything with eyes."

"You are a vegetarian?" Blanca smiled - this strange boy became more interesting the more she got to know him. "I thought you might be."

"I couldn't eat anything that had been alive. I wouldn't want anything nice to die just to give me something to eat."

"Do you feel close to all living things?"

"All the time. And look at Alice, she was part of us today." Jamie paused, felt his cheeks grow warm. "We were a bit like a family, all of us down there in the water."

"Yes, we were." Blanca looked up at the sky again, at the little tufts of cloud against the endless, infinite blue. "She, Alice, really knew what she was doing. And, that, well that frightens me."

"Why?"

"Because of what Malcolm Stewart said before I left Oban. He was very interested in my camera. He wants to look at the video, but I don't think for a very good reason. I am sure that when he knows that the *calamar* is real, he will try to catch it."

"They'll all like that. My father's the same. They want to study Alice, pull her apart. It makes me sick." Jamie took in a deep breath. "Will you help me stop them?"

"Yes, but how can we do that?"

"We've just got to find a way."

"It will not be easy."

"I know it won't, but if we work together, we'll come up with something."

"I hope so, and believe me I will do all I can."

Jamie stared at her, his heart lifting. At last he'd got someone who was truly on side. "We'll find a way," he said, his voice determined. "We'll save Alice. We'll get her out of here as soon as we can." Then he turned away, looked out at the sea, wondering where she was hiding.

It took Malcolm Stewart an hour to contact Charlie Coots, editor of the *Oban Times*. He finally got phone call through to the thin, white-haired journalist at the bar of the Glencruitten club-house, where he'd just finished a round of golf with an old friend, John Forrester, a seasoned reporter from Inverness. Both were into their second pint, and the interruption wasn't welcome.

"You take some finding," Malcolm said. "I thought journalists were on the job twenty-four seven."

"I was in a bunker on the eighteenth, using a seven when last I counted," Charlie replied crisply. He had little time for the Oban vet who fancied himself as a ladies' man, who once let his daughter's puppy die because he'd been too busy to take an x-ray, consequently failing to find a broken rib that punctured a lung. "If it was numbers you were after."

"I'm talking circulation. Greater numbers for that rag of yours."

"In that case call the office in the morning."

"Just thought I'd get to you first." Malcolm's snuffling laugh filtered through. "You're top dog on the *Oban Times*, aren't you?"

"If it's urgent there's an emergency service."

"I tried that," Malcolm replied. "And the girl there told me I'd find you at Glencruitten. So are you interested in what I've got to say or not?"

"Listen, Stewart," Charlie replied. "Unless World War Three has broken out, I suggest you stick to snipping balls off cats."

"You listen to me, Coots. This is something special. If you turn it down you could be sorry for the rest of your reporting life, which might suddenly turn out to be short."

"Oh, for Christ's sake, what are you getting at?"

"Something you could sell the rights to all over the world."

"Like what?"

"Like a sea creature that's been taking livestock down in Culloch."

"Oh, no! Not you too?" Charlie resisted the desire to snap his phone shut. "First it's crop circles on calves? Then it's ectoplasm that takes the shape of alien warriors? Or chewing gum that no one's cleaned up? What's going on down there? Something in the water that's sending everyone round the bend?"

"Something in the water's right." Malcolm's voice tightened. "And if you're not interested, there are others I could get in touch with."

"Angus Douglas, by any chance?"

"Why not?"

"I'd be careful of him, if I were you. He was on the phone a few days ago with a story about men from the moon." Charlie shrugged at John Forrester. "I think he's been hitting the booze too hard."

"Forget about Angus Douglas. What I have is evidence, real *evidence*. Including a lab report confirming this creature's existence." Malcolm Stewart's words were bitten off. This sardonic editor wasn't going to push him aside. "What's more, the creature's being filmed at this very moment."

"By Alfred Hitchcock, back from the dead?" When Angus Douglas phoned, Charlie felt some sympathy for a man down on his uppers. Even though the idea of crop circles as a tourist attraction was patently ridiculous, he'd treated an old friend gently. But this pushy vet was merely a nuisance. "Get with it, Stewart. I'm not interested in fantasy. We're a family paper. Try somewhere more appropriate. How about a sci-fi channel? They might listen to you there."

"Just one moment..."

"I'm sorry. Good-bye." With that Charlie Coots cut the phone conversation short. "A local vet," he explained to Forrester. "Trying to sell me something about monsters from the deep."

"On a Sunday?" Forrester raised his bushy eyebrows. "Where?"

"Culloch. I know they've had a bad time recently. What with Mad Cow Disease, fishing cuts and bloody awful weather. But now they've roped in an Oban vet with a story about something taking livestock. It's a pathetic attempt to kick-start the tourist trade."

"Poor sods, it can't be easy, they've had it rough."

"They're desperate. Someone even claimed to have seen Nessie floating down the local stream."

"Really?" Forrester raised his bushy eyebrows, wondering if the story had some mileage after all. Charlie knew what he was doing, he'd been in the game long enough, but you never knew with something like this, it could be worth a paragraph or two. "A couple of malts," he said to the barman, planning ahead. "Make them doubles, while you're at it."

—⚏—

After the conversation was cut short Malcolm Stewart stared at his phone, not quite believing he'd been so readily dismissed.

"The arrogant shit," he said aloud. "I'll show him."

But he had nothing to show anyone yet, nothing to back up his claim. The book on squids he'd ordered from Amazon, hadn't yet arrived. And there were only two other people in the world who knew anything about recent events. One, an over-excited girl in New Zealand, was too far away to be of any use. The other, Will McCory, was a man he wanted to keep in the dark for as long as possible. He hadn't even told him the sample he'd taken had been positively identified.

The only thing to do is catch it, he told himself. *And fast.*

He'd been thinking along those lines ever since he'd heard of *Architeuthis*, wondering if the creature could be tranquillised. But the size of it, the amount needed, and the administering of the drug were major problems. He'd considered using underwater search-lights, in the hope of hypnotising the squid. Fish were drawn to light at night, perhaps this giant member of the aquatic family would react in the same manner. But, that too, would be an almost impossible task and, what's more, would let everyone know what was being attempted.

"If that stupid bloody editor had listened to me a minute more, I've have got my name in the paper." Malcolm muttered, the phone still clutched in his furious hand. "Then everyone would know who the credit belonged to. Wouldn't even have had to catch it to get the recognition I deserve. Well, to hell with him and his goddamned newspaper. I'll catch it, that'll show them. Using bait. Like the way they tied goats to trees in the old days in India, hunting tigers. The squid takes livestock," he went on, convincing himself. "I'll bait a net with a lamb carcass. That should do the trick. Get Douglas to help. Bring it ashore. Then they'll see. By Jesus, then the whole bloody world will see. They'll know who to thank for the first giant squid ever displayed alive. They'll know who to honour for that."

And what about Blanca's video? he added, his mind a whirl. *Can't wait to I get my hands on that.*

SQUID

The giant squid hung in a network of kelp, quietly content with what had occurred. Her injured tentacle ached a little, but that was nothing compared to the joy she'd found in dancing with the starfish. It had been wonderful, playing with him and his companion, although *she* had been disappointing. Perhaps it was like that with females in his tribe, they were less animated than their partners. The way some male fish were more colourful than those they bred with.

As for the offspring, it had shown no signs of life at all. It reminded Alice of the egg cases her relatives stuck to rocks on the ocean floor, where they stayed until the young came out to lead their own little lives. What's more, the solid silver block containing the embryo looked as unappetising as the egg case she, herself, had come from, as cleverly disguised as her own protective shield. Perhaps, by now, the mother had found a niche to leave it in. Alice hoped so, as the female had seemed quite exhausted when she took it out of the water.

There was much to think about, Alice realised, as she settled comfortably amongst the kelp, especially as far as the future was concerned. Her curiosity had been satisfied, she now knew what life was like out of the water, away from the world she was used to. As well, she'd recently consumed a good-sized thorny skate, which she'd caught without much effort as it ventured too close. Although she'd had to pick through a number of sharp little spikes along the spine, it was good to get back to decent food again. The porbeagle had shown her that. The prey ashore wasn't as plentiful, or nearly as tasty, as that which came from the sea. And the vicious creature that had hurled her into the stream, when she was quite prepared to retreat, made her wonder whether it was worthwhile venturing out of the water.

But she *did* want to see the starfish again, if only to dance for him one more time. The thing to do, she told herself, was to wait until he clicked the stones, called her from her refuge. There were other things she could do for him. She could stretch out, show him how long she was, tentacles in front, reaching as far as they could, her tail trailing behind. Then she'd withdraw everything, curl herself into a ball and roll around him, spinning through the water. The thought gave Alice a tingle of pleasure. She blinked her incredible eyes, put her arms about herself, and waited to see what would happen next.

"Well do it tonight," Billy told two of his friends in the car-park of the *Black Watch*. "No point in waiting any longer. We've got what we want."

"Thought you reckoned tomorrow," said Brian, who had to keep wiping his nose. "When the tides were good."

"The tides aren't bad tonight, mate. And the weather's packing up."

"All right," agreed Ed, a tall lad with a straggly beard. "Let's do it." He giggled, it'd be fun to stir up some real shit. "Let's get the stuff when it's dark."

"Be careful, that's all," Billy said, coughing, spitting on the ground. He'd smoked some weed that tasted like cow pats and hadn't done anything for his head. He'd settle with the creep from Glasgow later. In the meantime he'd better get things moving here. One of his clients, as he liked to call them, had seen a copper up at Harry Carter's this afternoon. It looked like the old fart was getting cold feet. In that case, he couldn't afford to waste any more time. If he was going to make a name for himself, he had to put the DDT in the water tonight. But there was no way he could do it on his own, so he'd brought these two deadheads along. And he couldn't have them messing up. He'd have to keep his eye on them. "We don't want no trouble, you understand. So be extra bloody careful."

"Course not." Brian pulled a dirty handkerchief out of his pocket. "Just want to get it done so you can give us what you promised."

"Trouble?" Ed pulled on his beard, stuck out his chest. "That's me middle name."

"Not tonight, it isn't." Billy wondered if he'd made a mistake. But it was too late to change anything now. "Just keep it cool."

TWENTY-TWO – seeing is believing

"Hello, come in," Jamie said, opening the front door to see Blanca González looking great. She'd obviously had a hot bath - her hair was damp, there was colour in her cheeks. She was a different person to the one who'd climbed shivering out of the sea, and the sight of her got all sorts of things buzzing around inside him. "Have you looked at the tape?"

"I have been too busy getting warm. We can to see it together now," Blanca replied, before following him into the living room where his parents and a large policeman, who half-rose from his chair, were waiting. "Hello," she added brightly. "I hope you were not too worried about us?"

"I was frankly terrified," admitted Molly McCory. "When you dropped Jamie off on your way back I wanted to put him to bed and keep him there forever."

"She's kidding," Jamie said. "She was fine."

"To tell you the truth, neither of us were," said William, with a rueful smile. "However, let me introduce you to Sergeant Croft. If your tape's anything like Jamie says, we'll need his help to keep the crowds under control. Once the news gets out there'll be chaos."

"That's true enough," said Croft, after shaking Blanca's hand. "Even if this, ah, creature's disappeared by then, they'll be down in their droves to see where it was."

"That's why we've got to work fast," said Jamie, taking the tape from Blanca, putting it in the video player. "Just wait till you all see this."

His mouth dried as he watched the set warm. He was bursting to see what Blanca had filmed. He glanced at his parents – their faces were stiff with expectation. They'd stared at him, open-mouthed with disbelief, when he tried to tell them what had happened after he got home. He wasn't all that good with words, but talking about Alice he'd sounded worse. In the end he'd given up, asked them to wait until Blanca arrived so they could see for themselves. Then the sergeant came in, and they'd settled down a bit. Now Blanca was here and they were about to learn what Alice was like. Christ, he was going to explode if the images didn't come up clear and sharp.

"Before we start, let's get one thing straight," said Molly, as her son's thumb hovered over the remote control. "There's something I want made clear. I can't take any more surprises. Did this squid actually pull you through the water?"

"Yes, I told you that."

"You told me a great number of things, most of which were incredible," Molly replied. She didn't want to put Jamie in a bad light, especially in front of Sergeant Croft, but what he'd said when he arrived home trembling – she still wasn't sure if it had been due to cold or excitement – had made her shake her head in disbelief. He was a strange boy, she accepted that, but what he'd said was amazing. She'd made no further comment then, just seeing him in one piece had been enough. She'd hugged him, given him hot Ovaltine, which was all he wanted – he'd been too excited to eat. He was bubbling over to tell them what had happened. She'd managed to keep quiet while he described what Alice, but when he mentioned the shark, she'd exploded. She couldn't help herself, this whole business was going from bad to worse. In spite of the fact he'd insisted that the squid was good, that it had saved him, she thought she was losing her mind. William had comforted her; she'd breathed deeply, tried to control her fear. And when Jamie said that Alice got hold of him and pulled him through the water, she'd bit her tongue, knowing if she didn't she'd become hysterical. Now, before she saw the tape, she wanted one thing made absolutely clear - how could this giant creature, which had eaten livestock, pull Jamie through the water and leave him unharmed? Such an act was beyond belief; she couldn't hold her tongue any longer. "Did it touch you? Grab you with its tentacles?"

"Yes, Mum. Two or three times."

"And *you* did nothing to stop it?" Molly turned to Blanca. She should have talked to the Spanish girl earlier, but Blanca had been grey with cold when she brought Jamie home, and only had time to let him out of the car before rushing off to *Rose Cottage*. "I mean, why didn't you interfere?"

"There was no danger, really," Blanca replied, fully understanding Molly's concern. She'd often heard her own mother chastising her brother for bringing her home covered in scratches, not looking after her as he should. "You will see it on the video."

"Come on then, let's look at it," said William quickly - they'd get nowhere until they'd seen the tape. He turned to Jamie. "Go ahead, start it."

No one said anything when the tape began, simply sat quietly, eyes fixed on Jamie diving for stones. They watched him bang them together without comment. Then the camera turned, wobbled as it recorded Blanca's reaction to the arrival of the squid. There were gasps and murmurs as Alice stopped in the water with a sudden swirl, spun toward the screen, her great arms open, suckers all down their length.

"Oh, God," Molly burst out. "That's....horrible."

"It's all right, Mum," Jamie said. "She didn't hurt me."

"Weren't you frightened?"

"No way."

"I was afraid at first," Blanca admitted. "It was so much bigger than Jamie."

"Yet, you did nothing?" Molly spluttered. "Heavens, how could you...?"

"Watch, Mum," Jamie said quickly. "Alice was frightened too."

Once more there was an uneasy silence as the squid changed from a red to grey, as if the warmth of welcome had been switched off. The camera moved forward. The squid hesitated before making a cautious approach. It turned sideways, one great eye staring at the lens, examining it carefully. Then as if satisfied, with a quick flowing movement it dashed away, returned in its former glowing red and began to spin. It circled Jamie carefully, finally reaching out to touch the boy.

"No," cried Molly. "Let him go."

"She's just playing, Mum," Jamie said. "Watch, she's having fun."

No one uttered another word while the squid performed her amazing routine. All were gripped by the way the enormous creature, so much bigger than they had imagined, so much more unreal than anything they knew, swayed in the water, came close and dashed away, spun on its tail and changed colour from red to blue to green, the iridescence of its hues caught by the camera in the clear and sparkling sea.

Molly moaned, tried to move forward as the tentacles took Jamie by the shoulders, pulled him along like a surfboard. William put an arm around her, held her until the games were done, until all the spinning, pirouetting, acrobatic move had been exhausted and Jamie dived for the stones again. This time he clapped them together slowly, and the giant squid seemed to understand. It paused for a moment, then gently floated away. One moment it filled the screen, huge eyes and arms everywhere, the next it was gone. As it went the trembling of Blanca's hands began to blur the images, the tape went black.

"Amazing," William whispered, completely overawed. He turned to Blanca. "I must congratulate you, there's never been anything like this filmed before."

"I'm glad you like it," Blanca said, her eyes dancing with joy. "But some of it is bad. I had no gloves, and my hands got very cold."

"Are you all right now?" asked William, finding it easier to ask a simple question than say anything about the scene. "Have you warmed up again?"

"Sarah ran a big bath for me at *Rose Cottage*. I feel normal now."

"My dear," Molly murmured, moving closer, putting an apologetic hand on Blanca's arm. "I'm sorry for what I said earlier, I see why you behaved the way you did. I had no right to jump down your throat like that."

"Hey, what about Alice?" demanded Jamie. He couldn't believe they were talking about anything else. *That's the trouble with grown ups. They hide.* "Don't you believe me now? She is good, she didn't hurt me. She's not dangerous, is she?"

"No, she isn't, lad," said Sergeant Croft, slight tremor in his voice. "What she did was incredible. Even better than *Free Willy*." He turned to Blanca. "You did a fine job with that camera."

"It was Jamie. He is very brave."

"But what about *Alice*?" Jamie couldn't believe it. They were off-track again. "What are we going to do for her? You've seen what she's like."

"We have," said William. "And I agree with you absolutely now. We really have to try and save her. Make sure she avoids being captured."

"We've got to send her away. I don't want her to go but..." Jamie paused, the thought of never seeing Alice again was heartbreaking, but anything was better than letting her die. "She can't stay here."

"Could you send her off with those stones? The way you banged them at the end?" William asked, thinking that if a dog could remember two hundred words, this *Architeuthis* was bright enough to follow Jamie's signals a second time. "Do you think that might work?"

"I don't know," Jamie said. "She likes it here."

"What the devil's a thing like that doing around Culloch anyway?" Sergeant Croft asked briskly. The tape was impressive, but left too many questions that needed replies. His policeman's mind demanded answers. "That's what I'd like to know."

"I wanted to know the same thing," Blanca replied, her face unusually thoughtful. "While I was in Oban I checked through some references. I think I know why."

"For the food?" Croft turned to William. "You told me that's why it came ashore."

"I did," William admitted, watching Jamie run the tape back slowly, seeing everything in reverse. "Now I'm not so sure. Perhaps something sent her here."

"I'm sure it did," said Blanca. "And I know what it was."

"What?"

"There was a ship from Portugal that sank off the coast a few months ago. It was carrying medical supplies. I remember the incident. I checked the facts again before I came down here."

Blanca recalled the sinking, it had reminded her of the ill-fated *Prestige*, whose oil slick had blackened the beaches along the northern coast of Spain. She remembered the thick clogging layers, dripping off the rocks like tar, birds pulled from the sea, their feathers glued, their eyes frantically appealing for help. Her brother had joined the thousands who spent their Christmas holidays, white-coated and exhausted, scrubbing the coastline from dawn to dusk, only to be frustrated as fresh tides brought in new layers of black clinging sludge. Children asked their parents why they'd been punished, why the sea brought in *carbón*, the coal the disobedient were threatened with when the Three Kings arrived with gifts for the good. On some beaches black crosses were erected in protest against the mishandling of the whole disastrous affair.

"The ship had, as part of its cargo, oestrogen," she went on. "I think that might have had a bad effect on the wildlife. I think that's what drove the squid away."

"I remember the sinking," muttered Croft. "We got a report from the Coastguard. In case anything got washed up. There were no survivors, were there?"

"No, everyone died."

"But could oestrogen have had such a disastrous effect?" asked William, frowning. "I mean, it would have become diluted pretty quickly."

"Of course, but we don't know how contaminated this squid became. Or what affect the drug had on its glands."

"Oestrogen?" William persisted. "That's prescribed for women with menstrual problems. But, on a squid, I'm not sure it would have any effect at all?"

"That's the whole point – we just don't know. It can completely change the mood of some people. Alter the way their bodies function, even the way they think." Blanca ran fingers through her long dark hair. "With horses it makes them mature earlier."

"Of course, I've used it to induce ovulation in mares."

"That is precisely why that particular hormone is so successful." Blanca smiled briefly. "It is known to have a powerful romantic effect."

"On giant squids?"

"I think this squid is female. That is why Jamie calls her Alice," Blanca replied with a smile. "But nobody knows what a concentrated dose of animal-based oestrogen could have on a sea creature that has never been exposed to it before. It can enhance the ability to sense odours enormously. Perhaps that's why this *calamar* could detect the smell of food from so far away. And, as you say, it causes an increase in sexual desire in many mammals."

"No way!," exploded Molly. "Are you actually suggesting that this giant squid has fallen in love with my son?"

"Mum, come on," Jamie said quickly. "I told you, we're just friends."

"And why is this the only squid affected?" asked William putting out a hand to calm his wife. "Why aren't there hundreds of them?"

"Why aren't they all over the place, dancing and singing and clapping hands?" asked Molly. She knew she sounded hysterical, but the strain was beginning to tell. "There must be others."

"Perhaps there are," said Blanca. "But they haven't been discovered yet."

"Alice is here because she's intelligent. She wanted to see what the land is like, maybe the others aren't the same" Jamie said – they were getting nowhere fast. "Anyway, it doesn't matter *why* she got here. She's here now. We've got to so something. We've got to send her away."

"Then we'd better do it pretty quickly, lad," said Tony Croft. It was all very well to talk about theories, but there was real work to be done. "You'd better know it, my boy, there are a couple of other parties not all that keen on letting her go. One wants to poison the water. The others would like to put her in a tank and invite the world to see her."

"Who?" Jamie's heart gave a desperate lurch. "Who are these bastards?"

—⚏—

"Dropped in a bit early," Angus Douglas said breezily, his portly figure framed by the door of Malcolm

Stewart's apartment. *Catch the sod on the back foot. Get there before he's ready*, he'd told himself, drinking a large scotch in the bar of the *Royal Hotel* where he'd taken a room for the night. He had no intention of getting breathalysed driving back to Culloch in the dark. "That all right with you?"

"Of course." Malcolm glanced at his watch. It was a little after five, almost an hour earlier than agreed. "Come in. Can I get you something?"

"If you had a single malt, I wouldn't say no." Angus looked around the comfortable room. It had a view across to Mull. "Nice digs," he added, with a sound that might have been a laugh. "Must say you vets live high on the hog."

"Thank you." Malcolm went to the bar. Still smarting from his dismissal by Charlie Coots, he'd sent his wife and twin daughters the cinema, intending to tackle Douglas alone. He wasn't quite ready, but that didn't matter. Enough scotch and this domineering lump of lard would be putty in his hands. "I've *Oban* or *Tomatin*, which would you prefer?"

"*Tomatin* would suit me nicely. After all, we've really got something to celebrate, haven't we Mister Stewart?"

"Have we?" Malcolm poured a large whisky for Douglas, a smaller one for himself. "Last time we spoke you were threatening me with sedition."

"The treat might still hold. Depends what you tell me."

"About what?" Malcolm handed Douglas, now ensconced in a leather armchair, his drink. "What did you have in mind?"

"Let's not get onto the silly-bugger circuit again." Angus sipped a little *Tomatin*, nodded his approval. "Just plonk yourself down and tell me everything you know about the Kraken that's taken up residence in Culloch."

"I, ah," stammered Malcolm, startled enough to pause when Angus held up a pudgy hand. "Before you begin a load of bollocks about conger eels, giant cockles or Nessie, even though she might have her place in all this, listen to me a moment," the Chairman of the Town Council said firmly, then went on to reveal what he'd discovered in his extensive library, what *The Natural History of Norway* had disclosed about Kraken. "So, let's not beat about any more bushes," he concluded. "We both know what we're talking about, what took the foal, the calf and my Blackface ram. And we both know what we want to do with this creature from the deep."

"I see," Malcolm muttered, still trying to gather his thoughts. This Douglas character was more than just an unattractive face. If he'd got that close to the truth without any scientific training, it wouldn't take long before half the world knew what was in Culloch harbour, and were forming their own plans to entrap the beast. "What do *you* want, exactly?"

"I want the Kraken in a tank. Right down there on the waterfront. I want this creature, dead or alive, to put my town back on the map." Angus drank the rest of his whisky, held out his glass. "And you, if I'm not very much mistaken, would like all the glory you can get. That's good scotch, by the way. How about another."

"Of course." Malcolm refilled both glasses, realising that Douglas could probably drink the entire bottle without showing any effect. "In that case, what are we going to do?" he asked carefully, returning to his chair. "Got anything in mind?"

"This is where you come in, Mister Stewart. You're the expert. You must have some experience of trapping animals. A wild cat, perhaps? An unruly dog? So, tell me how would you go about catching a giant squid?"

"They won't waste much time once they put their heads together," Croft said, after telling Jamie that the Chairman of the Town Council had gone to Oban to meet Malcolm Stewart. "It's not like Douglas to hang about. He's off for the entire night. That means he's up to something serious."

"They'll have it all sorted out by midnight," agreed William. "By then they'll know exactly what they're going to do."

"Then we've only got tomorrow to protect her," said Jamie. He glanced at the window, the sky was beginning to darken. "It's too late to do anything now."

"It still doesn't give us much time, lad." said Croft. "Especially as we have no plans how to go about it." He chewed thoughtfully. "It could take days to get any sort of trap set up."

"What exactly would they do with the squid?" asked Blanca. "She has done very little harm."

"Angus would like to display her like a set of antlers on a wall," explained William. "That'd show everybody how clever he is. What's more, a display like that would bring in bus-loads of tourists, make our town and its chairman celebrities all over the world."

"But, why? If they want to show off Alice, can't they use Blanca's tape?" asked Jamie. "You said it was amazing. There'd never been anything like it before."

"Silly, isn't it?" William gave an ironic smile. "We've got all they need, but can't show it to them yet. Not until Alice is sent away."

"But..." Jamie pulled his hat down tighter. It looked as if he was on his own. *Why can't we tell these people to back off? Get the hell away from here.* "But what about the vet in Oban, Dad? Doesn't he like animals?"

"There isn't much doubt that Malcolm Stewart is in it for the glory. Every drop he can get."

"That is true," Blanca agreed. "He is not a very nice man."

"And they're both very clever," murmured Croft, opening a fresh packet of gum, which he offered around but all declined. "And we're stuck until we know what they're going to do."

"Can't we find out?" muttered Jamie, his voice tight. "Give Stewart ring, Dad. Ask him."

"I'll try, but he's not likely to give away very much"

"Shit," Jamie muttered, but nobody seemed to mind. "That's one lot," he said, turning to the sergeant. "You said there were two. The others were going to use some sort of poison."

"Aye, I did," Croft replied. "Harry Carter and Billy the Dealer have a drum of DDT. But Constable Roberts is taking care of that. I think he's got it under control."

"Nothing's under control," Molly McCory interrupted impatiently. She'd remained simmering while she listened to Sergeant Croft, said nothing as Jamie's determination grew, but had to put stop to her son's endeavours before something really dreadful happened. "I've had enough of this, I really have. God alone knows what's going on in this little town. But, as for *poison*, that's the limit." She swung savagely to Jamie. "I don't want you going near the water again. Is that clear? I'm sorry about Alice, but I don't want you back in the sea."

"Mum...?"

"Give me your word on that." Molly stared at Jamie, wishing she could soften the pain in his eyes, but she'd had enough. He'd already told her he'd almost been attacked by a shark. She'd seen for herself what this enormous squid was capable of. She'd been appalled by the size of the creature, yet had said little when it tossed him about like a toy. But now, with talk of poison in the water, she had more than she could bear. There wasn't going to be any more. This was the end of it. It didn't matter if Jamie never spoke to her again, he wasn't going back into the water, at least not until this was all over and done. "Not even near the coast. Is that understood?"

"Yes, Mum."

"You promise me that?"

"Yes, Mum, I do."

After that there was a long silence in the room.

TWENTY-THREE – the tide turns

"It's getting dark," whispered Billy the Dealer from under a tree in the Common, where he huddled with Brian who kept wiping his nose with the back of his hand, and Ed who was so tall he had to stoop to hear him. "We could do it now."

"You know where it is?" asked Ed, resisting a desire to giggle. This was totally exciting. "This....what'd you say it was?"

"DDT. Used to kill everything. So deadly it got banned."

"Then what's it going to do to me?" sniffed Brian, asking himself if it was worth it - even though Billy had promised him freebies for a week. "Shit, I know you want to make a name for yourself, but what if it gets all over us?"

"It won't." Billy pulled three pairs of rubber gloves out of his pocket. "I looked it up in the cyber-cafe. Put these on and you'll be all right."

"Great. No prints, either." Ed laughed as he eased a hand into a glove, wiggled his fingers. "Nurse, pass me the scalpel."

"Come on, let's make a start." Billy looked up the darkening road in the direction of Harry Carter's stables, where he'd last seen the DDT. It was his game now – he and his mates were leaving Harry out of it, going it alone. "Just up here. It's not far."

"Up where?" Brian asked. "Who's got the stuff?"

"Harry Carter. But don't worry about him. He's probably pissed by now."

"Yeah, most likely." Despite the warmth of the evening, Brian was beginning to shiver. "But when we get it, what are we going to do?"

"Piece of cake, I've got it all worked out," replied Billy. He'd decided about mid-afternoon to tackle the job himself, made up his mind after he heard from one of his clients that Harry was losing his bottle. Seems that Constable Roberts had been sniffing around. Okay, if the old boy had lost it, he'd use these two. He only hoped they kept their heads. They'd have to be real careful with that rusty drum. Decent knock and it'd be squirting all over the place, but if they watched themselves they'd be all right. "First we get hold of it. Then we roll it over the grass and pour it in the river."

"That's it?" queried Ed, running his fingers through his straggly beard. "No keyholes to pick?"

"That's all. Just be quiet when we get there."

"Yeah," muttered Brian. "We could go to jail for this."

"Got to catch us first." Ed released a giggle, held up a rubber-gloved finger. "Wait for me, nurse. Keep nice and warm. Be back as soon as this's over."

Shuffling, looking over their shoulders, they set off up the road.

Blanca González felt wonderfully alert as she walked up the hill to *Rose Cottage*. She had remained later than expected at the McCory's, going over her schedule for the following day with William, who became quietly efficient while he worked. After the awkward pause, when Jamie was forbidden by his mother to go near the water, the boy said goodnight and went to bed, muttering that no one really cared about Alice, that no one wanted to help. Soon after that Sergeant Croft left, saying he'd do his best to find out what Angus Douglas and Malcolm Stewart were planning, and let William know. Molly, silently, went into the kitchen to make sandwiches. Blanca, on the other hand, was unable to remain quiet, her mind was too full of the dancing squid, and her heart went out to Jamie. She understood why his parents had retreated into everyday tasks, hid behind the work they understood, but she sensed they were bristling beneath the skin, that there was a great deal more to be said.

"Is there nothing we can do?" she finally asked, putting aside the timetable they'd prepared. "I feel so sorry for Jamie. He wants to save Alice so much."

"So do I," William replied. "But handling a creature that size is impossible."

"Isn't there some animal protection agency we could contact?"

"For a giant squid?" He shook his head. "Anyway, that would only make matters worse."

"How?"

"Word would get out. Any publicity, good or bad, would have people here by the thousands. That might be what Angus Douglas wants, but it'd do Alice a great deal of harm."

"I feel so helpless."

"Well, neither of us can do anything tonight. And tomorrow we're busy. The Chattans think they've got a new case of Mad Cow Disease. I have to go up there first thing. I could lose my licence if I don't. As for you,

you've a full day ahead." He tapped her ample list. Many of the locals, keen to meet the new vet, had put off appointments until she began. There were half a dozen small animals that needed to be vaccinated against rabies or distemper, some that had to be treated for respiratory conditions. At mid-day she was to perform keyhole surgery to neuter a female cat. "And, as I said, whatever we did would involve others. Before we knew it, the place would be crawling with politicians and marine biologists, all wanting their piece of the pie."

They talked a little longer, then Molly came in with a plate of sandwiches, cups of tea, saying she'd offered Jamie cheese and Vegemite grilled on toast, but he didn't even look at it. She'd found him sitting in front of his computer, a purplish-red *Architeuthis*, the size of a bus, filling the screen.

"I feel dreadful making him promise to stay out of the water," she'd murmured. "But I couldn't do anything else. You do understand that, don't you, Will?"

"Yes, the sea's far too dangerous at the moment."

"It's... it's all become so *awful*. I couldn't believe it when Tony Croft talked about poison. It sent shivers down my spine." She looked down at her cup of untasted tea, replaced it on the table. "Oh, I wish that *thing* had never come near the place. I wish Jamie had never set eyes on Alice."

"It's not the squid's fault," Blanca said. "It's like all the other animals that come close to us. They do what we make them do."

"I suppose so, but..." Molly stared at Blanca. "There's nothing *you* could do? I mean, you seem to know so much?"

"There's nothing any of us can do at the moment," said William. "And Blanca's going to be tied up all day tomorrow. Let's hope the police can put a stop to it. At least, as far as the poison is concerned."

Soon after that Blanca had left, walked up the hill to feel warm air beginning to blow in from the south. That is not a good sign, she told herself. If this place is anything like Cantabria, we will have rain tomorrow. Gales too. Perhaps that will help. It might send Alice away. She paused a moment, looked across the seemingly tranquil town, then went on wondering what the new day would bring.

Harry Carter heard them coming. He listened intently as three hushed voices in the uneven dark turned into shadowy figures, keeping close to garden fences, hopping beneath street lights, making their furtive way up the road to his stable. He'd been expecting them ever since Constable Roberts found him sitting on the drum of DDT, after he put it around that he wanted a word with Billy. But, until now, the little bugger kept well away - like a crow that has seen a farmer with a gun.

Finally, after the sun went down, Billy turned up as expected - with a couple of mates. Harry grunted with satisfaction when he recognised the Dealer – the little sod would get a welcome he wasn't expecting. Harry was sitting in the darkness behind the stable door, a double-barrelled shotgun across his knees, not a drop of scotch in sight. It was time he pulled his finger out, he'd kept telling himself all afternoon, time he got back to where he'd been when he started up the stables, before the booze began to destroy him, when he still had plenty of grit.

"Right, lads show yourselves," he said, as one of his horses gave a nervous whinny. "Let me see how fast you can run."

"This is it," said Billy, still confident. One line of coke had been enough to set him off – like he said, he wasn't a user, but there were times when a line was needed. Only thing, though, he should've given Brian more, the poor bugger had the shakes. "The big building up on the corner."

"You cover the front. I'll take the back," whispered Ed, tugging his beard, unable to stay still for the excitement. "That sound good to you?"

"Keep quiet and follow me. If anyone's there, I'll do the talking."

"Right, gov. You give the orders."

"Are you sure we should be doing this?" sniffled Brian. "I mean, what the fuck? They catch us, we're in deep shit."

"We're doing a bit of public good," replied Billy. He could see that the door of the stable was open. There was no sign of Harry or anyone else. "We're cleaning up the place."

"Yeah." Ed giggled. "Doing a bit of good for the planet."

"Come on. Let's get our hands on the drum."

Harry Carter waited until they appeared at the door - three uncertain figures peering into the gloom - then he emerged, shotgun carefully hidden by his side. "Looking for something, Billy?" he barked, and watched them jump like they'd shit themselves.

"That you, Harry?" Billy the Dealer stammered, trying to work out what had gone wrong. The old fart should be staggering drunk by now, or snoring his head off somewhere. "How you doing?"

"I'm fine. Fuck off."

"Let's get out of here," Brian spluttered, turning to go, but Ed caught him by the shoulder. "Hang on, mate," he said. "There's three of us."

"Thought we'd do the job without you, Harry." Billy lifted his voice, encouraged by Ed's remark. "Get rid of that drum you were worried about."

"The drum's fine, thanks."

"Bit dodgy though, isn't it?" Billy took a half-step forward, Ed beside him, holding Brian. "Could start leaking any minute. Decent kick and who knows what. Be spilling all over the place. Get into the horses. You wouldn't want that, would you now? Messing up your stable?"

"How about your whisky?" said Ed. "Run out, has it? I could get you a bottle if you like."

"You trying to take the piss, you little prick?"

"Not taking nothing. Not little, either. Six foot two in me socks."

"We don't have to do business like this," said Billy with an exaggerated shrug. "All you got to do is look the other way. When you turn round, the drum's gone."

"Magic." Ed fluffed out his beard. "Hocus pocus."

"I'll give you hocus-fucking-pocus, sunshine." Harry produced the gun, both barrels pointing at the lads. "If you're not out of here before I count to three, you'll find yourself in Kingdom Come."

"If you use that, you're in real trouble," Billy said defiantly – he wasn't going to give in now. "Remember what happened to...what's-his-name."

"One..." began Harry

"Come on, Harry. We talked about this, remember? We're working for Culloch. Getting rid of them sea-slugs that've been taking stuff. Doing some good round here." Words poured from Billy in an attempt to get the Harry to cool down. *Christ, he was losing a great chance to get really known. Business would go through the roof if he pulled this off.* "Think what they'd say about you? Local hero. Whisky galore? That'd only be the start of it."

"Two..."

"I think he's serious." said Ed, coming down fast, beginning to strip off his gloves. "We better take some notice."

"If he shoots us, he goes to jail."

"If I shoot you, you'll go to Hell. Three..." Harry fired one barrel into the air with a blast that rang through the stable, startling the horses, turning the three lads into athletes racing down the road. Ed, long legs pumping, was out in front. Billy the Dealer in the middle, Brian trailing way behind. "Don't come back," Harry shouted. "Don't even think about it."

"Well, we've got that sorted," Constable Roberts said to Jack, barman from the *Harbour Light*, as he watched the three lads turn a bend of the road, huffing and puffing as they ran away. "The sergeant will be well pleased about that."

"You going to do anything about Harry?" Jack asked, moving away from the tree he and Roberts had used as cover. "Firing a gun inside town limits?"

"Not really. If he turns up with the drum in the morning, we'll call it quits."

"Think he'll do that?"

"Sure of it. Harry's learnt a lesson or two." Roberts was pleased the old chap had come to his senses - less concerned that he, the hard-nosed copper, was turning soft. It was a nice feeling, really. "All I got to do now is find out what Angus Douglas and his mate are up to. Croft's not told me yet. But that shouldn't be too difficult. He'll give his hand away soon enough."

Jamie stared at the image on the screen, at the giant creature known as *Architeuthis*, at the report he'd turned up about a sailor in the nineteen-sixties who had seen a squid lying beside his ship. The size of the *thing*, as he called it, had amazed him. He reckoned its body was so enormous he couldn't have got his arms around it.

"Alice is like that," Jamie whispered. "There's so much life in her."

The eyes of the beast had also impressed the sailor. He thought they were looking right back at him, staring up as he stared down.

"Course they were," Jamie added. "They were seeing what sort of *thing* you were. Working out if you were safe or not."

He changed the image to a section of skin from a sperm whale, showing sucker-marks left by a giant squid, after a *life-and-death* battle. It made him think of how Alice had come to his rescue when the porbeagle was circling around.

"She helped me," he said. "And I've got to do something for her now."

Jamie clicked again and found a report on the largest squid ever brought ashore. It measured fifty-five feet from the tip of its tentacles to the end of the tail, and had been caught by three fishermen who dragged it onto the beach and tied it to a tree. When the tide went out the great creature was found to be dead. Later, it was cut up for dog meat.

"They're not going to do that to you, Alice. I've promised Mum I wouldn't go back into the water again, but I've got to do what I can."

After that Jamie read the article on the latest catch – the one they were calling the Colossal Squid, which had been pulled out of the depths near Antarctica. The fishermen who brought it aboard were reeling in their line, having hooked a Patagonian toothfish, when they realised that something had caught their catch. It took them two hours to haul the moribund squid out of the water. It died soon afterwards, but the scientific world couldn't get over the fact that it had been the first intact male ever landed. Saddened by the fate of this great living creature, one that could have known Alice, Jamie finally turned out his light, lay in bed thinking about the morning. Before he went to sleep he ate the cheese on toast his mother had left him. It was cold, but tasted all right. He thought he'd better do something for her. She wasn't going to be too happy with what he had in mind for the morning.

By midnight, the bottle of *Tomatin* behind them, the *Oban* whisky begun, Angus Douglas and Malcolm Stewart had decided what to do. They'd not come to a conclusion easily. For several hours the vet had wavered, reluctant to reveal to this arrogant pot-bellied politician what he had in mind. But slowly, coming to realise that he could do little on his own, he'd outlined his scheme and agreed to work with the Culloch chairman, who said he could provide the necessary boats, nets, knowledge of the coastline, and several pairs of capable hands. Without them the plan wouldn't work.

"It's still going to take some doing," Malcolm said, when they finally reached agreement. "They're delicate creatures, no matter how big they are. The flesh would tear if you used a hook."

"I don't want it minced," Douglas replied, holding out his glass for more. "I want it alive in a tank. Swimming around for the world to see."

"Have you thought about talking to Dun..stiff..ah, Dunstaffnage?" Malcolm asked, aware that the scotch had thickened his tongue. "They're the experts."

"I don't want anyone to know anything about it, apart from you and me. Didn't I make that clear?" Angus had had enough of this weasel with the funny laugh who couldn't hold his scotch. "Stop buggering about and tell if there's anything more I should know about the Kraken."

"What, ah, are you going to do when you've got it?" Malcolm poured two more whiskies, his own very small. "While you're building your tank?"

"That's simple, Mister Stewart. I'll get all the boats in the quay to block up the harbour entrance. Our little catch will be quite happy there until we can get it a better home. Now, have you got anything else to tell me? If not, I'll be on my way."

After that remark, little was said. Both men sipped their final whisky planning what to do next. Malcolm doubted if the squid would remain in the harbour, entrance blocked or not. It'd probably find a way of escape, or simply lift itself back into the sea. But that wasn't important. He'd be credited with capturing the first live and healthy *Architeuthis* in the history of the beast, and that would be enough for him. Angus also felt he had little to lose whatever happened after the creature was caught. If they got this thing ashore he'd have his picture taken with it. Dozens of angles, dozens of times, film, tape, wherever they had. Let the whole world know where Culloch was. He'd be the one they'd have to thank when they visited the museum, the theme park or whatever he had constructed in the name of Angus Archibald Douglas. Fame was beckoning in the distance. There was a knighthood around the corner.

"I'll give Tommy Tranter a bell when I get back to the *Royal*," Angus said, pushing himself out of the leather armchair he'd remained in all evening, apart from standing when the vet's wife and twin daughters arrived with plates of cheese and biscuits to say good-night. "He's my handyman. His brother, Freddy, has a boat. Nets and, what else did you say you wanted, a fresh-killed lamb as bait?"

"That'll do fine," Malcolm replied, seeing two huge Angus Douglases. "What time do we leave in the morning?"

"First thing. Make sure you don't oversleep."

TWENTY-FOUR – broken lines

Early next morning, before it was light, the giant squid moved into Culloch harbour. She'd waited all night by the Tombstone hoping the starfish would appear. But there had been no call, no clicking of stones, and her hearts had sunk lower and lower. From time to time she'd slept a little, half-dozing, moving just enough to keep herself in place, but would have instantly become alert had there been any sign of the friend she waited for. And all the while, in the waters flowing steadily by, she became aware of a change in the weather.

There was an easing of pressure around her, a slow and increasing swell, which told her things were altering in the world she knew. It was a warning she was accustomed to, a foretelling of when to plunge deep to avoid the crashing waves that lashed the surface, the violence released by the wind. Like most animals, on land or sea, her sensitivities were her counsellors – there had been times when they saved her life.

She should leave, she knew. It was time to depart these shores. But the desire to see the starfish one last time made her stay, even say goodbye to his female companion with the child - though, she hoped that by now the offspring in its egg-case had been placed in a safe dry niche, had begun to breathe on its own.

So, instead of obeying her instincts, of returning to the depths, Alice had remained in the kelp until morning.

SQUID

Then, in the hope of a final farewell, she returned to the harbour, to the river mouth where she'd first come ashore. This time, however, her approach was not due to any urge from below, the strange intensity in the currents, that had altered her life, was barely detectable now. Nor did the promise of delicious food bring her close to shore. This time the decision came from the heart. She had become, in the past few days, her own person, someone who could think for herself.

She really did want to see the starfish one last time, even if she couldn't dance for him; she needed a moment of close contact to send her back to the depths. As for those silly ideas of bonding, they belonged to an immature past. But the gentle touch of his tiny tentacles, perhaps a small surge together through the waves, would allow her to leave content. With that in mind she was incapable of resisting a return to the river mouth and, although she'd only ever left the sea under the cover of the darkness, Alice wasn't afraid of the approaching light. She felt sure that she'd be safe.

"That was Tommy Tranter on the phone, Angus Douglas's handyman," Sergeant Croft said to Constable Roberts as he came out of his office, opening a new packet of gum. "The chairman called him late last night. Told him he wants his brother, Freddy's, boat with half a mile of full strength net, ready to go out by mid-morning."

"What's the old bugger up to now?" Roberts asked. Croft hadn't revealed nearly enough. Even when they'd talked about how Harry Carter had dealt with Billy and his mates, there'd been little more than a crisp, *well done*. Fine, that was his way of saying thanks, but it was time to tell the full story. The waterfront was buzzing with gossip. A couple walking home after the pubs closed last night said they'd seen Nessie in the harbour. "Going into the bait business, is he?" Robert asked with a knowing look. "Going to catch himself a conger eel?"

"What makes you say that?"

"I've got a pretty good idea what's going on, sir," Roberts replied, knowing he'd hit the mark. "What with all the talk that's been flying around, I didn't think the old codger would waste any time."

"You been talking to Will McCory?"

"I don't really need to, sir. But I think it's time you filled me in. When things get moving, and that could be any moment now, we'll need all the help we can get."

"Well, I'll tell you what I know so far," the sergeant said, realising he had no choice. Alice would soon be front-page news, and there was little point in keeping quiet any longer. He began by describing what Blanca González had taped in the water, went on to talk about the hours he and Will had spent considering their options, and finally admitted that said he was on Jamie's side, wanted to save the squid as much as anyone, even though it might cost him his job. However, he added, neither he nor Will knew what Douglas and Stewart were planning. They guessed the pair would attempt to catch the squid, but had no idea how. Though it looked as if the request for Freddy's boat, a net, fresh lamb for bait, made their intentions clear. "My guess is, they'll try their luck about noon," Croft added. "There's a full tide then."

"What you want me to do?" Roberts asked when the sergeant stopped to pop in a stick of gum in his mouth. He'd listened with increasing excitement while Croft related what he knew. The whole business was fantastic, sent a shiver down his spine. My God, he was actually taking part in an amazing event. He was in the front line now. "Would you like me to get my mates together?"

"Yes, but don't do anything rash at the moment."

"What about a stand-by craft?" Roberts asked. "Something with an outboard motor? So we can move fast if we have to?"

"Good thinking, Sergeant," Croft replied. "Now, I'll see if I can get hold of Will McCory. He'll need to know what's going on."

William McCory, however, was out of touch. At that very moment he was pinned between a split-pine gate and an Ayrshire the Chattan twins thought might be suffering from Mad Cow Disease. The cow certainly had all the symptoms. It was standing awkwardly, its back bowed low. When William tried to get close it lurched toward him, pushing him against the gate, smashing his mobile phone.

"Bloody hell," said Ian. "Did it get you?"

"No, I'm all right." William replied. "The horn went into the wood. Though I heard something snap." He pulled the broken phone out of a jacket pocket. "Shit, it's useless now."

"Sorry," said Alec. "Put it on the bill."

"I'll see about that," William replied dismissively, easing himself away from the Ayrshire, which stood unsteadily in the corner of the pen. "I can't do much for the cow, I'm afraid. I don't think it's Mad Cow, but we shouldn't take any chances."

"Christ," muttered Alec. "That's all we need, another outbreak here."

"It's been bad enough with the weather," added Ian, his country face creased with concern. "Just got the blueberry shelter up again, now it's looking like there's more gales on the way."

"As for that thing the other night that took the calf." His brother scratched his short grey hair. "They're saying it was Nessie. Any truth in that?"

"The town's full of rumours," William muttered. "Now, about this cow, I'm afraid we've got to put her down." He went on to explain that the only way to determine whether it was Mad Cow Disease or not was to slaughter the animal, remove its head and have the brain tissue checked. "I'm sorry, but we've got no choice. In the meantime, you must contain the rest of the herd. They can't be moved off your land."

"I thought there was a new test," said Ian, wanting to know as soon as he could, afraid if the result was positive they'd lose all the cattle they had. "One you can do on the spot."

"Only if you have the equipment," William replied. "You need about five minutes with an electrocardiogram. The results go into a special program on a laptop. It gives you a pretty accurate reading, but I don't have anything like that with me now."

"Couldn't you get hold of what you need?"

"It might be faster if we got to work straight away. I could put her down now, if you like."

"Is there no alternative?"

"Not really, the government rules are strict. And the faster you get a negative result, the faster you'll clear the herd." William regretted the pressure he was putting them under, but knew he had no choice. "You'll get compensation."

"Money's not going to replace old Bess," said Alec, his hand on the cow. "We've had her since she was a calf."

"Then, let's wait. I'll get the equipment."

"No," said Ian, facing the facts. "Do it now. We want to be absolutely sure."

Half an hour later, William was driving back to Culloch, the cow's head in a plastic bag, his heart going out to the Chattans, his concern for his son rising. Jamie said he wouldn't go into the water, but the promise had come hard.

Jamie McCory answered the house-phone as soon as it rang. There was no one else around. His father was out at work. His mother was shopping. He'd got up early, eaten his breakfast, given his mother a smile saying how good the new muesli was. Pretty soon his father went into the surgery to get Blanca started and then set out to see someone's cow. His mother, after kissing him lightly on the cheek, said she had to go down to the supermarket.

"You'll be here when I get back?" she'd said, making as little of the question as possible, even though it knotted her stomach. "There's a new dish I was reading about. Mushrooms with melted goat's cheese. I thought I'd try it for your lunch."

"Sounds good, Mum."

"Any plans for this morning?"

"I'm looking up things on the web." It wasn't exactly a lie, there was a ton of stuff he wanted to look at. "Just to see what I can find."

"Yes, well..." Molly stood awkwardly for a moment. "I won't be long."

Shortly after she'd gone, while Jamie stood indecisively, torn between obeying his mother and what he knew he had to do, the telephone rang. He snatched it up to hear Sergeant Croft's voice asking for his father. "I couldn't get through on his mobile. Have you any idea where he is?"

"He's looking at a cow."

"Do you know where?"

"He didn't say."

"What about your mother, is she around? There's something..."

"If it's got anything to do with Alice, you can tell me about it," Jamie interrupted. "Is it anything about the poison?"

"No, I'm glad to say that's been taken care of."

"What then? Is it about the others? Those two who were going to catch Alice? Have you heard anything about them?"

"I have, as a matter of fact." For the second time that morning Tony Croft decided not to conceal from what he knew about Douglas and Stewart. Anyway, there was every chance that Will would call, and the boy could pass the message on. "They'll be down at the quay about mid-day with a boat and a net. It looks as if they're going to try and catch the squid."

"What can we do to stop them?"

"I'm not sure. That's why I wanted to talk to your dad."

"Can't you arrest them?"

"I doubt it. It's not illegal to fish."

"It's illegal...." Jamie was going to say *murder*, but that didn't make sense. No one else felt the same as he did about Alice. No one really understood. Except maybe Blanca, and she was busy in the surgery. He was on his own, like he was when he smashed Alf's speargun. He had to do what he could. "Aren't there any rules?" he persisted. "Common Market regulations, things like that?"

"None that I know of."

"There should be," Jamie said vigorously, knowing he was wasting his time. *I'll leave a note*, he was about to add, but that would give the game away. "I'll see if I can find Dad," he muttered. "Let him know you want to talk."

"Good lad. Now, don't do anything on your own."

"I'll try to get in touch with Mum," Jamie replied, ignoring the remark.

"If you find her, get her to call me."

"I'll do that."

Both put down the phone, their expressions grave. Croft was worried what the boy might do. Jamie knew he had no choice.

At that very moment, John Forrester, seasoned reporter from Inverness, who'd been with Charlie Coots at the Glencruitten Golf Club when Malcolm Stewart rang in an attempt to interest the *Oban Times* in Alice, was reading an item he'd sent to his own paper, headed: NESSIE IN CULLOCH?

After returning to Inverness, Forrester decided to do the piece. Charlie was a competent editor, but could be awfully stubborn at times. He obviously had little respect for the vet and his tale about deep sea monsters lurking in the Firth of Lorne. However, there might *just* be something in it. And Nessie was always good news. After driving home, Forrester knocked out a few hundred words, sent them off STOP PRESS, and here they were this morning in the *Inverness Gazette*.

"Should, at least, make the Oban vet happy," the reporter murmured, reaching for the phone. "Pity I didn't get his name."

A few moments later he was speaking to Davie Forbes, a photographer in Culloch, who made a living snapping weddings, christenings and the occasional stag-night do. However, because of the awful weather, business hadn't been too good of late.

"You could be in for a bit of luck," Forrester told him, after the initial greetings were over. "Try hanging around the port today. You never know what might turn up."

"This anything to do with your bit in the *Gazette*?"

"Could be, Davie, could be. What have you heard about Nessie?"

"Too bloody much, if you want the truth." Davie was a thin, balding man, who doubted that anything existed unless he saw it through a well-focussed lens. "The town's full of it. Some layabout claims to have seen her swimming down the Orchy. A drunken couple saw her in the port."

"Then keep your camera ready. If you get anything, give me a ring."

Wondering at Forrester's interest, Davie put down the phone, checked his camera bag and locked the shop. There was a fresh wind blowing, white-caps were beginning to form out at sea. If he got nothing else, there might be a shot or two of waves cracking into the harbour wall, masts making interesting angles - something to sell to the tourists if they ever showed up again.

The first day's work for Blanca González began smoothly. She liked the surgery, it was neatly arranged, and she immediately warmed toward Lucy, William

McCory's competent nurse. After he left them together, Lucy welcomed her eagerly, saying how badly they needed help, as Mister McCory was out so much. What's more, there was a sudden rise in the number of cats and dogs requiring attention.

"I think they want to see you, really," Lucy added, smiling shyly. "They don't know quite what to expect. I heard some of them practising their Spanish in the waiting room. Though, I think they'll be too shy to use it."

"It is good they have confidence in me," Blanca replied. "Sometimes, you know, they like to wait and see if a new person is what they expected."

"Oh, you've been given an excellent report by Mister McCory." Lucy tapped her grey hair, making sure the bun was in place. She liked this girl, who looked very competent in her leaf-green uniform, and seemed eager to get started. "Now, let's see, the first person on your list is Missus McPherson. Her cat's got the sniffles, she says."

"The sniffles?"

"It's nose is running. It might be diabetes, but you'd be the best judge of that."

"We'll take a few tests and see."

With that Blanca began - lifting small animals out of cages, weighing the creatures on digital scales, checking rectal temperatures, examining mouths, ears and eyes, feeling for broken bones. It was good to be back at work again, even if some of the locals were almost impossible to understand. Lucy, however, translated and the morning sped rapidly by, even though her mind kept returning to Jamie McCory. She also wondered what Malcolm Stewart was doing. He'd phoned but she hadn't taken his call.

TWENTY-FIVE – the calm before...

Malcolm Stewart drove down to Culloch, dark glasses clamped over red-rimmed eyes, head splitting, stomach threatening to turn over. Each time he swung around a bend, his BMW following Angus Douglas's Bentley like a puppy behind its master, he was sure he was going to throw up. Last night's whisky had poisoned him. Today's events had made things worse. He'd been unable to get hold of Blanca González, had no idea what she'd got on tape, and when he met Douglas, saw how bright-eyed and bushy-tailed he was, he was almost sick on the spot - last night's drinking had had no effect, the overweight man was whistling.

"Here at last, are we?" Angus had said, when Malcolm arrived at the *Royal Hotel*, pointedly looking at his watch. "You're half an hour late."

"There were a few things I had to do."

"Like drinking black coffee, making a few trips to the loo, and taking a couple of aspirins." Angus chortled. "Pity they're such a blinding white."

"Is everything ready in Culloch?" Malcolm asked, trying to gain some ground. "The boat, the bait, everything we need?"

"It will be when we get there." Angus was delighted with the vet's condition. It separated the men from the boys. "If you still think you're up to it, let's be off."

Without any further delay they began to drive south, Angus coasting with a certain abandon, recklessly swinging through tight corners, his eye on the rear-view mirror, expecting at any moment to see the expensive sports car behind him stop, the driver's head come out the window, and the colour of its paintwork abruptly alter.

"So far, so good," he grunted, as the miles spun by. "But, let's see what you're like when we're out at sea. There's a fine wind blowing."

The thought made him frown, he glanced up at the sky. It was low and grey, the weather rapidly closing in. Freddy's trawler was less than thirty feet, it'd bob like a cork in the swell. Still, he and his brother, Tommy, knew how to handle it, could lay out a net under almost any conditions. As for him, he'd been on and off boats most of his life.

"All we really need from you, Mister Stewart," he said, as the Culloch harbour came in sight. "Is to show us where this Kraken is. After that you can spew your guts out."

Behind him, Malcolm drove doggedly on, more than ever determined to be credited with the capture of the first live and healthy *Architeuthis*. It was a pity the sun wasn't shining, photographs of him presenting his catch to the world would have looked better against a brilliant sky. Still, whatever the weather, there was a reasonable chance the species would be named after him.

The state of the skies made Jamie McCory uneasy. He worried as much about the coming storm as he did about Alice. He'd been in rough water before and knew what to do - you had to go with it, watch the draw-back when you were getting out, but he had little idea what effect high seas would have on his friend. She'd arrived on a night that was pouring with rain. He didn't know if more bad weather would send her away, or bring her closer. He had to check for himself.

"I've got to help her," he told himself, as he hurried up the hill overlooking the Grotto. "If I don't, they'll get her, and God knows what they'll do."

Sergeant Croft's phone call had been frightening enough, told him he had little time. At mid-day that old fart, the boss of the Town Council, and the vet from Oban would be out in a boat with a net trying to catch Alice. They'd kill her, he had no doubt about that. He had seen her, dancing in the water like a mermaid in one of those stories he'd read as a kid, and knew she'd never survive in a net. She'd struggle, fight to get out the way she'd fought the porbeagle. She'd perish almost straight away. Even with those thoughts buzzing through his head, his heart pounding, he'd waited until the last minute hoping his father would phone or his mother return, but neither of them did. In the end, when he knew he couldn't wait any longer, he left with his diving gear.

"Squids die when they're caught," he said as a seagull, tossed by a gust of wind, spun over his head. "You can't keep them alive in a tank."

As for one the size of Alice, she'd end up like those horrible lumps he'd seen in pictures. Spread on the floor, as white and shapeless as a piece of dough. Arms and tentacles, stretched out like rope. Usually with someone grinning as though he was king of the world.

"Those two bastards will be the same," he told the gull, as it made another squawking turn. "All they want is their picture taken. They don't give a shit about Alice."

SQUID

Simmering with anger, he scrambled down the hill, jumping from rock to rock. He had to work quickly now. The tide was coming in, the wind rising. He could see that the water was still quite clear, but would soon get cloudy. Then he mightn't be able to pick out Alice, even if she was right beside him. She could change colour whenever she wanted to, make herself almost invisible.

"Get in and find a couple of stones," he told himself as he threw off his clothes, pulled on his wet-suit. "Send her a message."

He hurried to an edge where he could slide down quickly, catch a wave as it was going out, no creeping in like he usually did. He put on his weighted belt, checked the quick-release, tugged on his fins, spat on the inside of his goggles, spread it around to stop the lenses steaming over, slipped them on and adjusted the snorkel. Even if he was in a hurry, he had to be careful, do things right. Then, with a final glance at the menacing sky, he went into the water.

"Come on," he breathed through a stream of bubbles. "Find her fast."

He only hoped he had enough time.

The giant squid hovered on the edge of the trough that ran into Culloch harbour, her splendid eyes searching the water. For hours she'd circled the little port, at times approaching the river mouth - that fountain of tastes and savours - but nothing had tempted her ashore. On each occasion she'd moved away, back into the deep, where amongst the wreckage of fishing boats and other jetsam from the town, she'd waited in the hope of seeing the starfish again.

Yet, as time swirled on, she began to wonder if entering the harbour had been such a good idea. She'd never seen the starfish swimming in this grubby seascape, it had the sense to search for whatever it needed where the water was clean. On the other hand, this must be where it lived, where it and its family sheltered. What's more, now that she'd met the partner and the incubating child, and danced for them, wasn't it reasonable to expect that she'd be welcomed on their doorstep?

Alice drifted about uneasily, uncertain whether to go or stay. Even though she'd spent her adult life making decisions, she found it beyond any previous experience to know what was best – to live with her lovely memories or see the creature that had captured her hearts for one last time. As a result of her indecision, she hung and hovered, hoping for the best, and was on the point of finally leaving when she became aware of something delicious in the water.

Her first reaction was to resist. This was the taste that had coaxed her in the past; it brought back memories of younger days, scrumptious bits from passing cruise-liners. And, even though she'd recently discovered that whatever the land provided it was never as delicious as food from the sea, this was close, and would require little effort to reach. There was the scent of fresh blood all around her, so it couldn't do any harm to have a look. What's more, it seemed especially yummy. In her depressed condition a little pick-me-up might be exactly what she needed.

Alice moved back into the harbour, toward the lamb lowered into the water, hooked in a net.

William McCory kicked the wrecked tyre on his four-wheel drive and let out an unusually foul oath. He'd been driving down the road from the Chattan farm with the cow's head – which urgently needed to go to Edinburgh, be tested for Mad Cow's Disease - when one of the front tyres blew out. He leapt from the vehicle, examined the damage and swore loudly again.

"Fuck it," he shouted. "I'll have to change the bastard."

Hurrying along the uneven track, worried about almost everything, he skidded, smacked against a rock and the vehicle came to a halt. He'd been distracted, wondering what Jamie was doing, if he had kept his promise. His thoughts also centred on his wife, knowing Molly would be biting her nails, regretting she'd put the boy under so much pressure not to return to the sea. His mind had been too busy to keep his eyes on the road.

"Couldn't have come at a worse moment," he muttered, pulling the jack out of the car. "Christ, there's so much to get done."

He also needed to know if Tony Croft had learnt anything more about Angus Douglas's activities, and whether those idiots with the DDT had been stopped from poisoning the harbour. Just as important was Blanca González. On her first morning in the clinic she'd be completely on her own. Not quite, Lucy would be there, but he had hoped to spend an hour or two beside her, introducing her to those who arrived with their pets.

"She'll be all right, I'm sure," he grunted, lugging the spare off the vehicle, rolling it though the mud. "But I should have been with her."

It would take half an hour to change the wheel, get back to town. Then he'd have to contact an delivery service to take the cow's head to Edinburgh. That was something else he couldn't waste time over. After giving the

Chattans little choice in the matter, he couldn't keep them waiting. Above all, he was without his mobile phone. *God*, he thought. *How I've come to rely on it.*

"Get going," he urged himself. "Fast as you can."

Cursing steadily, William McCory struggled with the wheel-brace, found the bolts difficult to shift. They'd been tightened under pressure in a garage, and resisted stubbornly as he struggled against time, as he sweated beneath increasingly cloudy skies.

"Have you seen the *Gazette*?" asked Davie Forbes, the photographer, his balding head peering in through the police station door. "Forrester's bit about Nessie?"

"We have," replied Constable Roberts. He'd just taken care of Harry Carter's DDT. The stable-owner had delivered the drum half an hour earlier, muttering apologies, saying he was giving up the booze, hoped to do more work in the community. Murdoch would believe that when he saw it but, in the meantime, gave credit where it was due. "What's it got to do with you?" he asked, surprised to see the photographer, who seldom came to the station. "You involved in any way?"

"I am, as a matter of fact. Just had a call from Forrester," replied Davie. "Told me to get out my Box Brownie."

"In that case you'd better have a chat with the sergeant." Murdoch jerked his thumb over his shoulder. "He'll want to know what's going on."

Davie Forbes found Tony Croft peering at a weather pattern on a TV screen that showed winds pushing up from the south, cold air coming down from the polar region, all of which promised to produce a perfect mess when they finally met.

"Pretty shitty, isn't it?" Croft said without looking up. He knew who it was, had heard Forbes' voice at the front desk. "Going to take its photo?"

"If I can't find anything better."

"Think you might? I heard you mention the *Gazette* when you were talking to Constable Roberts." Croft hadn't been too disappointed to see the piece about Nessie in the Inverness paper; at least the story was out in the open. With any luck there'd be no more meetings behind closed doors, where everyone was told to keep silent. "Have you any idea what's happening?"

"Sort-of, but not enough." Davie dumped his camera bag on the sergeant's desk. "The *Gazette* wants pictures of the waterfront, and whatever's going on down there. I'd like to think we could work together. That's why I came."

"There's nothing I'd like more, but without any bullshit. There've been too many rumours, too many people playing silly games." Croft turned away from the TV screen. "Angus Douglas, our esteemed Chairman of the Town Council, and Malcolm Stewart, an over-zealous vet from Oban, are out in a boat in the harbour right now."

"They've gone fishing, with a storm coming in." Davie Forbes screwed his eyes up shrewdly. "Must be after something big?"

"Not Nessie exactly, as the paper said, but another monster from the deep," Croft replied, relief in his eyes. It was about time everyone knew the truth. "A giant squid, if you want to know. One of those creatures you read about in books that scare the pants off you."

"Bloody hell, that's real news." Davie smiled widely for the first time in days. Business could be looking up.

A few shots of a giant squid and his troubles would be behind him. From now on, stag-parties could photograph themselves – though he'd still keep weddings and christenings, there was a certain charm in that. "So why are we waiting here?"

"We're not, we're on our way." Croft reached for his cap, a pair of binoculars. "Come on. There's already a crowd along the harbour wall."

By the time Sergeant Croft and Davie Forbes left the police station, Freddy Tranter and his brother Tommy were beginning to lay out a heavy-gauge net. Angus Douglas was at the wheel of the trawler, trying to hold a steady course through the rising swell. Malcolm Stewart clung to a hand-rail, his face an unsavoury green.

"Stay where you are," Freddy yelled at him as he moved to watch the lines uncoil. "If you see anything, give a shout."

"Don't worry about me," Malcolm replied grimly. "Just look after the net."

"When I want your advice, I'll ask for it," Freddy replied brusquely. "Now, for Christ's sake, keep out of the way or you'll end up in the drink."

Unlike his brother, Freddy hadn't spent most of his life at someone else's beck and call. There had been a time when, with a crew of two, he'd caught herrings by the boat-load, white fish by the ton, but not any more. Now he went after prawns, brought in crabs which made him a living, but the golden days were over. So, when Douglas offered a few hundred quid to go out with a net, a lamb carcass for bait, even though he thought the old bastard was crazy, it was a job he couldn't refuse.

However, he didn't want this pasty-faced prick from Oban telling him what to do.

"That's enough," he said, swinging away to his brother, after a couple of hundred yards of net were out. "Let's put the bait down. Here, in the middle of the run."

"Are we out far enough?" Tommy queried, hoping that everything went right. He'd been in serious trouble since the Blackface ram disappeared and was desperate to get back into the laird's good-books. Sarah had done her bit, twice as a matter of fact. They'd be all right if this stunt worked, but they'd better make sure it did. "I mean, the thing's supposed to be the size of a bus."

"We could catch a train in this net if we had to." Freddy didn't believe they were going to catch anything with dead lamb, but there was no point in arguing about that. He glanced toward Douglas, struggling with the wheel. "Keep her on course," he shouted. "I'll tell you when to turn."

Angus nodded, having no doubt they'd catch the squid. The air carried the tang of promise. All the elements were in place. That article in the *Inverness Gazette* couldn't have come at a better time. There'd be no need to phone Charlie Coots again. The editor of the *Oban Times* would be the one who made the calls from now on. Angus chuckled, lifted by the coming storm, confident the weather would add the necessary touch of drama. What's more, Malcolm Stewart had assured him the monster would still be around. He was certain the squid would be starving by now, would head for the bait.

"These things need a hundred pounds of food a day. Some even more," Stewart had said, as they waited on the quay to board the trawler. Even though the mere thought of what a squid consumed made his stomach turn. "It hasn't eaten anything we know of since it took your ram."

"Could pick up something in the sea, couldn't it?" Douglas grunted, thinking that this little shit from Oban had better be right or it'd be his carcass they dragged aboard and spread out for the world to see. "There's still plenty of stuff in the water round here."

"That's possible, but it wouldn't be enough," Malcolm replied, determined not to be out-pointed now. The cephalopod would be captured as a result of his brilliant calculations. Whether it turned up dead or alive didn't matter, he'd have his name in all the books, become a part of history. "Especially as it's developed a taste for livestock," he added, swallowing uncomfortably. "Believe me, it'll still be there. It'll come running for the bait."

Those were the last words he spoke before staggering on board. Now, he held on as best he could as the sea began to heave more strongly, as the waves started to break at their crests. He desperately wanted the whole business over as the lamb was placed the net.

Although Malcolm Stewart was right in nearly all his calculations, he was unaware that the giant squid was so close to the trawler. However, in spite of her size, she was almost impossible to see in the turbulent sea. The tantalising taste of fresh meat had drawn her on. And even though she knew it might not live up to expectations, it was almost within reach. So, she moved cautiously through the shallower water, swam slowly over a broken bedstead, past a tangle of shopping carts, searching for the source. Then, quite suddenly, she realised there was something obscuring her splendid vision. Through the murk she could see a mist of fine fibres, like a weed that had grown in a regular pattern, hanging between her and the tempting lamb. But, although this misty stuff was irritating, gave her a warning tingle, she decided to take a closer look, this time from above. Very cautiously, she came to the surface, keeping her back low, her arms and tentacles together. She raised head above the water and examined the outside world. For a moment she remained, her enormous eyes on a small craft coming toward her, wondering what it meant. Unfortunately, although she made herself visible for a mere few seconds, they were enough.

"There, look. Look, it's there," shouted Malcolm Stewart, catching sight of *Architeuthis*, as a great roar went up along the waterfront, as Alice vanished beneath the waves once more. "Get a hook. A gaff, get anything. Catch it while you can."

"What's that?" demanded Freddy Tranter, one of the few who hadn't seen the creature; he was busy with the net. "I told you to stay out of the way."

"I saw it. It's *Architeuthis*. ."

"Arky-who? What the fuck are you talking about?"

"The squid. On the other side of the boat." Malcolm Stewart lurched across the deck. "Out here. I saw it. Get something to catch it with. Quick."

"Get back, you daft bastard."

"No, look. For Christ's sake, look."

With those words Malcolm waved a wild arm, slipped on a piece of seaweed and, shouting from the depths of his lungs, fell headfirst into the water. The steady breeze carried his gurgled cries to all those along the waterfront.

"Well, bugger me," Sergeant Croft said to Davie Forbes, whose eye was glued to his camera. "That's a start. What happens next?"

"I'll tell you when I've got it."

TWENTY-SIX – stormy weather

Jamie McCory swam toward the Grotto as fast as he could, his heart beating rapidly, his stomach tense. It was after mid-day. He'd waited too long. By now Angus Douglas and Malcolm Stewart would be out in the boat like Sergeant Croft had said. He should have left as soon as he was told what they were doing, given himself more time. But he'd hesitated, wishing his father would turn up, or his mother returned from the shops. But neither came home, even though he'd hung on as long as he could.

In the end he'd gone on his own, running up the hill, jumping down the other side. He'd put on his gear, got into the water quickly, worrying all the time. He had no idea where Alice was, hated the thought of her going into a net. They'd probably bait it with something that would tempt her. It was his fault really. He should have sent her away the last time they were together. Not kept her playing like she was his pet. As he hurried through the choppy seas all sorts of things buzzed around his head, mainly about Alice, but his mother too - he hadn't wanted to break his promise.

"She'll understand," he muttered, as a wave broke over his snorkel. "She'll have to." He blew the water out. "But, shit, what if she doesn't?"

He'd have to find a way around it, doing dishes, weeding, stuff around the house. *But that was in the future*, he told himself, coming closer to the Grotto, to the shelf of limestone where he'd first seen Alice. *I got to find her first.*

He paused, treading water, took a dive and peered into the gloom below the shelf. The swell was moving things around. He couldn't see any lobsters or spider crabs. They knew how to take care of themselves when the weather was foul. They'd be tucked away, clinging to something solid. There were a few prawns skipping about, and some seaweed waving. But there was no sign of Alice.

Jamie went back up, cleared his lungs and dived again looking for a couple of stones. The only thing to do was click them together, hoping she hadn't forgotten what it meant. She'd responded before, but he wasn't sure it'd work again. Though, he'd read the other day that someone in Edinburgh had proved fish have good memories - some remembered how to escape from a net, a trick they'd learnt a year earlier. If fish could do it, Alice could. She'd shown him how clever she was.

"Come on, girl," he breathed, banging the stones together in the slow rhythm he'd used to contact her before. "It's time to say good-bye."

He left the Grotto, there was no point in waiting, turned toward the harbour where they were laying out the net. If he found Alice anywhere, it'd be near the bait. That's if they hadn't already pulled her out of the water. *Then, shit, what was he going to do? No, don't even think about it*, he told himself. *You've got to get there and stop them. Make her go away.* Concern growing by the minute, clicking as he went, Jamie paddled through the rising swell.

"I am surprised the McCorys have no *mascotas*, ah, pets," Blanca González said to Lucy, as she checked the fallopian tubes of the female cat she'd just neutered. At the beginning of the operation, the cat comfortably tranquillised, she'd made a small incision in a shaved area of the abdomen, eased out the tubes, snipped them in two, and then tied the ends with thread that would dissolve internally. She had also removed the ovaries so the creature would never be on heat again. "You know, they seem to like animals very much."

"They had a dog until recently," replied Lucy, impressed by the skill of Blanca's hands. Mister McCory was good, but this girl had especially clever fingers. "Willy, he was called. He died, and they haven't got another. Not yet, anyway."

"That is sad." Blanca made sure the tubes weren't bleeding, showed no sign of leakage as a new thought filtering in. "Was Jamie very close to Willy?"

"He was, you know. When the dog was younger they were together all the time. But in the last few years it had trouble with its legs." Lucy peered through her pebble glasses as Blanca replaced the tubes, slipped them back into the abdominal cavity, regretting she'd never be able to do anything as skilled as that. The Spanish girl had added something exciting to the clinic, and she was such a friendly person to work with, she chatted all the time. "There's a cat that comes round each morning to be fed."

"Has it got a name?" Blanca reached for needle and suture, wondering if Jamie's affection for Alice had anything to do with the dog, when the door of the surgery was abruptly opened and Molly's head appeared. "Where is he?" she asked, her voice trembling. "Jamie? Where's he gone?"

"He's not in here" Lucy replied, alarmed by the interruption. It was most unlike Missus McCory to come into the clinic, especially during an operation. What's more, Jamie frequently went off on his own. "Is something wrong?"

"That's what I'm trying to find out. I told him not to go into the water. He promised he wouldn't. I don't know what's happened. I can't get through to Will. There's something wrong with his mobile phone. I...I..." Molly choked, tears filling her eyes. "I'm...worried about him. I don't know where he is. Someone's trying to poison the harbour. And there's that *thing* he calls Alice out there. My God, where is he? Doesn't anyone know?"

"I'm...I'm sure he's all right, Missus McCory" Lucy stammered, genuinely moved by Molly's distress. "I mean, he must be..."

"I think I know where might have gone," Blanca interrupted, needle in hand. "In a minute, I will look for him, if you like."

"Back into the water? Is that what you think?" Wiping her eyes, Molly turned to the Spanish girl. "Did he say anything to you?"

"I have not spoken to him this morning, but...." Blanca paused, put a comforting hand on the cat, which was beginning to stir on the operating table. "Can you finish this, please, Lucy," she added, handing needle and thread to the nurse. "It will need one stitch, or maybe two. Then, put her in the cage. Tell the owners they can take her home this afternoon."

"Yes, of course. Is that all?"

"Make sure there is plenty of anti-biotic powder on the incision. Put on a bandage and an Elizabethan collar, so she cannot lick it." Blanca smiled calmly, even though her mind was a whirl. "They will have to bring her back in a week to take the stitches out. But tell them that everything went well."

"You know where he is, don't you?" Molly persisted, trying to restrain her nerves. She couldn't afford to go to pieces now. "Tell me where's he's gone."

"It is just an idea," Blanca replied, giving the cat a final pat. It was a black and orange-flecked, the colour her mother called thunder-and-lightning. Then, with a reassuring smile at Lucy, she moved to the door. "I will look for him where we went before," she told Molly. "But, if he is not there, I have no idea where else he could be."

"You *do* think he's gone back into the water?"

"Come, we will go and see."

Both women left the surgery. Blanca trying to reassure Molly, saying Jamie was an excellent diver. She was sure, even if he had gone back into the water, he could take care of himself. Molly made no reply, just pressed her desperate lips together, attempting not to cry. Alone, Lucy began stitching the cat, murmuring softly while she worked, trying to put all other thoughts aside. She'd been deeply impressed by Blanca's keyhole surgery, the operation had taken less than half an hour from start to finish. Fortunately, for her peace of mind, she knew nothing about Alice, or how the cephalopod was being treated.

When the giant squid saw Malcolm Stewart splash into the sea she fled. Tail first, arms and tentacles trailing, her powerful jets shot her away from the net, the bait and this new member of the starfish tribe. This specimen was far less competent than the one she knew, or its partner - it seemed to be dying in the water, sending out cried for help. And there were other unpleasant sounds around her, sharp crashes, motors starting up. Usually, the water carried the ocean's voice for miles, but the harbour had become an impenetrable battery of frightening clamour.

It was clearly time she went away, returned to the world she knew. These incompetent creatures, incapable of living in the sea, were in turmoil. They reminded her of the breeding frenzy that destroyed all logic in her tribe, a ritual that had an aspect which was quite repellent if you weren't involved. Now, something similar seemed to be clouding the vision of those who lived ashore. With no idea of what might happen next, Alice had no choice in the matter - she must get away fast.

She spun over the broken furniture, the bottles, cans and seabed garbage, over the lip of the trough into cleaner water. There she hung, wondering if this was the end of the affair. If this was the last she was to see of the land that surrounded her continent, of the starfish that had touched her innocent hearts.

That tender feeling, the rather absurd idea that one day they might have bonded, held her a moment on the edge of the deep. Even if nothing else were possible, it would have been nice to have said good-bye, to have touched his strange unyielding skin, to have done a final twirling dance together. But, if that was not to be, she might as well go as quickly as she could - the sound of the motors was coming closer, the awful banging was getting louder by the second.

With what could have been a giant sigh, Alice turned toward the ocean. It was wonderful to have known the starfish, to have seen, in spite of moments of jealousy, his partner and their child. Ah, well, she would always have her memories. With that half-comforting thought Alice shot out another jet, moved further off-shore, was about to leave for the oceans' depths when she heard the barely distinguishable clicking of Jamie McCory's stones. They seemed to be beating out a steady rhythm, the signal he sent as a greeting, yet the message was so clouded by all the other noises she'd have to move closer to be sure.

Quite calmly, Alice swam toward to the sound, wondering what further turns and twists awaited her in this alien world.

What Alice failed to see, by leaving the harbour quite so soon, was Malcolm Stewart being fished out of the water. Gasping, spluttering, still wildly shouting that the giant squid was in the harbour, exactly as he'd predicted, his bedraggled figure was hauled aboard Freddy Tranter's trawler.

When he'd plunged into the sea, arms waving, eyes on Alice, his life had been saved by the net. The back-wash from the boat swung him into the mesh. Instinctively he clung to it, his face pressed against the lamb carcass, lungs threatening to burst.

"What the fuck he think he's doing," cried Freddy, turning to Angus Douglas at the wheel. "Hold it steady, for Christ's sake. Your friend's just gone over."

"Shows what a twat he is," shouted Douglas, elated by what he'd just seen. The giant squid had shown itself. That's all that mattered now. In the few moments it had been out of the water, he'd noticed a battery of camera flashes. There'd be a record of the creature, photographs enough to bring in tourists by the hoard. He'd have more evidence than had ever been produced for Nessie, every chance of putting Culloch on every map in the world. As for Malcolm Stewart, reduced to the clumsy fool he was, he could drown for all the Chairman of the Town Council cared. "What's he trying to do?" He chuckled. "Catch the bugger by hand?"

"Jesus Christ, this is turning into a fucking circus." Freddy turned to his brother. "Bring the net in," he cried. "The silly bastard's in it. Get him on board. Then get these arseholes off my boat. I never want to see the pricks again."

"I'd throw him back, if I were you," called Angus. "He's rather small." His grin widened as he watched Tommy catch the back of Malcolm's jacket with a boathook, drag him out of the sea. "On the other hand, now that we've landed him, we might as well take him home. Davie Forbes is on the quay. He'll get his picture in the paper. Probably be honoured like those chaps he was babbling about last night." Douglas's laughter rose to a roar. "What was it they were credited with? Herring farts?"

"Exciting stuff," said Sergeant Anthony Croft, focussing his binoculars on Malcolm Stewart being hoisted aboard the trawler, watching the Oban vet shout a few garbled words before being violently ill over the side. "At least there aren't any casualties. You got all that, I suppose?"

"I got shots that'd make your hair curl." Culloch's photographer slapped his balding pate without taking his eye off the viewfinder, snapping the action frame by frame. "I was right on that thing when it came out. What the hell was it, anyway? Nessie? In that case, I've struck it rich."

"It wasn't Nessie, but you'll do all right." Croft took a fresh packet of chewing gum out of his pocket, looked at it then put it back. His stomach would give little trouble from now on. "I think that really was a giant squid. Not that I know much about them."

"Who does?"

"That poor sod chucking his heart out. But I'd talk to Will McCory if I were you. He's the one who got onto it first. The creature's been taking livestock round here. Will'll tell you all you want to know."

"Why isn't he here?"

"Good question." Croft glanced around, but saw no sign of the local vet. "I tried to get him earlier, but it seems he's out of touch. I wouldn't worry though. He'll turn up soon as he knows what's going on. By God, this'll put his mind at rest."

William McCory was already in Culloch, but in anything but a tranquil frame of mind. Increasingly concerned about the whereabouts of his son, angry over the delay caused by the tyre he'd had to change, frustrated by the crowds filling the streets, he'd never felt so harassed. On top of everything, it was almost impossible to find transport for the cow's head, he'd brought from the Chattan farm, to Edinburgh for testing. The roads leading down to the quay were blocked, reducing progress to a trickle. He cursed, banged on the horn, ignored the protests of those who moved reluctantly out of his way, to finally arrive at the taxi rank where nobody wanted to miss the excitement on the waterfront.

"Do I have to go?" the driver he spoke to said, a beefy man with cautious eyes. "That means I won't find out what's going on?"

"What is going on?" William asked, waving an arm at the waterfront - it was black with people. "What's all this about?"

"It's Freddy Tranter," the driver replied. "He's gone out to catch something big."

"In the harbour?

"Looks like it, doesn't it." The driver took the keys out of the taxi, began locking to doors. "I'm going down to see."

"You're going to Edinburgh, like it or not," William said sharply. "This plastic sack's got the head of an animal that might have Mad Cow Disease. Don't worry, it's sealed, but refusal to deliver it's against the law. It could cost you your licence."

"For Christ's sake, why me?" With a surly shrug the driver opened the boot of the taxi, watched William place the cow's head inside with eyes that were now hostile. "I'm going to lose out here."

"I know how you feel, but I'll see that your fare is doubled."

With those words, he hurried home convinced that Malcolm Stewart and Angus Douglas were making at attempt to catch the giant squid, that while hurrying back to Culloch from the Chattan's farm he'd missed the opportunity of a lifetime.

"Shit," he gritted through clenched teeth. "I could throttle both of them."

He never got the chance. When he finally pulled up outside his house he found Molly and Blanca González about to get into the Spanish vet's Ford. Blanca was wearing her diving gear, putting Jamie's air-bottle in the back. Both gave him a startled look when he asked what they were doing.

"It's Jamie," his wife replied, her voice rising. "He's gone."

"Where?"

"We don't know. We think he's in the water."

"By God, I hope not," William said, his own frustration dying. He put a comforting hand on Molly's arm - he'd never seen her so upset. Her eyes were red with unshed tears "You sure he's not on the waterfront? Half the town's down there."

"He went before all the fuss began."

"He could be there, you know"

"He's not, I just know it. Jamie's wet-suit and diving things have gone." Molly clenched her fists, wanting to strike out at everyone. "Where have you been? I tried to call you several times. Why didn't you answer your phone?"

"It's smashed." William glanced at the sky, at the cloud lowering along the horizon, then turned to Blanca. "You're obviously going after him. Do you know where he is?"

"I think so," Blanca replied, trying to appear calm even though she was worried about getting into the water. It was rough, but that wasn't her main concern. She had an air-bottle and could stay down low, but was deeply unsure about confronting the enormous *Architeuthis* on her own. It had been friendly enough when Jamie was near, but with her alone anything could occur. However, she mustn't let that stop her now. Molly looked as if she was on the edge of a nervous breakdown. William was very tense; the lines in his face were deep. "Come with me, we will go to the place I saw Alice before." She waved them into the Ford. "Maybe Jamie's clothes are there. If they are, I will look for him. That is all I can do. But, come quickly. The weather, it is getting very bad."

"Are you sure you'll be all right?" asked William.

"Stop it," shouted Molly. "Let's just go and do what we can."

Without another word they drove off, harbouring their fears, their heads turning toward the waterfront as a great and boisterous roar went up when Malcolm Stewart was dumped ashore.

TWENTY-SEVEN – the long good-bye

Jamie McCory swam against the rising waves, through water that was increasingly cloudy. He could barely see more than a few yards in any direction. The state of the sea made clicking the stones difficult. He lost rhythm frequently - sometimes tapped out a quick signal, at others a slow beat, realising that if Alice could hear him she might not know what he wanted.

Come on, he told himself. It was impossible to speak now, his snorkel kept filling with water. For the first time since he'd been struck by lightning, he was beginning to feel the cold. *You know it's me. You've got to listen.*

He left the Grotto, went down the coast. It was the only direction that made any sense. She had to be somewhere along the shore - if she hadn't gone already. In a way, he hoped she had, even though it made him sad. But, if she hadn't, he must find her. Make her say good-bye. She had to be sent away. Everybody would know she was in Culloch by now. They'd be coming from all over, with whatever they could lay their hands on, to try and bring her in.

Shit, what are they going to do with her? Put her in a tank and charge people to come and watch? Let them throw in coins and cigarette butts, see what she would do?

The thought was sickening, it made his stomach crawl.

Jamie pushed himself on. It wasn't far to the harbour entrance. He had to go around the point, that's all. He'd done it before on sunny days to see how long he could stay in the water. There was a deep trough near the shore, there'd been times when he'd seen big fish swimming in and out of it. It was on the edge of the trough the basking shark had swum over his shoulder. That had been great, he'd felt close to it. Not as close as he felt to Alice, but she was special.

He struggled on through the murky water, hoping she'd turn up. If she didn't, then he'd have to find out what was happening on the waterfront. Just a quick look would be enough to see if they'd already caught her. And if they had, then he didn't know what on Earth he could possibly do.

On the waterfront Angus Douglas puffed out his substantial chest, about to take credit for what the crowd had just witnessed. He would make history for himself as he claimed to be the discoverer of *Architeuthis cullochus*, the only giant squid to be seen alive and kicking in Scottish waters. In crisp and clear sentences he would proudly let them know that this mysterious creature from the deep had actually come ashore and taken livestock, but had been sent back to the depths where it belonged through a process that he, solely and almost single-handedly, was responsible for initiating. What's more, its presence had been recorded for posterity, and his act was now well and truly registered on film by a hundred different cameras and mobile phones. This great event had come about due, almost entirely, to his foresight as Chairman of the Town Council. His vision of things to come belonged to the long lineage of leadership that he alone possessed. He was, he silently told himself, about to play another blinder.

Those who'd assisted would, of course, be rewarded. Davie Forbes would be proclaimed official photographer of the town; Sergeant Anthony Croft recommended for promotion. He'd give generous thanks to Malcolm Stewart, the vet from Oban, who played a valiant part, albeit in a secondary role. Culloch's own veterinary surgeon, William McCory, had provided essential information; may he continue to practice for years to come. Yet his role was also that of an assistant, however valuable it might have been. The man would be given an official recognition when the Angus Archibald Douglas Marine Park was opened. However, all who lived in or visited Culloch would have no doubt who to thank for the value that *Architeuthis cullochus* had bestowed on the town, a renascence which would bring Culloch out of its current depression, guarantee prosperity for the decades ahead.

Unfortunately, Angus intended to add, this was a single event. The almost mythical creature had shown itself briefly, then vanished beneath the waves. The monster was unlikely to return according to Malcolm Stewart, who would be given a moment to say something in confirmation if he ever stopped vomiting. The poor man was now wrapped in a blanket, shivering as his photograph was taken by many along the quay. Angus also intended to mention McCory's new assistant, a Spanish vet, who was said to have recorded video sequences of the squid in action. If her material lived up to expectations, she'd be taken care of, Angus hoped, in more ways than one.

He noted, however, as he cleared his throat, about to begin, there was no sign of Blanca González at the moment or of Will McCory, for that matter. No doubt they'd turn up sooner or later, he told himself, weeping copiously at having missed the fun. With that small jolt of heart-warming self-satisfaction, as their absence left him alone on the stage, Angus Douglas began his address and, as he had predicted, played a champion's role.

Blanca González sat on the edge of a rock ready to enter the water, reluctant to get in - a quick thread of fear running down her spine. It wasn't the state of the sea that held her back, or any great nervousness as far as Alice was concerned - for all she knew the squid had gone. What worried her more than anything was the thought that she'd never find Jamie in the rising tides. Or, if she did, he would no longer be breathing. She only hoped, to God, she wasn't too late.

When she'd finally arrived, with his nervous parents, at the place where she and Jamie had dived the day before, they discovered his scattered clothes, tossed aside where he'd thrown them off. Getting down to the rocks hadn't been easy. Abandoned cars blocked the roads near the waterfront - their drivers had to be found to clear the way. When they eventually escaped of the surging crowd, the skies had begun to darken; the wind was blowing gusts that tore leaves off swaying trees.

"He, he can't be out in this," Molly had said, getting out of the car, picking up Jamie's clothes, folding them carefully. "He wouldn't be, would he, Will?"

"It's not that bad" Her husband glanced at the menacing clouds. "Jamie knows what he's doing."

"In weather like this?"

"He's been out in bad weather before," William replied, trying to lessen his wife's concern. "I remember him telling me once..."

"Oh, for God's sake...." Molly turned to Blanca, who was shrugging the air-bottle onto her back. "What do you think...oh, I'm sorry, let me help you with that."

"Thank you." When the bottle was firm, Blanca picked up the rest of her gear, put it on quickly. "Don't worry," she said. "I am sure he will be all right."

"You be careful," called William, he'd never felt more useless. There was nothing his capable hands could do - he'd drown in five minutes in that water. "I mean...well, you know what I mean."

"Yes, I do."

With that, Blanca moved to the edge of the sea, made sure everything was in place then, with a quick wave at the parents, slipped into the water. Immediately a wave slapped her down. Below, the water was dirty; seaweed ran loose in the swell. She quickly became aware that her only chance of finding the boy was swimming close to the surface, hoping to catch sight of his snorkel, his fins beating as he swam through the unwelcoming sea.

"*Dios mío,*" she whispered to herself. "Let me see him soon."

The giant squid hovered on the edge of the trough at the entrance of Culloch harbour. Although she remained unseen, vibrations in the water told her there was a great deal of danger near the shore. More motors were running. More banging and slapping the sea rang through her sensitive skin. She couldn't be sure if this was to drive her into the mesh with the bait, or send her away. Nevertheless, there was one sound about which she had no doubt – the clicking of the starfish, even though the increased disturbance was making it more and more difficult to detect where it was coming from. At times it seemed to be very close, at others way out in the deep. She had little idea where to find him.

Jamie pushed on steadily, trying his best to keep his signal even but the waves made it hard, and his hands were getting cold. *Funny*, he thought. *Haven't been like that for ages*. He wondered if it had anything to do with the way he felt. He wasn't enjoying the water like he usually did. He wasn't visiting as a friend, dropping in to have a look around. He was here on a mission. He knew that sounded wierd, but that's what it was - he was doing what he could to save Alice, and he was doing it alone.

He hadn't heard anything from his father before the left the house. His mother hadn't returned from the shops. In a way, that was good - he'd never have got out of the place if she'd been there. She wouldn't have let him near the water. Which made him think of his promise, and he began to feel really bad. She'd been good to him. She was the best friend he had, and it was rotten what he was doing to her now. But he had no choice, and only hoped one day she'd understand, even forgive him.

Swimming as fast as he could, Jamie came to the rocks at the end of the point running out from the harbour. In a few minutes he'd be able to see what they were doing in there. If nothing was happening he'd turn round and have another look in the Grotto. But if Alice was being pulled out of the water, struggling for her life in a net, he had no idea what he'd do. That'd be the end of everything. He'd never get there in time to save her. And with everyone yelling and screaming, the way they always did when they caught something big, who was going to take any notice of a kid telling them to put her back. He hated to think what would happen once she'd been hauled out of the sea. Christ knows what they'd do with her. He felt helpless on his own, but he wasn't going to give up now.

A shiver of depression went through him, and he wondered if he was kidding himself, if all this was hopeless. How could he possibly find her with seas like this, with all that shouting and banging in the harbour, and no one to give him a hand? Perhaps it was time to give in. Then, out of the corner of an eye, he saw something in the water. Or thought he did. He couldn't be sure. It was a shape that moved through the clouds in the sea. One second it looked like Alice, the next it was gone as another patch of stirred-up silt drifted across like a curtain, blocking it out. He wasn't certain if it was her or not. He didn't know. Maybe he was seeing things because he wanted to. Maybe he was going out of his mind.

Alice? he tried to say, but couldn't. The sea was too rough. *Is that you?*

He continued clicking, beating out an uneven rhythm.

"We'll lose both of them now, won't we?" Molly McCory said, her breath steaming over a window in Blanca's Ford, where they'd been forced to take shelter from the wind. It was coming over the water in gusts that brought tears to their eyes. "We shouldn't have let her go."

"She'll be all right. She's got the bottle. There's plenty of air in it," William said, doing his best to sound reasonable, talking of things he knew. "I had it filled the other day."

"That doesn't mean she'll be all right. Look at the water."

"She knows what she's doing. She's dived before."

"What about Jamie? So has he, but that doesn't make me feel any better." Molly vigorously wiped the window clean. "I shouldn't have tried to stop him. I should have taken him. With all the things he needed. Then he'd have been all right. I made a mistake, making him promise not to go into the water."

"You did what you thought was best."

"I've been...I've been too strict."

"You were trying to protect him."

"You should've been more helpful. There've been times when you could have done more. Listened to him, not been so sarcastic."

"I'll try to be more tolerant in future."

"He's got to come back first, or...." Molly put a hand over her lips. There was no point in going on like this. Both desperately wanted their son back, neither had anyone else to blame. "Blanca will find him," she whispered. "She'll find him soon."

"I'm sure she will."

Blanca González reached the Grotto, the first place she could think of to search. Once there, she came to the surface, glanced around but there was no sign of Jamie's snorkel. All she could see was a white plastic bottle that had been washed out to sea. She dived again, peered under the ledge where Jamie said he'd first seen Alice. It was dark, there were a few fish darting about, but no sign of the giant squid. She edged back, wondering where to look next. He might have gone down to the harbour, or further north along the coast. He could even have swum out to sea. She hoped he hadn't, it would be impossible to find him there. Trying not to worry, Blanca turned south, toward the harbour.

The giant squid picked up the clicking again, heard its uneven sound. It came from a direction she knew so well, the place where the starfish had entered her life, paddling along incompetently, looking quite absurd. Now, he seemed to be back there again, making his distinctive noise. Even though she wasn't quite sure what it was saying, it could only mean he was trying to contact her.

For a moment she hung, calculating whether to seek him out or not. It wasn't easy. He may, like some of his fellow creatures, want to frighten her with that misty net, yet that was most unlikely. On the other hand, he could be asking for help. Alice hovered, trembling with indecision as waves rolled over her enormous body. Then, she shot away.

Jamie didn't see Alice until she was beside him. He didn't know she was there until a tentacle came out and touched. He'd almost reached at the end of the point running out from the harbour, when he felt a gentle caress on his shoulder, like the way he used to stroke his dog. But it was more inquisitive than that, seemed to be asking whether she'd be welcome or not, whether he wanted her to stay. He turned quickly, his heart leaping with joy to find her beside him - she was so close he could see his own reflection in her great lidless eyes. He was so delighted he dropped the stones and swallowed a mouthful of water.

"Alice. You're alive," he spluttered, removing the snorkel and gasping for air. "I thought I'd lost you. I thought you'd gone."

He reached out for her and went under. *This was crazy. Here she was, looking great, and I'm losing my way in the water.* With an effort he struggled back to the surface.

Alice swam around the starfish trying to assess his strange reaction – she wasn't sure if it was a peculiar form of welcome or whether he was attempting to say goodbye. But his performance didn't surprise her, after all, she had given him a fright. And, on a day like this with the weather so foul, she understood why he wasn't at his best in the water. If he'd had any sense he'd have stayed ashore. Nevertheless, he did seem pleased to see her.

In an effort to cheer him up she changed colour, turned bright red, added a line of luminescent blue down either side, rolled over and showed him her tummy. He responded, put out an arm, his tiny tentacles grasping her own, and for a few precious seconds they clung together, then she knew from his touch he was telling her it was time for her to leave – there was great danger in the harbour..

He was telling her there were other starfish trying to catch her, those who had lured her in with their tempting bait. If they failed with the net, they intended to drag her out of the water with cruelly sharpened hooks. She'd seen it happen elsewhere, it was an ugly sight. It was quite clear now, from the way her starfish was acting, from the messages that flashed between them, that she must leave as soon as she could. What's more, she realised that he had braved these unfriendly seas to see that she was safe, to say farewell. A wave of gratitude swept through her, turning her a brighter red, and she was about to embrace him with her eight strong arms when she realised he was failing in the water. There was less strength to his touch; his breathing was uneven. And she knew she couldn't abandon him in the sea in this condition. He must to be taken back to the life he was accustomed to, so she could return to hers.

Alice put her tentacles out again, took Jamie in tow and began to lead him toward the Grotto. Once there she could release him, and try to forget what he'd meant to her.

Jamie relaxed as Alice took hold. He knew she was pleased to see him again. She'd turned colours he'd not seen before. That was great. She was still safe and well; no one had hurt her; she hadn't been caught in the net. He breathed more easily as she pulled him through the water, close to the surface, his snorkel catching air. It was terrific, it couldn't be better. He was feeling tired now, so he floated, paddled a little, allowed himself to be tugged along. They were going back to the Grotto. He didn't know what would happen when they got there, but it didn't matter any more. He'd found out all he needed. She was untouched. He had to make sure she stayed that way, no matter what happened to him.

He felt happy about everything as he was pulled along; he felt a little numb but wasn't cold any more. The water was soft around him, the waves didn't hit so hard. In fact, he began to wonder what it would be like if he spent the rest of his life with Alice.

It wouldn't be bad, he thought. *Be away from all those people trying to kill her. Be with the fishes, in a way. Even if they ate me up.*

The thought made him laugh, he spluttered, and remembered other things. He didn't have a lot to go back for, he didn't have many friends. There were one or two mates he was fond of, but they were few. And he'd always been happier in the water than standing around on street corners or playing computer games. On top of everything, he'd broken his promise to his mother. He'd never done that before. She'd be hopping mad, and he had no excuses. He was better off where he was.

Blanca was okay, he thought of her as he went with Alice. She'd asked him if he believed in God, and he told her that he didn't know. It wasn't a thing he thought about, not often anyway. Well, maybe he was going to discover something now. Maybe that's where Alice was taking him, some place where he'd find out more.

That's the trouble with people. They don't try to learn what they don't know, he said to himself, as they approached the Grotto, Alice not going too fast, the water not as violent as it had been before. *But, this was different. He was on a journey. This was a voyage of discovery.*

TWENTY-EIGHT – the creature rests

"The weather's getting worse," Molly cried, her heart in her throat as she peered through the window of Blanca's Ford. "We should do something. Get help. We can't sit here doing nothing."

"I've been thinking the same." William reached into the back of the car, fumbled through Jamie's clothes. "I hope he brought his phone with him. Mine's smashed, and you don't have one."

"Who can you call? The Coastguard?"

"Tony Croft. I know his number."

To his relief William found Jamie's phone and made the connection. As soon as the sergeant knew who it was, he began by saying, "Where the hell have you been, Will? You've missed all the fun. If you'd been here, you could have seen the squid for yourself."

"Did they catch it?"

"I'm happy to say, they didn't. Though not for want of trying. There's a dozen boats still out there having a go." Croft laughed. "But we saw it, and that got everyone excited. Especially Angus Douglas. He's down of the quay giving a press conference now. Wouldn't be surprised if..."

"Listen, Tony, any chance of sending out a lifeboat?" William interrupted. "Jamie's in the water. He went off looking for the squid."

"Bloody hell, I wondered where he was." Croft's voice altered sharply. "I'll see what I can do. Constable Robert has an inflatable on standby. Do you know where Jamie is?"

"Probably near the harbour. The excitement would have got him there."

"We'll look there first." Croft glanced at the weather, it was getting worse by the minute. "Don't worry, I'll send Roberts off now."

"Be as quick as you can." William McCory closed Jamie's phone, turned to his wife. "Tony's on to it," he said. "There'll be a boat out soon."

Molly closed her eyes. "I'm sure they'll do all they can," she replied, but couldn't bring herself to add anything more.

Not quite believing the sight was real, Blanca González looked up through the water to see Jamie McCory above her, towed along by the *calamar*. The great creature was swimming backwards, its arms trailing behind, its gigantic tentacles holding the boy, nursing him through the waves.

Her first reaction was relief, knowing he was alive. Then she realised that the giant squid had seen her too, and was eyeing her with some concern. It paused, released Jamie, came down to where she was, hung massively before her, and her heart turned over in her chest.

It will not hurt me, she told herself. *It knows I am a friend.* Then something quite absurd came to mind. Dios mío, *it could be jealous.*

The squid swam around her, darkening in colour, opening its arms as it had for the camera, showing its huge suckers. Blanca remained as still as she could, hoping it wouldn't touch her the way an octopus had clung to her when she was fishing with her father. It had grabbed her shoe; when she tried to remove the tentacle it snaked up her arm, making her pull away in dread.

That did not know what it was doing, she reassured herself. *Alice does, she is helping Jamie. She will know I want to help him too.*

Alice didn't exactly share the thought – in fact, she resented the sudden appearance of the female companion. Her rescue had been progressing steadily, and soon they would have reached their goal. The starfish had been quite at ease in the water, and she knew it wouldn't be long before she could leave him, when his partner arrived and spoilt everything.

However, her initial resentment faded quickly when she saw that the female was behaving herself. She remained where she was, made no attempt to take hold of her companion and, as her hands were empty, had obviously found somewhere safe to leave the child. Perhaps the starfish-world was similar to her own - where the women of the tribe had more sense than the males, knew how to take care of matters far better than their counterparts, made the wisest decisions. This one had arrived with the thing on her back which enabled her to stay down longer. That showed real intelligence, especially on a day like this. A pity her friend hadn't had more sense.

Alice hovered, not quite sure what to do, assessing the female with her questioning eyes. Blanca waited, trying to control her fear.

From the surface Jamie peered down, wondering why his journey through the water had been abruptly cut short. Seeing Blanca and Alice face to face, he understood why, and realised he'd better do something about it. He took several deep breaths to clear his lungs, refilled them, and then went down through the surging seas, aware that he had to be quick. He'd been in the water a long time now and was beginning to lose all sense of space and time. It was great of Blanca to come after him - she really was a good person. He had to let her know he was grateful, but he had to make Alice understand he didn't want to leave her. Given the choice he'd rather be with her.

He stopped between them, turned to Alice. But, as he put out a hand to touch her, she backed away. *She's frightened*, he thought. *Just when it was going so well.* He faced Blanca and saw that her eyes were wide with concern. *I'm all right*, he tried to tell her, giving her the OK signal, though it was difficult now, he was beginning to shiver, and his fingers didn't move that way he wanted them to.

Recognising his condition, Blanca knew she had to get him out of the water fast. He mightn't know it, told her he didn't feel the cold, but he was beginning to lose body heat. If it got any worse he could die. Her heart beating furiously, one eye on the giant squid, which seemed to be waiting, assessing the situation, Blanca took hold of Jamie, swam him back to the surface. He gasped when he got there, the snorkel slipped from his mouth. He swallowed water as a wave slapped his face.

"Come on, Jamie," Blanca said, giving him her mouthpiece. He took it, breathed, coughed and cleared his throat. "I will take you. Now, let's go back."

"No," Jamie spluttered. It was funny this, like some sort of stupid dream. He had to choose between Blanca and Alice. *You're being ridiculous*, he told himself, but all he could say was, "No."

"It is not far." Blanca turned him onto his back, put an arm across his chest and, making sure his snorkel was clear of the water, replaced her mouthpiece and began swimming toward the Grotto, braving the swelling seas. All she could think of, as she ploughed along, was how clever her mother had been when she'd insisted on life-saving classes in the swimming pool at Cabezón de la Sal. *Not long*, she reassured herself, even though this was more difficult than anything in a pool. *It will not take long to get there.*

"I..." Jamie spluttered. There were so many things he wanted to say, but couldn't. Not now. It was over now. Alice was safe, he was sure of that. He felt sleepy all of a sudden. "I...want..."

There must be somewhere to get out, Blanca told herself. She could see the shoreline, the waves breaking over the rocks, spilling white foam. It looked magnificent from a distance, but would make leaving the water a deadly task. *There has to be somewhere to land.*

Alice watched the female take hold of the starfish and had to admit that the method she used made sense. Her partner was exhausted, had become something of a burden; even Alice had trouble dragging him along. What's more, being a land animal, she would have had put him ashore, although she had little idea how. Whatever, she'd have found a way. They weren't too complicated these air-breathing things, they lived simple lives. They didn't even need to hunt for food. It was in cages all around them.

Still, as poignant as it was, Alice realised that her visit was now over. The female starfish was doing quite well in the water, and should have little trouble when she reached the shore. So Alice wasn't especially unhappy about the way things had turned out. Apart from one or two rather unpleasant experiences with animals that were too large to eat, some of which had turned very nasty when she'd fancied their young, she'd discovered some wonderful things during the past few days. Most important of all was that many of these land-dwelling starfish were quite nice when you got to know them. They behaved decently on the whole.

With these pleasant thoughts, and feeling hungry again - it had been quite a taxing morning, Alice, the giant squid, waved an unseen tentacle at the two ploughing along on the surface, issued a cloud of jet-black ink, spelling the end of all contact, and shot out to sea. She swam away from the coastline, down into the trough and sped into the ocean's depths. The water was clean now, the strange force that had sent her wandering seemed to have gone for good. In time, as she'd suspected from the start, she'd find a partner more suited to her way of life. Then, she'd make every effort to be happy, as content and fulfilled as any other creature, large or small, with a secret love in its heart.

On the surface Blanca struggled. She was strong, in spite of her slightness, but as Jamie became more sluggish, pushed less with his fins, she could see that the shoreline wasn't getting any closer, in fact it seemed to be drifting away. Each time she glanced at the rocks they appeared more distant, as if some unseen hand was pulling them back. She wondered if it was the Corrievreckan current she'd heard about, one of the most dangerous in this part of the world. Each year it added to its victims, sucked boats down, spewed them out empty onto the rocks

It does not matter what it is, she thought, as it began to rain. *We must get through it, or we will both be dead.*

She had already removed Jamie's weighted belt, let it sink to the bottom. He floated well enough without it but, being more buoyant, was more easily moved by the waves. And her arms were beginning to tire. She'd changed over once, replacing one with the other over his chest, and was wondering how long her air would last when a sudden surge tore the boy from her grasp, sent him floundering away.

No, she shouted to herself. *I will not let that happen.*

She swam after him, managed to grasp his hood, pulled his head out of the water. He coughed, spat, heaved and tried to get away.

"Stop it," she cried, shaking him. "I am here to help you."

"No," he muttered. "I want...."

"Do what I tell you to do," she shouted, echoing of her mother's strict voice. "If you don't do what I say, you'll be sorry."

"I...." he began, but she jammed the mouthpiece between his lips, pulled him close again. "You're coming with me, Jamie. Don't struggle, be a good boy and do what I tell you to."

"What...?"

"Relax, you're going to be all right. We'll be out of the water soon."

"You're....?"

"Keep quiet and do what I say."

Jamie closed his eyes, allowed himself to be pulled along, not sure who was doing it. Blanca or Alice? He wasn't certain which one he'd spoken to, but that didn't matter much. Whoever it was, was helping him. That was good. He didn't feel too bad. Saw lots of colours. And there was something on the water he'd hadn't noticed before, something black coming toward them. The one who was pulling him hadn't seen it yet, she was facing the other way.

"Look..." he tried to say, but only a mumble came out. "Look..."

Blanca González couldn't reply, she was too busy keeping Jamie's head above water, trying desperately to reach the shore.

"I think everything's going to be all right," Tony Croft said, calling the number William used to phone him earlier. "Murdoch's seen a couple in the water. About half a mile off-shore."

"Who?" the vet asked, Jamie's mobile clamped to his ear, eyes scanning the horizon – he could see nothing but breaking waves. "Could he identify them?"

"Not really, all wet-suits look alike. But he called to say he'd spotted a couple he was about to pick up. I wanted to get news to you as soon as possible. One of them must be Jamie. Who's the other one, you got any idea?"

"The new vet, Blanca González. She went looking for him."

"Good for her." Croft swept his binoculars over the water, trying to pick up Murdoch's boat. It wasn't easy. The quay was crowded. All around him people were pushing and shouting; rumours were flying fast. There was talk of Nessie taking the vet's boy. It was a pity, but the kid was always in the water. You had to keep an eye on lads like that. "I'd go home, if I were you," the sergeant suggested, having to shout into the mobile phone. "Murdoch will come back when he's finished out there." He paused and swallowed. "I'll let you know as soon as he lands."

"Thanks, Tony. Thanks for everything."

"Don't think of it. Just keep your fingers crossed."

William McCory closed the phone, turned to his wife, who sat facing away, her eyes on the surging sea. "That was Tony, as you must have gathered. Constable Murdoch's sighted Jamie. Blanca too. He's about to pick them up," he said quietly.

"Are they all right? Did he say anything about that?"

"He said to go home. Wait for them there."

"I'll run a hot bath." Molly pushed her hair into place, refusing to contemplate anything else. "There'll be water enough for two."

Blanca didn't see the boat until it was almost alongside her. When she did, she thought it was a *cayuco*, one of those flat-bottomed crafts that brought thousands of illegal immigrants ashore along the south coast of Spain, many of whom drowned at sea. She heard voices, saw a uniform and thought the Guardia Civil had come to her rescue.

"*Gracias*," she said, as willing hands pulled Jamie out of the water. "*Pensaba que me iba a morir*. Oh, thank you" she added, realising who it was. "I thought I would die."

"Not today, Miss," replied Murdoch as he helped her out, thinking she looked very pretty, even though half-drowned. "Well, not you, anyway. The lad's not too clever, though. We better get him home as fast as we can."

"He is cold." Blanca put her cheek against Jamie's. "But not too bad. Have you got a blanket? A coat, anything?"

"We certainly have." Murdoch reached beneath a seat and pulled out a rug. "We've got all you need. You'll be safe with us."

"That will help, he'll be all right now," Blanca said, tucking the blanket around Jamie, then she smiled at the fresh-faced young man with cheeky eyes. "I do not know how to thank you."

"Don't worry, Miss, we'll find a way." Murdoch winked at Jack, the barman, who was working the outboard. "Let's get out of here," he said. "Give her all you've got."

An hour later, Jamie sat before the fire his mother had lit while he'd soaked himself in the bath. His father had examined him, listened to his heart, his breathing, said he needed no more than a good night's rest, should be fine in the morning.

"Feeling any better?" Molly asked, from where she sat on the arm of his chair. She'd offered him food but he wanted nothing. There was an untouched mug of Ovaltine beside him. They were alone in the room. Blanca González had returned to *Rose Cottage*; William gone to thank Sergeant Croft. "Are you starting to warm up now?"

Jamie nodded. He'd said little since being taken out of the water, only a word or two when asked if his fingers and toes felt all right, shook his head when someone suggested calling the doctor.

"You were lucky," Molly said, as wind blew hail against the window-pane. "Blanca too, you know. My God, we owe that girl so much. She was incredibly brave."

For a moment Jamie could not reply. Then, pulling his wool hat down to his eyes, whispered, "She's gone. I'm never going to see her again," He burst into sniffling sobs.

"Blanca? She's just gone to fetch dry clothes."

"Alice. She's not coming back."

"Jamie, she's safe." Molly rubbed the back of his neck, wanting to hold him close, yet knew that this was not the moment. All she could do was offer consolation; helplessly watch the tears flow. "Nobody's going to hurt her now."

Jamie McCory nodded, but continued to cry. He said nothing more, just kept his eyes on the flames as they danced in the grate - they looked like Alice's arms.

A year later he was smiling. He'd not cried for long the day Alice left, although he stayed quiet for a week or more. In the end he accepted it had turned out for the best, was the only way the adventure could have ended. He didn't go back to the sea that summer, but when the storms were over and the water warmed he returned to the Grotto, the Tombstone, the Castle and the Place where the Pollock was Murdered, saw some fishes he knew, others that were to become his friends. Even though there was no sign of Alice, her wonderland welcomed him.

Now, a year later, he was smiling broadly. It was the opening of the Angus Archibald Douglas Marine Park. Nearly all the citizens in Culloch were there to see the magnificent model of Alice hanging from the ceiling. Based on Blanca's video - which had its own special room where everyone could watch the giant squid dance - the model was more ferocious than Alice had been, but Jamie didn't mind that. At least they could see her, have some idea what she was like. With her arms outstretched, her tentacles at full extent, she reached from one end of the hall to the other.

Jamie turned to look over the crowd. His mother was smiling as she listened to Anthony Croft, now promoted to Inspector. With them was Angus Douglas, looking splendid in kilt and sporran, holding a glass of malt whisky. Even Malcolm Stewart was part of the group, having wheedled his way back in. William was talking to the Chattan twins, whose cow had been clean - she'd probably fallen and hit her head when Alice entered the stable. But nobody blamed the giant squid for anything now, she'd bought fame and fortune to Culloch, made the little town on the Argyll coast a place where tourists were flocking in, where biologists from all over the world were coming to examine *Architeuthis cullochus*, see if their theories about what the creature was like had been right or wrong.

"It was all because of you," said Blanca González, who appeared beside Jamie to give him a hug. "This would not be here if you had not cared so much."

"It was your video that made the difference." Jamie eased away, she was looking great and he didn't want to get another hard-on. *It'd be stupid*, he told himself. *Anyway, she's seeing that copper who saved us. Angus*

Douglas had sniffed around for a bit, but she'd sent him packing. She's a person who knows what she wants. She's cool. "What about all that stuff you shot?"

"Let us say that we did it together."

"Yeah, we did." Jamie looked up and smiled at Alice. "We did it together, didn't we, girl."

Around him people murmured approval, nodded and gazed and expressed delight. Passing drinks from hand to hand all were quite sure that, in some way or another, they were responsible for the sun that now shone on Culloch. All believed they'd played their part in the rebirth of the town, had encouraged Alice, however briefly, out of her waterland. Through their efforts, part of her had come to stay.